"There is lots of room here. There's a guest room."

Logically, Jessica knew she could not stay. But it felt so good to be here. It felt oddly like home to her, even if it didn't to Kade. Maybe it was because she was aware that for the very first time since she had been attacked in her business, she felt safe.

And so tired. And relaxed.

Maybe for her, home was where Kade was, which was all the more reason to go, really.

"Okay," she heard herself saying, without nearly enough fight. "Maybe just for one night."

THE PREGNANCY SECRET

BY
CARA COLTER

Published in Great Britain 2015
by Mills & Boon, an imprint of Harlequin (UK) Limited,
Eton House, 18-24 Paradise Road, Richmond, Surrey, TW9 1SR

© 2015 Cara Colter

ISBN: 978-0-263-25132-6

23-0515

Harlequin (UK) Limited's policy is to use papers that are natural, renewable and recyclable products and made from wood grown in sustainable forests. The logging and manufacturing processes conform to the legal environmental regulations of the country of origin.

Printed and bound in Spain
by CPI, Barcelona

Cara Colter shares her life in beautiful British Columbia, Canada, with her husband, nine horses and one small Pomeranian with a large attitude. She loves to hear from readers, and you can learn more about her and contact her through Facebook.

To my friend, and mentor, Joan Fitzpatrick,
whose wisdom and compassion have guided
and inspired me for three decades.

CHAPTER ONE

A BLOCK AWAY from a destination he had no desire to
reach, it pierced Kade Brennan's distracted mind that
something was wrong.

Very wrong.

There were no sirens, but the strobes of the blue and
red bar lights on top of half a dozen police cruisers were
pulsing strenuously. It was jarringly at odds with the
crystal clear morning light that filtered, a suffused lime
green, through the unfurling spring leaves of the huge
cottonwoods that lined the shores of the Bow River.

Now, above the sounds of a river bloated with spring
runoff, above the sounds of the cheerful chirping of birds,
above the sounds of the morning rush of traffic, Kade
could hear the distinctive static of emergency frequency
radios. A robotic female voice was calling a code he did
not understand. It looked as if there was an ambulance
in that cluster of emergency vehicles.

Kade broke into a run, dodging traffic as he cut across
the early-morning crush of cars on Memorial Drive to
the residential street on the other side.

It was one of those postcard-pretty Calgary blocks
that looked as if nothing bad could ever happen on it.
It was an older neighborhood of arts and crafts–style

houses, many of them now turned into thriving cottage businesses. Nestled under the huge canopies of mature trees, Kade noted, were an art-supply store, an organic bakery, an antiques shop and a shoe store.

This neighborhood was made even more desirable by the fact it was connected to downtown Calgary by the Peace Bridge, a pedestrian-only walkway over the river that Kade had just crossed.

Except at this moment the postcard-pretty street that looked as if nothing bad could ever happen on it was completely choked with police cars. People walking to work had stopped and were milling about.

Kade, shouldering through them, caught bits of conversation.

"What happened?"

"No idea, but from the police presence, it must be bad."

"A murder, maybe?" The speaker could not hide the little treble of excitement at having his morning walk to work interrupted in such a thrilling fashion.

Kade shot him a dark look and shoved his way, with even more urgency, to the front of the milling crowd, scanning the addresses on the cottagey houses and businesses until he found the right one. He moved toward it.

"Sir?" A uniformed man was suddenly in front of him, blocking his path. "You can't go any farther."

Kade ignored him, and found a hand on his arm.

Kade shook off the hand impatiently. "I'm looking for my wife." Technically, that was true. For a little while longer anyway.

"Kade," Jessica had said last night over the phone, "we need to discuss the divorce." He hadn't seen her for more than a year. She'd given him the address on this street, and he'd walked over from his downtown condo, annoyed at what his reluctance about meeting her was saying about him.

All this was certainly way too complicated to try to explain to the fresh-faced young policeman blocking his way.

"Her name is Jessica Brennan." Kade saw, immediately, in the young policeman's face that somehow all these police cars had something to do with her.

No, something in him screamed silently, a wolf howl of pure pain, *no*.

It was exactly the same silent scream he had stifled inside himself when he'd heard the word *divorce*. What did it mean, he'd asked himself as he hung up his phone, that she wanted the divorce finalized?

Last night, lying awake, Kade had convinced himself that it could only be good for both of them to move on.

But from his reaction to this, to the fact all these police cars had something to do with her, he knew the lie he had told himself—that he didn't care—was monstrous in proportion.

"She's okay, I think. There's been a break-in. I understand she was injured, but it's non-life-threatening."

Jessica injured in a break-in? Kade barely registered the non-life-threatening part. He felt a surge of helpless fury.

"She's okay," the young cop repeated. "Go that way."

It was upsetting to Kade that his momentary panic and rage had shown in his face, made him an open book to the cop, who had read his distress and tried to reassure.

He took a second to school himself so that he would not be as transparent to Jessica. He looked up the walk he was being directed to. Twin white lilacs in full and fragrant bloom guarded each side of a trellised gate. The house beyond the gate was the house Jessica had always wanted.

It was a cute character cottage, pale green, like the fresh colors of spring all around it. But it wasn't her home. A sign hung over the shadowed shelter of an inviting porch.

Baby Boomer, and in smaller letters, Your Place for All Things Baby.

Jessica had given him only the house number. She hadn't said a word about *that*.

And he knew exactly why. Because, for a moment, that familiar anger was there, overriding even the knife of panic that had begun to ease when the young cop had said she was okay. *Hell's bells, did she never give up?*

Or was the anger because the house, her new business and that phone call last night were evidence that she was ready to move on?

It was not as if, Kade told himself sternly, he wasn't ready to move on. In fact, he already had. He was just completely satisfied with the way things were. His company, Oilfield Supplies, had reached dizzying heights over the past year. Without the complication of a troubled relationship, he had been able to focus his attention intensely on business. The payoffs had been huge. He was a man who enjoyed success. Divorce did not fit with his picture of himself.

Divorce.

It was going to force him to face his own failure instead of ignore it. Or maybe not. Maybe these days you just signed a piece of paper and it was done. Over.

Could something like that ever be over? Not really.

He knew that from trying to bury himself in work for the past year.

If it was over, why did he still wear his ring? He had talked himself into believing it was to protect himself from the interest of the many women he encountered. Not personally. He had no personal life. But professionally he met beautiful, sophisticated, *interested* women every day. He did not need those kinds of complications.

He was aware, suddenly, he did not want Jessica to see he was still wearing that ring that bound him to her, so he took it off and slipped it in his pocket.

Taking a deep, fortifying breath, a warrior needing the opponent—when had Jessica become the opponent?—not to know he had a single doubt or fear, Kade took the wide steps, freshly painted the color of rich dairy cream, two at a time.

In startling and violent contrast to the sweet charm of the house, the glass had been smashed out of the squares of paned glass in the door. The door hung open, the catch that should have held it closed dangling uselessly.

Inside that door Kade skidded to a halt, aware of glass crackling under his feet. His eyes adjusted to the dimness as he burst out of the bright morning light. He had entered into a world more terrifying to him than an inhabited bear den.

The space was terrifying because of what was in it. It was the world he and Jessica had tried so hard to have and could not. It was a world of softness and light and dreamy hopes.

The stacks of tiny baby things made other memories crowd around Kade, of crying, and arguing, and a desperate sense of having come up against something he could not make right. Ever.

He sucked in another warrior's breath. There was a cluster of people across the room. He caught a glimpse of wheat-colored hair at the center of it and forced himself not to bolt over there.

He would not let her see what this—her injury, this building full of baby things—did to him.

Unfortunately, if he was not quite ready to see her, he had to take a moment to gather himself, and that forced him to look around.

The interior dividing walls within the house had been torn down to make one large room. What remained for walls were painted a shade of pale green one muted tone removed from that of the exterior of the house. The large space was connected by the expanse of old hardwood, rich with patina, and yet rugs and bookcases had been used to artfully divide the open area into four spaces.

Each was unique, and each so obviously represented a nursery.

One was a fantasy in pink: the crib was all done in pink flowered bedding, with pink-striped sheets and a fluffy pink elephant sprawled at the center. A polka-dot pink dress that looked like doll clothes was laid out on a change table. The letters *g-i-r-l* were suspended by invisible threads from the ceiling. A rocking chair, with pillows that matched the bedding, sat at right angles to the crib.

The next space was a composition in shades of pale blue. The crib and its bedding, again, were the main focus, but the eye was drawn to the vignette of boyish things that surrounded it. There were toy trains and tractors and trucks displayed on the shelves of a bookcase. Miniature overalls and an equally miniature ball cap hung on an antique coatrack beside it. A pair of impossibly small work boots hung from their laces off the same rack.

Next was one all done in lacy white, like a wedding dress, a basket on the floor overflowing with white stuffies: lambs and polar bears and little white dogs. The final display had two cribs, implying twins, and a shade of yellow as pale as baby duck down repeated in the bedding and lamp shades and teeny outfits.

Kade stood, sucking air into his chest, taking it all in and fighting the unmanly desire to cut and run.

How could Jessica do this? Work every day with the thing that had caused her, and him—and them—such unbelievable heartache? He felt all that anger with Jessica solidifying inside his chest. *Now* he was ready to face her.

He narrowed his eyes and looked to the cluster of people. They were at the very back of the old house, behind a counter with an old-fashioned cash register perched on it. Feeling as if his masculinity and size could damage the spaces, he passed through them quickly, holding his breath and being careful not to touch anything. Kade edged his way to the back of the room, inserting a firmness into his step that he did not feel.

It was unnecessary, because she didn't open her eyes as Kade arrived at the back of the store. Jessica was strapped to a wheeled gurney. Her eyes were tightly shut. A uniformed medic was leaning over her, splinting her right arm below her shoved-up sleeve. Two police officers, a man and a woman, stood by, notepads out.

Seeing Jessica would have been, at any time, like taking a punch to the stomach. But seeing her like this was unbearable.

It reminded him of the hardest lesson his marriage

had taught him: even though it was his deepest desire, he had been unable to protect her.

Studying her now, without her awareness, Kade could see subtle changes in her. She looked oddly grown-up in a buttoned-up white blouse and a gray pencil skirt. Her slender feet were encased in a pair of very practical and very plain flat pumps. She looked professional, and yet oddly dowdy, like that British nanny on television. Her look, if it could be called that, filled him with a certain sense of relief.

Jessica was obviously not out to capture a man.

But she looked so serious, not that he expected her to be upbeat, given the circumstances. She looked every inch the pragmatic businesswoman she had evidently become, rather than the artist she had always been. He was pretty sure the only day he'd ever seen Jessica out of jeans was the day they'd gotten married.

Her hair was the same color, untouched by dye, wheat ripening in a field, but had been bobbed off short, in a way that made her features seem elegant and chiseled and mature rather than gamine and friendly and girl-ish. Or maybe it was because she had lost weight that her features, especially her cheekbones, seemed to be in such sharp relief. She had on not a drop of makeup. Again, Kade felt a completely unwanted niggle of relief. She was obviously not making the least effort to play up her natural beauty.

Despite the fact she looked both the same and different, despite the fact she looked pale and bruised and despite the fact she was dressed in a way that suggested she did not like drawing attention to herself, Jessica did what she had always done, even though he tried to steel himself against reacting to her.

From the first moment he had seen her laughter-filled face on campus, he had been captivated. She had been sitting with friends at an outdoor picnic area. She had looked his way just as he was crossing a huge expanse of lawn, late for class.

His heart had done then exactly what it did now. It had stood still. And he had never made that class. Instead, he had crossed the lawn to her and to his destiny.

Jessica—then Clark—hadn't been beautiful in the traditional way. A little powder had not done anything to hide her freckles, which had already been darkening from the sun. Her glossy hair, sun streaked, had been spilling out of a clip at the back of her head. She'd been supercasual in a pink T-shirt and jean shorts with frayed cuffs. Her toenails had been painted to match her shirt.

But it was her eyes that had captivated him: as green as a leprechaun's and sparkling with just as much mischief. She had, if he recalled correctly, and he was sure he was, been wearing just a hint of makeup that day, shadow around her eyes that made them the deep, inviting green of a mountain pond. Her smile had been so compelling, warm, engaging, full of energy, infused with a force of life.

But two years of marriage had stripped her of all of that effervescent joy. And he could see, from the down-turned line around her mouth, it had not returned. Kade welcomed the iciness he felt settle around his heart.

He had not been enough for her.

Still, even with that thought like an acid inside him, he could not stop himself from moving closer to her.

He was shocked that he wanted to kiss her forehead, to brush the hair back from the smoothness of her brow. Instead, he laid his palm over her slender forearm, so aware his hand could encircle it completely. He saw that she was no longer wearing her rings.

"Are you okay?" The hardness Kade inserted in his voice was deliberate. There was no sense anyone knowing the panic he had felt, just for a moment, when he had thought of a world without Jessica. Especially not Jessica herself.

Jessica's eyes flew open. They were huge and familiar pools of liquid green, surrounded by lashes so thick they looked as if they had been rolled in chocolate cake batter. She had always had the most gorgeous eyes, and even her understated look now could not hide that. Unbidden, he thought of Jessica's eyes fastened on him, as she had walked down the aisle toward him… He shook off the memory, annoyed with himself, annoyed by how quickly he had gone *there*.

Now her beautiful eyes had the shadows of sorrow mixed with their light. Still, for one unguarded moment, the look in her eyes when she saw it was him made Kade wish he was the man she had thought he was. For one unguarded moment, he wished he was a man who had an ounce of hope left in him.

CHAPTER TWO

Wariness took the place of what had flared so briefly in Jessica's eyes when she had seen it was him, Kade. A guard equal to the one he knew to be in his own gaze went up in hers.

"What are you doing here?" Jessica asked him, her brow knit downward.

What was he doing here? She had asked him to come. "Did she hit her head?" Kade asked the ambulance attendant.

Jessica's frown deepened. "No, I did not hit my head."

"Possibly," the medic said.

"What are you doing here?" Jessica demanded again. It was a tone he remembered too well, the faintest anger hissing below the surface of her words, like a snake waiting to strike.

"You asked me to come," Kade reminded her. "To discuss—" He looked at the crowd around them, and could not bring himself to finish the sentence.

"Oh!" She looked contrite. "Now I remember. We were meeting to discuss…" Her voice drifted away, and then she sighed. "Sorry, Kade, I truly forgot you were coming." Apparently she hadn't lain awake last night contemplating the *d-i-v-o-r-c-e*.

"It's been a crazy morning," she said, as if it needed clarification.

"So I can see," he said. Jessica. Master of the understatement.

"Who are you?" the woman police officer asked.

"I'm her husband." Well, *technically*, he still was.

Kade was only inches from Jessica, but he was so aware that the small physical distance between them was nothing compared with the emotional one. It could not be crossed. That was what hissed right below the surface of her voice. There was a minefield of memory between them, and to try to negotiate it felt as if it would be risking having them both being blown to smithereens.

"I think her arm is fractured or broken," the medic said to Kade, and then returned his attention to Jessica. "We're going to transport you. They'll do X-rays at the hospital. I'm going to call ahead so they'll be ready for you in the emergency department."

"Which hospital?" Kade asked.

"You don't need to come," Jessica said, and there was *that* tone again, her apology apparently forgotten. She glared at Kade in warning when he frowned at her.

She was right. He did not *need* to go with her. And he could not have stopped himself if he tried.

"Nonetheless," he said, "I'd be more at ease making sure you were okay."

"No."

Kade knew that tone: she had made up her mind and there would be no getting her to change it.

No matter how stupidly unreasonable she was being.

"I thought he was your husband," the woman police officer said, confused.

"You don't need to come to the hospital," Jessica said.

She tried to fold her arms over her chest. The splint on her right arm made it awkward enough that after three attempts she gave up. She glared at her arm accusingly, and when that brought her no relief, she switched her glare to him.

To what he could tell was her chagrin, he accomplished what she had not been able to. He folded his arms firmly over his chest.

Battle stations.

What did this mean that he was insisting on accompanying Jessica to the hospital? That he was accepting responsibility for her?

Had he ever stopped feeling responsible for her?

"I thought he was your husband," the police officer said again.

"I am," Kade said, and heard the same firmness in his voice as that day that felt as if it was so long ago when he had said, "I do."

Jessica felt a shiver travel up and down her spine.

Her husband.

She watched Kade standing there, so close she could smell the familiar heady scent of him, his arms folded firmly over the deepness of that chest. He looked grim and formidable when he took that stance.

And even with that intimidating scowl drawing his dark brows down and pulling the edges of his mouth? Kade was the most magnificently made man Jessica had ever encountered. And she was pretty sure the female police officer wasn't immune to that fact, either.

Jessica had never tired of looking at him, not even when their relationship had become so troubled. Sometimes it had made her anger even more complicated that she still liked to look at him when he was so aggravating!

But gazing at him now, she felt resignation. This morning Kade had on a beautifully cut summer suit that she was certain was custom made. With it he had on a plain white shirt, possibly Egyptian cotton, and a subdued, expertly knotted tie, the slight luster of it screaming both silk and expense.

The ensemble made him look every inch the president and CEO of one of Calgary's most successful companies. Despite a rather mundane name, Oilfield Supplies did just that. It supplied the frantic oilfield activity of Alberta and beyond. With Kade's work ethic, ambition and smarts, the company's rise, in the past few years, had been mercurial.

And yet there was nothing soft looking about the man. There was none of the slender build or office pallor of a desk worker about him. He had learned his business from the bottom up, working on rigs to put himself through university. Despite the beautiful clothing, that rugged toughness was still in the air around him. Kade Brennan, with those long legs and those broad shoulders, and that deep chest, radiated pure power.

He had mink-dark hair. It managed, somehow, to look faintly unruly, no matter how short he cut it. And right now, that was very short.

He was clean shaven—Jessica had never known him not to be—and the close shave showed off the masculine perfection of his face: great skin, high cheekbones, straight nose, full lips, faintly jutting chin.

And his damn eyes, sexy and smoldering, were the deep sapphire of the ocean water. It was a color she had seen replicated only once, off the southernmost tip of the Big Island of Hawaii, where they had gone for their honeymoon.

But well before she'd had that reference point, from practically the moment she had met him, Jessica had spent an inordinate amount of time dreaming what their baby would look like. Would it have his eyes or hers, or some incredible combination of both?

The knife edge of that familiar pain was worse than the pain that throbbed along the length of her arm, despite the ice packs splinted in with her limb that were supposed to be giving her relief from pain.

Her husband.

She could feel her heart begin a familiar and hard tattoo at all that had once meant, and at all she knew about this man, the delicious intimacies that only a wife could know.

That he had ticklish toes, and loved the smell of lemons, and that if you kissed that little groove behind his ear, he was putty—

Jessica made herself stop, annoyed that she had gone *there* so swiftly. With everything between them, how was it she could feel this when she saw him? As if she had made the slow, chugging climb up the roller coaster and was now poised at the very summit, waiting to plunge down?

With everything between them, it felt like a betrayal of herself that she could feel such a deep and abiding hunger for the familiar feeling of his arms around her, for the scrape of his cheek across her own, for his breath in her ear, for the gentle savagery of his lips claiming her lips and his body claiming her body.

Her husband.

She felt weak. Where was her newfound sense of herself when she needed it most? Where was her fledgling self-respect? Where was her feeling that her life was working, and that she could have dreams she had set aside when Kade had walked away from her?

Jessica had discovered she could be responsible for her own dreams. It was really much easier without the complications of a man! In fact, she had decided the things she was dreaming would be so much more attainable without a man, especially one like him, who was just a little too sure that he knew the right answers for everybody.

Jessica was certain Kade would not approve of the secret she held inside herself. It was a secret that gave her pure joy, just as once an ultrasound picture tucked in a pocket close to her heart had. She had made a decision to adopt a baby.

It was at the very initial stages, little more than a thought, but she wanted things between her and Kade finalized before she even started the application process. She reminded herself that she needed to be strong for this meeting with Kade, and she despised the unexpected weakness of desire.

She'd rehearsed for a week before she'd called him, striving for just the right all-business tone of voice, planning this morning's meeting so carefully...

Of course, being caught in the middle of a breaking and entering had not been part of her plan! She could not believe, in all the chaos, she had totally forgotten he would be coming.

That was it. That explained the way she was feeling right now. She'd just had quite the shock. The pain in her arm was throbbing mercilessly, and despite denying it to the medic, it was possible she'd hit her head in the scuffle. Maybe, just maybe, a tiny bit of weakness in the department of her husband was acceptable.

Except right now she needed to be strong around him, not weak!

She stole another look at him. There was no missing how ill at ease the store made him. Something in his closed expression even suggested anger. At that realization, that he was angry, something in her hardened. She had known he might react like this when she'd invited him here.

And she had told herself firmly that it was a test she needed to pass. Divorcing Kade, not just on paper, but with her heart, would involve not caring what he liked or didn't like about her choices.

Her lawyer was absolutely right. It was time to tie up some loose ends in her life. And the lawyer was not even aware of *all* the reasons why it had become so important. Her lawyer knew only about her thriving business. Her decision to adopt was a secret, for now.

But it was a secret that required her to acknowledge that Kade Brennan, the husband she had been separated from for more than a year, was one gigantic loose end!

"What happened here?" Kade asked, but typical Kade, he wasn't asking. He was demanding, ready to take charge.

And she was never going to admit what a relief it would be to let him. "Really, Kade, it's none of your business."

The female officer, in particular, looked taken aback at her tone. "I thought he was your husband," she said again, almost plaintively.

"We're nearly divorced," Jessica explained, trying for the cavalier note of a career woman who didn't care, but she had to physically brace herself from flinching from the word.

Divorced.

She'd rehearsed that word, too, trying to take the bitter edge out of it, the sense of loss and finality and failure.

"Oh." If she was not mistaken, Officer—Jessica squinted at her name tag—Kelly took to that information like a starving hound scenting a bone.

"What happened here?" Kade asked again.

Jessica glared at him. To her relief, the medic announced they were ready to go, and she was wheeled out past Kade before having to give in to his demand for answers. Behind her, to her annoyance, she could hear the police officer filling him in on what had happened. She glanced back to see the female officer blinking helpfully at Kade and checking her notes.

"She came in to do paperwork this morning, six o'clock. Someone broke in around seven thirty."

"Don't come to the hospital," Jessica called over her shoulder, feeling a childish desire to get in the last shot. "I don't need you."

She glanced back one more time just as they crossed through her doorway to outside, where throngs of people seemed to be gathered in front of her house. But she didn't really even notice. What she noticed was that her arrow had hit home.

Kade looked momentarily stricken by her words.

That she didn't need him.

And instead of feeling happy that she had drawn blood, she felt sick about it, and some little demon inside her had to try to repair it, and let him know he was needed after all.

"Actually, Kade, can you find a way to secure everything? Please?"

Really, after her remark that she didn't need him, he should tell her to go get stuffed. But he didn't.

"And if you could put up a closed-for-the-day sign over that broken window I'd be most appreciative."

He snorted, but didn't say no.

"I can't just leave things. The door is broken. He could come back. Anybody could come in and just start helping themselves to everything in here."

All her hopes and dreams. It was a strange twist that she was being forced to ask Kade to rescue them.

"Never mind," Jessica said, appalled that she had even asked him. "I'll call someone."

She didn't need him. She didn't! Why was she giving him this mixed message: "I need you. I don't need you." She had the stunning realization she was not as clear of her soon-to-be ex-husband as she thought she was!

"I'll look after it," he said.

She should have protested harder, but there was no denying what a relief it was to have Kade Brennan, her husband for a little while longer, say that he would look after things.

CHAPTER THREE

JESSICA WAS WHEELED out to the ambulance, and Kade prowled through her shop looking for items to repair her door. Finally, in a back drawer in a tiny kitchen area he found a hammer and regarded it thoughtfully.

"This isn't really a hammer," he muttered to himself. "It's more like a toy, a prop for one of her fake nurseries."

In a dank cellar, he found some old boards. Thankfully, they had nails in them that he could pull and reuse. Why did women never have the essentials? Nails, screwdrivers, hammers, duct tape?

He boarded up the broken front door and found a square of thick wood to write a few words on.

He had to nail it up over the broken window because of the lack of duct tape. A determined thief could still get in, but the repair, though not pretty, actually looked quite a bit more secure than her old door with its paned glass.

He surveyed his work briefly, and recognized it as temporary but passable. Then he called his personal assistant, Patty, to tell her he would be very late today, if he made it in at all. "I need you to find me a simple surveillance system. I think there's a kind that alerts to your phone. And then could you find a handyman? I need a door fixed, a window replaced and that surveillance system installed. Have him call me for the details.

"And also if you could have my car dropped at Holy Cross Hospital? Whoever brings it can just give me a call when they get there, I'll meet them for keys." He listened for a moment. "No, everything is fine. No need for concern."

Kade walked out to Memorial Drive and was able to flag a cab to take him to the hospital.

He found Jessica in a wheelchair, in a waiting room in the X-ray department.

"How are you doing?"

It was obvious she was not doing well. Her face was pale, and she looked as if she was going to cry.

He could not handle Jessica crying. There was nothing he hated more than the helplessness that made him feel. To his detriment, he had not reacted well to her tears in the past.

He felt ashamed of the fact that she felt it necessary to suck in a deep, steadying breath before she spoke to him.

"They've done an X-ray. I'm just waiting for the doctor. It is broken. I'm not sure if they can set it, or if it will need surgery." She looked perilously close to tears.

Kade fought an urge to wrap his arms around her and let her cry. But he'd never been good with tears, and it felt way too late now to try to be a sensitive guy. It would require him to be a way better and braver man than he knew how to be.

She knew his weaknesses, because she set her shoulders and tilted her chin. "You didn't have to come."

He shrugged. "Your store is secure," he told her. "I put up a sign."

The struggle—whether to be gracious or belligerent—

was evident in her eyes. Graciousness won, as he had known it would. "Thank you. What did it say?"

"Baby bummer, temporarily closed due to break-in."

A reluctant smile tickled her lips, and then she surrendered and laughed. "That's pretty good. Even though it's a major bummer, not a baby one."

Kade was pretty pleased with himself that he had made her laugh instead of cry.

"It could have been a much more major bummer than it was," he said sternly. "Tell me what happened."

Jessica couldn't help but shiver at the faintly dangerous note in Kade's voice. She could not be intimidated by it!

"Isn't it fairly obvious what happened?" she asked coolly. "I was doing some paperwork, and there was a break-in."

"But he came through the front door."

"So?"

"Is there a back door?" Kade asked. That something dangerous deepened in his tone.

"Well, yes, but we just surprised each other. Thankfully, I called 911 as soon as I heard the glass break."

"Don't you think you could have run out the back door and called 911 from safety?"

Jessica remembered what she didn't like about Kade. Besides everything. She needed a good cry right now and she was sucking it back rather than risk his disapproval. On top of that, he was a big man at work. It made him think he knew the answers to everything.

Which was why she didn't even want him to know about adoption. He was certain to have an opinion about that that she would not be eager to hear.

"Hindsight is always twenty-twenty," she informed him snootily.

"How did you end up hurt?" Kade asked.

Jessica squirmed a bit.

"Um, we scuffled," she admitted. "I fell."

"You scuffled?" Kade asked, incredulous. "You *scuffled* with a burglar? I would have thought it was hard to scuffle while running for the back door."

"I was not going to run away," she said.

"That is nothing to be proud of."

"Yes," she said, "it is. Don't you dare presume to tell me what to be proud of."

From their shared laughter over the bummers of life just moments ago to this. It was just like the final weeks of their marriage: arguments lurked everywhere.

"Why are you proud of it?" he asked, that dangerous something still deepening in his tone, that muscle jerking along the line of his jaw that meant he was *really* annoyed.

"I'm proud I took on that scrawny thief," Jessica said, her voice low, but gaining power. "I lost my mother when I was twelve. I've lost two babies to miscarriage."

And she had lost Kade, not that she was going to mention that. In some ways the loss of him had been the worst of all. The other losses had been irrevocable, but Kade was still there, just not there for her.

"Sorry?" he said, reeling back slightly from her as if she had hit him with something. "What does that have to do with this?"

"I am not losing anything else," she said, and could hear the tautness in her own voice. "Not one more thing."

He stared at her, and she took a deep breath and continued.

"You listen to me, Kade Brennan. I am not surrendering to life anymore. I am not going to be the hapless victim. I am making the rules, and I am making my own life happen."

Kade was shocked into silence, so she went on, her tone low. "So if that means scuffling with someone who was trying to take one more thing from me, then so be it."

"Oh, boy," he said, his voice low and pained. "That's not even sensible."

"I don't care what you think is sensible," she said with stubborn pride.

Though, she did plan to be more sensible soon. Naturally, there would be no more scuffling once she had adopted a baby. She would think things all the way through then. She would be the model of responsible behavior.

She hoped there were no questions about how one would handle a break-in on the adoption application.

"So you weren't running for the back door," he deduced, regaining himself. "Not even close."

"Nope." The new Jessica refused to be intimidated. She met his gaze with determination. She was not going to be cowed by Kade. She was not one of his employees. She was nearly not even his wife. In a little while, they would practically be strangers.

At the thought, a little unexpected grayness swirled inside her—she was willing to bet that was a result of her injury, a bit of shock—but she fought it off bravely.

"I was not letting him get away," Jessica said. "The police were coming."

For a moment he was stunned speechless again. He clenched that muscle in his jaw tighter. She remembered she hated that about him, too: the jaw clenching.

His voice rarely rose in anger, but that muscle, leaping along the hard line of his jaw, was a dead giveaway that he was *really* irritated about something.

"Are you telling me—" Kade's voice was low and dangerous "—that you not only scuffled with the burglar, but you tried to detain him?"

"He was a shrimp," Jessica said defiantly.

"In case you haven't looked in the mirror recently, so are you. And he could have had a knife! Or a gun!" So much for his voice rarely being raised in anger.

"I wasn't going to stand by and let him steal from me!" At the look on Kade's face, she backed down marginally. "Okay, so maybe I didn't think it all the way through." Something that was definitely going to have to change once she embraced motherhood.

"Maybe?"

She was not sure why she felt driven to defend herself, even when she knew Kade was right and she was wrong. Not just defend herself, but goad him a little bit.

"Break-ins started on this block a few nights ago. No one can sleep at night. We all go down there and check our businesses. That business is everything to me now. It's my whole life."

He heard the unspoken, she was sure. That the business had replaced him as her whole life.

The jaw muscle was rippling beneath the line of his skin. She watched it, fascinated despite herself. He was *really* angry.

"You've been going down there in the middle of the night to check your business?"

It didn't seem nearly as clever now with Kade glaring at her.

"Yes, I have," she said, refusing to back down. "And I'll probably do it again tonight, since he got away."

Well, actually, she probably wouldn't, but there was no sense Kade thinking he could order her around, could control her with even a hint of his disapproval. Those days were over.

"You are not going down there tonight," Kade said. "For God's sake, Jessica, haven't you ever heard of security cameras?"

"Of course I've thought of security cameras. And security companies. But the options are many and the selection is huge," she said. "I've been trying to figure out what is best for me and my budget. Not that that is any of your business. And you don't have any say in how I decide to handle it. None whatsoever. You and I only have one thing left to discuss. And that is our divorce."

And unbidden, the thought blasted through her that *that* was a major bummer.

And the doctor, a lovely young woman, chose that moment to come out, X-rays in hand, and say, "Mr. and Mrs. Brennan?"

Mr. and Mrs. Brennan. That should not fill her with longing! That should not make Jessica wonder if there would ever be another Mrs. Brennan taking her place.

It was over. Their brief marriage was over. They were getting divorced. Kade's life was no longer any of her business, just as hers was no longer any of his.

She would probably change her name back to Clark. She could be Ms. Clark instead of Mrs. Brennan. The baby would be a Clark.

She wasn't thinking about a first name. She knew better than that. Or at least she should know better than that. A memory knifed through her: Kade and her poring over the baby-name books. Deciding on Lewis for a boy and Amelia for a girl.

And then the first miscarriage. And somehow, she could see now, in retrospect, what she had not seen then. From the moment Kade had asked her not to name that little lost baby, a crack had appeared between them.

No, she was determined to enjoy the success of her baby nursery design business and her new storefront as a means to an end. She could have it all.

She could fill her life with the thrill of obtaining those adorable outfits no other store would carry, those one-of-a-kind over-the-crib mobiles, those perfect lamb-soft cuddly teddy bears that everyone wanted and no one could find.

And someday, maybe sooner than later, the outfits would be for her own baby. She would design a nursery for her own baby.

"Don't," he'd whispered when she had started painting the walls of their spare room a pale shade of lavender the second time. "Please don't."

But now she didn't need his approval. She could do it all her way. She could finally, finally be happy. All the pieces were in place.

Weren't they? If they were, why did Jessica feel a sudden desire to weep? It was that crack on her head. It was the throbbing in her arm. It was her day gone so terribly wrong, nothing according to her plan.

"Mr. and Mrs. Brennan?" the doctor asked, again, baffled by the lack of response.

"Yes," Kade said.

"No," Jessica said at the very same time.

He looked stubborn, a look Jessica remembered well.

She didn't think she should admit a sudden urge to kill him in front of the doctor, so she shrugged. "We're nearly divorced," she informed the doctor. "He was just leaving."

Kade gave her a look, and then got to his feet and prowled around the small waiting area.

"Well, if you could come with me."

Jessica stood up from the wheelchair to follow the doctor. She wobbled. Kade was instantly at her side.

"Sit down," he snapped.

Really, she should not tolerate that tone of voice from him, that tendency to bossiness. But the sudden wooziness she felt left her with no choice.

Kade pushed her down the hallway with the doctor, and they entered a small examining room. The doctor put the X-rays up on a light board.

"It's not a complicated break," she said, showing them with the tip of her pen. "It's what we call a complete fracture. I'm going to set it and cast it. I think you'll be in the cast for about four weeks and then require some therapy after to get full mobility back."

Four weeks in a cast? But that barely registered. What registered was that this was her arm with the bone, showing white on the X-ray, clearly snapped in two. Her wooziness increased. She had to fight an urge to put her head between her knees.

"Is it going to hurt?" Jessica whispered, still not wanting Kade to see any sign of weakness from her.

"I wish I could tell you no, but even with the powerful painkiller I'm going to give you, yes, it's going to hurt. Do you want your husband to come with you?"

Yes, part of Jessica whimpered. But that was the part she had to fight! Aware of Kade's eyes on her, she tilted her chin. "No, I'm fine. Kade, you don't have to wait."

CHAPTER FOUR

YOU DON'T HAVE to wait was not quite as firm as *you can leave now.* Jessica forced herself not to look back at him as the doctor took her to a different room. But she had to admit she felt grateful that he did not appear to be leaving.

A half hour later, her arm in a cast and immobilized in a sling, with some prescription painkillers and some instructions in her other hand, Jessica was pushed by a nurse back to the waiting area. Her feeling of wooziness had increased tenfold.

Because she actually felt happy that Kade was still there. He sprang from a chair as soon as he saw her, and then shoved his hands into his pockets.

"You didn't have to wait," Jessica said in stubborn defiance of the relief.

"I'll make sure you get home safely," he said. "I had someone from the office drop off my car for me while I waited. I'll bring it around to that door over there."

And then, before she could protest on a number of fronts—that she didn't need him to drive her and that she was going back to work, not home—he was gone.

She didn't want to admit how good his take-charge attitude felt sometimes. By the time he'd arrived at the door, she'd realized there was no way she was going to work. She was also reluctant to concede how good it felt when he held open the door of his car for her and she slid from the wheelchair into its familiar luxury. Moments later, with the wheelchair returned, he put the car in gear and threaded through what was left of the morning rush with ease.

Why did she feel glad that he didn't have a different car? She shouldn't care at all. But he'd bought the car after they'd graduated from university, well before he'd been able to afford such a thing.

"But why?" she'd asked him when he had come and shown it to her. The high-priced car had seemed as if it should not be a priority to a recent university graduate.

"Because when I marry you, this is what we're driving away in."

And then he'd shown her the ring he couldn't afford, either. Three months later, with the roof down and her veil blowing out the back, they had driven away to a shower of confetti and their cheering friends.

One of her favorite wedding pictures was of that scene, the car departing, a just-married sign tacked crookedly to the back bumper that trailed tin cans on strings. In that picture Kade had been grinning over his shoulder, a man who had everything. And she had been laughing, holding on to her veil to keep it from blowing off, looking like a woman embracing the wildest ride of her life.

Which marriage had definitely turned out to be, just not in the way she had expected. It had been a roller-coaster ride of reaching dizzying heights and plummeting into deep and shadowy valleys.

Jessica took a deep breath. She tried to clear her head of the memories, but she felt the painkilling drugs were impeding her sense of control. Actually, she did not know which impaired her judgment more: sitting in the car, so close to Kade, or the drugs.

She had always liked the way he drove, and though it felt like a weakness, she just gave herself over to enjoying it. The car, under his expert hand, was a living thing, darting smoothly in and out of traffic.

They pulled up in front of the house they had once shared. It was farther from downtown than her business, but still in a beautiful established southwest neighborhood with rows of single-story bungalows, circa 1950.

Oh, God, if getting in his car had nearly swamped her with memories, what was she going to do if he came into the house they had once shared? There was a reason she had asked him to meet her at her business.

"Kade," she said firmly, wrestling the car door open with her left arm, "we need to get a divorce."

Kade made himself turn and look at her, even though it was unexpectedly painful having her back in the passenger seat of the car.

He forced himself to really look at her. Beneath the pallor and the thinness, he suspected *something*.

"What aren't you telling me?"

She wouldn't look at him. She got the car door open, awkward as it was reaching across herself with her left arm.

"You could have waited for me to do that," he said, annoyed, but she threw him a proud glare, found her feet and stepped out.

But her fighting stance was short-lived. She got a confused look on her face. And then she went very white. And stumbled.

He bolted from the car and caught her just as her legs crumpled underneath her. He scooped her up easily and stared down at her. And there he was, in the predicament he would have least predicated for the day—with Jessica's slight weight in his arms, her body deliciously pliant against his, her eyes wide on his face. She had a scent that was all her own, faintly lemony, like a chiffon pie.

She licked her lips, and his eyes moved to them, and he remembered her taste, and the glory of kissing Jessica.

She seemed to sense the sudden hiss of energy between them and regained herself quickly, inserted her good hand between them and shoved. "Put me down!"

As if he had snatched her up against her will instead of rescuing her from a fall. He ignored her and carried her up the walkway to the house.

Their house.

He was not going to carry her across the threshold. The memory of that moment in their history was just too poignant. He set her down on the front steps and her legs folded. She sat down on the top stair, looking fragile and forlorn.

"I don't feel well and I don't know where my keys are," she said.

He still had one, but he wasn't sure if he should use it. It felt presumptuous. It didn't feel as if he should treat it like his house anymore.

"I must have left my purse at the shop," she said, trying to get up.

"Sit still for a minute," he said.

It wasn't an order, just a suggestion, but she folded her

good arm over the one in the sling. He half expected she might stick her tongue out at him, but she didn't.

"You've lost weight," he said, watching her sit on the stoop.

"A little," she admitted, as if she was giving away a state secret. "You know me. Obsessed about my projects. Right now it's launching Baby Boomer. Sometimes I forget to eat."

He frowned at that. She was always obsessed about something. Once, it had been about him.

"What's your sudden panic to get a divorce?" he asked.

She choked and glared at him. "Over a year is not a sudden panic."

"Have you met someone?" His voice sounded oddly raw in his own ears.

Jessica searched his face but he kept his features cool.

"Not that it is any of your business, but no." She hesitated. "Have you?"

He snorted. "No, I'm cured, thanks."

"I am, too!" She hesitated again, not, he guessed, wanting to appear too interested in his life. "I suppose you're playing the field, then?"

"What? What does that mean, exactly?"

"Seeing lots of women."

He snorted and allowed himself to feel the insult of it. Jessica was painting him as a playboy? "You have to know me better than that."

"You live in that building. It has a reputation."

"The condominium has a reputation?" he asked, astounded. "The building I live in? River's Edge?"

"It does," she said firmly. "Lots of single people live there. Very wealthy single people. It has a pool and that superswanky penthouse party room. The apartments are posh."

"How do you know all that?" he asked.

She turned red. "Don't get the idea I've been sneaking around spying on you."

"That is the furthest from any idea I would ever get about you," he said drily.

"The newspaper did a feature on it."

"I must have missed that."

"It seems like a good place for a single guy to live. One who is, you know, in pursuit of fun and freedom."

That was what Jessica thought he was in pursuit of? Jeez. Well, let her think it. How could it be that she didn't know him at all?

"Rest assured—" he could hear the stiffness in his voice "—I live there because it is a stone's throw from work, which by the way is where I spend the majority of my waking hours." He hesitated, not wanting to appear too interested in her life, either. "So are *you* playing the field?"

"Don't be ridiculous," she said.

"How come it's ridiculous when I ask but not when you ask?" And there it was, the tension between them, always waiting to be fanned to life.

"I already told you I'm obsessed with my business. I don't have time for anything else."

"So you are not in a new relationship, and apparently not looking for one. You want a divorce why?"

She sighed with what he felt was unnecessary drama. "We can't just go on indefinitely like this, Kade."

He wanted to ask why not but he didn't.

"All those hours I spend working are paying off. My business is moving to the next level."

He raised an eyebrow at her.

"I did over a hundred thousand in internet sales last year."

He let out a low appreciative whistle. "That's good."

"I think it could be double that this year with the store-front opening."

So she was moving up as well as on. Well, good for her. No sense admitting, not even to himself, how happy he was that her moving on did not involve a new guy moving in.

"My lawyer has advised me to tie up any loose ends."

He managed, barely, not to wince at being referred to as a loose end. "So your lawyer is afraid of what? That you'll be wildly successful and I, as your legal partner, will come in and demand half your business?"

"I suppose stranger things have happened," she said coolly.

"I think my business is probably worth as much as your business if we were going to start making claims against each other."

"We both know your business is probably worth a hundred times what my little place is worth. It's not about that."

"What's it about, then?" He was watching her narrowly. He knew her so well. And he knew there was something she wasn't telling him.

She sighed heavily. "Kade, we don't even have a separation agreement. We own this house together. And everything in it. You haven't even taken a piece of furniture. We need to figure things out."

He rolled his shoulders and looked at *their* house, the hopeless little fixer-upper that she had fallen in love with from the first moment she had laid her eyes on it.

"It's like the cottage in *Snow White*," she had said dreamily.

It hadn't been anything like the cottage in *Snow White*. Except for the decorative shutters, with hearts cut out of them, the house had been an uninspired square box with ugly stucco. The only thing Snow Whitish about it? It needed seven dwarfs, full-time, to help with its constant need for repair.

She had not done one thing to the exterior since he had left. They hadn't been able to afford too much at the time, so they had rented one of those spray-painter things and redone the stucco white. The black shutters and door had become pale blue.

"Isn't the color a little, er, babyish?" he had asked her of the pale blue.

Her sigh of pure delight, as if the color was inviting a baby into their house, seemed now, in retrospect, as if it might have been a warning.

Their strictly cosmetic changes were already deteriorating.

Was it the same inside as it had been? Suddenly he felt driven to know just how much she had moved on. It felt as if he needed to know.

He looked on his chain and acted surprised. "I have a key."

And a moment later he was helping her into the home they had shared. He had thought she would, if sensible, rip out every reminder of him.

But she was the woman who had scuffled with a burglar, and she had not done the sensible thing.

Their house was relatively unchanged. He thought she might have tried to erase signs of him—and them—but no, there was the couch they had picked out together, and the old scarred wooden bench she had fallen in love with and used as a coffee table. She hadn't even gotten rid of the oversize fake leather burgundy recliner with the handy remote control holder built into it. He had thought it would go. When people had come over she had referred to it, apologetically, as the guy chair, her nose wrinkled up with affectionate resignation. She had even named it Behemoth.

In fact, as far as Kade could see, the only change was that the bench contained only a mason glass jar spilling purple tulips. It was not covered with baby magazines. Oh. And there was one other thing changed. Their wedding pictures, her favorite shots in different-size frames, were not hung over the mantel of the fireplace. The paint had not faded where they had hung, and so there were six empty squares where once their love for each other had been on proud display.

The fireplace didn't actually work. He remembered their excitement the first time they had tried to light it, the year's first snow falling outside. The chimney had belched so much black smoke back into the house they had run outside, choking on soot and laughter. There was still a big black mark on the front of it from that.

He led her through the familiar space of the tiny house to the back, where the kitchen was. One day, they had hoped to knock out a wall and have open concept, but it had not happened. He made her sit at the table, another piece of furniture they had bought together at the second-hand stores they had loved to haunt on Saturday mornings. Without asking her, he fetched her a glass of water, finding the glasses with easy familiarity.

He remembered trying to paint the oak cabinets white in an effort to modernize the look of the kitchen. It had been disastrous. They had fallen asleep tucked against each other, propped against a cupboard, exhausted, covered in more paint than the cabinets. The cabinets looked as awful as they always had, the old stain bleeding through the white. They'd never bothered to try painting them again. The truth was, he liked them like that, with their laughter and ineptitude caught for all time in the hardened paint dribbles. And he thought she probably did, too.

The memories all felt like a knife between his eyes.

CHAPTER FIVE

BUT OF COURSE, Kade knew, those happy memories of renovation disaster had all happened before everything went south. After Jessica had discovered she was pregnant the first time, renovation had slammed to a halt.

Chemicals. Dust. The possibility of stirring up mouse poo.

Jessica took a sip of the water, watching him over the rim. "We need to make a decision about the house."

"You can have it," he said. "I don't want it."

"I don't want you to give me a house, Kade," she said with irritating patience, as if she was explaining the multiplication tables to a third grader. "I actually don't want this house. I'd like to get my half out of it and move on."

She didn't want the house with the fireplace that didn't work and laughter captured in the paint dribbles? She'd always loved this house, despite its many flaws.

There was something more going on that she was not telling him. He always knew. She was terrible at keeping secrets.

"I'll just sign over my half to you," he repeated.

"I don't want you to give it to me." Now she sounded mad. This was what their last weeks and months together had been like. There was always a minefield to be crossed between them. No matter what you said, it was wrong; the seeds were there for a bitter battle.

"That's ridiculous. Who says no to being given a house?"

"Okay, then. I'll give it to you."

"Why are you being so difficult?"

He could not believe the words had come out of his mouth. Their favorite line from *Beauty and the Beast*. In the early days, one of them had always broken the fury of an argument by using it.

For a moment, something suspiciously like tears shone behind her eyes, but then the moment was gone, and her mouth was pressed together in that stubborn "there is no talking to her now" expression.

"Can't we even get divorced normally?" she asked a little wearily, sinking back in her chair and closing her eyes.

"What does that mean?" he asked, but was sorry the minute the words were out of his mouth.

Of course, what it meant was that they hadn't been able to make a baby *normally*.

But thankfully, Jessica did not go there. "Normal— we're supposed to fight over the assets, not be trying to give them to each other."

"Oh, forgive me," he said sarcastically. "I haven't read the rule book on divorce. This is my first one."

Then he realized she was way too pale, and that she wasn't up for this. "You're not feeling very good, are you?"

"No," she admitted.

"We need to talk about this another time."

"Why do you always get to decide what *we* need?"

That stung, but he wasn't going to get drawn into an

argument. "Look, you've had a tough morning, and you are currently under the influence of some pretty potent painkillers."

She sighed.

"You should probably avoid major decisions for forty-eight hours."

"I'm perfectly capable of making some decisions."

"There is ample evidence you aren't thinking right. You've just refused the offer of a house."

"Because I am not going to be your charity case! I have my pride, Kade. We'll sell it. You take half. I take half."

He shrugged, and glanced around. "Have you done any of the repairs that needed doing?"

Her mutinous expression said more than she wanted it to.

"Nothing is fixed," he guessed softly. "You're still jiggling the toilet handle and putting a bucket under the leak in the spare bedroom ceiling. You're still getting slivers in your feet from the floor you refuse to rip out, even though it was going to cost more to refurbish it than it would to put in a new one."

"That's precisely why I need to sell it," she said reasonably. "It's not a suitable house for a woman on her own."

Again, he heard something Jessica was not telling him.

"We'll talk about selling the house," he promised. "We'll probably get more for it if we do some fixes."

He noted his easy use of the word *we*, and backtracked rapidly. "How about if I come back later in the week? I'll have a quick look through the house and make a list of what absolutely has to be done, and then I'll hire a handyman to do it. My assistant is actually tracking one down to fix the door on your shop, so we'll see how he does there."

"I think the real estate agent can do the list of what needs to be done."

She'd already talked to a real estate agent. He shrugged as if he didn't feel smacked up the side of the head by her determination to rid herself of this reminder of all things *them*.

"Your real estate agent wants to make money off you. He is not necessarily a good choice as an adviser."

"And you are?"

He deserved that, he supposed.

"Okay. Do it your way," Jessica said. "I'll pay half for the handyman. Do you think you could come in fairly quickly and make your list? Maybe tomorrow while I'm at work?"

He didn't tell her he doubted she would be going back to work tomorrow. Her face was pale with exhaustion and she was slumped in her chair. No matter what she said, now was not the time for this discussion.

"I'm going to put you to bed," Kade said. "You're obviously done for today. We can talk about the house later." He noticed he carefully avoided the word *divorce*.

"I am exhausted," she admitted. "I do need to go to bed. However, you are not putting me to bed." She folded her one arm up over her sling, but winced at the unexpected hardness of the cast hitting her in the chest.

"I doubt if you can even get your clothes off on your own."

She contemplated that, looked down at her arm in the sling. He knew at that moment, the reality of the next four weeks was sinking in. In her mind, she was trying to think how she was going to accomplish the simple task of getting her clothes off and getting into pajamas.

"I'll go to bed in my clothes," she announced.

"Eventually," he pointed out, "you're going to have to figure out how to get out of them. You're going to be in that cast for how long?"

"A month," she said, horror in her features as her new reality dawned on her.

"I'll just help you this first time."

"You are not helping me get undressed," she said, shocked.

He felt a little shock himself at the picture in his mind of that very shirt sliding off the slenderness of her shoulders. He blinked at the old stirring of pure fire he felt for Jessica. She was disabled, for God's sake.

It took enormous strength to wrestle down the yearning the thought of touching her created in him, to force his voice to be patient and practical.

"Okay," Kade said slowly, "so you don't want me to help you get undressed, even though I've done it dozens of times before. What do you propose?"

Her face turned fiery with her blush. She glared at him, but then stared at her sleeve, bunched up above the cast, and the reality of trying to get the shirt off over the rather major obstacle of her cast-encased arm seemed to settle in.

"Am I going to have to cut it off? But I love this blouse!" She launched to her feet. He was sure it was as much to turn her back to him as anything else. She went to the kitchen drawer where they had always kept the scissors and yanked it open. "Maybe if I cut it along the seam," she muttered.

He watched her juggle the scissors for a minute before taking pity on her. He went and took the scissors away and stepped in front of her. Gently, he took her arm from the sling, and straightened the sleeve of the blouse as much as he could.

There was less resistance than he expected. Carefully, so aware of her nearness and her scent, and the silky feel of her skin beneath his fingertips, he took the sharp point of the scissors and slit the seam of the sleeve.

She stared down at her slit-open sleeve. "Thanks. I'll take it from here."

"Really? How are you going to undo your buttons?"

With a mulish expression on her face, she reached up with her left hand and tried to clumsily shove the button through a very tight buttonhole.

"Here," he said. "I'll help you."

She realized she could not refuse. "Okay," she said with ill grace. "But don't look."

Don't look? Hell's bells, Jessica, we belong to each other. Instead of getting impatient, he teased her. "Okay. Have it your way." He closed his eyes and placed his hand lightly on her open neckline. He loved the feel of her delicate skin beneath his fingertips. Loved it.

"What are you doing?" she squeaked.

"Well, if I can't look, I'll just feel my way to those buttons. I'll braille you. Pretend I'm blind." He slid his hand down. He felt her stop breathing. He waited for her to tell him to stop, but she didn't.

It seemed like a full minute passed before Jessica came to her senses and slapped his hand away.

He opened his eyes, and she was looking at him, her eyes wide and gorgeous. She licked her lips and his gaze went to them. He wanted to crush them under his own.

That old feeling sizzled in the air between them, the way it had been before her quest for a baby had begun.

"Keep your eyes open," she demanded.

"Ah, Jessica," he said, reaching for her buttons, "don't look, but keep my eyes open. Is that even possible?"

"Try your best," she whispered.

"You are a hard woman to please." But, he remembered, his mouth going dry, she had not been a hard woman to please at all. With this memory of how it was to be together, red-hot between them, his fingers on her buttons was a dangerous thing, indeed.

Kade found his fingers on the buttons of her shirt. She stopped breathing. He stopped breathing.

Oh, my God, Jessica, he thought.

He did manage to keep his eyes open and not look. Because he held her gaze the whole time that he undid her buttons for her. His world became as it had once been: her. His whole world was suddenly, beautifully, only about the way the light looked in her hair, and the scent of her, and the amazing mountain-pond green of her eyes.

His hands slowed on her buttons as he deliberately dragged out the moment. And then he flicked open the last button and stepped back from her.

"There," he said. His voice had a raspy edge to it.

She stood, still as a doe frozen in headlights. Her shirt gapped open.

"You want me to help you get it off?"

She unfroze and her eyes skittered away from his and from the intensity that had leaped up so suddenly between them.

"No. No! I can take it from here."

Thank God, he thought. But he could already see the

impracticality of it. "I'm afraid you'll fall over and break your other arm struggling out of those clothes," he told her. "The blouse is just one obstacle. Then there's, um, your tights."

"I can manage, I'm sure." Her tone was strangled. Was she imagining him kneeling in front of her, his hands on the waistband of those tights?

He took a devilish delight in her discomfort even while he had to endure his own.

"And I'm not sure what kind of a magician you would have to be to get your bra off with your left hand," he said.

She looked stricken as she went over the necessary steps in her mind.

"If you let me help you this time…" Kade suggested, but she didn't let him finish.

"No!"

"Okay." He put his hands in the air—cowboy surrender. And suddenly it didn't seem funny anymore to torment her. It just reminded him of all they'd lost. The easy familiarity between them was gone. The beautiful tension. The joy they had taken in discovering each other's bodies and the secrets of pleasing each other. In those first early days, he remembered chasing her around this little house until they were both screaming with laughter.

She blushed, and it seemed to him each of those losses was written in the contrived pride of her posture, too. Jessica headed for the hallway, the bedroom they had shared.

If he followed her there, there was probably no predicting what would happen next. And yet he had to fight down the urge to trail after her.

What was wrong with him? What could happen next? She was on drugs. Her arm was disabled. She was being deliberately dowdy.

The simple truth? None of that mattered, least of all the dowdy part. Around Jessica, had he ever been able to think straight? Ever?

"While you're in there," he called after her, trying to convince her, or maybe himself, that he was just a practical, helpful guy, and not totally besotted with this woman who was not going to be his wife much longer, "you can pick what you're going to wear for the next four weeks very carefully."

"And while you're out there, you can start making a list of the fixes. Then you won't have to come back later."

To help her. He would not have to come back later to help her. He mulled that over. "I'm not sure how you can do this on your own. Think about putting on tights one-handed. It would probably be even more challenging than getting them off."

"I can go bare legged," she called.

"I don't even want to think about how you'll get the bra on," he said gruffly. He couldn't imagine how she was going to struggle into and out of her clothes, but that was not a good thing for him to be imagining anyway.

CHAPTER SIX

JESSICA BOLTED THROUGH her bedroom and into the safety of her bathroom. She did not want Kade thinking about her bra, either!

But the reality of her situation was now hitting home.

Oh, there were practical realities. How was she going to manage all this? Not just dressing, which was going to be an inconvenience and a major challenge, but everything? How was she going to take a shower, and unpack boxes at Baby Boomer? How was she going to butter toast, for heaven's sake?

But all those practical realities were taking a backseat to the reality of how she had felt just now with Kade's hand, his touch warm and strong and beautiful, on her neck, and then on her buttons.

That was just chemistry, she warned herself. They had always had chemistry in abundance. Well, not always. The chemistry had been challenged when they—no, she—had wanted it to respond on cue.

Still, it was easier to feel as if she could control the unexpected reality of Kade being in her home—their home—while she was comfortably locked in her bathroom.

Just to prove her control, she locked the door. But as

she heard the lock click, she was very aware that she could not lock out the danger she felt. It was inside herself. How did you lock that away?

"Focus," Jessica commanded herself. But life seemed suddenly very complicated, and she felt exhausted by the complications. She wanted out of her clothes and into her bed.

She wanted her husband out of her house and she wanted the stirring of something that had slept for so long within her to go back to sleep!

Even if it did make her feel alive in a way she had not felt alive in a long, long time. Not even the excitement and success of her business had made her feel like this, tingling with a primal awareness of what it was to be alive.

Even the most exciting thing in her life—contemplating adopting a baby, and starting a family of her own—had never made her feel like this!

"That's a good thing," she told herself, out loud. "*This* feeling is a drug, a powerful, potent, addicting drug that could wreck everything."

But what a beautiful way to have it wrecked, a horrible uncontrollable little voice deep inside her whined.

"Everything okay in there?"

"Yes, fine, thanks." No, it wasn't fine. *Go away. I can't think clearly with you here.*

"I thought I heard you mumbling. Are you sure you're okay?"

"I'm fine," she called. She could hear a desperate edge in her own voice. Jessica was breathing hard, as if she had run a marathon.

Annoyed with herself, she told herself to just focus on one thing at a time. That one thing right now was removing her blouse. By herself.

Her nightie was hanging on the back of the bathroom door. She should not feel regret that the nightwear was mundane and not the least sexy. She should only be feeling thankful that it was sleeveless.

For a whole year, she had not cared what her sleepwear looked like. As long as it was comfortable she hadn't cared if it was frumpy, if it had all the sex appeal of a twenty-pound potato sack.

For a whole year, she had told herself that not caring what she slept in, that not spending monstrous amounts of money on gorgeous lingerie, was a form of freedom. She had convinced herself it was one of the perks of the single life.

"Focus on getting your blouse off!" she told herself.

"Jessica?"

"I'm okay." She hoped he would not hear the edge in her voice. Of course, he did.

"You don't sound okay. I told you it was going to be more difficult than you thought."

What? Getting dressed? Or getting divorced?

One of the things that was so annoying about Kade? He had an aggravating tendency to be right.

"Focus," Jessica commanded herself. She managed to shrug the blouse off both her shoulders, and peeled the sleeve off her left arm with her teeth. But when she tried to slide the newly slit sleeve over the cast, it bunched up around it, and refused to move.

By now, Jessica was thoroughly sick of both Kade's tendency to be right and the blouse. It wasn't one of her favorites anymore. How was she going to ever wear it again without imagining his hands on the buttons?

She tugged at it. Hard. It made a ripping sound. She liked that sound. She tugged at it harder.

"Argh!" She had managed to hurt her arm.

"Okay in there?"

"Stop asking!"

"Okay. There's no need to get pissy about it!"

She didn't want him telling her what to get pissy about! That was why she needed to divorce him.

She investigated the blouse. It was bunched up on the cast, and she had tugged at it so hard it was stuck there. She was afraid she was going to hurt her arm again trying to force it back off. Gentle prying was ineffectual. It refused to budge. The shoulder was too narrow to come down over the cast, and the fabric had ripped to the seams, but the seams held fast.

"That will teach me to buy such good quality," Jessica muttered, then waited for him to comment. Silence. One-handed, she opened every drawer in the bathroom looking for scissors. Naturally, there were none.

She would just have to forge ahead. So with the blouse hanging off her one arm increasing her handicap substantially, and by twisting herself into pretzel-like configurations, she managed to get the tights off. And then the skirt. She was sweating profusely.

Once the bra was off, she thought, it would be fairly simple to maneuver the nightgown over her head.

She reached behind her with her left hand and the bra gave way with delightful ease. She stepped out of it and let it fall in the heap with her tights and skirt.

The nightgown should be simple. If she left it hanging up as it was on the back of the bathroom door, she could just stick her head up under it, and it would practically put itself on. She grunted with satisfaction as she managed to get inside her nightie, put her left hand through the armhole and release it from its peg.

The nightie settled around her like a burka, her head covered, her face out the neck hole. That was okay. This angle should be good for getting her right arm up through the right armhole.

She tried to get her casted arm up. The nightie shifted up over her head as she found the right armhole and shoved. Of course, the blouse bunched around the cast prevented it from clearing the hole. It snagged on something.

So she was stuck with her arms in the air, and her head inside her nightgown.

She wiggled. Both arms. And her hips. Nothing happened.

With her left hand, she tried to adjust the nightie. She tugged down the neckline. Now half her head was out, one eye free. She turned to the mirror and peered at herself with her one uncovered eye. Her nightgown was hopelessly caught in her blouse, and her arm was stuck over her head.

And it hurt like the blazes.

She plunked herself down on the toilet seat and wriggled this way and that. She was sweating again.

There was a knock at the door.

She went very still.

"I made that list."

"Good," she croaked.

"Nothing on it I didn't expect. What do you think about the floors?"

She could not think about floors right now! She grunted as she tried again to free herself from her nightgown.

"Everything okay in there, Jessica?"

"I told you to stop asking!"

"I heard a thumping noise. You didn't fall, did you?"

"No."

"Are you okay?"

"Um—"

"It's a yes-or-no answer."

"Okay, then," she snapped with ill grace. "No." She unlocked the door.

He opened it. He stood there regarding her for a moment. She regarded him back, with her one eye that was uncovered, trying for dignity, her nightie stuck on her head, and her arm stuck in the air. "Don't you dare laugh," she warned him.

He snickered.

"I'm warning you."

"You are warning me what?" he challenged her.

"Not to laugh. And don't come one step closer."

Naturally, he ignored her on both fronts. Naturally, she was relieved, about him coming over anyway. Her arm was starting to ache unbearably. The smile on his lips she could have lived without.

Because there was really nothing quite as glorious as Kade smiling. He was beautiful at the best of times, but when that smile touched his lips and put the sparkle of sunshine on the sapphire surface of his eyes, he was irresistible.

Except she had to resist!

But then the smile was gone. Kade was towering over her. It occurred to her, from the draft she felt and the sudden scorching heat of his eyes, that the nightie was riding up fairly high on her legs.

Wordlessly, the smile gone, his expression all intense focus, he reached for where the blouse was stuck in the right-hand armhole of her nightgown. He began to unwind it. It gave easily to the ministrations of his fingers.

She said nothing.

"You see," he said softly, "there's nothing you can threaten me with that will work. Because the worst has already happened to me."

"What's that?" she demanded. How could he say the worst had happened to him when she was the one sitting here, humiliatingly trapped by her own clothing?

"You're divorcing me," he said softly. And then his face hardened and he looked as if he wanted to choke back the words already spoken.

CHAPTER SEVEN

THE NIGHTGOWN BROKE FREE, and her casted arm went through the right hole and the rest of the garment whispered around her. She used her left hand to tug the hem down to a decent level over her legs.

He bent his head and put his teeth on the fabric of her blouse, and the stubborn seam released. With one final, gentle tug that did not hurt Jessica's arm at all, the blouse was free from the cast.

"A good tailor can probably fix that," he said, laying the destroyed blouse in her lap.

"I'm not divorcing you," she said. "We're divorcing each other. Isn't that what you want?"

He found where her sling was discarded on the floor and looped it gently over her head.

"It seems to be what you want all of a sudden," he said. "There's something you aren't telling me, isn't there?"

She felt suddenly weak, as if she could blurt out her deepest secret to him. How would it feel to tell him? *Kade, there is going to be a baby after all.*

No, that was not the type of thing to blurt out. What would be her motivation? Did she think it would change things between them? She didn't want them to change because of a baby. She wanted them to change because he loved her.

What? She didn't want things to change between them at all. She was taking steps to close this door, not reopen it! She was happy.

"Happy, happy, happy," she muttered out loud.

"Huh?"

"Oh. Just thinking out loud."

He looked baffled, as well he should!

"Go to bed," he told her. "We'll talk later. Now is obviously not the time."

He had that right! Where were these horrible, weak thoughts coming from? She needed to get her defenses back up.

With what seemed to be exquisite tenderness, he slipped her cast back inside the sling, adjusted the knot on the back of her neck.

His touch made her feel hungry for him and miss him more than it seemed possible. He put his hand on her left elbow and helped her up, and then across the bathroom and into the bedroom.

He let go of her only long enough to turn back the bedsheets and help her slide into the bed. She suddenly felt so exhausted that even the hunger she felt for her husband's love felt like a distant pang.

He tucked the covers up around her, and stood looking down at her.

"Okay," she said. "I'm fine. You can leave."

He started to go, but then he turned back and stood in the bedroom door, one big shoulder braced against the frame. He looked at her long and hard, until the ache came back so strong she had to clamp her teeth together to keep herself from flicking open the covers, an invitation.

Just like that, the intimacies of this bedroom revisited her. His scent, and the feel of his hands on her heated skin, his lips exploring every inch of her.

"Are you okay?" he asked. "You're beet red."

Flushed with remembered passion, how embarrassing.

She would do well to remember all that passion had not been able to carry them through heartbreak and turbulence.

She had bled all the passion out of this bedroom. She had become, she knew, obsessed with having a baby after the two miscarriages. It had become so horrible. Taking temperatures and keeping charts, and their lovemaking always faintly soured with her desperation.

Seeing him standing in the doorway, she remembered she had stood in that very spot watching him pack his things after their final night together.

"Please don't," she'd whispered.

"I can't stay."

"But why?"

Those cruel words that were forever a part of her now.

"Jessica, you've taken all the fun out of it."

"Out of making love?" she had asked him, stricken.

"Out of everything."

These were the things she needed to remember when a weak part of her yearned, with an almost physical ache, to be loved by him. To be held by him. To taste his lips again, and to taste faint salt on his skin after they'd made love. To feel the glory of his well-defined muscles under her fingertips. To smell him fresh out of the shower, to laugh with him until she could barely breathe for the ecstatic joy of it.

No, she needed to remember the pain, not the glory, the loneliness and the disappointment, and all the hurtful things. She needed to remember when she had needed him—when she had felt so fragile it had seemed as if a feather falling on her could have cracked her wide-open—Kade had been unavailable in every way.

"I'm fine," she said to Kade now. "Please go."

He heard the coolness in her tone and looked offended by it, but she told herself she didn't care. She told herself she felt nothing but relief as she heard him close the door of the house behind him, and then lock the dead bolt with his key.

She told herself she didn't care that he had gone and that she was alone again. For a woman who was happy, happy, happy, she felt an overwhelming need to cry. With her good arm she grabbed her pillow and put it over her face to try to stifle her desire.

Desire. Why had that unfortunate word popped into her head? This further evidence of her weakness made her fight harder not to cry.

It was weak—it was not the woman she wanted to be. Today hardly even rated as a bad day. She'd had two miscarriages. *Those* had been bad days. She'd had the husband she loved madly leave her. *That* had been a bad day.

But despite her every effort to talk herself out of them, the tears came, and they came hard, and they came for every bad day Jessica had ever had.

Kade left the house and stood on the front step for a moment. There was a little peekaboo view of the downtown skyline. It was the only place on the property that had any kind of a view, and he and Jessica used to sit out here with a glass of wine on a summer's night, planning the deck they would build someday to capitalize on their sliver of a view.

But that had been before the pregnancy quest. Then wine, along with renovations, had been off her list.

He didn't want to go there.

He glanced at his watch and was shocked how early it was in the day. It wasn't even noon yet. It felt as if he had put in a full day, and a hard day, too. Still, there was a place he could go when he didn't want to go *there* for that walk down memory lane.

Work.

He called his assistant. The handyman had already been dispensed to Jessica's business. If he went and liked the guy's work, he could surrender the list. It might minimize encounters like the one he had just had.

He decided he liked the handyman, Jake, and he liked his work. Patty had provided him with the surveillance and security system she had found, and it was already installed when Kade arrived.

"It's really cool," Jake said. "It's motion activated, but you can program it to only send an image to your phone if a door or window is touched. Give me your phone number."

Kade had the fleeting thought it should be Jessica's number that he gave him, but on the other hand, how could he trust her not to rush right down here if her phone alerted her to an intruder?

He gave him his number, and they chortled like old friends as they experimented with setting the alarm and then touching the door, watching their images come up on Kade's phone. Along with the alarm system, a new door was nearly installed, and Jake had matched the old one very closely and even gotten one with shatterproof glass. He was reinforcing the frame so that the dead bolt would not break away.

But somehow when Kade left, the list for the fixes at the house he and Jessica shared was still in his pocket. He had not surrendered it to the obviously very capable handyman.

Why? He suspected it was not because he had not got an answer from her about the floors.

He mulled it over as he drove into the office. Somewhere between her house and there, he had decided he was doing the fixes himself.

But why?

He wasn't particularly handy. The state of the kitchen cupboards over there and the fireplace that did not work were ample evidence of that.

Then he knew. It was time to finish it. Not just the house, but all that house represented. It was time to finish his relationship with Jessica. She was absolutely 100 percent right about that.

And as much as he wanted to, he could not hand those finishes off to someone else. It would be cowardly. And he sensed it would leave him with a sense of incompletion that he could never outdistance.

He would go over there, and he would do all the fixes on the list in his pocket, and then they would get a real estate agent in to appraise the place, and then they would put a for-sale sign on it, and it would sell, and it would sell, and that last thing that held them together would be done.

And how should he feel about that?

"Happy, happy, happy," he said.

Though when Jessica had muttered that, obviously under the influence of whatever, she had looked about the furthest thing from happy! And he was aware that happy, happy, happy was about the furthest thing from how he was feeling, too.

But that just showed him how true it was and how urgent. They needed to be done. He called his assistant and did something he had not done for a long, long time.

He asked her to clear his weekend.

It wasn't until he hung up the phone that he was aware that, for someone who wanted to finish things, another motivation lurked just behind his need to fix the house.

Was Jessica going to be okay after being mugged? Not her arm. That would heal. But her. She had always had that artistic temperament, ultrasensitive to the world.

If he knew Jessica—and he did—she was not nearly as brave as she was trying to be.

So, on Saturday morning, feeling a little foolish in his brand-new tool belt, Kade knocked on the door of the house he had shared with Jessica. He was certain she had said she would be at work, but she opened the door.

He could see why she wasn't at work. She would scare people away from her fledgling business in the getup she had on. She was wearing a crazy sleeveless dress that was at least four sizes too large for her.

But, in truth, it was her face that worried him. Just as he suspected, her drawn features hinted she might not be doing well. There was the gaunt look of sleeplessness about her, as well as dark circles under her eyes.

"It's a maternity dress. I have three of them." Her tone was defensive. "They're easy to get on. See the buttons down the front? That is a very hard thing to find in a dress."

"I didn't say anything." Her arm was in the sling. At least she was following doctor's orders.

"But getting dressed was not that easy, even with the buttons. I'm running late."

He noticed her cast had been decorated with all kinds of signatures and drawings.

In college, she had always been surrounded by friends. But then marriage had done something to her. Her world, increasingly, had become about him and their house. When the pregnancy quest had begun, Jessica had quit the job she'd had since earning her arts degree. Admittedly, it had not been the best job. She had barely made minimum wage at that funky, fledgling art gallery in east Calgary.

At first, he'd liked it that Jessica was home, and doted on him. He'd liked it quite a lot, actually. Maybe he'd liked it enough he'd encouraged it. Who didn't want to come home to fresh-baked bread, or roast beef and Yorkshire pudding or three dozen chocolate-chip cookies still warm out of the oven?

Who didn't want to come home to the most beautiful woman in the world waiting for him, with some newly inventive way of showing she loved him? Once it had been rose petals floating in a freshly drawn tub. Another time it had been a candlelit wine tasting in the back garden, a garden that she had single-handedly wrested from a weedy demise.

But slowly, all her devotion had begun to grate on him. He was so aware that Jessica's world was becoming smaller and smaller: paint colors for rooms rather than canvases. She was always trying new recipes. She discovered shopping online and was constantly discovering useless bric-a-brac that he was supposed to share her enthusiasm for.

It had pierced even his colossal self-centeredness that she was becoming a shadow of the vibrant person she had once been. The obsession with the baby had just intensified the sense he didn't know who she was anymore.

She'd started buying things for a baby they didn't have: little shoes just too adorable to pass up, hand-crocheted samplers for the walls of a nursery they didn't have yet. The magazine racks—God forbid a magazine was left conveniently out—were stuffed with parenting magazines.

She was forever showing him articles on the best baby bottles, and strollers, and car seats. She wanted him to go over fabric samples with her because she had found a seamstress to custom make the crib bedding. But it didn't matter which one he picked. The next day she had more for him to look at. She was acquiring a collection of stuffed animals that would soon need a room of their own, not to mention require them to take out a second mortgage to pay for them all.

"Jessica," he remembered shouting at her, "nobody pays three hundred dollars for a teddy bear."

She had looked crushed, and then unrepentant.

The anger, he knew in retrospect, though he had no idea at the time, had nothing to do with the teddy bear. It had to do with the fact he felt responsible for the awful metamorphosis taking place in her. It had to do with the fact that he was aware, in her eyes, he was not enough for her.

She brought him back to the present. "You didn't have to say anything about the dress. I can see in your face how you feel about it."

He was fairly certain it was the memory of the three-hundred-dollar-teddy-bear fight that had been in his face, so he tried to banish those thoughts and stay in the mo-

ment. "I'm not sure why you would wear something so…
er…unflattering."

"Because I don't care what you think, that's why!"

Or, he thought looking at her, she was trying very,
very hard to make it appear that she didn't care what he
thought.

CHAPTER EIGHT

"I LIKE THE CAST, though," Kade told Jessica.

And he did. He liked it that she had a bigger world again. All the scribbling on the cast was evidence of friends and coworkers and a life beyond the house. Okay, it grated a bit that she had managed to make a bigger world without him, and somehow it was still about babies.

"The dress is what I could get on by myself. See? Buttons down the front."

"About the dress," he said, deadpan. "Are they all that color? What would you call that color?"

"Pink?" she suggested.

"Nausea, heartburn, indigestion…" It was the slogan of a famously pink stomach-relief medication.

"The other ones are worse—"

"No, no, they can't be."

"Spiced pumpkin and real-woods camo."

"A camo maternity dress? I guess my next question would be, how are sales?"

"They are very, very popular."

"Tell me it ain't so," he groaned.

"They are part of an extraoversize line."

"Look, you are scaring me with the visual."

"Well, your visual is a little scary, too," she said,

standing back from the door to let him by her. "A tool belt? And what is that you're driving?"

"I borrowed a truck."

"A truck worthy of a camo-wearing pregnant lady, too."

"I needed it for the vibrating floor sander I rented to refinish the floors."

"A floor sander. The scariness increases. You always thought we should just replace the floors," she reminded him.

"You always thought we should refinish them."

"But it doesn't matter now!" she said, but it felt as if it did. It felt as if it was part of all that was unfinished. In the house, and between them. But Kade did not tell her that.

"What do you know about refinishing a floor?" she asked, looking at her watch.

"Oh, ye of little faith," he said. "I went on the internet. It's easier than you think."

Jessica looked insultingly doubtful.

"I think that refinishing will be less time-consuming than ripping out the old floor and putting down a new one," he told her. He didn't add it might be more in keeping with his skill set.

"Why are you tackling it? Why didn't you just hire someone? That guy you hired to install my door was excellent. By the way, I owe you some money for that."

"Yeah, whatever."

She looked as if she was going to argue, but then remembered she already was in the middle of one argument with him and decided to stick to that one. "I mean this is not exactly your line of work, Kade. It's certainly not in keeping with your current lifestyle."

"What lifestyle is that?" he asked her.

"You know."

"I don't."

"CEO—chief everything officer—at a prestigious company, resident of River's Edge."

"I already told you I work all the time."

"That's exactly what I'm trying to say. You work all the time, and not at renovations. You have a very sophisticated lifestyle. You move in very high-powered circles. I don't understand why you want to do this."

"I started it," he said grimly. "And I'm going to finish it."

She looked at him, and he knew she got it. She got it at every level that he had meant it at.

"Well, I'd love to stay and help—"

He could tell she meant it to sound sarcastic, but instead they both heard the wistfulness there, and Jessica blushed.

"—but I have to go to work. It already took me nearly forty-five minutes longer to get ready than I thought it would, and my part-time staffer can only stay until noon today."

"You slept in," he guessed.

Jessica looked as if she was going to protest, but then didn't. She sighed. "I had trouble sleeping."

"I thought you would."

"What? Why?"

"There aren't very many people who could walk away from being assaulted without being affected by it. And you've always been more sensitive than the average person anyway."

She smiled wanly and gave in, just a little bit, to the fact that he was her husband. He *knew* her. "I'm okay till I lie down, then I feel as if I hear glass breaking. I jump at the sound of the furnace turning on, and that tree branch outside the bedroom scraping the window. Then, since I'm awake anyway, I contemplate how to protect my shop, and hate how helpless I feel."

He drew in a deep breath. The warrior in him wanted to devote his life to protecting her.

But she looked as abashed at her confessions as he was at his reaction to them. Jessica glanced again at her watch. "Yikes! Would you look at the time! Sorry, again. I can't help."

"It doesn't matter. There is a lot of legwork before I actually do anything. I have to move furniture before I get started on the floors."

She cast a look at Behemoth. She was obviously thinking moving furniture was a two-person job, but he had also rented a dolly this morning with that recliner specifically in mind.

But Jessica surprised him. The practicalities of moving furniture were not what was on her mind.

"Remember the day we brought that home?" she asked softly.

These were the conversations he didn't want to have. Because the truth was that he remembered everything.

"You protesting the whole way home how ugly it was," Kade reminded her. He thought her exact words had been that it didn't fit with her *vision* for their house. He hadn't become totally jaded with the vision yet. Or maybe he had started to, because he had brought home the chair over her strenuous protests.

"And then we couldn't get it in the door. It weighs about a thousand pounds—"

"Well, maybe fifty," he corrected her wryly.

"And I was trying to hold up one end of it and you were trying to stuff it through the door. I told you it was a sign the house did not want it, and then you shoved extra-hard. The frame of the door cracked and Behemoth catapulted into the house and nearly crushed me."

"Except I saved you," he said.

She looked at his face. Her eyes were very wide. She looked as if she was going to step toward him.

Suddenly, he remembered how they had celebrated getting that chair into the house. On the chair. And she had seemed affectionately tolerant of Behemoth after that.

The memory was between them, liquid and white-hot. It didn't mean anything that she still had the chair, did it?

"Go to work," Kade said gruffly, deliberately stepping back from her. "You probably wouldn't be of any help in your delicate state anyway."

Too late, he realized that a delicate state usually referred to pregnancy, and that, of course, was the topic that was a minefield between them.

Thankfully, she seemed a little rattled, as he was himself, by the Behemoth memory. He didn't intend to share the secret of the furniture-moving dolly with her. She would come home, and the floors would be completely done, and the furniture back in place and she would be filled with complete admiration for his adeptness in all things masculine.

And she would be so sorry things had not worked between them.

That thought blasted through his brain from nowhere that he could discern.

"Where should I put the furniture?" he asked hastily.

"Oh. Good question. Try the guest room. I use it as an office. It probably has the most room in it right now."

"Okay."

She cast one last rather insultingly doubtful look around the living room, but then looked at her watch and made a squeaking noise. She disappeared and came back in a few minutes, her look improved ever so slightly by a nice handbag, ultrahigh heels and dark glasses that hid the circles under her eyes.

"All right," she called. "Good luck. See you later."

Then she turned and, with her heels clacking sexy defiance of that horrible dress, went through the kitchen and out the back door. The door seemed to snap shut behind her. Was he mistaken, or had she been eager to get away from him?

Jessica could not wait to get out of that house! Her husband was an attractive man. His executive look—the tailored suits and linen shirts and silk ties, the manicured nails and the beautifully groomed hair—was enough to make any woman give him a second glance.

And yet the man he was this morning felt like *her* Kade. Casual in jeans faded to nearly white, his plaid shirt open at the beautiful column of his throat, his sleeves rolled up over the carved muscle of his forearms, a faint shadow of whiskers on his face. It was who he had been in private—dressed down, relaxed, so, so sexy.

Add to that the tool belt riding low on his hips, his easy confidence about pitting all that masculine strength against Behemoth…

Behemoth. Back in the day. When everything was still *fun*.

Good grief, she had wanted to just throw herself

against him this morning, feel his heart beating beneath her cheek, feel his arms close around her.

The robbery had left her far more rattled than she ever could have believed. Her sleep was troubled. She started at the least sound. Her mind drifted back to that morning if she let down her guard for even a second. And she felt dreadfully alone with the stress of it.

It was making her weak. The fact that he *knew* how she would react made her lonely for him, even though the sane part of her knew wanting to lean on Kade was an insane form of weakness. She had already tried that once, and he wasn't good at comforting her. Probably what had stopped her from throwing herself at him this morning was uncertainty. Would he have gathered her to him, rested his chin on the top of her head, folded his arms around her? Or would he, after an uncomfortable moment of tolerating her embrace, have stepped away?

She did not think it would be a good idea to make herself vulnerable to Kade again.

But even with that resolve strong within her, Jessica arrived at work feeling rattled.

Her stomach was in knots.

"Good grief," said Macy, her part-time staffer, stopping in her tracks. "Where'd you get that dress?"

"You know perfectly well I got it from the rack of Poppy Puppins at the back."

"It looks horrible on you."

Jessica didn't want to look horrible. She hated it that Kade had seen her looking horrible, even though she had deliberately worn the outfit to let him know she did not care one whit what he thought of her.

Sleep deprivation, obviously, was kicking in, plus it was some kind of reaction to being the victim of a crime, just as Kade had said, because Jessica felt as if she was fighting not to burst into tears.

"It has buttons on the front!" Jessica exclaimed for the second time that day. Ignoring the pitying look from Macy, she headed to office and slammed the door behind her.

She could not focus, even before she had *the* thought. *The* thought made her stomach feel as if it had become the lead car on the world's biggest roller coaster. It plunged downward and then did a crazy double loop. She bolted out of her office and into the store.

"Jessica? What's wrong?"

Jessica stared at Macy, not really seeing her. This was the thought that was tormenting her: Had she told Kade to put the furniture in the guest room? But she used that room as an office! And if she was not mistaken, she had the names of adoption agencies and lawyers who specialized in that field strewn all over the desk.

"Are you okay?" Macy asked. She dropped a tiny stuffed football and rushed to Jessica's side. "Are you going to faint?"

Jessica looked down at the bill of lading she still had clutched in her hand. She did feel terribly wobbly. "I think I'm okay," she said doubtfully.

"I was supposed to babysit for my sister at noon, but if you want, I'll see if my mom can do it instead."

Jessica was ashamed that her distress, her weakness, was that obvious to her employee. But her soon-to-be ex-husband had always had a gift for rattling her world, in one way or another.

What did it matter if he knew she was contemplating adoption? But at some deep, deep level, she did not want him to know.

So though usually Jessica would have said a vehement no to an offer like Macy had just made, she didn't. Usually, she would have pulled herself together. She could just phone and tell Kade to put Behemoth in her bedroom instead of the office.

She looked at her watch. He'd been there, in her house, for an hour and a half. It was possible he was already in the office, poring over her personal papers, uncovering her secrets.

"Oh, Macy, could you? I'd be so grateful." She shoved the bill of lading into Macy's hand.

And it wasn't until Jessica was halfway home that she realized she had not even waited for Macy's answer, but had bolted out the door as if her house was on fire.

Which, in less than half an hour, it would be.

CHAPTER NINE

JESSICA PULLED UP to the front of her house. She usually parked in the back, but such was her sense of urgency, she had decided to cut seconds by parking out front instead.

Her sense of her life spiraling out of her control deepened at what awaited her. All the living room furniture was on the front lawn, with the exception of Behemoth, which, as she already knew, could not fit through the front door. At least she hoped the furniture on the front lawn indicated there had been no invasion of her office.

Gathering herself, Jessica went up the steps. The front door to her house was open. She peered in. Her living room was emptied of furniture.

Kade was glaring down at some instructions in his hand. There was a machine there that looked like a huge floor polisher, only it had a bag attached to it, like a lawn mower. Though it felt like further weakness, she stood there for a minute regarding him, loving the look of him.

He looked big and broad and strong. He looked like the kind of man every woman dreamed of leaning on. But that was what Jessica needed to remember.

When she had needed someone to lean on, and when that person should have been her husband? Kade had not been there. At first he had just been emotionally absent, but then he had begun working longer and longer hours, until he was physically absent, too.

By the time Kade had made it official and moved out, her abandonment by her husband had already been complete.

Remembering all that as a defense against how glorious he looked right now, Jessica cleared her throat.

"It's not for sale," he said, without looking up.

"What?"

He did look up then. "What are you doing back?" he asked with a frown.

"What's not for sale?"

"The furniture. People keep stopping and asking if there's a yard sale. The coffee table is generating quite a lot of interest."

"I always told you it was a good piece."

He was silent for a moment. She knew she had left herself wide-open for him to tease her about what a *good piece* meant to him as opposed to what it meant to her. When he didn't follow that thread—once he had found teasing her irresistible—she was not sure how she felt. But it was not relieved.

"If Behemoth was out there," Kade said, "people would be throwing their money at me. I'd be at the center of a bidding war. The newspaper would probably be here by now to find out what all the fuss on Twenty-Ninth Avenue was about."

"Which brings me to my next question," Jessica said. "Why exactly is everything out on the lawn?"

He lifted a shoulder. "Faster to toss it out there than move it all down the hall."

"Toss?" she said.

"I meant gently move."

Despite the fact it meant he had been careless with her possessions, no matter what he said—and what was to stop anyone from taking whatever they wanted?—she felt relief that he had obviously not been anywhere near the spare bedroom that served as her office. She would know by looking at him if he had seen that adoption stuff, but obviously he was preoccupied with the machine in front of him.

It didn't surprise her that he would throw her things out on the lawn if that was faster than maneuvering them down the hallway. He had always had intensity of focus. When he wanted something, he simply removed the obstacles to getting it. It had made him a tremendous success in business.

It was how he had wooed her. She had been bowled over by him. But then that same attitude had become a toxin in their relationship.

A baby wasn't going to happen? Cut your losses and move on.

"How come you're home?" he asked again.

"Things were slow," she, who never told a fib, lied with shocking ease. "I shut it down a bit early. It seemed to me I should be helping out here. After all, I started it, too."

"I don't really see how you can help. You're kind of handicapped at the moment." He regarded her with a furrowed brow. "You still look not quite right. Pale. Fragile."

"I'm fine."

He brightened as he thought of a use for her. "I know what you could do! You could order pizza. Is Stradivarius still around the corner? God, I've missed that pizza. I haven't had it since—"

His voice trailed away. *Since you left me.* Had he missed her? At all? Or had even pizza rated higher than her?

It didn't matter. Their lives were separate now. She was moving on. Which reminded her of why she had rushed home. And it was not to order him a pizza!

She sidled by Kade. She passed close enough to him to breath in the wonderful familiar scent of him, mixed with something unfamiliar. Sawdust from the floor?

It was tempting to lean just a little closer and breathe deeply of the intoxication that was his scent. But she didn't.

"I'll just go, um, freshen up." She didn't mean changing her clothes. Changing clothes had become a rather daunting undertaking with one arm out of commission. What she really meant was she would go to her office and put her life away from his prying eyes just in case he did make it in there.

Behemoth, it turned out, was in the bathroom, not her office. It would be necessary to climb over it if she was really freshening up, which she wasn't. How far did she need to take the ruse? Did she need to climb over that thing and flush the toilet?

It seemed as if it would be endangering her other arm, and unnecessarily, because when she glanced back down the hall, Kade was not paying the least bit of attention to her.

As always.

The thought was edged with so much bitterness she could practically taste it, like chewing on a lemon peel.

Jessica went into her office. The papers were all out, just as she had remembered, but they were undisturbed. She slid them into the top drawer of the desk. She considered locking it, but it fell under the category of him not paying any attention to her. She doubted Kade would find her interesting enough to pry into her closed desk.

"Interesting placement of Behemoth," she said when she came back into the living room.

"I was thinking it might start a trend. Every man would like a recliner in the bathroom. Some kind of recliner-toilet combination is probably a million-dollar idea just waiting to be developed."

"That is gross."

"It isn't. It's combining practicality with extreme luxury. You have to admit there is nothing particularly comfortable or luxurious about a toilet seat."

She remembered this about him with an ache of longing: that easy irreverence that made her want to be stuffy and disapproving, but she always gave in and laughed instead.

She could feel her lips twitching. He saw it, too.

"Think about it," Kade pressed on. "We could offer designer colors. Pickled pumpkin and redneck camo. We could throw in a free matching dress with every purchase."

She tried to be stern. She giggled. He smiled at her giggle. She succeeded in smothering her giggle. He succeeded in smothering his smile.

"I think," she said severely, Mother Superior to misbehaving novice, "we should try to get the floors done before we tackle anything else together."

"Oh, right. Okay. So come and look at this."

She went over to where he was glaring at the floor. "What do you think?"

"About what?"

"That was what I was afraid of," he groaned. "I already sanded this part. Not much is happening. I just went out and got a different grit of sandpaper. I'm going to try it again. Cover your ears."

Obediently, Jessica put her hands over her ears. The machine roared to life. It was like standing next to a jackhammer.

To her relief, Kade stopped it after a few seconds. "Better," he said, "but still…" A light came on in his face. "It's not heavy enough."

"Huh?"

"The sander. It isn't heavy enough to really dig into those floors. Get on."

"What?"

"Come on. Sit on the front of it."

"Have you lost your mind?"

"You wanted to help. You can't do much with your arm like that. Come sit on the sander."

Why hadn't she just gone and ordered a pizza? Against her better judgment, she moved a little closer. "Sit on it?" She tapped it. "Here?"

He nodded eagerly.

Oh, jeez, it had always been hard not to get caught up in his enthusiasm.

She kicked off her shoes, gathered her skirt underneath her and sat down regally on the sander. She planted her feet firmly on a part of it that looked like a front fender. "Do not do anything that will jeopardize my other arm," she warned him.

"Don't worry." Grinning happily, he started the sander. A quiver ran through her. And then a tremble.

"Oh, my God." Her voice came out shaking, as if she was trying to talk from under water. In the midst of an earthquake. With her good hand, she clutched wildly at the side of the sander. She braced her front feet.

"Ready?"

Ready? *Sheesh, Jessica, run for your life!* Instead, she clung like a bronc rider waiting for the gate to open. She nodded her head.

The machine lurched across the floor.

"That's better," Kade called. "It's working!" He swung the huge machine slowly back and forth over the floor.

"I feel like I'm on one of those machines from a seventies gym," she yelled. Her voice sounded as if she was a cartoon character. Her whole body was vibrating crazily. She could see the flesh on her arms and legs jiggling rapidly.

She started to laugh. Even her laughter was shaking. Kade also gave a shout of pure glee.

He abandoned the slow sweeping motions in the corner and swiveled the machine outward. He raced across the living room, pushing the machine in front of him. Jessica glanced over her shoulder. A wide swath of sanded wood showed behind them, like the wake behind a boat.

They rocketed toward the front door.

An older woman put her head in. Her glasses slipped down her face and her mouth fell open. She was followed by her husband. His mouth fell open, and he grabbed her arm and tried to push her back out the door, as if protecting her from a sight unsuitable for a lady.

She was having none of it, though. She stood her ground, taking in the sight, wide-eyed.

Kade jerked the machine to a halt so quickly Jessica was nearly launched. He turned off the machine. Jessica pulled her skirt down—the vibrating had made it ride dangerously up her thigh—and tried to quit laughing.

An undignified snort, caused by the suppressed laughter, came out of her mouth.

"Yes?" Kade asked their visitors, his voice dignified, as if not a thing was amiss.

"Uh, we were wondering if there's a yard sale," the man said when it was evident his wife was still shocked speechless. "We wondered about the bench."

"Not for sale," Kade said, and then Jessica heard a familiar wickedness enter his tone. "However, I'll give you a good deal on the world's best vibrator."

The woman staggered backward out the door. The man's mouth fell open so hard, his chin hit his chest.

"Sorry to disturb you," he cried as he backed out the door after his wife.

Jessica waited until they were gone. She glared up at the man who was her husband, but she could not stir any genuine annoyance with him. Instead, she remembered how funny and spontaneous he was, she remembered that irreverent edge to his humor.

A smile was tickling his lips. And then she remembered that oh-so-familiar grin. And realized she had never really forgotten that.

Kade gave a shout of pure delight and devilment. And then the laughter spilled out of Jessica, too, and they were both laughing. Hard. Until they were doubled over with it, until the walls of their little house rang with it.

Until the laughter flowed between them like a river that connected them to everything they had once been.

CHAPTER TEN

KADE LOOKED AT Jessica and realized how much he loved to make her laugh. He always had. That was what he had missed most when their relationship had begun to go sideways. Her laughter.

"Goodness," Jessica said a little breathlessly. "I have not laughed like that in a very long time."

"Me, either," he admitted.

"It reminds me of when we were younger," she said.

"Me, too."

"Before…" Her voice faded away. But he knew what she meant. Before the loss of the first baby. And then the second one. Her laughter had leached out of her like bloodred wine leaking from a wineskin with a small puncture in it.

And when she had stopped laughing, and when he had realized how powerless he was to fix that, nothing had seemed worth laughing about to him anymore, either.

Now he watched as she scrambled off the sander, brushing at that ugly skirt with her good arm. The laughter had lightened the strained look around her eyes and mouth.

But when she faced him, a different kind of strain was

there. And it wasn't, for once, the strain of remembering everything that had transpired between them.

This had been lost, too, this deep and delicious sense of awareness of each other. Or maybe not lost. Maybe it had gone underground, like a creek that ran below the surface. It didn't matter that right now, Jessica's surface was encased in that thoroughly revolting dress. Kade could see, with utter ease, to what was underneath. And not her underwear. Her spirit. He could sense that beautiful, sensual awareness of each other, a longing to touch and explore.

In their marriage, it felt as if that had gone, too. It had gone the same place the laughter had gone—into that lonely abyss. It was as if the raft of life that they had shared had snapped in two, and they had stood by helplessly, with no paddles, drifting farther and farther away, not able to stop it.

"Why babies?" he asked softly.

"What?"

She actually looked frightened by the question.

"Why Baby Boomer? Why is your business about all things baby when that caused us so much heartache?"

"Oh." She relaxed visibly. "I'm not sure it was even intentional. You know some of my friends had seen the nursery you and I—" Her voice drifted away and she squinted, as if looking at something in the distance. Then she cleared her throat. "Nicole Reynolds asked me if I could do something for her. A mural on the wall of her nursery. It was a forest scene, with rabbits and birds and a deer. It was an immersion and it kind of snatched me back from the brink. Gave me purpose and a reason to get up in the morning. I liked being part of what was happening in their family, that circle of joy and expectation. It just kind of snowballed."

He was so aware he had caused her that pain. Well, not all of it. The miscarriages had put her in a space he couldn't reach. And then she'd wanted to try again. To plunge herself into that pool of misery he could not rescue her from again. He'd thought it was his job to make her happy. To make her world perfect. At some point, to his grave detriment, he had given up trying.

"I'm sorry, Jessie. I'm sorry it wasn't me who snatched you back from the brink."

Her eyes skittered to him and then away. For a moment it looked as if she would cross that abyss between them, throw herself into his embrace, come home.

But that moment passed even before he recognized completely what was blooming inside him.

Hope.

Shouldn't he know by now that that was the worst trap of all? To hope?

She seemed to recognize it, because smiling way too brightly, she said, "How about if I go order that pizza now?"

"Oh, yeah, sure."

She retreated to the kitchen; he looked at the floors. With the extra weight on the sander, wood had disappeared quickly. The wood was bare, but wavy. If he put a level on it, it would probably rock like the little horse in one of her nursery displays. He was fairly certain that the damage caused by her wild ride on the sander was something wood filler could not fix.

But he was aware of *liking* this kind of problem over the other kind. The baffling problems of the heart.

"What kind of pizza?" she called.

"The usual," he said, before he remembered they really didn't have a usual anymore, not since their lives had become unusual.

But she didn't miss a beat, and he heard her talking into the phone, ordering a half pepperoni and mushroom and a half anchovies and pineapple and ham.

He went into the kitchen and watched her. The afternoon sunshine was painting her in gold. Even in that horrible dress, she looked beautiful. He remembered what it was to share a life with her and felt the pang of intense loss.

And suspected she was feeling it, too. Jessica had hung up the phone, but she had all the old take-out menus out of the kitchen drawer—she'd actually allowed them to have a junk drawer—and was studying them hard.

"You're too heavy," he said when she glanced up at him.

"Excuse me? Then maybe pizza isn't the right choice!"

"Oh, for heaven's sake. Not like that."

"Not like what?"

"You," he said, and could hear the gruff sincerity in his voice, "are perfect. You are too heavy for the sander! We dug some pretty good ruts in the floor."

"Oh." She blushed and looked back at the menus. She was pleased that he thought she was perfect. And he was pleased that he had pleased her, even though the road they were on seemed fraught with danger. "You should have hired it out."

"Very unmanly," he said.

"You," she said, and he could hear the sincerity in her voice, "couldn't be unmanly if you were wearing this dress."

He was pleased that she thought he was manly,

though the sense of danger was hissing in the air between them now.

She was right, and not just about the manly part. He
should have hired the floor job out. The truth, he wouldn't
have missed those moments of her laughter for the world.
Even if the floor was completely wrecked, which seemed
like a distinct possibility at the moment, that seemed a
small price to pay.

"I just need something lighter than you to put on the
sander." He deliberately walked away from the building
tension between them and went out the back door to their
toolshed. He found an old cinder block. He didn't miss
the look on her face when he came back in hefting it, as
her eyes found the bulge of his biceps and lingered there
for a heated moment.

He slowed marginally, liking her admiration of his
manliness more than he had a right to. Then he went into
the living room and found and pitted himself against a
nice comforting problem, one that he could solve. How
did you get a cinder block to sit on a sander?

Kade finally had it attached, and restarted the
machine. It wasn't nearly as much fun as waltzing around
the room with Jessica. And it wasn't nearly as dangerous, either.

Or that was what he thought until the precise moment he smelled smoke. Frowning, he looked toward the
kitchen. They were having pizza. What was she burning?

He shut off the sander, and went into the kitchen doorway, expecting crazily to find her pulling burned cookies from the oven. She had gone through a cookie phase
when she had made her world all about him. Who had
known there were so many kinds of cookies?

Once or twice, he had tried to distract her from her

full-scaled descent into domestic divahood. He had crossed the kitchen, breathed on her neck, nibbled her ear...

He remembered them laughing when he'd lured her away and they'd come back to cookies burned black. She had taken them out of the oven and thrown the whole sheet out into the yard...

But now there were no cookies. In fact, Jessica was standing right where he had left her, still studying all the take-out menus as if each one represented something very special. Which it did, not that he wanted to go there now. Kade did not want to remember Chinese food on the front steps during a thunderstorm, or a memorable evening of naked pad thai, a real dish that they had eaten, well, in the spirit of the name.

"Don't distract me," he snapped at her, and that earned him a wide-eyed look of surprise.

"What are you burning?"

"I'm not burning anything."

He turned away from her, sniffing the air. It wasn't coming from in here, the kitchen. In fact, it seemed to be coming from the living room. He turned back in and the sanding machine caught his attention. A wisp of something curled out of the bag that caught the sawdust coming off the floor.

And in the split second that he was watching it, that wisp of phantom gray turned into a belch of pure black smoke.

"The house is on fire!" he cried.

"That's not funny," she said.

He pushed by her and opened the cupboard by the stove—thank God she had not moved things around—and picked up the huge canner stored there. He dashed to the sink, then remembered the canner didn't fit well under the faucet. He tilted it precariously and turned on the water. It seemed it was filling in slow motion.

She sniffed the air. "What the—"

He glanced back at the door between the kitchen and the living room. A cloud of black smoke billowed in, up close to the top of the door frame.

"Get out of the house," he yelled at her. He picked up the pot and raced out to the living room. The first flame was just shooting out of the sawdust bag on the sander. He threw the pot of water on it. The fire crackled, and then disappeared into a cloud of thick black smoke that was so acrid smelling he choked on it.

He threw the pot on the floor, and went to Jessica, who, surprise, surprise, had not followed his instructions and had not bolted for the door and the safety of the backyard. She was still standing by the menus with her mouth open.

He scooped her up. He was not sure how he managed to think of her arm under these circumstances, but he did and he was extracareful not to put any pressure on her injured limb. He tucked her close to his chest—and felt a sense, despite the awful urgency of this situation, of being exactly where he belonged.

Protecting Jessica, looking after her, using his superior strength to keep her safe. She was stunned into silence, her green eyes wide and startled on his face.

And then he felt something sigh within her and knew she felt it, too. That somehow she belonged here, in his arms.

He juggled her to get the back door open, then hurtled down the back steps and into the yard. With reluctance, he let her slide from his arms and find her own feet.

"Is the house on fire?" she asked. "Should I call 911?"

"I want you to make note of the technique. First, you get to a safe place, then you call 911."

"But the phone's in there."

"I have one," he tapped his pocket. "But don't worry. The fire's out. I just didn't want you breathing that black guck into your lungs."

"My hero," she said drily. "Rescuing me from the fire you started."

"It wasn't exactly a fire," he said.

She lifted an eyebrow at him.

"A smolder. Prefire at best."

"Ah."

"The sander must be flawed. Sheesh. We could sue them. I'm going to call them right now and let them know the danger they have put us in." He called the rental company. He started to blast them, but then stopped and listened.

He hung up the phone and hung his head.

"What?"

Kade did not want to admit this, but he choked it out. "My fault. You need to check the finish that was on the floor before you start sanding. Some of the finishes become highly flammable if you add friction."

She was smiling at him as if it didn't matter one bit. "You've always been like that," she said. "Just charge ahead, to hell with the instructions."

"And I'm often left cleaning up messes of my own making," he said. "I'm going to go back into the house. You stay out here. Toxins."

"It's not as if I'm pregnant," she said, and he heard the faint bitterness and the utter defeat in those words.

And there it was, the ultrasensitive topic between

them. There was nothing to say. He had already said everything he knew how to say. If it was meant to be, it would be. Maybe if they relaxed. It didn't change how he felt about her. He didn't care about a baby. He cared about her.

So he had said everything he could say on that topic, most if it wrong.

And so now he said nothing at all. He just laid his hand on her cheek, and held it there for a moment, hoping she could *feel* what he had never been able to say.

CHAPTER ELEVEN

JESSICA DID SEEM to be able to feel all those things he had never been able to say, because instead of slapping his hand away, she leaned into it, and then covered it with her own, and closed her eyes. She sighed, and then opened her eyes, and it seemed to him it was with reluctance she put his hand away from her.

And so they went into the house together and paused in the doorway.

"Wow, does that stink," Jessica said. She went and grabbed a couple of dish towels off the oven handle. "We need these over our faces, not that I can tie them."

Kade took the towels from her and tied one over the bottom half of her face and one over his.

"Is mine manly?" he asked. "Or did I get the one with the flowers on it?"

He saw her eyes smile from under her mask. Now Jessica was in an ugly dress *and* had her face covered up. But the laughter still twinkled around the edges of her eyes, and it made her so beautiful it threatened to take his breath away far more than the toxic cloud of odor in the room.

Firmly, Kade made himself turn from her, and aware he looked ridiculous, like an old-time bandito, surveyed the damage to the living room.

All that was left of the sander bag was ribbons of charred fabric. They were still smoking, so he went over and picked up the sander and threw it out the front door, possibly with a little more force than was necessary. It hit the concrete walkway and pieces shot off it and scattered.

"That gave me a manly sense of satisfaction," Kade said, his voice muffled from under the dish towel. He turned back into the room.

The smile deepened around her eyes. How was this that they had narrowly averted disaster, and yet it felt good to be with her? It was as if a wall that had been erected between them was showing signs of stress, a brick or two falling out of it.

There was a large scorch mark on the floor where the sander had been, and a black ugly film shining with some oily substance coated the floor where he had thrown the water. The smoke had belched up and stained the ceiling.

"I think the worst damage is the smell," Kade said. "It's awful, like a potent chemical soup. I don't think you're going to be able to stay here until it airs out a bit."

"It's okay. I'll get a hotel."

"You're probably going to have to call your insurance company. The smell is probably through the whole house. Your clothes have probably absorbed it."

"Oh, boy," she said, "two claims in one week. What do you suppose that will do to my premiums?" And then she giggled. "It's a good thing the furniture is on the lawn. It won't have this smell in it. Do you think I'm going to have to repaint?"

"You don't have to go to a hotel," he said. "I've got lots of room."

Son, I say, son, what are you doing?

She hesitated. There was a knock at the door.

"Pizza," they said together.

Jessica contemplated what she was feeling as Kade looked after the pizza delivery. He cocked his head slightly at her, a signal to look at the delivery boy, who was oblivious, earbuds in, head bobbing. He didn't seem to even notice that he was stepping over a smoldering piece of machinery on the front walkway to get to the door. If he noticed the smell rolling out of the house, it did not affect his rhythm in any way.

As they watched the pizza boy depart, she felt like laughing again. That was impossible! She'd had two disasters in one week. She should be crying, not feeling as if an effervescent bubble of joy was rising in her.

Shock, she told herself. She was reacting to the pure shock of life delivering the unexpected. Wasn't there something just a little bit delightful about being surprised?

"Of course I can't stay with you, Kade," she said, coming to her senses, despite the shock of being surprised. "I'll get a hotel room. Or I can stay with friends."

"Why don't we go to my place and eat the pizza? You don't make your best decisions on an empty stomach. We'll figure it out from there."

Other than the fact it, once again, felt good to be *known*, that sounded so reasonable. She was hungry, and it would be better to look for a place to live for the next few days on a full tummy. What would it hurt to go to his place to have the pizza? She had to admit that she was curious about where Kade lived.

And so she found herself heading for the borrowed truck, laughing at the irony of him carefully locking the door when all her furniture was still on the lawn. Except for her precious bench, which at the last moment, she made him load into the box of the truck, they just left everything there.

She suspected leaving her furniture on the lawn was not nearly as dangerous as getting into that truck with him and heading toward a peek at his life.

His condo building sat in the middle of a parklike setting in a curve in the Bow River. Everything about the building, including its prime nearly downtown location, whispered class, wealth and arrival. There was a waterfall feature in the center of the circular flagstone driveway. The building was faced in black granite and black tinted glass, and yet was saved from the coldness of pure modern design by the seamless blending of more rustic elements such as stone and wood in the very impressive facade.

A uniformed doorman came out when Kade pulled up in front of the posh entryway to the building.

"Hey, Samuel, can you park this in the secured visitor area for me?"

Kade came and helped her out of the truck, and she was aware of the gurgle of the waterfall sliding over rocks. Something in the plantings around it smelled wonderful. Honeysuckle?

If the doorman was surprised to have a pickup truck to park among the expensive sports cars and luxury vehicles, it certainly didn't show in his smooth features.

"It's underground," Kade said to Jessica, when the truck had pulled away. "You don't have to worry about your bench."

The truth was she was so bowled over by her surroundings, the bench had slipped her mind.

Though the incredible landscape outside should have prepared her for the lobby, she felt unprepared. The entryway to the building was gorgeous, with soaring ceilings, a huge chandelier and deep distressed-leather sofas grouped around a fireplace.

No wonder he had never come home.

"Wow," Jessica said, gulping. "Our little place must seem pretty humble after this. I can see why you were just going to give it to me."

Kade looked around, as if he was puzzled. "I actually didn't pick the place," he said. "The company owns several units in here that we use for visiting executives. One was available. I needed a place to go and we had one vacant. I rent it from the company."

She cast him a glance as they took a quiet elevator up to the top floor. He really did seem oblivious to the sumptuous surroundings he found himself in. Once off the elevator, Kade put a code into the keyless entry.

"It's 1121," he said, "in case you ever need it."

She ducked her head at the trust he had in her—gosh, what if she barged in when he was entertaining a girlfriend?—and because it felt sad that she knew she would never need it. Well, unless she did stay for a couple of days until the disaster at her place was sorted.

Already, she realized with wry self-knowledge, her vehement no to his invitation was wavering.

Maybe that wasn't so surprising. Kade was charming, and he could be lethally so. She needed to remember charm was not something you could take to the bank in a relationship.

He opened the door and stood back.

"Oh, my gosh," Jessica said, stepping by him. The sense of being seduced, somehow, increased. She found herself standing in a wide entryway, floored in huge marble tiles. That area flowed seamlessly into the open-space living area, where floor-to-ceiling windows looked out over the park and pathways that surrounded the Bow River.

The views were breathtaking and exquisite, and she had a sense of being intensely curious and not knowing where to look first, because the interior of the apartment was also breathtaking. The furnishings and finishes were ultramodern and high-end. The kitchen, on the back wall of the huge open space, was a masterpiece of granite and stainless steel. A huge island had the cooktop in it, and a space-age stainless-steel fan over that.

"Let's eat," Kade said. He'd obviously gotten used to all this luxury. The fabulous interior of his apartment didn't create even a ripple in him. "Maybe on the deck? It's a nice night. I'll just get some plates."

Jessica, as if in a dream, moved out fold-back glass doors onto the covered terrace. It was so big it easily contained a sitting area with six deeply cushioned dark rattan chairs grouped together. On the other side of it sat a huge rustic plank table with dining chairs around it. It looked as if it could sit eight people with ease.

Huge planters contained everything from full-size trees to bashful groups of purple pansies. She took a seat at the table and wondered about all the parties that had been hosted here that she had not been invited to. She looked out over the river.

She felt as if she was going to cry. The apartment screamed to her that he had moved on. That he had a life she knew nothing about. After all their closeness this afternoon, she suddenly felt unbearably lonely.

Kade came out, juggling dishes and the pizza.

"What?" he said, sliding her a look as he put everything down.

"Your apartment is beautiful," she said, and could hear the stiffness in her own voice.

"Yeah, it's okay," he said. She cast him a look. Was he deliberately understating it?

"The kitchen is like something out of a magazine layout."

He shrugged, took a slice of pizza out of the box and laid it on her plate, from the pepperoni half, just as if they had ordered pizza together yesterday instead of a long, long time ago.

"I think I'll look for open concept in my next place," she said. She bit into the pizza and tried not to swoon. Not just because the pizza was so good, but because of the memories that swarmed in with the flavor.

"Don't," he said.

Swoon over pizza?

"It's not all it's cracked up to be, open concept."

"Oh," she said, relieved. "You don't like it?"

"You can't be messy. Everything's out in the open all the time. Where do you hide from your dirty dishes?"

"That would be hard on you," Jessica said. She remembered painful words between them over things that now seemed so ridiculous: toothpaste smears on the sink, the toilet paper roll put on the "wrong" way. "But I didn't see any dirty dishes."

"Oh, the condo offers a service. They send someone in to clean and make the beds and stuff. You don't think I'm keeping all those plants alive, do you?"

"Very swanky," she said. "Kind of like living at a hotel."

"Exactly. That is probably why this place," Kade said, "has never felt like home."

Jessica felt the shock of that ripple through her. This beautiful, perfect space did not feel like home to him?

"I've missed this pizza," he said.

"Me, too," she said. But she knew neither of them was talking about pizza. They sat out on his deck and watched the light change on the river as the sun went down behind them. The silence was comfortable between them.

"I should go," she finally said. "I have to make some phone calls. It's probably getting late to call a friend for tonight. I'll go to a hotel and arrange something for the rest of the week."

"You shouldn't bother. It sounds as if it's going to be a lot of hassle. There is lots of room here. There's a guest room."

Logically, Jessica knew she could not stay. But it felt so good to be here. It felt oddly like home to her, even if it didn't to Kade. Maybe it was because she was aware that, for the very first time since she had been attacked in her business, she felt safe.

And so tired. And relaxed.

Maybe for her, home was where Kade was, which was all the more reason to go, really.

"Okay," she heard herself saying, without nearly enough fight. "Maybe just for one night."

The logical part of her tried to kick in. "I should have packed a bag. I don't know why I didn't think of it."

"I told you," Kade said with an indulgent smile, "you don't think well when you're hungry. I thought of it, but then I wondered if your stuff was going to smell like that burning sander. Don't worry. Like I said, the place is set up for visiting execs. The bathrooms are all stocked up with toothbrushes and toothpaste and shampoo and stuff. And you don't need pajamas."

She could feel her eyebrows shoot up into her hairline.

He laughed. "The guest bedroom has its own en suite, not that I was suggesting you sleep naked. You can borrow one of my shirts."

Good grief, he was her husband. Why would she blush like a schoolgirl when the word *naked* fell, with such aggravating ease, from his gorgeous lips?

CHAPTER TWELVE

"AND WHAT SHOULD I do for clothes tomorrow?" Jessica asked. Her voice felt stiff with tension.

But Kade did not seem tense at all. He just shrugged, and then said, his tone teasing, "We will figure something out. It's not as though we could do worse than what you have on."

We.

She ordered herself not to give in to this. It was a weakness to let him look after her. It was an illusion to feel safe with him.

But she did. And she was suddenly aware she had not really slept or even eaten properly since the break-in. Exhaustion settled over her.

"One night," she decided. "My place will probably be aired out by tomorrow."

"Probably," he said insincerely.

"I think I have to go to bed now."

"All right. I'll show you the way, and find you a shirt to wear for pajamas."

"I'll put away the dishes."

"No, I'll do it. I've gotten better at picking up behind myself."

Was that true, or would the maid come and pick up

after them tomorrow? She found she just didn't care. She was giving herself over to the luxurious feeling of being looked after. Just for one night, though!

And then she found herself led down a wide hallway and tucked inside a bedroom that was an opulent symphony of grays. She went into the attached bathroom. Her mouth fell open. There was a beautiful bathtub shaped like an egg in here. And double sinks and granite, and a walk-in shower. And this was the guest room.

Why did she feel such comfort that he didn't feel as at home here as he had in the humble little wreck of a house they had shared?

Just tired, she told herself. As promised, there was everything she needed there, from toothbrushes to fresh towels.

When she went out of the bathroom, she saw he had left a shirt on the bed for her. Unable to stop herself, she buried her face in it, and inhaled the deep and wonderful scent of her husband. She managed to get the oversize buttons undone on the dress and get it off.

She pulled his shirt on. His buttons weren't quite so easy to do up, but she managed. When she noticed they were done up crooked, she didn't have the energy to change them. She tumbled into the deep luxury of that bed, looked out the window at the lights of the city reflecting in the dark waters of the river and felt her eyes grow heavy.

She realized, for the first time since her shop had been broken into and she had been injured in her ill-advised scuffle with the perpetrator, she was going to get to sleep easily. She suspected she would sleep deeply.

Only it wasn't really the first time in a week.

It was the first time in a year.

* * *

Kade was so aware that Jessica was right down the hallway from him. He wished he would not have made that crack about her sleeping naked.

Because a man did not want to be having naked thoughts about the wife he still missed and mourned.

But he had developed ways of getting by all these painful feelings. He looked at his watch. Despite the fact Jessica was in bed—she had always handled stress poorly, and he suspected she was exhausted—it was still early.

And he had his balm.

He had work. Plus, he had nearly wrecked her house today. He needed to look after that. He liked the sense of having a mission. This time, though, he decided to call the guy who had fixed her shop door, at least for the floors.

Jake, like all good carpenters and handymen in the supercharged economy of Calgary, was busy.

But willing to put a different project on hold when he heard Jessica's situation, and that Jessica's furniture was currently residing on the lawn.

His attitude inspired confidence, and Kade found himself sharing the whole repair list with him. Jake promised to look at it first thing in the morning, even though it was Sunday, and get back to him with a cost estimate and a time frame.

"Can she stay out of the house for a couple of days? The floor sanding and refinishing causes a real mess. It's actually kind of a hazardous environment. Even the best floor sander can't contain all the dust, and it's full of chemicals. Plus it'll be easier for me to work if she's not there."

"Oh, sure," Kade said, thinking of Jessica staying here

a few days. She probably wouldn't. She would probably insist on getting a hotel.

But for a little while longer, anyway, he was still her husband. And he liked having her here, under his roof. He liked how protective he felt of her, and how he felt as if he could fix her world.

So he gave Jake the go-ahead.

As he disconnected his phone, Kade realized he needed to remember, when it came to larger issues, there was a lot he could not fix. This sense of having her under his protection was largely an illusion. They had tried it over the fire of real life, and they had been scorched.

Tomorrow, he would get up superearly and be gone before she even opened her eyes. He would solve all the helpless ambivalence she made him feel in the way he always had.

He would go to work.

He would, a little voice inside him said, abandon his wife. The same as always.

But it didn't quite work out that way. Because in the night, he was awakened to the sound of screaming.

Kade bolted from his bed and down the hall to her door. He paused outside it for a minute, aware, suddenly, he was in his underwear.

He heard a strangled sob, and the hesitation was over. He opened her door, and raced to her side. The bedside lamp was a touch lamp, and he brushed it with his hand.

Jessica was illuminated in the soft light. She was thrashing around, her hair a sweaty tangle, her eyes clenched tightly shut. When the light came on, she sat up abruptly, and the jolt to her arm woke her up.

She looked up at him, terrified, and then the terror melted into a look he could have lived for.

Had lived for, once upon a time, when he still believed in once upon a time.

"Are you okay?" he asked softly.

"Just a dream," she said, her voice hoarse.

He went into the adjoining bathroom and found a glass wrapped in plastic that crinkled when he stripped it off. Again, he was reminded this place was more like a hotel and not a home. He filled the glass and brought it to her.

She was sitting up now, with her back against the headboard, her eyes shut. "Sorry," she said.

"No, no, it's okay." He handed her the water. "How long have you been having the nightmares?"

"Since the break-in." She took a long drink of water. "I dream that someone is breaking into my house. My bedroom. That I wake up and—" She shuddered.

Kade felt a helpless anger at the burglar who had caused all this.

"Are you in your underwear?" she whispered.

"Yeah." He wanted to say it was nothing she had never seen before, but she looked suddenly shy, and it was adorable.

"You know I don't own a pair of pajamas," he reminded her.

He sat down on the bed beside her. Everything about her was adorable. She looked cute and very vulnerable in his too-large shirt with the buttons done up crooked. Her hair was sticking up on one side, and he had to resist the temptation to smooth it down with his hand. He noticed her eyes skittered everywhere but to his bare legs.

Sheesh. How long had they been married?

She seemed as if she might protest him getting in the bed, but instead, after a moment's thought, she scooted over, and he slid his legs up on the mattress beside her.

He felt the soft familiar curve of her shoulder touching his, let the scent of her fill up his nose.

"I'm sorry about the nightmares," he said.

"It's silly," she said. "I think I'm getting post-traumatic stress disorder. It's shameful to get it for a very minor event."

"Hey, stop that. You were the victim here. The person who should be ashamed is whoever did this. Jessica, do these people not have any kind of conscience? Decency? Can they not know how these stupid things they do for piddling sums of money reverberate outward in a circle of pain and distress for their victims?"

He felt her relax, snuggle against him. "I feel sorry for him."

He snorted. "You would."

"I don't think you or I have ever known that kind of desperation, Kade."

Except that was not true. When she had wanted to have that baby, he had been desperate to make her happy. Desperate. And her own desperation had filled him with the most horrifying sense of helplessness.

He reached over and snapped off the light. His hand found her head, and he pulled it onto his shoulder, and stroked her hair.

"Go to sleep," he said softly. "I'll just stay with you until you do. You're safe. I'll take care of you. Why don't you lie back down."

"In a minute," she said huskily. "You know what this reminds me of, Kade?"

"Hmm?"

"Remember when we first met, how I was terrified of thunderstorms?"

"Yeah," he said gruffly, "I remember."

"And then that one night, a huge electrical storm was moving over the city, and you came and got me out of the bathroom where I was hiding."

"Under the sink," he recalled.

"And you led me outside, and you had the whole front step set up. You had a blanket out there, and a bottle of wine, and two glasses, and we sat on the step.

"At first I was terrified. I was quivering, I was so scared. I wanted to bolt. The clouds were so black. And the lightning was ripping open the heavens. I felt like Dorothy in the *Wizard of Oz*, as if I could be swept away.

"And then you put your hand on my shoulder, as if to hold me to the earth. You told me to count the seconds between the lightning bolt and the thunder hitting and I would know how far away the lightning strike was."

He remembered it all, especially her body trembling against his as the storm had intensified all around them.

"It kept getting closer and closer. Finally, there was no pause between the lightning strike and the thunder, there was not even time to count to one. The whole house shook. I could feel the rumble of the thunder ripple through you and through me and through the stairs and through the whole world. The tree in the front yard shook."

"Yeah, I remember."

"The whole night lit up in a flash, and I looked at you, and your face was illuminated by the lightning. You weren't even a little bit afraid. I could tell you loved it. You loved the fury and intensity of the storm. And suddenly, just like that, I wasn't afraid anymore. I loved it, too. Sitting out on the front steps with you, we sipped that wine, and cuddled under that blanket, and got soaked when the rain came."

She was silent for a long time.

"And after that," he said gently, "every time there was a storm, you were the first one out on that step."

"It's funny, isn't it? It cost nothing to go sit on those steps and storm watch. They came from nowhere. We couldn't plan it or expect it. And yet those moments?"

"I know, Jessica," he said softly. "The best. Those moments were the best."

"And today," she said, her voice slightly slurred with sleep, "today was a good day, like that."

"I nearly burned your house down."

"Our house," she corrected him. "You made me laugh. That made it worth it."

It made him realize how much pain was between them, and how much of it he had caused. He had a sense of wanting, somehow, to make it right between them. It bothered him, her casual admittance that she did not laugh much anymore. It bothered him, and he accepted responsibility for it.

So it could be a clean goodbye between him and Jessica. They could get a divorce without acrimony and without regret. So they could remember times like that, sitting in the thunderstorm, and know they had been made better for them. Not temporarily. But permanently.

He was a better man because of her.

CHAPTER THIRTEEN

PERHAPS, KADE THOUGHT, he was not the man he had wished to be or hoped to be, but still, he was better than he had been. Because of her, and because of the love they had shared.

Was there a way to honor that before they said goodbye? What if tomorrow, Sunday, he wasn't going to go to work after all?

Kade could tell something had shifted. Her head fell against his chest heavily, and he heard her breathing change.

And he knew he should get up and move, but there was something about this moment, this unexpected gift of his wife trusting him and being with him, that felt like one of those best moments ever, a moment just like sitting on the front step with her watching thunderstorms.

And so he accepted that he was reluctant to leave it. And eventually he fell asleep, sitting up, with Jessica's sweet weight nestled into him and the feel of the silk of her hair beneath his fingers.

Jessica woke to the most luxurious feeling of having slept well. The sun was spilling in her bedroom window. When she sat up and stretched, she saw that through the enormous windows of the bedroom, she had a view of the river and people jogging down the paths beside it.

Had she dreamed Kade had come into her room and they had talked about thunderstorms? It seemed as if she must have, because things had not been that easy between them for a long, long time.

And yet, when she looked, she was pretty sure the bedding beside her had been crushed from the weight of another person.

Far off in that big apartment, she heard a familiar sound.

Kade was whistling.

She realized she was surprised he was still here in the apartment. She glanced at the bedside clock. It was after nine. Sunday was just another workday for Kade. Usually he was in the office by seven. But not only was he here, he sounded happy.

Like the Kade of old.

There was a light tap on the door, and it swung open. Jessica pulled the covers up around her chin as if she was shy of him.

"I brought you a coffee."

She *was* shy of him. She realized she had not dreamed last night, because she had a sudden and rather mouth-watering picture of him in his underwear. Thankfully, he was fully dressed now, though he was still off the sexiness scale this morning.

It was obvious that Kade was fresh out of the shower, his dark hair towel roughened, a single beautiful bead of water sliding down his cheek to his jaw. Dressed in jeans, he had a thick white towel looped around his neck, and his chest and feet were deliciously bare.

She could look at that particular sight all day: the

deepness of his chest, the chiseled perfection of his muscles, the ridged abs narrowing and disappearing into the waistband of jeans that hung low on slender hips. Her mouth actually went dry looking at him standing there.

He came in and handed her the coffee. It smelled wonderful—though not as wonderful as his fresh-from-the-shower scent—and she reached out for it. Their fingers touched, and the intensity sizzled in the air between them.

She knew that no part of last night had been a dream. He had slipped onto the bed beside her, and they had talked of thunderstorms, and she had fallen asleep with his big shoulder under her head.

She took a steadying sip of the coffee. It was one of those unexpectedly perfect moments. Kade had always made the best coffee. He delighted in good coffee and was always experimenting with different beans, which he ground himself. It had just the right amount of cream and no sugar.

He remembered. Silly to feel so wonderful that he remembered how she liked her coffee. The luxury of the bed, the sun spilling in the window, the coffee, him delivering it bare chested—yes, an unexpectedly perfect moment.

"I just talked to Jake," he said, taking a sip of his own coffee, and eyeing her over the rim of it.

"Who?"

"Jake. The contractor who fixed the door at your shop. He's over at your house."

"He's at my house at, what is it, seven o'clock on Sunday morning? How do you get a contractor, especially a good one, to do that?"

"I used my substantial charm."

"And your substantial checkbook?" she asked sweetly.

He pretended to be offended. "He's going to do the list of all the things that need fixing—the leak in the roof and the toilet handle and the floors, which really need refinishing now. And he'll fix the new smoke damage on the ceiling, too. That's the good news."

"Uh-oh, there's bad news."

"Yeah. There always is, isn't there? It's going to take him the better part of a week to get everything done. And he says it will go a lot smoother if you aren't there."

She concentrated hard on her coffee. "Oh," she finally squeaked out. A week of this? Coffee delivered by a gorgeous man whom she happened to know intimately? Who had joined her last night in bed in his underwear? She'd be a basket case. "Look, obviously I can't stay here. I'll call a friend. Or get a hotel."

"Why is it obvious you can't stay here?" he asked.

"Kade, we're getting a divorce. We're supposed to be fighting, not setting up as roommates." Certainly she should not be feeling this way about the near nudity of a man she was about to divorce!

"'From where the sun now stands, I will fight no more forever,'" he said softly.

"I hate it when you quote Chief Joseph." No, she didn't. She loved it. She loved it as much as she loved that he had made her coffee exactly as she liked it, without even having to ask.

She loved that he remembered she had once bought a piece of art—that they couldn't afford—with a part of that quote as its name. She remembered that he hadn't been mad. He'd turned the piece over in his hands—a shard of gourd, burned with an Appaloosa galloping across it toward the sun—and he'd smiled and said, "Worth starving for a few weeks."

And, of course, they hadn't starved.

But of course, that had been at the beginning, when her staying home and having a house of her own and a husband to look after had been so novel. Later, it seemed as if Kade was nothing but annoyed when she bought things for the house. She thought of reminding him of that.

But it seemed too petty. She slid him a look now. Was he quoting that because they were turning over a new leaf? Because they were not going to squabble anymore?

Everybody squabbled when they got divorced.

"You want to do something fun today?" he asked. "Since fixing the house has been removed from our list?"

No, she did not want to do something fun! She wanted to get a divorce. She wanted to sell the house they had shared. She wanted to cut ties with him. She wanted to adopt a baby and get on with her life, without him. Fun? Who had fun in the middle of a divorce?

"I thought I took the fun out of everything," she said. She put the coffee down and folded her arms over the largeness of his shirt, which she suddenly wished was at least a little sexy. She recognized the treachery of her thoughts.

He looked bewildered. "You took the fun out of everything?"

"That's what you said. The day you left."

Kade looked genuinely shocked. "I didn't say that."

"Yes, you did." The words, in fact, felt burned into her, as if they had become part of who she was.

"Are you sure?"

"Oh, yeah."

He looked genuinely distressed, but she found she couldn't let it go.

"So," she said, trying for a bright, light note, "what do you do for fun? You're probably an expert at it, now that the dead weight isn't around your neck anymore."

"Jessica, I don't remember saying that. It must have been one of those mean, in-the-heat-of-the-moment things. I'm sorry."

She shrugged, as if it didn't matter one little bit, as if she had not mulled over those words every single day for a year.

"So if we *were* going to do something fun today—and I'm not saying that we are—what would you suggest?" Did it sound as if she was forgiving him? *Was* she forgiving him? "Remember, I have one arm out of commission. Skydiving is out. Ditto for rock climbing. And bull riding."

"I said that? That you took the fun out of everything?"

"Yes! And then you packed your bag, and you left, and you never looked back."

"I thought you'd call, Jessica."

"Why would I call? You were the one who left." She hesitated. She tried to strip any hurt from her voice. "I thought you'd call."

"I didn't know what to say."

"Neither did I. I wasn't going to beg you to come back."

"Why would you beg me to come back?" he asked wearily. "And I guess that's why I didn't call, either. We had reached a complete impasse. We were utterly and exhaustingly miserable. We just seemed to go in endless circles. You wanted a baby. I'd had enough."

She could see the very real pain in his face. For the first time? Had she really been so wrapped up in herself and what she wanted that she could not see what it was doing to him? She'd accused him of being insensitive to her, but she saw now it had been a two-way street. She felt an odd little shiver of awareness go up her spine.

"So," Jessica said carefully, trying to navigate the minefield between them without getting blown up, "answer the question. What do you do with a one-armed woman for fun?"

His eyes fastened on her lips.

"Stop it," she said.

"Stop what?" he asked innocently.

"Looking at me like that. I think *that* would be quite a challenge one armed."

"What?" he asked innocently.

"You know."

He smiled wickedly. "I think *that* could be quite a lot of fun.

"I think it would be darn near impossible."

"I don't. I like a challenge. I like figuring things out."

Good grief, she could not stay here for days with this kind of delicious sensual tension in the air between them.

"I could start by offering to help you shower," he said, his voice a low growl.

She threw the pillow at him. It was a clean miss, but he dodged anyway, managing to save his coffee. He laughed and made a face at her. "So are we agreed? We'll do something fun today?"

"I suppose, if you promise to be good," she said warningly, reaching for the other pillow.

"Do I have to? Okay, okay." And then he backed away from her, closed the door and was gone.

She freshened up in the bathroom and put on the maternity dress. When she saw her reflection in the full-length mirror of his opulent guest bathroom, she felt she had succeeded just a little too well in her goals.

She had wanted to look as if she didn't care! She was not sure she had wanted to look quite this bad! She looked like a waif abandoned outside an orphanage. Still, defiantly, refusing to give in to the temptation to win his approval in any way, least of all by trying to make herself attractive to him, she stepped out of the bathroom.

The truth was she hadn't brought anything else anyway. She had thought her stay here was going to be brief. Given the shakiness of her resolve, looking pathetic seemed as if it could only be a good thing.

He was behind the kitchen counter putting croissants—obviously freshly delivered—on a plate.

"Wow. Excuse me while I pluck out my eyes. I'd forgotten the full ugliness of that dress. Or maybe I blocked it. Trauma."

"It is not that bad." He still had not put on a shirt. In the "life was unfair" department, this seemed to rate quite high: that he wanted to pluck out his eyes and she wanted to gaze at him endlessly.

"It is. That bad. Believe me. At least its awfulness helps me figure out the agenda for the day. We need to go shopping first."

"I am not going shopping. I love this dress." She didn't actually. She thought it was quite hideous. "I'm sorry you'll be embarrassed by me, but that's the way it is."

"I'm not embarrassed by you. But in the 'find something to be grateful for' department—"

She squinted at him suspiciously. He was not a "find something to be grateful for" kind of guy.

"I'm just glad you didn't bring the camo one. If we end up in the woods today, I don't want to misplace you."

"What are the chances we'll end up in the woods?"

"Anything can happen when you just let the day unfold."

She should not feel nearly as thrilled by that as she did! But spontaneity had not been part of her world for a long time, and Jessica suddenly felt eager for it.

CHAPTER FOURTEEN

ONE THING THAT Jessica remembered about Kade with complete fondness was that he always seemed open to what the world could bring him.

They had a simple breakfast at his apartment. He had had the still-steaming croissants and preserves delivered, and they sat out on the terrace and ate in the new warmth of the spring light. What was it about spring that brought hope to even the most wounded heart?

He seemed to forget she looked ugly. She seemed to forget he looked gorgeous. The old comfort rose up between them.

They talked as if nothing had ever gone wrong between them. It was like the old days, when spending time with him felt as if she was spending time with her best friend. The conversation flowed easily and naturally, words spilling out of them, as if they were anxious to catch up. They talked about mutual friends, his aunt Helen and her cousin Dave. They talked a bit about their businesses.

And then they left his place and walked downtown. Jessica became self-consciously aware of the ugliness of her dress again as she walked beside him. Kade was dressed casually in a sports shirt and summer khaki pants, and yet she could not help but notice how he got *that* look from women. Interested. Admiring. Hungry for a taste of that particular delight. They would glance at her, too, and then dismiss her.

When he came around to her good arm and his hand found hers, her own sense of hunger deepened. She was so aware of how much she had missed this, the small intimacies that made a relationship, the feel of his hand, strong, closing possessively around her own, sending that message to all who passed: *taken*.

She was determined to make a go of it on her own, but that simple thing, him taking her hand, filled her with a longing that felt physical in its intensity, like a shiver going up and down her spine that would not go away.

If she was smart, she would drop his hand and turn and run.

But smart seemed to have abandoned her. She wanted these moments. It felt as if she was stealing them to store away, as a part of her, for when she did not have him anymore. She actually felt thankful that *these* memories might overlay the old ones. Their history, leading up to the separation, was so filled with bitterness and anger and frustration that it had become as if the dark colors of a new painting had completely obliterated the light of the old painting that existed right underneath it.

They entered the downtown. It was a beautiful day so they avoided the Plus 15 Skywalk and instead strolled the pedestrian mall on Stephen Avenue. Downtown did not have its weekday bustle, the throngs of men and women in business attire, but there was still a colorful conglomeration of shoppers and activities on the streets.

A cowboy-hatted busker had set up close to Stephen Avenue Walk and was singing lustily. They stopped and watched for a few minutes. Kade dropped a five into his guitar case and they moved on.

They enjoyed the historic sandstone buildings of one of Canada's few designated National Historic Sites. Calgarians had been conducting their commerce here on Eighth Avenue for over a hundred years. They passed the building where Kade worked, in the heart of Calgary's financial district, and then walked along the column-fronted arcade of the very impressive Hudson's Bay Company building. The building had always anchored Calgary's downtown core.

"How about there?"

She looked at the store Kade had paused to point out. It was a tiny but very upscale boutique called Chrysalis, which Jessica knew of but had never set foot in. "I can't go in there."

"Why?"

Mostly because of how she was dressed right now! "I can't afford anything in there."

"I can."

"No."

"Come on. It will be fun. Remember that scene we liked in that movie?"

"Pretty Woman?" she guessed.

He nodded happily. "Let's reenact that."

"I'm no Julia Roberts," she said, but she could feel herself being drawn into his playfulness. Where had all the playfulness gone between them?

"You are way better than her," he said, and he looked at her with such genuine male appreciation that she nearly melted.

They went into the shop. It was understated and tasteful. But the salesclerk was a very chic young woman with an outrageous purple streak in her blond hair. She rushed at them, probably, Jessica thought, to get rid of her, the same as in the movie.

"My first customers of the day," she said gleefully. Then she eyed Jessica with the look of a seasoned fashion aficionado. Rather than judgment or snobbery, Jessica sensed friendliness and very genuine concern. "What is that you are wearing?"

In a tone that should be reserved for "I'm so sorry to hear about the death in your family."

"I'm having a little trouble with my arm," Jessica said defensively.

"Even so, you're lovely! And just a little bit of a thing. You have to show off your assets!" She cast Kade a look that clearly said, "Especially if you are with a guy who looks like that," and that she clearly considered him an asset worth keeping.

"Thank you. We'll just have a quick look around," Jessica said.

"No, no, *no*. I am going to guide you through your Chrysalis experience."

"Oh, dear," Jessica mumbled, and sent Kade a pleading look. *Get me out of here.* But Kade folded his arms over his chest and shrugged slightly. *Let's just go with it.*

"I will have you fixed up in no time. In fact, I will love working with you. Caterpillar to butterfly, as our name suggests. I'm Holly, by the way."

The girl's enthusiasm was so genuine that Jessica could not even stir herself to annoyance at being called, basically, an insect pupa.

"Usually, I would ask about your lifestyle, but today I think you're looking for some things that are easier to get in and out of, aren't you?"

Kade frowned at Holly. "We were hoping for some-one more like the salesclerk in *Pretty Woman*. You know? If you could just be snotty, and then I flash my gold card at you and you fall all over yourself trying to help us out."

Holly laughed. "Well, I like the gold card part. And I always fall all over myself trying to help people out." She looked at Jessica. "How would you feel if I just put you in a change room and found some things that I think would work for you?"

Jessica should be insulted. She was obviously being told she could not be trusted to pick out her own things, but given the dress she had on, could she blame the girl?

"I like to encourage everyone to let me pick some things for them," Holly said. "You know, people get in shopping ruts."

Out of the corner of her vision, Jessica saw Kade roll his eyes at the near religious fervor Holly apparently had for the shopping experience.

Undaunted, Holly went on. "They pick variations of the same thing for themselves over and over. Sometimes a fresh eye can be amazing. And then, you can model what I pick out for you for your extremely handsome boyfriend."

"Husband," Kade said. "Though I like the handsome part."

"Oh, sorry. No rings," Holly said. She squinted at him. "Though you look as though you've had one on recently."

Jessica's gaze flew to Kade's ring finger. Sure enough, a white band of skin marked where his wedding ring had been. The band had been there recently, obviously, since such marks faded rather quickly. What did it mean that he had worn his ring so recently?

Stay in the moment, she ordered herself sternly. She had one mission today. To have fun. To let go. To be free. And if she ended up, with Holly's help, looking a little bit better than she looked right now, she'd go with that, too.

For once, Jessica felt no desire at all to hide behind their upcoming divorce.

She followed Holly obediently to the back of the store. There was a classy sitting area there for Kade, complete with a comfy deep upholstered chair and a huge flatscreen TV. Holly handed him the remote, and then shooed Jessica into an opulent change room.

Minutes later, she was back. "I don't mean to be presumptuous, but I brought you this." She held up a bra. "Front closing."

And sexy as all get out. Jessica took the bra with her good hand and suddenly ached to put it on. To give herself permission to be feminine and beautiful.

She had not felt like a beautiful woman since her husband had left her. Despite career success, somehow she carried loneliness and defeat within her.

A thought, unwelcome, came out of nowhere.

Had she been planning on using a child to combat her pervasive feeling of inadequacy? She shook off the shadow that passed over her. Today was just about fun. She had given herself over to introspection quite enough in the past year.

"You are a lifesaver," Jessica told Holly, and then surrendered to the process. She allowed herself to be spoiled completely. Holly did have an exceptional eye for fashion, and along with the bra, she had soon provided Jessica with a stack of clothing topped by a filmy jade silk top.

None of it was anything Jessica would have chosen

for herself. She had become the master of understated. Almost all her clothes were in neutrals, grays and taupes, as if, she realized with a start, she was trying to make herself invisible.

Jessica fingered the silk and felt a pure and simple longing. To be pretty.

It occurred to her she had not cared about being pretty since long before Kade had left her. Since she had lost the second baby.

"This will be amazing with your eyes. And look— Velcro fasteners!"

"You found a top with a Velcro closure? Is this really silk? Where's the price tag?"

"Your Prince Charming out there told me to take the price tags off."

"Humph," she said, but she didn't feel nearly as annoyed as she should have. She didn't have to buy it, she reminded herself. She just had to have fun with it.

Soon, the ensemble was completed with an easy-to-pull-on skirt with a flirty hemline and a delicate pair of sandals that Jessica could just slip her feet into.

"You look awesome," Holly said. "Go show him."

Jessica stared at herself in the mirror. "Um, I think I look a bit too young." Plus, the blouse was extremely sheer, which explained Holly bringing a sexy bra with it.

"Nonsense."

"This looks like something a teenager would wear. Don't you think the skirt is a little, um, short? Not to mention the blouse is a little, er, see-through."

"When you have legs like that? Show them off, girlfriend. Same with your other assets. Now go show him! He'll let you know how right that look is for you."

Feeling strangely shy about sharing this oddly intimate moment with Kade, the same as she had felt this morning sharing space with him, Jessica exited the change room. Kade had found a football game on TV and didn't even look impatient. He looked content.

And then he noticed her. He flipped off the sound. His eyes darkened. She suddenly didn't care how short the skirt was or if the blouse was see-through. She did a saucy little spin.

"Wow," he said, his voice hoarse. "You look incredible. Two thumbs-up to that one."

Jessica didn't just feel beautiful for the first time in a long time. She felt sexy. It felt unbelievably good to feel sexy with no agenda, no calendar lurking in the back of her mind, no temperature to take. It felt, well, fun. And after that, she just gave herself over to the experience completely.

It was fun, having Holly help her in and out of outfits, and then modeling them for Kade, who was a great audience. He raised his eyebrows, and did low wolf whistles and louder ones. He made her feel as if she was not only sexy and beautiful, but as if she was the only woman in the world he felt that way about.

But even so, Jessica had to draw the line somewhere, and she drew it at an evening dress Holly hauled in.

"I have absolutely nowhere to wear such a thing," she said. Still, she touched it wistfully. Like everything in Chrysalis, the cut and the fabric were mouthwatering. "I won't be able to get it on over my arm."

"Sure you will," Holly said. "It's back fastening, so I'll just drop it over your head, like this, and poof. Ooh, butterfly."

It took a bit more work for them to get her arm out

the sleeve, but then she was standing there looking at herself, stunned.

Her hair was flyaway from all the in-and-out of trying on clothes, but somehow that added to the sense of electricity in the air. The dress, the color of licking flame, fit her like a glove, then flared out at the bottom in a mermaid hemline.

"Here." Holly crouched at her feet. "Let me slip these on you."

As if in a dream, Jessica lifted one foot and then the other. She stared at herself in the mirror. The heels had added three inches to her height. The cast and sling on her arm might as well have disappeared, the outfit was so attention grabbing, especially with a very deep, plunging neckline.

Holly stood back and looked at her with satisfaction. "*This* is exactly what I envisioned from the moment you walked through the door. Go show him."

Should she? What was the point? It didn't feel fun anymore. It felt strangely intense, almost like the moment she had walked toward him down that long aisle in her wedding dress.

She was going to protest, but when Holly held open the door for her, Jessica sucked in her breath and walked out. Holly slid away.

Kade didn't look right away. "Don't drop it!" he yelled at the TV. And then he turned and saw her. Without taking his eyes off her, he turned off the remote. The television screen went blank. He stood up. His mouth fell open and then he shut it, and rocked back on his heels, looking at her with eyes narrowed with passion.

This was what she had missed when that moment she had glided down the aisle toward him had been replaced by the pressures of everyday living, by disappointments, by hurts, by misunderstandings.

"Jessie," he whispered.

This was what she had missed. She leaned toward him.

CHAPTER FIFTEEN

JESSIE LEANED TOWARD HIM, looking at him with heavy-lidded eyes.

*Pretty woman...walking down the street...*The music seemed to explode into the small dressing room and waiting area. Jessica gasped and put her hand to her throat, wobbled on the high heels.

Kade was in front of her instantly, looking down at her with concern.

"Sorry," she said. "I keep startling from loud noises."

He cocked his head at her. The room flooded with Roy Orbison's distinctive vocals. Kade took one step closer to her. He held out his hand, and she didn't hesitate, not for one second. She took his hand. Kade drew her to him and rocked her against him.

And then, as if they had planned it, as if they had never stopped dancing with each other, they were moving together. Even though the tempo of the song was fast, they did not dance that way.

They slow danced around the waiting area, their bodies clinging to each other, their gazes locked. The music faded, but they didn't let go, but stood very still, drinking each other in, as if they could make up for a whole year lost.

Holly burst in. "How cool was that, that I found—" She stopped. "Whoa. You two are *hot*."

Kade's arms slid away from Jessica. He stepped back. He swept a hand through his hair. "We'll take it," he said.

"That dress?" Holly said.

"No. Everything. Every single thing she tried on."

Jessica's mouth opened, but the protest was stuck somewhere in her throat, and not a single sound came out. She turned and went back into the change cubicle.

"Wear this one," Holly suggested, following her in. She dug through the pile of clothing to the very first outfit Jessica had tired on, the jade top and skirt.

But she didn't want to wear that one. Her world felt totally rattled by what had just happened, by how spontaneously she and Kade had gone into each other's arms. She wanted to feel safe again.

"Where's the dress I came in here with?"

Holly giggled. "He told me to throw it away."

"What?"

"Yeah, he said to grab it at my first opportunity and dispose of it."

"And you just listened to him? That's outrageous."

"He's very masterful," Holly said with an unapologetic sigh. "Besides—" she winked "—he's the one with the credit card."

Jessica thought of the frank male appreciation in his eyes as she had modeled her new outfits, and she contemplated how she was feeling right now.

Alive. One hundred percent in the land of the living, the life force tingling along the surface of her skin. Did she really want to go back to safety? To reclaim that familiar wooden feeling she had lived with for so long?

Why not, just for today, embrace this? That she was

alive? And that her life was alight with the unexpected element of fun? And with the unexpected sizzle of attraction between her and the man she had married.

They left the store with Kade's arms loaded with parcels, and with her feeling fresh and flirty and like a breath of spring in the first outfit she had tried on. He had paid for everything.

"I'll pay you back," she said. He had insisted on buying every single thing she had donned, even the evening gown.

Since the theme of the day was fun, she'd given in. But buying the gown? That was just silly. She had nowhere to wear an evening gown. Her future plans did not involve anything that would require formal wear. In fact, she needed to be stocking up on comfy pants and sweatshirts that could hold up to baby puke and other fluids associated with the delights of motherhood.

But she had been so caught up in the moment, and the dress had made her feel so uncharacteristically glamorous—sexy, even—that she had actually wanted to be silly. She had wanted to purchase that piece of silk and gossamer that had made her feel better than a movie star.

She should have protested more—she knew that when the bill was totaled—but the look in his eyes when he had seen her had sold every single outfit to her. She'd had a ridiculous sense of *needing* those clothes, though in her heart, she knew what she wanted was the look in his eyes. "Once we sell the house, I'll pay you back," she said firmly.

"Whatever. Hey, this stuff is already heavy. Look. There's one of those rickshaw things being pulled by a bike. Have you ever been in one of those?"

"No."

He juggled the packages to his left arm, put his two fingers to his lips and let out a piercing whistle. The driver, a fit-looking twentysomething guy, pulled over.

"Where to?"

"Ah, we aren't sure yet. I think we need you for the day. Have you got a day rate?"

"I do now!"

Jessica knew she should have protested when the driver named his rate, but somehow she just couldn't. She and Kade piled into the narrow seat of the rickshaw, squished together, all their packages bunched in with them.

"Where to?"

"We need a picnic lunch," Kade decided. "And a bottle of wine. And a forest. Maybe Yan's for the lunch. Do you feel like Szechuan?"

She thought of all those menus she had sorted through yesterday, each one representing a memory. She loved Szechuan-style Chinese food. "Two orders of ginger beef," she reminded him.

Their driver took off across the downtown, darting in and out of traffic, getting them honked at, shaking his fist and yelling obscenities at drivers of vehicles.

It was hysterically funny, and she could not stop laughing. That wondrous feeling of being alive continued to tingle along the surface of her skin.

"You're going to get us killed," she said with a laugh as a cab they had cut off laid on the horn. She clung to Kade's arm as the rickshaw swayed violently, and then their driver bumped up on a curb. "Or get my other arm broken."

He twirled an imaginary moustache. "Ah, getting

you right where I want you. Helpless. And then I can ply my lethal charms against you."

Kade flopped down on the blanket that he had purchased. The driver had found them a quiet spot on Prince's Island, and had managed to make himself scarce while Kade and Jessica enjoyed their picnic under a leafy tree, with the sound of the river in the background. Now, after too much food, and most of a bottle of wine, Kade felt sleepy and relaxed.

"Two orders of ginger beef," he moaned. "It's masochistic."

"Nobody was forcing you to eat it."

"You know why we always have to buy two, though." *Always*, as if there was not a yearlong blank spot in their relationship, as if they could just pick up where they had left off. He considered where they had left off, and thought, despite his current level of comfort with Jessica, why would they want to?

"Yes, we always have to buy two because you eat the first one by yourself, and most of the second one."

"Guilty," he moaned. "My tummy hurts, Jessie."

"And three spring rolls," she reminded him. "And most of the sizzling rice." Despite the sternness in her tone, when he opened one eye, she was smiling. She looked as utterly content as he could remember her looking in a long, long time.

He lifted up his shirt and showed her his tummy. She sighed, and scooted over beside him, that teeny-tiny skirt hitching way up her legs, and rubbed his stomach with gentle hands.

"Ah," he said, and closed his eyes. Maybe it was because he had not slept well last night, or maybe it was because he had eaten too much, or maybe it was because his world felt right for the first time in over a year, but with a sigh of contentment, he went to sleep.

When he woke up, she was sleeping curled up beside him. He slid his arm around her shoulders and pulled her into his side, being careful of her arm.

"Did we fall asleep?" she asked.

"Yeah."

"Is our driver still here? Or did he take off with all my new stuff?"

Kade got up on one elbow. He could see the rickshaw over by the riverbank. When he craned his head, he could see the driver tapping earnestly at his phone with his thumbs.

"I haven't paid him yet. He's not going anywhere." He slid his own phone out of his pocket and checked the time. "Holy, it's four o'clock already."

"It's been a perfect day," she said.

"Agreed. What was the best part for you? The shopping? I love the long dress."

"I don't have a single place to wear a dress like that," she said. "I shouldn't have bought it."

"Yes, you should have. I want you to accept it as a gift from me. You can pay me back for the rest of that stuff if you insist—"

"Which I do!"

"But I want to buy that dress."

"Why do you want to buy me a dress that I probably will never wear?"

"Wear it around the house. Put a movie on, and wear it to watch it. Eat popcorn in it."

She laughed. "That seems eccentric and foolhardy. What if I got butter on it?"

"That's what I liked about it. You know what it re-minded me of, Jess?"

"No. What?" She held her breath.

"It reminded me of those paintings you used to do, the ones that were all swirling colors and amazing motion."

"I haven't thought about those for years," she said.

"Save the dress and wear it to the unveiling of your first art show."

She laughed a little nervously. "I'm not having a first art show."

"But that's what I've always wondered. Where did that part of you go?"

"I paint murals," she said. "That's my creative outlet."

"I don't think bunnies on walls do justice to your gifts," he said.

"I don't care what you think!" she snapped. "Sorry. Let's not ruin the moment with you telling me how to live my life."

She was right. This was not any of his business, not anymore. Maybe it never had been.

"Is there any ginger beef left?" he asked wistfully.

"No."

"How about sizzling rice?"

And then the moment of tension was gone, and she laughed and passed him the container. It seemed like the most natural thing in the world to go home to his place together. And then to say good-night with unnatural for-mality and to go to their separate bedrooms.

The next morning, they both got up. He ordered crois-sants again. She came out to eat one in the too-large shirt.

"I guess I should have been shopping for pajamas in-stead of evening dresses," she said.

What kind of kettle of worms would it open up, he

wondered, if he said he liked what she had on—his shirt—way better than pajamas?

"Are you coming back here after you've finished work?" he asked her. He was holding his breath waiting for her reply.

"I guess," she said, and he heard in her voice the very same things he was feeling. What were they reopening, exactly, by living under the same roof? What were they moving toward? Were they putting a framework in place for their future relationship? Was it possible they could be one of those rare amicably divorced couples who were friends?

He hoped things would become clear in the next few days, because he did not like uncertainty. And at the moment, his future seemed murky, like looking into a most uncooperative crystal ball.

CHAPTER SIXTEEN

MONDAY, AFTER WORK, Jessica returned to Kade's apartment. She was somewhat ashamed that she had not done a single thing to make new living arrangements for herself. And now here she was, aware she was waiting for the door of the apartment to open.

Why? Kade never came home at regular hours. What was she waiting for? Hadn't this been part of their whole problem? That she waited, as if her whole life depended on him, and he had a whole life that had nothing to do with her?

Surely she'd come further than this, still waiting for him to come home! It was pathetic, and she was not being pathetic anymore. And so, instead of sitting in the apartment, she went and explored his building.

There was a good-size pool that they were conducting a kayaking class in, and beside that was a climbing wall. She went and sat on a bench and watched people climb the wall.

A good-looking man came over and introduced himself as Dave and asked her if she was going to try it.

She held up her arm. "Already did," she said, deadpan. He laughed and flirted with her a bit, and she realized whatever had happened when she had put on all those clothes had been good. She was wearing one of her new outfits, and it seemed to fill her with confidence she hadn't had for some time. Dave went up the wall, obviously showing off, and she was content to let him.

She watched for a while, and decided as soon as her arm got better, she would try climbing. The wall looked really fun.

After doing a thorough tour of the building and the gorgeous gardens outside, which included that impressive waterfall at the front, she wandered back to the apartments.

Kade was there. Did he look pleased when she let herself in using the code he had given her?

"Hey," he said. "How was your day?"

"Oh, I struggled through."

"Work late?"

"Oh, no, I've been back for a while. I thought I'd check out your building. It's great. I love the climbing wall."

"Really? I've never been on it. Is that one of the outfits we bought yesterday?"

"Yeah, I've had lots of comments on it. A guy named Dave, down at the climbing wall, stopped to talk to me. I don't think he normally would have mistaken me for his type."

She felt just the littlest thrill of pleasure that Kade could not hide his annoyance at Dave's attention.

"Want to order something for dinner? I don't have much here to cook." He snapped his fingers. "Unless you want an omelet."

He'd always made the best omelets.

"Perfect," she said.

And it was perfect. After dinner they watched the

news together, and it felt so utterly easy, as if they were an old married couple.

Which they were, sort of.

Of course, when they'd been a newly married couple, they hadn't sat around watching television. They couldn't keep their hands off each other. Later, when that stage had passed—or when she'd killed it, by bringing out the dreaded chart—they had played cards sometimes in the evening.

She suddenly longed for that.

"You have a deck of cards, Kade?"

"Why? You want to play strip poker?" he asked with such earnest hopefulness she burst out laughing.

"No!"

"How about a strip Scrabble game, then?"

"How about just an ordinary Scrabble game?" she said, trying not to encourage him by laughing.

"Can we use bad words?"

"I suppose that would be okay. Just this once."

"How about if we use only bad words?"

She gave him a slug on his arm. "That falls into the 'give him an inch and he'll take a mile' category."

Suddenly, she wanted to play a bad-words Scrabble game with him. She wanted to not be the uptight one, the stick-in-the-mud. "A bad-words Scrabble game it is," she said.

"I don't actually have a Scrabble board."

"That figures."

"But I bet we can find it on the computer."

And so that was what they did, sat side by side on his sofa, playing a bad-words Scrabble game on the computer until she was laughing so hard it felt as if she could die from it.

"So," he said casually, after he had just played *phaut*, "tell me why you want a divorce all of a sudden."

"I told you, it's not all of a sudden."

"But there's something going on."

And, maybe he'd done this on purpose, reminded her of what it was like to have a best friend, because she wanted to tell him. Crazily, she wanted to know what he thought.

"I'm thinking of adopting a baby," she said quietly.

He was staring at her. "Aw, Jess," he said, not as if he was happy for her, but as if he pitied her.

"What does that mean?" she asked.

"It's the Old English spelling of *fart*," he said. "*P-h-a-u-t*. You can challenge it if you want. But you miss a turn if you're wrong."

She had just told him something very important! How could he act as if the stupid word he'd made up was more engrossing?

"Not *that*. What does 'aw, Jess' mean?"

"Never mind. I'm sorry I said it."

She saw, suddenly, that he was using his stupid made-up word as a way not to get into it with her. "No, I want you to tell me."

"But then when I do, you'll be mad," he said, confirming his avoidance strategy.

"Will I?" When had she become that person? The one who invited opinions, but then was angry if they were not what she wanted to hear? She wanted it not to be a truth about her, but in her gut, she knew it was.

"You don't want to hear what I have to say, but maybe I'm going to say it anyway, for the sake of the baby."

She felt as if she was bracing herself.

"A baby isn't supposed to fill a need in you, Jessica," he said quietly. "You're supposed to fulfill its needs."

Jessica felt the shock of it. She felt as if she should be very, very angry with him. But she was not. Instead, she remembered the revelation she'd had in the change room of Chrysalis, the one she had tried to shake off.

That she was using a child to try to fight off her own pervasive feeling of inadequacy. Instead of being angry with Kade, Jessica was, instead, sharply aware she had carried a certain neediness in her since the death of her mother. The miscarriages had made it worse.

So Kade had called a spade a spade. She saw, from the look on his face, it was not a put-down at all. She had a deep sense of his courage, that he had handed her a simple truth, knowing it might make her angry, but also believing she needed to hear it. And maybe also believing she would know what to do with it.

Jessica remembered how before she had hated everything about Kade, she had loved everything about him. And this was one of the things she had loved, that he had a way of seeing right to the heart of things. He would have shrugged it off, uncomfortable, if she called it intuition, but that was exactly what it was.

It was part of what made him so good at business. He was brilliantly insightful. Before things had gone sideways between them, Jessica had loved his input, so different from her own.

"I've been too blunt," he said. "I'm sorry."

"No, Kade," she said, "it's what I needed to hear, even if it's not what I wanted to hear."

She suspected this was why she had not wanted to tell him about the adoption, because he could shed a light on her plans that could change everything.

"You and I," she said, "we've always been so different. It's as if we each have the pieces of half of a puzzle.

It's when we're together that we can piece together the whole thing."

She thought of those adoption papers at home, and it occurred to her this was what he had shown her: she was still wanting a baby to fill gaps in her life.

She had probably never been less ready for a baby than she was right now.

"I'm very tired now," she whispered, feeling as if she was holding the remnants of another shattered dream within herself. "I'm going to bed."

"Jess, I'm sorry. I didn't want to hurt you."

She smiled wanly. "Oh, Kade, I don't think we ever wanted to hurt each other. And yet, somehow we always do."

And yet, over the next few days it was as if something had broken free between them; a wall of ice had crumbled, and what was held behind it flowed out. As they shared his beautiful space, there were moments of spontaneous laughter. And quiet companionship. As they shared meals and memories and old connections, they rediscovered their comfort with one another. And caught glimpses of the joy they had once shared. And relaxed into that rare sensation of having found someone in the world with whom it was possible to be genuine.

And so when Jake called Kade on Thursday afternoon and told him that the house was done, Kade felt not happy that the work had been finished so quickly, but a sense of loss. He wanted to give Jake a list of ten more things to do. No, a hundred. No, a thousand.

He brought her the news after work. Jessica had arrived at the apartment before him. She was wearing one of the outfits they had bought together—a lively floral-print dress with a belt and a wide skirt that reminded him of something someone might wear to dance the jive.

She had her arm out of the sling and was wiping down his counters. Once it had bugged him so much that she felt driven to wipe up every crumb.

But now, watching her, he could see it gave her a kind of contentment to be bringing order to her space, and he found he liked watching her.

She looked up and saw him standing there, and she smiled a greeting.

"Hey! You are not supposed to be out of that sling yet."

"You know me."

It was the most casual of statements, but it filled him with some sense of satisfaction that, yes, he did know her.

"I could not handle the mess on the counter. I needed both hands free to wring out the dishcloth."

"You've always been such a stickler for tidy."

"I know. You used to protest daily, *too many rules*."

"Did I? I don't remember that."

Jessica cast Kade a look. Could he really not remember the mean things he had said to her?

"You called me the sock Nazi," she remembered ruefully. Was she hoping he would apologize? He didn't. He cocked his head at her, and looked at her in that way that made her stomach do the roller-coaster thing.

"I couldn't understand the changes in you," he said. "We said 'I do' and overnight you went from being this kind of Bohemian free-spirited artist to Martha Stewart's understudy."

"And you," she reminded him, "resisted me at every turn. It drove me crazy. If I put out a laundry hamper, you would throw your dirty clothes on the floor beside it."

It had driven her crazy that she had been creating this perfect little nest for them—a perfect world, really—and he'd resisted her at every turn. He'd left his socks in the living room. He'd hung his towels crooked in the bathroom. He'd left dishes in the sink, and if he'd been working outside and forgot something in the house, he'd just traipsed in, leaving a pathway of leaves and grass and mud in his wake.

"I know I could be inconsiderate," he said, but he didn't sound very remorseful. "I felt as if you were trying to control me all the time, I felt as if you thought the way you wanted to live was the only correct way, and what I wanted, to be a little relaxed in my own space, didn't count at all."

Jessica felt shocked by that. It was certainly true. She had always wanted things her way.

"And then I'd come home from working all day, and you'd have some elaborate meal all prepared and candles on the table and the best dishes out. I would have been just as happy with a hamburger and my feet up on the coffee table in front of the TV. Not that I was allowed to put my feet up on the coffee table, even though it was really a bench that was sturdy enough to have survived one war, a fire and two floods."

She was aghast at the picture he was painting. He looked as if he was going to stop, but now that the floodgates were open, he was completely unable to.

"I wanted to talk to you the way we had always talked—about ideas and dreams and your art. I wanted to laugh with you and be lighthearted.

"But suddenly all you wanted to talk about was paint

colors for the nursery and could we please get a new sofa, and did I think there was too much tarragon in the recipe. *Tarragon*, Jess."

And so this was how their relationship had started to show cracks, she thought. She had known it was all going dreadfully wrong.

"I wanted to shake you, and say, 'Who are you and what the hell have you done with Jessica?'"

It wasn't until after he'd gone from her life that she realized how stupid it had been to make an issue out of the very things she then had missed.

"But you—" Jessica's defensive response died on her lips. She considered the possibility he was right. Instead of feeling defensive, she let what he had just said sink in. Suddenly, for the first time, it occurred to her maybe she should be the one who was sorry. If she was going to move on, if she was going to be a good parent—no, a great parent—to a child someday, she had to start working on herself now. And part of that meant facing her role in the relationship going wrong.

Up until this point, had she really told herself she had no part in it? That it was all his fault?

"What happened to you?" he asked. "And worse, what did I have to do with it?"

"Nothing," she said softly, and with dawning realization. "You had nothing to do with it. I think, Kade, ever since my mom died, I longed to have *that* world again.

"I was only twelve when she was diagnosed with a rare form of cancer. She went from diagnosis to dead in three weeks."

"I know that," he said, reminding her he knew so much about her.

"But what you didn't know—maybe what I didn't

even know until this minute—was that I wanted my world back. After she died, it was just my dad and my brother and me. Everything went south. The house was a catastrophe. We ate takeout and macaroni and cheese. I couldn't even invite a friend over, our house was such a disaster. I wanted my lovely, stable family back."

"Oh, Jessie," he said. "I probably should have figured that out."

"And then we got married," she said slowly, "and I already had this idea in my head what a perfect life looked like, and I set out to make our life together look like that. And when I could sense you were dissatisfied, I thought it was because we needed to take the next step—to solidify ourselves as a family."

"You decided you wanted to have a baby."

"Didn't you want to have a baby?" she asked.

"Of course I did," he reassured her. "But maybe not for me. I wanted you to be happy. It didn't seem as though paint chips and the creative use of tarragon were making you happy. It certainly didn't seem as though I was making you happy."

CHAPTER SEVENTEEN

So here was a painful truth looking Jessica in the face. She'd had a wonderful husband who loved her, and somehow she had managed to manufacture misery.

Not that their challenges had not been real, but why hadn't she been able to focus on everything that was right and good, instead of working away at the tiny cracks until they had become fractures between Kade and her?

As painful as this conversation was, Jessica was relieved by it. This was the conversation they had needed to have a year ago, when everything had fallen apart so completely between them. Maybe if they had had it even before that, they could have stopped things from progressing to a complete fallout.

"When the first miscarriage happened," Jessica admitted softly, "I think it was a cruel reminder of what I'd already learned from my mother's illness—I was not in control of anything. And yet instead of surrendering to that, I fought it hard. The more out of control I felt, the more I started trying to control everything. Maybe especially you."

"Jessica," Kade said, and his voice was choked, "I always saw the failure as mine, not yours."

Her eyes filled with tears. It was not what she needed to hear, not right now, just as she was acknowledging her part in their marriage catastrophe.

"When I married you," Kade said, his voice low and pain-filled, "it felt as if that was a sacred vow and that I had found my lifelong duty. It was to protect you. To keep you safe. To stop bad things from happening. I felt as if my love should be enough to protect us—and you—from every storm.

"When it wasn't? When the growing chasm between us was made impassable by the two miscarriages, I could not enter your world anymore. I felt as if I was losing my mind. Those miscarriages, those lost babies, made me admit to myself how powerless I was. I couldn't do the most important thing I'd ever wanted to do. I could not save my own babies.

"And that compounded the fact I was already dealing with a terrible sense of failure at lesser levels."

"What levels?" she asked.

"I had failed to even make you happy. I wanted you to stop trying to get pregnant. But you wouldn't. It made me feel as if I was not enough to meet your needs. It felt as if the bottom fell out of our whole world. When you wanted to keep trying—keep subjecting yourself and us to that roller-coaster ride of hope and joy and grief and despair—I just couldn't do it. And so I retreated to a world where I could be in control."

"And abandoned me," she whispered.

"Yes," he said quietly. "Yes. Yes, I did abandon you. But I think not nearly so thoroughly as you abandoned yourself. It was as if a baby was going to become your whole reason and your whole life."

She realized that she had not been ready then, and she

was not really ready now, either. She began to cry. She had vowed no more losses, and now she faced the biggest one of all. Somehow in marriage, she had lost herself. She had become the role she played instead of the person she was.

Kade had always hated tears.

Always. If they argued and she started crying, he left.

Except when they had lost the first baby. They had crawled into bed together and clung to each other and wept until there were no tears left.

But after that, it was as if he steeled himself against that kind of pain, against feeling so intensely ever again. Even after the devastation of the loss of the second baby, he had been capable of only a few clumsy claps on the shoulder, a few of the kinds of platitudes she had come to hate the most.

It had seemed as if her grief had alienated him even more, had driven him away even more completely.

The tears trickled down her cheeks. She could not stop them now that they had been let loose.

She expected him to do what he had always done: escape at the first sign of a loss of control on her part. But he didn't.

"Jessie," Kade said softly. "In retrospect, we weren't ready for those babies. Neither of us was. We thought our relationship was on firm ground, but at the first stress, it fractured, so it wasn't. Babies need to come into a stronger place than that."

He came and he put his arms around her. He drew her deep against him, doing what she had needed so desperately from him all along. He let her tears soak into his shirt.

"I'm okay now," she finally sighed against him. "Thank you."

"For what?" he growled.

"For holding me. It's all I ever needed. Not for you to fix things, but for you to be there, as solid as a rock, when things went sideways."

He looked at her. He nodded. She could see the regret in his face. She could see that he got it. Completely.

And then something changed in his eyes, and he reached down and lifted a tear off her cheek with his finger, and scraped his thumb across her lip.

Jessica could feel the move into the danger zone. And she should have stepped back from it. But she could not.

A part of her that would not be controlled missed him—and missed this part of their life together—with a desperation that made her think she knew how heroin addicts felt. The *need* overshadowed everything. It overpowered common sense and reason. It certainly overpowered the need to be in control and the need to be right.

They were all gone—common sense and reason, control and the need to be right. They were gone, and in their place his thumb scraping across her lip became her whole world. Her lips parted, and she drew his thumb into her mouth. His skin tasted of heaven.

He went very still. She gazed up at him. And then she stood on her tiptoes, and she pulled his head down to her. She kissed that beautiful, familiar little groove behind his ear. He groaned his surrender and placed his hands on each side of her face and looked down at her, and then lowered his mouth to hers.

Welcome.

Welcome home.

His hunger was as apparent as hers. He crushed her lips under his own. His tongue found the hollow of her mouth, and she melted against him as he devoured her. His lips moved away from hers and he anointed the hollow of her throat and the tip of her nose and her eyelids.

"Jessica," he said hoarsely. "Oh, Jessica."

He scooped her up in his arms and went to the hallway to his bedroom. He tapped open the partially closed door with his foot, strode across the room and laid her on his king-size bed. It gave luxuriously under her weight. She stared up at him.

And wanted her husband, Kade, as she had never wanted anything else in her entire life. The wanting sizzled in her belly, and curled around her heart, and came out her lips as a moan of desire and invitation. She held out her good arm to him.

And he came willingly down to her, laying his body over hers, careful to hold his weight off her broken wing. He found the lobe of her ear and nipped it with delicate precision. He rained tiny kisses down on her brow and her nose and her cheeks and her chin.

Finally, when she was gasping with wanting and longing, he captured her lips and nuzzled teasingly. And then he took her lips more deeply, laying his claim, stoking the fire that was already there to white-hot.

"I am going to melt," she said hoarsely.

"Melt, then," he whispered. "Melt, and I will come with you."

His mouth on hers became a fury of possession and hunger. His tongue plunged the cool cavern of her mouth, exploring, darting, resting, tasting. He left her mouth and trailed kisses down the open collar of her shirt. He laid his trail of fire down her neck and onto her breastbone. His fingers found the buttons of her blouse and released them one by one. His lips found the nakedness of her flesh where it mounded above her bra, then blazed down the rise of her ribs to the fall of her belly. His lips went to all the places on her that only his lips had ever been before.

She did not melt. Rather, the heat built to a near explosion. The first of July, Canada Day, was weeks away, but the fireworks had begun already. They started, always, with the smaller ones, delightful little displays of color and noise, smoke and beauty. But they built and built and built to a fiery crescendo that lit the entire sky and shook the entire world.

It was obvious from the need that ached within her, from the way her body arched against him in welcome and anticipation, that this particular set of fireworks was heading toward only one possible climax.

"My arm— I don't know…" she whispered. It was her only uneasiness. She felt no guilt and no regret. He was her husband, and they belonged to each other in this way. They always had.

Kade took his weight off her and drank her in deeply.

"Do you want to do this?" he asked, and his voice was a rasp of raw need.

She knew her answer, her certainty, was in her face, and vibrating along the whole length of her body.

"I do. It's just with my arm like this, I don't know how we're going to manage," she said.

"I do," Kade whispered, his voice a growl of pure and sensual need. He had, intentionally or not, echoed their vows. *I do.* "Do you trust me, Jessie?"

"Yes."

"I know exactly how we are going to do this," he told her.

And he did. And so did she.

When they were done, in the sacred stillness that followed, the truth hit her and hit her hard.

It was not that she loved her husband again. It was that she had never stopped. Cradling the warmth of that truth to her, in the arms of her beloved, *home* for the first time in more than a year, Jessica slept.

Kade woke deep in the night. Jessica was asleep beside him, curled tightly against him, like a puppy seeking warmth. He felt tenderness toward her unfurl in him with such strength it felt as if his throat was closing. He'd known, in some deep place inside himself, ever since he'd seen the police cars in front of her store that morning, that he still loved her.

That he could not imagine a world without her. Not just *a* world. *His world.*

Something buzzed by his ear, and Kade realized it was that sound that had woken him up, and he was momentarily confused. His phone was automatically set to Do Not Disturb during the evening hours. He picked it up off the nightstand and squinted at it. It was four-thirty in the morning.

The phone buzzed again, vibrating in his hand. It was not his normal ring. Suddenly it occurred to him they had programmed the alarm at Baby Boomer to this phone to override his do-not-disturb settings. He unlocked the screen. Sure enough, there was a live-feed image of someone at the door of Baby Boomer.

Glancing at Jessica and seeing how peaceful she looked, Kade slipped from the bed, grabbed his clothes off the floor and went out into the hall. He called 911, with his phone tucked in against his ear, pulling on his pants at the same time. He explained what was happening, but the operator sounded particularly bored with his news of an alarm going off and a possible break-in in progress.

He thought of Jessica with her arm immobilized and he thought of her ongoing sleep disturbances and about the way she startled every time there was a loud sound. Even in the cubicle of the dress shop, when the music had started unexpectedly, she had nearly jumped out of her skin. Thinking of that, Kade felt really, really angry. Dangerously angry.

Jessica needed to know that he would look after her. That he would protect her. If her world was threatened, he would be there. He would put his body between her and a bullet if he had to.

And so, like a soldier getting ready to do battle for all he believed in, Kade went out the apartment door, got in his car and headed at full speed to her store.

At first it appeared no one was there. But then he noticed the newly repaired door hanging open and a sliver of light moving inside the store.

Without a single thought, he leaped from the car and took the stairs two at a time. He burst in the door and raced across the room and tackled the shadowy figure by the cash register.

Jessica was right. The thief was scrawny! Holding him in place was ridiculously easy. The anger at all the grief this guy had caused Jessica seemed to seep out of him. The thief was screaming, "Please don't hurt me."

He seemed skinny and pathetic, and just as Jessica had guessed, desperate with a kind of desperation Kade did not know.

Kade heard sirens and saw flashing lights, and moments later the police were in the doorway, telling *him* to put his hands in the air. It seemed to take forever to sort it all out, but finally, he finished filling out reports and doing interviews.

It was now nearly seven. Jessica was probably awake and probably wondering where he was.

He called her, and could hear the anxiety in her voice as soon as she answered the phone.

"Where are you?"

"The alarm at your business alerted to my phone a couple of hours ago. I headed over here."

"*You* answered the alarm?"

"Well, I called the police, but I just wanted to make sure they caught him." He laughed, adrenaline still coursing through his veins. "You were right, Jessie. He was scrawny."

She cut him off, her voice shrill. "You caught the thief?"

"Yeah," he said proudly.

"But you are the one who lectured me about being foolhardy!"

He frowned. He wanted to be her hero. He wanted her to know her world was safe with him. Why didn't she sound pleased? Why wasn't she getting the message?

"You could have been killed," she said. "He could have had a gun or a knife. You're the one who pointed that out to me."

"Jessica, it all worked out, didn't it?"

"Did it?" she said, and he did not like what he heard in her voice. "Did it, Kade?"

"Yes!"

"Kade, being in a relationship means thinking about the other person."

"I *was* thinking about you."

"No, you weren't."

"How about if you don't tell me what I was thinking about? We had a great night last night. It doesn't mean you own me. It doesn't mean you get to control me. You know what this conversation feels like? *Here we go again*."

"Does it?" she said, and her voice was very shrill. "Well, try this out—here we *don't* go again!"

And she slammed down the phone. He stared at his phone for a long time, and finally put it back in his pocket. He already knew, when he got back to his apartment, she would be gone.

CHAPTER EIGHTEEN

JESSICA HUNG UP the phone. She was shaking violently. She hugged herself against the feeling of being cold.

And she faced an awful truth about herself. Her courage was all used up. She did not have one drop left. This love made her feel so vulnerable, and she did not want to feel that way anymore.

She thought of how it had been last night, of Kade's heated lips anointing every inch of her fevered flesh.

In the cold light of dawn, her heart swelled with loving him.

But it didn't feel good at all. It felt as if that love could not make her whole and could even destroy what was left of her.

It was her curse: her mother, whom she had loved so deeply, taken from her. And then each of those babies, whom she had loved madly and beyond reason, without even having met them, gone from this earth.

Loving Kade felt as if it was leaving herself open to one more loss. And he could be reckless. Impulsive. Look what he had just done! That could have been a far different phone call. It could have been the police calling to tell her Kade was dead.

Was he right? Was she trying to control him? Whatever—she had a deep sense that she could not sustain one more loss.

Quietly, Jessica walked through his beautiful apartment. With each step a memory: pizza and warm croissants and sitting on the sofa and playing a Scrabble game. She went back to the guest room, put on the nearest thing she could find, but left all the rest of the clothing they had bought together, because it, too, held too many memories.

Of dancing with him in Chrysalis. She should have recognized the danger right that second, before rickshaw rides, and Chinese food in the park, and falling asleep on a blanket with the trees whispering their names. Before it had all built to that moment last night of unbridled passion, of *hoping* for the most uncertain thing of all.

The future.

Feeling like a thief who had stolen the most precious thing of all, a moment of the pure pleasure of love, Jessica slipped out the door of Kade's empty apartment and locked it behind her. She went down to the lobby and had the concierge call her a cab.

In minutes, she was being whisked through the dawn-drenched city. As soon as they pulled up in front of her house, she wished that she had thought to go to a hotel.

Because this was more of them, of her and of Kade. It was the house they had chosen together and lived in together and loved in together.

And fought in together, she reminded herself, and watched love make that torturous metamorphosis to hate.

She could not survive that again. She could not survive losing him again.

When she let herself in the house, she felt relief. It wasn't really *their* house anymore. Though all her familiar furniture was back, except her bench, which was still in the back of a truck somewhere, everything else felt new.

Except Behemoth, which seemed to be squatting on the new floor glaring accusingly at her.

It even smelled new, of floor varnish and paint. The floors glowed with soft beauty; the walls had been painted a dove gray. The soot was gone from where they had tried to use the fireplace that one time, and it was gone off the ceiling.

Jessica went through to the kitchen, and it was as she had dreaded. She reached up and touched the cabinets. The oak stain was no longer bleeding through the white, and that, more than anything else, made her feel like crying.

She kicked off her shoes and passed her bedroom. There would be no going back to bed. She was sure of that. She went to her office and slid open the desk drawer.

Jessica took out all the documents she needed to start filling out to begin the adoption procedure, to get on with her dreams of a life in a way that did not involve him.

But as she stared at the papers, she realized she was terrified of everything that love meant, and especially of the built-in potential for loss and heartbreak.

She was not whole. She had never been whole. She had brought a neediness to her and Kade's relationship that had sucked the life out of it. And if she did not get herself sorted out, she would do the same to a child.

She thought of putting the documents back in the desk drawer, but it seemed to her they would be just one more thing to move, to sort through when the time came to leave here. It seemed to her she was not at all sure what she wanted anymore.

She dumped the papers in the garbage, and then she went and sat on the couch and hugged her knees to herself, and cried for who she was not, and what she was never going to have.

Finally, done with crying, done with Kade, done with dreams, she called the real estate office. An agent was there promptly, and Jessica calmly walked through the house with him as he did his appraisal. She felt numb and disconnected, as if the agent was on one side of a thick glass wall, and she was on the other. She didn't really care what price he put on the house. In fact, she barely registered the number he had given her. She gave him the listing, signed the papers, and he pounded the for-sale sign into her lawn.

She kept hoping her phone would ring, but it didn't. She and Kade had arrived at the same place, all over, an impasse that neither of them would be willing to cross. If it was a good thing, why did she feel so bereft?

After she had watched the agent pound the sign in in front of her house, she went outside and invited him to come by Baby Boomer and do the very same thing.

In the brutal light of this heartbreak, Jessica could see herself all too clearly. The business had risen from her neediness, from her need for something outside herself to fill her. It had been part of that whole obsession that she had not been able to let go of, not even after it had cost her her marriage to the man she loved.

Jessica expected to feel sad when the for-sale sign went up in front of Baby Boomer.

Instead, she felt relief. She felt oddly free.

It was going to be different now. She thought about what she really wanted, and she remembered when she had first met Kade, before she had lost herself, who she had been. An artist, not drawing pictures of bunnies on nursery walls, but drawing from a place deep within her.

That night, after she had closed the shop for the day, she went into the art-supply store next door. As soon as she walked in the door, the smells welcomed her—the smell of canvases and paints and brushes.

It smelled of home, she told herself firmly, her true home, the self she had walked away from again and again and again.

But home conjured other images: Kade laughing, and Kade with his feet up on the coffee table, and Kade's socks on the floor, and Kade opening a box of pizza, and her sitting on a sander laughing so hard she cried. She shook that off impatiently.

She had made her vow, her new vow. And it was not to have and to hold. The vow she intended to obey was that she would not lose anything else. Not one more thing. And that meant not doing anything that would open her to loss.

Possibly more than any other single thing, loving Kade fell into that category.

Over the next weeks Jessica had to relearn a terribly hard lesson: you didn't just stop loving someone because you wanted to, because it had the potential to hurt you.

Love was always there in the background, beckoning, saying you can have a larger life if you risk this. But she thought maybe it was from living in the house they had shared together that she could not shake her sense of grief and torment.

Not even painting could fill her.

So she did other things she had always wanted to do and held back from. She signed up for a rock-climbing course, and a kayaking program, and a gourmet-cooking class. She had a sense of needing to fill every second so that she would not have time to think, to be drawn into the endless pool of grief that was waiting to drown her. Jessica was aware she was searching frantically to find things she could be passionate about that did not involve that sneaky, capricious, uncontrollable force called love.

But the more she tried to do, the more exhausted she became. If these efforts to fill her life were right, wouldn't she feel energized by them, instead of completely drained? At rock climbing, her limbs were so weak she could not hold herself on the wall. At kayaking—which was only in a local swimming pool for now—she fell out of the kayak and had a panic attack. At cooking class, she took one taste of her hollandaise sauce and had to run to the bathroom and be sick.

The feeling of weakness progressed. Jessica felt tired all the time. She had fallen asleep at work. She cried at the drop of a hat. Her stomach constantly felt as if it was knotted with anxiety.

Obviously, she had been absolutely correct when she had told him, "Here we *don't* go again." She took this as evidence that she was doing the right thing. If she was having this kind of reaction to a weeklong reunion with her husband, what would happen to her if they tried it for another year? Or two? And *then* it didn't work? Obviously, she could not survive.

"You need to go see a doctor," Macy said to her after finding her fast asleep, her head on her arms on her desk. "Something is wrong with you."

And so she went to see the doctor. She knew nothing was wrong with her. Love was not an ailment a doctor could cure. You could not take a pill to mend a broken heart. The doctor ordered a raft of tests, and Jessica had them all done, knowing nothing would come of it.

But then the doctor's office phoned and asked her to come back in. There were test results they needed to discuss with her in person.

And that was when she knew the truth. Jessica knew that, like her mother, she was sick and dying. Thank God she had not proceeded with her adoption idea. Thank God she had not proceeded with loving Kade.

It was just another confirmation that she could not allow herself to love. People could leave her, but she could leave people, too. It was all just too risky.

The doctor swung into the room, all good cheer. Jessica guessed he'd had a fantastic golf game that completely overrode the news he was about to give her.

She waited for him to remember the gravity of breaking it to someone that they were dying.

But that foolish grin never left his face!

"I have wonderful news for you," he said. "You're pregnant."

She stared at him. Life was too cruel. All those years of charts and temperatures and schedules, and now she was pregnant. Plus, she knew a terrible truth. Being pregnant did not necessarily mean walking away with a baby at the end.

Hadn't she decided she was unsuited for motherhood? She called Macy and told her she wouldn't be in for the rest of the day. She went home.

Her real estate agent was on the steps. "I've been trying to call you all morning. We have an offer on your house! A great offer."

Numbly she signed the paper he shoved at her. She went into the house and closed the door. Despite all her efforts to control everything, to keep change at bay, everything was changing anyway.

What was she going to tell Kade?

Nothing. He would feel trapped. He would feel as if he had to do the honorable thing, be sentenced to a life of bickering with her.

No. There had been no pretense in their last night together. He did love her. She knew that.

And now they were in the same place all over again. Where that love would be tested by life. What would make it different this time? If they lost another baby, how would it be any better this time?

"It won't," Jessica told herself. "It won't be better. It will be worse."

She lay down on the couch and cried and cried and cried. She hoped she had cried until there were no tears left, but from experience, she knew. There were always tears left. There was always an event waiting to blindside you, waiting to make you find that place where you had hidden a few extra tears.

CHAPTER NINETEEN

KADE DISCONNECTED FROM the phone call. He was part owner in his and Jessica's house, so he had been notified. It had just sold. Jessica, apparently, could not even tell him that herself. That had been a secretary at the real estate company asking him to come in and sign some documents.

He had not seen or heard from Jessica since that night when they had made love, and then he had made the fateful decision to go and tackle the breaking and entering at her business himself.

For a guy who thought he had the emotional range of a rock, he was stunned by how he felt.

Angry. And then sad. Frustrated. Powerless. And then sad some more.

He loved his wife. He loved her beyond reason. They were two intelligent people. Why could they not build a bridge across this chasm that divided them?

He mulled over the news about the house. What was he going to do now? Should he be the one to try to cross the minefield between them? A man had to have his pride.

But it seemed to Kade pride might have had quite a bit to do with why they could not work things out in the first place.

Maybe a man didn't have to have his pride.

Maybe a man having his pride really had nothing to do with being strong, with doing what needed to be done, with doing the right thing. Maybe a man had to swallow his pride.

Jessica, Kade knew, would never take the first step toward reconciliation, and for a second he felt angry again.

But then he relived her voice on the phone that morning of the break-in. It occurred to him that Jessica had not been trying to control him. She had been genuinely terrified.

Suddenly, he felt ashamed of himself. Wasn't this part of what was destroying them? Pride? Okay, it was a guy thing. It was always all about him. Even when he told himself it was about her. For example, he would go and save her store. But it had really been about him. He'd wanted to be the hero. He'd wanted to see her eyes glowing with admiration for him.

Maybe it was time for him to grow up.

To see things through her eyes, instead of through the warp of his own colossal self-centeredness.

She had been terrified.

And right from the beginning, from the day he had first seen her again, after she had tried to take out the thief herself at her store, she had given him clues where all that terror came from.

I lost my mother when I was twelve. I've lost two babies to miscarriage. I am not losing anything else. Not one more thing.

Kade had seen what losing those babies had done to her. He had seen the intensity of her own love tear her apart.

He had seen photos of her when she was a girl. In her

fifth-grade class photo, she had been grinning merrily at the camera, all leprechaun charm and joyous mischief. But by the following year, when her mother had died, she had looked solemn and sad, the weight of the whole world on her shoulders.

He tried to imagine her at twelve, her sense of loss, her sense of the world being a safe place being gone.

The loss of each of those babies would have triggered that old torment, that sense of the world not being safe.

As would the man she loved putting himself at risk.

And suddenly, he despised himself. So what if she tried to control him?

"Kade," he said and swore to himself. "Don't you get it? It's not all about you."

He loved her. He loved Jessica Clark Brennan, his wife, beyond reason. He had cut her loose to navigate her heartbreaks on her own. When she had disappeared into that dark world of her own heartache, instead of having the courage to go in with her, to help her find her way back out, he had abandoned her.

That was not love.

But how was he going to make her see that he understood that now? He suspected she had spent the past weeks building up her defenses against him—against love. How was he going to knock them back down?

They had just sold a house together. The most natural thing in the world would be to bring a bottle of champagne over there and celebrate with her.

And it was time for honesty. Not pride. Pride didn't want her to know how he felt, pride did not want to be vulnerable to her.

But love did. Love wanted her to know how he felt and love wanted to be vulnerable to her.

Pride had won throughout their separation.

Now it was time to give love, their love, a chance. A second chance.

With his mind made up, a half hour later, Kade knocked on the door of the house they had shared. He saw Jessica come to the window, and then there was silence. For a moment, he thought she was not going to open the door.

But then she did.

What he saw made him feel shattered. She was in one of those horrible dresses again. He thought she had been kidding about one being available in camo, but no, she hadn't been. Aside from the horror of the dress, Jessica looked awful—tired and pale and thin.

"Hello, Jessica," he said quietly. His voice sounded unnatural to him.

"Did you come to get your check?"

"My check?" he asked, genuinely confused. Obviously there would be no money yet from a house that had barely sold.

"I told you I'd pay you for those clothes from Chrysalis once the house sold."

"You didn't even take the clothes with you."

"What? Are you wearing them?"

"Are you crazy?"

"Because if you're not, I'm paying for them."

"Okay," he said. "I am, then. Wearing them."

Just a glimmer of a smile, before she doused it like a spark of a fire in a tinder-dry forest. Still, despite her look of studied grimness, was there a shadow of something in her eyes? Something that she did not want him to see? Despite all her losses, and despite the fact she wanted not to, he could tell she *hoped*.

And her hope, to him, was the bravest thing of all.

"Well, then, did you bring back my bench?"

"No."

"What are you doing here, then?"

"Isn't it obvious? I brought a bottle of champagne. I thought we should celebrate the sale of our house."

"Oh."

"This is the part where you invite me in," he told her gently.

"What if I don't want you to come in?" she said.

But he could still see that faint spark of hope in her eyes.

"We still have some business to complete, Jessie." Ah, she'd never been able to resist him when he called her Jessie.

She stood back from the door, her chin tilted up in defiance of the hope he had seen in her eyes. He went in.

He tried to hide his shock at what he found inside the house. The house was not a reflection of Jessica. And it wasn't just that the floors had been refinished, either. There were things out of place. There was a comforter and a pillow on the sofa. Empty glasses littered the coffee table. There were socks on the floor.

Really? It was all very frightening. "Are you okay?" he asked her.

She went and sat down on the sofa, crossed her arms over her chest in defense. Against him. "I'm fine. What do you want to discuss?"

"Ah." He went through to the kitchen with his bottle of wine. "How's your arm?" he called. Maybe that was the explanation for the mess. She was not completely able-bodied.

"It's okay. The cast has been off for a bit. I have some exercises I do to strengthen my muscles."

The corkscrew was in a familiar place. How was it this kitchen felt so much more like home than his own masterpiece of granite and stainless steel? He opened the bottle, got glasses down and poured. He hated it that the cabinets had been fixed.

He went back and handed her a wineglass, and sat down beside her. He noticed the black soot stain up the front of the fireplace had been fixed, too.

It was as if their memories were being erased, one by one. "Here's to the sale of the house," he said.

"To moving on," she agreed hollowly. But she set her glass down without taking a sip.

He took a sip of his own wine, watching her carefully over the rim of his glass. A bead of perspiration broke out over her lip, and her face turned a ghastly shade of white.

He set his glass down and reached for her, afraid she was going to tumble off the sofa. "Jessica?"

She slid away from his touch and found her feet. She bolted for the bathroom, and didn't even have time to shut the door. The sound of her getting violently sick filled the whole house.

No wonder the place was a wreck. She wasn't feeling well.

She came back into the room, looking weak and wasted. She sat on the couch, tilted her head against the back and closed her eyes.

"Why did you say you were fine? Why didn't you just tell me you had the flu?"

"Sorry," she mumbled. "I should have told you. I don't want you to catch anything."

Her eyes were skittering all over the place. She was

a terrible liar. She had the same look on her face right now that she'd had the year she'd denied buying him the golf clubs he'd wanted for a long time, when she really had.

But why would she lie about having the flu? Or maybe the lie would be that she didn't want him to catch anything.

He looked at her hard. After a long time, she looked back at him, proud and...right beneath that, what? *Scared?* Of what? Him?

Kade felt a strange stillness descend on him, the kind of stillness you might feel in a church with sun pouring through a stained glass window.

He *knew.* He knew right to the bottom of his soul. Jessica was pregnant. He was being given a second chance.

She looked away. "Yeah," she finally said, the word obviously an effort from the lie inherent to it. "The flu."

"Uh-huh."

Her eyes flew to his face, then moved away again.

"You're pregnant, aren't you, Jessica?"

She was silent for a bit and then she sighed with a kind of relief. "Imagine that," she said quietly. "All those charts and temperatures and schedules, all that taking all the fun out of it, and then one night. One single night..."

"Are you happy at all?" he asked her quietly.

"It's pretty hard to be happy when you're terrified," she said. "You know what the cruelest irony is, Kade? I'd just realized, with your help, that I am not ready for a baby!"

It came out very close to a wail of pure panic.

"Aw, Jess," he said quietly, "maybe that *is* when you are ready. When you can see your own imperfections and embrace them. Maybe it's when you can see it's an imperfect world, and instead of trying to impose perfection on it, you just embrace that, too. Maybe that's the only real lesson we can give a baby. It's the one I learned from the failure of us. The world is not going to be perfect. Life is not going to be easy. I can't control everything. But together, with love for each other, we can handle whatever it throws at us."

"We?" she whispered.

"Jessie, I am not leaving you alone with this. And maybe that's what I really wanted to say that night when you told me you were planning to adopt a baby. Not that you weren't ready, or that you had issues to work on, because who could ever be ready for a baby? And who does not have issues to work on? I guess what I was trying to say that night was that it's a lot to take on alone. I didn't want to think about you taking it on without me. It's going to take two people, stumbling through, to bring this baby into the world.

"I'm going to be there for you this time."

Her eyes went to his face, and this time they stayed there, wide and hopeful. She wanted to believe—the capacity for hope was there—but she was frightened, too. And who could blame her?

"I know my track record stinks," he said.

She didn't disagree with that.

"And I know I can't protect you from life. Or from loss. I know we're months away from holding a baby in our arms, and I know you're scared this is going to end like all the other times. All I can really protect you from is walking through difficult times alone."

She was crying now.

"Jessica, I've been given a second chance to be a better man. And I'm taking it. I'm proving to you—and to myself—that I can live up to those vows we took. I remember those vows. I remember each word of them. So listen to me. Because I'm doing this again. And I'm doing it right this time."

His voice was hoarse with emotion, almost a whisper at first, and then with it growing stronger and stronger, he spoke.

"I, Kade Brennan, take you, Jessica, to be my wife, my heart and my soul, my companion through life and my one and only love. I will cherish you and I will nurture a friendship based in trust and honor. I will laugh with you and, especially, I will cry with you. I will love you faithfully, today, tomorrow and forever. Through the best and the worst, through the difficult and the easy, whatever may come, I will always be there for you. I have given you my hand." Kade held out his hand to her, cleared his throat and said, "I have given you my hand to hold, and so I give also my life into your keeping."

To him, it seemed like forever that she looked at him, her eyes sparkling with unshed tears. And then her hand slipped into his, as if it had never left it, as if this was where her hand was meant to be.

Jessica spoke. Her voice was husky and tears were set free and flowed down her face, just as they had that day all those years ago, when he had cherished her tears instead of seeing them as a sign of his own powerlessness.

She said, "I, Jessica Clark-Brennan, take you, Kade, to be my husband, my heart and my soul, my companion in life and my one and only true love. I will cherish you and I will nurture our friendship, based in trust and honor. I will laugh with you, and, yes, I will cry with you. I will love you faithfully, today, tomorrow and forever.

Through the best and the worst, through the difficult and the easy, whatever may come, I will always be there. I have given you my hand to hold, and so I give also my life into your keeping."

She had her knuckles in her eyes, scrubbing like a child who just wanted the tears to go away.

But that was their past. Her tears had upset him and made him feel helpless and hopeless, and so he had turned away. And so she had begun to try to hide how she felt from him, the very one she should have been able to lean on, the one she should have been able to be completely transparent and completely herself with.

Not this time. This time he was walking right into the fire. He slid over on the sofa and crossed the small space that remained between them. Gently, he scooped her up and put her on his lap. She did not resist. She sighed against him as if she had waited her whole life for this moment.

To feel safe, to feel looked after, to feel as if there was a slight possibility everything would be okay. He tucked her head into his shoulder, and felt her tears soak through his shirt.

It wasn't until a long time later that he realized that it was not only her tears soaking his shirt. His own, locked inside him for way too long, had joined hers.

He could not know how this pregnancy would end. But he did know, however it concluded, they were in this together this time. For all time.

"I love you," he said. "Jessie, I love you."

And then he held his breath.

Until he heard the words he needed to hear.

"Kade, I love you."

At that precise moment, the sound of her voice and

her words washed over him, and he felt like a desert that had not seen rain for the longest time. He felt as if the moisture had come, fallen on the parched place that was his soul. He could feel the color and the life seeping back into his world.

CHAPTER TWENTY

"Hey, I like it."

"The dress?" Jessica said, turning to Kade. She was teasing. She knew he hated this dress, and every dress from her Poppy Puppins collection. But it did great as a paint smock, and it covered her growing girth beautifully. Jessica watched him shrug out of his jacket at the door.

"Of course not that dress." He wrinkled his nose. "I have to find your secret cache of those dresses. Every time I throw one out, three more appear."

She laughed. It was the small things that she had come to love the most: him coming through the door at night, playing a Scrabble game together, watching TV and eating popcorn together, him licking her fingers, slick with butter.

Sometimes she wondered, if they had never had a bad spell, if she had never known what it was like to live without him as part of her daily life, would she love these little things as much as she did? Would she have known to appreciate them?

She had moved into his place at River's Edge after her house had been turned over to the new owners. Eventually, after the baby was born, they would buy a house for the three of them.

But at the moment, they were both cautious about making decisions based on a baby. This caution remained, even though her due date was looming large. They didn't even have a nursery, and the guest room was untouched. No lavender paint or murals this time. No crib, no mobiles, no teddy bears.

They had a beautiful handmade crate they could line with blankets and put beside their bed. When the time came. She loved the idea of the baby sleeping next to them, so close they could breathe in each other's breath, exchange air, become even more a part of one another.

Kade came over and put his hand on the gentle swell of her belly under the paint smock.

He put his head down and spoke directly to her stomach. "Hello, baby. Do you hear me in there? Moving," he said with satisfaction. "A football player."

"Or a ballerina."

"Nah, it's a boy."

It was only in the past few weeks that they had dared to play this game, so afraid were they of jinxing this incredibly magical and miraculous experience. But this time, the fear was different. They would lie awake with it, deep into the night, holding hands, leaning on each other.

They had chosen not to know the sex of their child. This baby was a miracle, boy or girl. Besides, it was endlessly fun debating it, even as they carefully avoided the baby sections of the stores. It was like a superstition, but she did not care. She was not buying one thing for that baby until she had held it in her arms.

She had barely set foot in Baby Boomer since selling it to Macy. But she knew Macy had her covered. She knew there was a shelf there filled with things Macy was quietly selecting for her: bottles and blankets and tiny disposable diapers and little outfits. *If* the time came this time—that hope fluttered in Jessica's chest, they were so close now, and the doctor smiled and shook his head at Jessica's fears—they had a whole nursery that could be put in a box and delivered to them.

There was an unexpected new dimension to Jessica's relationship with Macy and with her old place of business.

Macy was selling paintings almost as fast as Jessica could produce them. Jessica was working largely in abstract, the colors and motion flowing out of her like rivers of light. It was as if this part of her, dammed up for too long, was bursting forth now that it had been set free.

And for some reason, that kind of art appealed to people shopping for baby stuff, not for nurseries, necessarily, though there was a whole move away from the cute traditional look of babies' rooms.

No, people having babies these days, and especially the ones who shopped at an upscale store like Baby Boomer, were largely established professional couples. They had whole gorgeous big houses to decorate, not just nurseries.

And the name Jessica Brennan was causing a surprising stir in the Calgary art scene.

"I like it," Kade said. Having greeted the baby, he turned his attention to the canvas. "What's it called?"

She didn't have a studio. The light pouring through the windows of his apartment had proved perfect. When it was too strong, she closed the curtains and had lights set up to point to the canvas. Between the canvases, paints, lights and paint tarps on the floor, the place looked very messy. Add to that a sock of Kade's, menus out on the counter and magazines on the coffee table, and the effect was one of moderate disarray. And she loved it.

Kade had, with gentle strength, helped her probe the origins of that terrible need to feel in control.

Perhaps, she thought, eyeing their space, she had gone a little too far the other way.

She lifted her shoulder. *Oh, well.*

She turned her attention to the canvas. She was not sure where this came from, this endless current of inspiration, but she was pretty sure it came from love.

"Today it's called *Joy Rising.*" She shrugged. "Who knows if it will still be called that tomorrow."

"Joy Rising," Kade said, and stood back from it.

The backdrop of the canvas was a light gray neutral. The rest of it was filled with hundreds of bubbles—like soap bubbles—rising, starting small at the bottom left of the canvas, growing larger at they reached the right-hand corner.

"It's good," he said. "Now, what's for dinner?"

It was a standing joke between them, a light tease about what she liked to call her Martha Stewart phase. "The pizza menu is on the counter."

He laughed.

And his laughter shivered along her spine. They had almost lost this. They had almost walked away from it. And that was what made it even more precious today.

And maybe that was what all loss did, if you were brave, if you were open to its lessons. Maybe all loss sharpened your sense of the now, of the gifts of this very moment.

He had moved over and was studying the menu.

"Kade?"

"Huh?"

Jessica put her hand to her swollen belly. "Ah."

He was at her side in an instant, scanning her face.

"It's time," she said. "Oh, my God, it's time."

And even this moment, with intense ripples of pain possessing her body, was awash with light, with joy rising. Jessica looked into the face of the man who was her husband, and she read the strength there and knew, together, whatever happened next, it would be just fine.

Kade woke up. His neck was sore. He had fallen asleep in the chair. For a moment, he was disoriented, but then he heard a little sound, like a kitten mewing, and it all came back to him.

His eyes adjusted to the dark, and there they were. His wife and his daughter, the baby on Jessica's chest.

He had thought over the past few months with Jessica as they came together as a couple again, as they celebrated their second chance, that he had come to know the depth and breadth of love completely.

Now, looking at his child, he knew he had only kidded himself. He had only scratched the surface of what love could be.

The baby made that mewing sound again.

Jessica stirred but did not wake.

Jessica. How could someone that tiny, someone who appeared that fragile, be so damned brave? Men thought they were courageous, but that was only until they'd seen a baby born. And then they had to admit how puny their strength was, how laughable this thing they had passed off as courage was.

Courage certainly was not tackling a thief!

Kade got up from his chair. Jessica needed to rest. She

had done her bit. Thirteen hours of the most unbelievable pain Kade could imagine.

How he had wanted to take that pain from her, to take her place.

But that was one of the lessons of this remarkable second chance. He could not take her pain away. He could not fix everything, or really, even most things.

He had to be there. He had to stand there in his own helplessness, and not run from it. He had to walk with her through her pain, not try to take it away from her. Admitting his own powerlessness sometimes took more courage than anything he had ever done before.

The baby mewed again, and stirred again.

He touched the tiny back of his baby girl. It was warm beneath his fingers. He could feel the amazing miracle of the life force in that tiny little bundle.

He had been the first to hold her, the nurse showing him how. He had looked into that tiny wrinkled face, the nose crunched and the eyes screwed tightly shut in outrage, and he had recognized her.

Love.

Love manifest.

And so, summoning his courage, he lifted the baby off the gentle rise and fall of his wife's sleeping chest.

He could hold her in the palm of one hand, his other hand supporting her neck, as the nurse had shown him.

Destiny.

They had decided to call her Destiny.

Her eyes popped open, a slate gray that the nurse had told him would change. They didn't know yet if she would have green eyes like Jessica's or blue like his, or some amazing combination of both.

The nurse had said, too, that this little baby probably could not see much.

And yet, as Kade held her, her eyes seemed to widen with delighted recognition.

"That's right, sweetie, it's me. Daddy."

Daddy. The word felt incredibly sweet on his tongue, and the baby squirmed in his hand. He drew her close to his chest and went and sat back down on the chair, awkwardly stroking her back.

He was so aware of how tiny she was, and helpless. How she was relying on him.

He felt a moment's fear. The world always seemed to be in such a fragile state. The weather changed and wars broke out, and floods came and fires.

People could be fragile, too, held in the trance of long-ago hurts, hiding the broken places within them.

There was so much that he was powerless over, and yet this little girl would see him as all-powerful. Her daddy.

This was what he needed to teach her: that yes, the world could be fragile and easily broken. And people could be fragile and easily broken, too.

But there was one thing that was not fragile, and that was not easily broken.

And that thing was love.

It was the thread that ran, strong, through all the rest. It was what gave strength when strength failed, what gave hope when it was hopeless, what gave faith when there was plenty of evidence that it made no sense at all to have faith. It was what healed the breaks, and made people come out of the trance and embrace all that it was to be alive.

"Welcome to this crazy, unpredictable, beautiful, amazing life," Kade whispered to his little girl. "Welcome."

He closed his eyes, and when he opened them, Jessica's hand was on his shoulder, and she was awake, looking at them both.

"I need to confess something to you," Kade growled.

"What?"

"I've broken one of my vows to you."

"Impossible," she whispered.

"No. You are not my one and only true love anymore. I have two of you now."

And the smile on Jessica's face—radiant, a smile that shamed the very sun—said it was worth it. Every piece of pain they had navigated was worth it.

Because it had brought them here.

To this place. To this moment.

Where they knew that all else might pass away, but that love prevailed.

* * * * *

She just stood there, staring up at Dalton as he took that last step that brought him up close and personal, and then put his warm, long-fingered hand over hers.

It felt good, his hand on hers. It felt really, really good.

"Um...here." Clara's voice kind of broke on the word. And then she slid her hand out from under his and clasped it, moving it to where she felt the kick. "Yeah." She smiled in spite of herself. "That's it."

"I feel it," he agreed as the baby poked at his palm, then poked again. He was watching their hands, all his attention on the movement beneath them. And then he lifted his gaze and met her eyes. His were the clearest, most beautiful blue right then. "Clara..." His voice was rougher now, even lower than usual.

She just stared up at him, still annoyed with him, and at the same time swept up in the moment, in the intimacy of it—their baby kicking, her hand over his. She should have glanced away.

But she didn't.

The Bravos Of Justice Creek:
Where bold hearts collide under Western skies

NOT QUITE MARRIED

BY
CHRISTINE RIMMER

Published in Great Britain 2015
by Mills & Boon, an imprint of Harlequin (UK) Limited,
Eton House, 18-24 Paradise Road, Richmond, Surrey, TW9 1SR

© 2015 Christine Rimmer

ISBN: 978-0-263-25132-6

23-0515

Harlequin (UK) Limited's policy is to use papers that are natural, renewable and recyclable products and made from wood grown in sustainable forests. The logging and manufacturing processes conform to the legal environmental regulations of the country of origin.

Printed and bound in Spain
by CPI, Barcelona

Christine Rimmer came to her profession the long way around. She tried everything from acting to teaching to telephone sales. Now she's finally found work that suits her perfectly. She insists she never had a problem keeping a job—she was merely gaining "life experience" for her future as a novelist. Christine lives with her family in Oregon. Visit her at www.christinerimmer.com.

For Gail Chasan,
because you are the very best!

Chapter One

At five fifteen on a sunny April afternoon, Dalton Ames sat on a bench in a park near his Denver corporate offices and told himself he was making a big mistake.

He should have gotten some answers before he agreed to meet with her. He should have made her tell him why, exactly, she had contacted him out of the blue and just *had* to speak with him in person. Because, honestly. What good could possibly come of seeing her now?

None. He knew that.

And yet here he was, briefcase at his feet, stomach in knots. Waiting. Irresponsibly, illogically, ridiculously eager just for the sight of her.

It could go nowhere. He knew that. And yet…

His racing thoughts trailed away to nothing as he spotted her approaching: Clara Bravo, more adorable than ever in a long white dress and a short jean jacket. Clara, with her shining sable hair, her tempting mouth so quick to smile. But she wasn't smiling now. Her expression was somber, her head tipped down.

Clara.

So beautiful.

And so very, very pregnant.

Seeing her so huge shocked him, though it shouldn't have. The detective he'd hired to find her back in early December, months after their summer romance, had reported that she was pregnant and engaged to marry the baby's father.

She glanced up and spotted him, those big eyes locking on him. Her soft mouth dropped open—and then snapped resolutely shut. She hesitated on the path, but then stiffened her spine and kept on coming.

He stood.

"Hello, Dalton." Her wonderful, slightly husky voice broke on his name.

He nodded. "Clara." His voice sounded calm. Reserved. It gave nothing away, which was as he'd intended. He took care not to glance down, not to ogle that big, round belly of hers. "It's good to see you," he lied.

It wasn't good. It hurt to see her. Even big as a house with some other guy's baby, she was much too appealing. He still wanted her. It turned a brutal knife inside him to have to look at her and know that she belonged to another man.

She lifted her left hand and nervously tucked a shining strand of dark brown hair behind her ear. No wedding ring. Odd.

And come on, it was too ridiculous, to pretend he didn't notice that giant belly. Stiffly, he said, "I see congratulations are in order…"

She kept her head up, those brown eyes unwavering. "Let's sit down, shall we?" Turning, she lowered herself to the bench, bracing an arm on the back of it to ease her way down.

He sank to the space beside her.

And then she drew in a big breath and started talking. Fast. "Please believe me. I don't want anything from you. I only think it's right that you know."

"Know?" He stared at her and wondered what in the world she could be babbling about.

She bobbed her head in a frantic little nod. "Yes. You have a right to know."

"Know what?" It came out as a threatening growl. He really needed to dial it back, but she…roused things in him. She made him feel things he didn't want to feel. Gruffness was his natural defense against such dangerous emotions.

And then she said, "I…got pregnant on the island, when we were together last year. This is your baby, Dalton."

His brain flickered, then reeled. "What did you just say?" He didn't mean to bark at her. But he must have.

Because she gasped and slid to the edge of the bench, as far from him as she could get without actually jumping up and racing away. He had to actively resist the imperative to grab her and drag her back closer to him. She repeated slowly, with care. "I said, it's your baby."

"By God. Yes, you did."

She pressed her lips together, sucked in a slow breath and aimed her chin high. "And, well, as you can see…" She put a hand on the hard, high swell of her belly. "I intend to keep this child, which is also *your* child."

It hit him again, like a boot to the solar plexus. She was saying it was *his* baby.

And she wasn't finished, either. "But of course I don't expect you just to take my word for it. Should you want proof, I'll be happy to cooperate with a paternity test as soon as the baby is born next month." A pause. He continued rudely gaping at her as she stumbled on. "And then, um, again, if you want nothing to do with this child, I'm fine with that, I…" Her voice wavered. But then she cleared her throat and forged on, "You don't have to worry about the baby's welfare. I have a supportive family and a large network of friends. Financially, I'm doing very well. So, after today, I won't bother you again. If you find you want to be involved, however much or little, well, that's something I'm open to, as we go along."

"As we…?" The ability to form a complete sentence seemed to have deserted him.

She rushed into the breach. "Um. Go along, yes. As we go along. I…look. I hate to do this to you." The big eyes filled. She gritted her teeth, blinked the moisture away. "I know you made it very clear, when we said goodbye on the island, that it was over, that we had an agreement and you wanted to stick to it, that you didn't want to see me anymore."

His eyeballs were suddenly dry as a pair of sunbaked stones. He blinked. "What? Wait a minute. That's not what I said. I said it wouldn't work between us, that I would only—"

She whipped up a hand, palm out. "Look. Whatever. All I'm saying is I know this has to be a huge shock for you and I'm so sorry, for everything. For getting pregnant in the first place, although God knows, we *were* careful." Her hand found her belly again. She lowered her head, shook it slowly back and forth. "I don't know how it happened, honestly. But it did. And I know I should have told you sooner, so I'm sorry for not doing that, too. I'm sorry for…" Her head shot up. She threw up both hands and cried, "Well, for everything. I'm sorry if this messes up your life. I'm *sorry*, all right? Just…I don't know. I'm not sure what else there is to say."

There was a whole hell of a lot to say as far as he was concerned. "I thought you married the baby's father in December."

Those big eyes got even bigger. "How could you know that?"

Smooth, Ames. Real smooth. He was a banker, born, bred and raised, president and CEO of Ames Bank and Trust, which had been serving the people of Colorado for almost a century. They said he was distant and a little bit cold. But always fair and calm and in command. He didn't feel in command right at the moment. Clearly, he *wasn't* in command and could blurt out any damn thing if he didn't get a grip.

He cast about for a good lie to tell her, but there really wasn't one that had a chance of flying. So he loosened his tie and settled for the truth. "I hired a detective to find you."

She gasped. "A detective?"

"That's what I said, yes. The detective told me that you live in Justice Creek, that you were getting married a few days before Christmas—and that several different sources had informed him that you were pregnant by your groom, Ryan McKellan. I remembered Ryan, of course, remembered what you'd told me about him." She made a soft, strangled sound, but then only gaped at him. He demanded, "You don't remember?"

"Remember…what?"

"That you told me about your friend Ryan on the island. You mentioned him more than once." Her best friend, she'd called the guy, twice. Both times she'd caught herself and blushed sweetly and said she was sorry for breaking their agreement to live in the moment and leave their "real" lives out of the time they were sharing. He'd shrugged and said she had nothing to apologize for, though really, he hadn't enjoyed the way her expression softened with fondness when she said that other guy's name. "That was kind of a shocker, to get the detective's report and find out that you and your good buddy Ryan were a whole lot more than friends."

"But we weren't!" she insisted on a rising inflection. And then she pressed her hands to her soft cheeks, as if to cool their sudden heat. "I don't get it. I... Oh, Dalton." Now she looked hurt. She whispered on a torn sigh, "You put a *detective* on me?"

He felt like a complete jerk and muttered defensively, "I wanted to find you. It seemed the simplest way."

Her soft lips trembled. "Wanted to find me, why?"

"I...couldn't seem to make myself forget you."

Her expression softened—but then, almost instantly, she stiffened again. "You're serious? You couldn't forget me?"

"No. I couldn't."

"But then what about your—?"

"Wait a minute." He'd just realized he'd been feeling like a douche-bag when, come to think of it, he wasn't any worse than she was. "How did *you* find *me*?"

"Well, I looked you up online and..." Her shoulders sagged. "All right. I see your point. You found me and I found you. What does it matter how? What does any of the rest of it matter?"

She had it right. It didn't matter, not to him, anyway. The baby mattered. *His* baby.

The baby changed everything. He demanded, "So, what about your husband, Ryan? Does he know that the baby isn't his?"

"He's, um, not my husband."

Could he have heard that right? "Not your—?"

"Not my husband. No. We decided not to go through with the wedding, after all."

"You're telling me you're *not* married." He tried to take in the enormity of that. All these months without a word from her, even though she was having his baby. Having his baby while planning to marry that other guy—and then *not* marrying that other guy, after all.

"Uh-uh. Being married just…isn't who we are together, Ryan and me."

"Together? You and he are together?" It came out in a dark, angry rumble.

"No, not *together*. Not in *that* way. We're together in a *friend* way."

"You live with him?"

"Of course not." She looked insulted. "I said we're friends." He didn't need to hear another word about the guy she'd almost married. But she told him more anyway. "Ryan hated the idea of the baby not having a dad."

"Hold it. What are you saying? The baby damn well does have a dad. *I'm* the dad."

"Yes, but…"

"What?"

"Dalton, you don't have to get so angry."

"I'm. Not. Angry."

She stared at him, wearing a stricken look. He felt like the overbearing ass she no doubt considered him. And then she said, with measured calm, "I'm just saying he was only trying to help me, that's all. But you're right. Ryan isn't the baby's father. Because, well, *you* are." And then, out of nowhere, she pushed herself to her feet. "And I think I've said what I came here to say."

"Wait a minute." He glared up at her. "You're leaving?"

"Yes."

"You can't leave yet. We're not through here. Sit back down."

She ignored his command and pulled a card from the pocket of her jacket. "Here. Address, phone numbers. It's all there. In case you... I mean, you know, should you choose to get in touch with me after this."

"After this? But we're not finished."

"Maybe you're not, Dalton. But I am. This wasn't easy. I've had enough for one day and I want to go home."

"But—"

"Please. Take the card."

He felt at a disadvantage, sitting there while she hovered above him. So he stood. She shoved the card at him again. He gave in and took it. Not that he needed it. He knew where she lived and he had all her numbers. The detective had provided all that. And Dalton had held on to the information, though he'd told himself he would never make use of it.

They stared at each other. He needed to keep her there until he could manage to collect his scattered wits. But he just wasn't dealing. His usually sharp mind felt dull as a rusty blade.

She said, "Well, goodbye, then."

His knees feel strangely rubbery. A baby. It was *his* baby she was having. Not that other guy's. *His* baby. And she *wasn't* married, after all.

And for all those months, he hadn't had a clue. Because she never bothered to tell him. Until now.

He couldn't decide if he was furious with her—or just desperate to know that she and the baby were both all right. She did look a little tired. There were shadows beneath those amazing eyes.

He asked, "Are you okay? The baby...?"

"Fine. Truly. We're both fine—and look. You just give me a call, anytime."

"Give you a call," he repeated numbly.

"Yeah. When—and if—you're ready to, um, talk it over."

"But didn't I just say I want to talk it over now?"

She gave a fierce little shake of her head. "Not now. Uh-uh."

"Why not?"

"I just…I need a little space, okay?"

"But—"

"I have to go, Dalton."

And with that, she turned and left him standing there. He wanted to go after her, to grab her and pull her back. But he didn't.

He just stood there by the bench, his mouth hanging open, watching her walk away.

Telling Dalton Ames that she was having his baby? Hardest thing Clara had ever done.

He'd seemed so angry. So stiff and pulled-together, wearing a gorgeous, perfectly tailored suit and Italian shoes, looking like the stuffed-shirt older brother of the amazing, tender, attentive man she'd known for those magical two weeks on the island. She'd barely kept herself from demanding, *Who are you and what have you done with the Dalton I knew?*

Twice during the drive home from Denver, Clara pulled off the road, certain she was about to throw up. The baby, not happy at all with the adrenaline cocktail surging through Mommy's system, kept kicking her. Somehow, though, she managed to make it home to her sweet little blue, maroon-trimmed Victorian on Park Drive in Justice Creek without losing her lunch.

It was after seven when she walked in the door. She knew she should eat, so she heated up some leftovers, poured a glass of juice and forced down a few bites of yesterday's chicken and a mouthful or two of seasoned rice. That was all she could take. She dumped the rest, rinsed the plate and stood at the sink staring out at her side yard, knowing she really, really needed to talk to a friend.

She'd kept it all to herself for much too long now. Even though her relationship with Dalton had been nothing but a foolish fantasy, it had only seemed right that she should face him, let him know that there would be a child and she was keeping it, before discussing the matter with anyone else.

So okay. She'd done what was right.

And now she needed support. She was calling in a good friend and telling all.

She considered calling Ryan. He'd been right there for her when she had no idea what to do next. He'd tried so hard to help her.

But come on. The last thing Rye needed now was her crying on his shoulder about some guy he'd never even met. Especially after everything she'd already put him through.

No. At a time like this, a woman needed a girlfriend. Her closest girlfriend.

So Clara called her favorite cousin Rory, aka Her Highness Aurora Bravo-Calabretti. Rory might be a Montedoran princess by birth, but at heart she was totally down-to-earth, someone you could trust with your deepest, saddest secrets. Rory lived with Ryan's older brother, Walker, at Walker's ranch, the Bar-N.

Once she'd made the call, Clara went out and sat on the front porch to wait.

Twenty minutes later, Rory pulled up to the curb. She

jumped right out, ran around the front of her SUV and hurried up the front walk. "Clara? What is it, darling? Are you okay?"

Clara rose and held out her arms. Rory went into them. They hugged good and tight, Clara's big belly pressed hard against Rory's flat one, and Clara whispered, "Ice cream. Chocolate Chunk Gooey Brownie."

Rory said, "I'm in."

So Clara led her inside and dished up the treat. They sat at the breakfast nook table. They'd each polished off half a bowlful before Rory asked, "So?"

And Clara took another creamy, chunky chocolaty bite, savoring the goodness of it, getting another shot of the comfort a girl can only get from a killer dessert, before she confessed, "Today I told my baby's father that he's going to be a dad."

Rory stopped with a bite of ice cream halfway to her mouth. She dropped the spoon back in her bowl. It clattered against the side. "Get off the phone."

"I did. I really did."

"Was it…?"

"Awful. It was awful. He was like some stranger. It was so bizarre. I kept wanting to ask him what he'd done with the man I knew—or *thought* I knew."

Rory pushed back her chair and circled the table to kneel at Clara's feet. "Give me your hands." She took them and gave Clara's fingers a comforting squeeze. "You are not only my favorite cousin in the whole world—you are the kindest, warmest, most supportive, loving friend around. Plus, you're totally hot."

Clara let out a laugh that sounded a lot like a sob. "Right. Just look at me. A human beach ball. Smokin'."

"Pregnant or not, doesn't matter. Either way, you are hot. If he treated you badly, it's his loss. You have a big family and they all love you, not to mention a large number of good friends. You need to remember that you are not alone, that you only have to call, anytime, day or night, and I'm here—and so is everyone else who adores you."

Clara shut her eyes for a minute. When she felt reasonably certain she wasn't going to burst into tears, she said, "I love you."

Rory squeezed her fingers again. "Love you, too. A lot."

"Now, go finish your ice cream before it's all melted."

Rory rose and went back to her chair. They both ate more of the to-die-for dessert. Finally, Rory said, softly, "I have to ask…"

"Go ahead." Clara gave her a wobbly little smile.

"I mean, is this it, then? Am I here because you're finally going to tell me how it all happened?"

Clara pushed her bowl away. "Yeah. This is it."

"Dear Lord. I need more ice cream. You?"

"I've had enough. But help yourself."

So Rory got up and got more—including another giant scoop for Clara, who insisted she didn't want it, but then picked up her spoon again and dug right in.

Rory said, "All right. I'm ready."

Where to even begin? "Remember when I went on that two-week Caribbean vacation last August?"

Rory was nodding. "Of course. Your thirtieth birthday getaway. I kind of suspected it might have happened then."

"You know how I was feeling then…"

"I remember. You were talking about burnout, that all you did was work. You really needed that vacation."

Clara had opened her restaurant, the Library Café, almost six years before. The café was a success by any standards. And she'd put in a whole bunch of seven-day workweeks to make it so. "I wanted a little glamour and pampering, you know? I wanted to reward myself for a job well done."

Rory suggested softly, "And maybe a little romance, too?"

"Oh, yeah. I had this fantasy that I might end up meeting someone amazing."

"And indulging in a crazy, fabulous tropical affair?"

"Exactly."

"And so your fantasy came true."

Clara smiled, feeling wistful. "That's right. I met him the first night. His name is Dalton. Dalton Ames. And just the sight of him—he's tall and fit, with black hair and piercing blue eyes. I felt like the heroine of the juiciest romance novel you ever read. I mean, you know how I am. You joke that I'm hot and all. But come on."

"Clara." Rory licked her spoon. "You *are* hot. Accept it."

Clara pulled her bowl back in front of her and took another melty, chocolaty, amazing bite. " I don't *feel* hot. I feel like I'm the solid one, the level-headed one. The family peacemaker. Guys tend to like me as a friend."

"A hot friend."

A snort of laughter escaped her. "Stop."

"Seriously, Clara. I know whereof I speak."

Clara purposely did not roll her eyes. "Anyway, when Dalton looked at me…I cannot tell you. It was like a sizzling shiver went all through me. *He* saw me as hot, I could see it in those heart-stopping baby blues of his. The sexual chemistry was immediate, unexpected—and like nothing in my life before. We danced and flirted. He said he was from Denver."

"Ah. Both of you from Colorado."

"Yeah." Seriously, what an idiot she'd been. She ladled on a little irony. "Like it was *meant to be.*"

"Don't make less of it," Rory chided. "I can tell from the way you talk about him that it was beautiful and special, that you felt a real connection with him."

"Ha."

"Tell me the story, Clara—and stop judging yourself."

Clara sighed. "He told me the trip was a getaway for him, that his work was demanding and he wanted a chance to live in the moment for a change."

"Just like you."

"Um-hmm. I told him that I was ready for an adventure, to live out a fantasy, to forget reality for a while. He said that sounded great to him."

"Okay, now I'm wondering..."

'What?"

"You weren't suspicious that it was all just a little too perfect?"

Clara shrugged. "Yeah. But only a little. The resort was like a tropical fairy tale, the beaches pristine, miles and miles of gleaming white sands. Not a cloud in the sky and the ocean went on forever. It all seemed so magical. And then I met this dreamboat of a man. I was kind of swept away—but at least I did have sense enough to ask him if he had a wife at home."

"Good for you. And?"

"He said he was recently divorced—and then he wanted to know if I had someone special. I told him there was no one. And then, feeling beautiful and wanted and thrilled to be getting a taste of exactly what I'd been dreaming of, I went to his suite with him and spent the night."

"Bold."

Even with all that had happened since then, the memory of that first night—of all the nights on the island—remained wonderfully sweet. "I thought so, yes. And it was the best, that night with him, better than anyone or any time before. In the morning, we agreed to spend the next two weeks together. We decided we would live completely in the now and not talk about our 'real' lives. And when the fantasy was over, we would go our separate ways."

Rory was chewing her lower lip. "Reality always intrudes, though, doesn't it?"

"Sadly, yeah," Clara admitted. "But for two incredible, perfect weeks, we were lovers. We were open and tender and passionate with each other—in the moment only, I mean. Mostly, we managed to keep our real lives out of it. The sex was just beautiful. And we climbed a volcano, went parasailing and scuba diving. Even bungee jumping. At night, we danced under the stars by the light of the moon. By the end, I knew I was falling in love with him."

Rory asked in a whisper, "Did you…tell him?"

Clara put her hand on her belly, rubbed it slowly and gently, feeling the love well up, the gratitude, in spite of everything. Her baby might not have a daddy. But she *would* be a good mother. Clara would make sure her child had a great start in life, with love and happiness to spare. "On the last night, I finally worked up the nerve. I told him I wanted to keep seeing him when we got back to Colorado…"

"Oh, my darling. And?"

"My fantasy crashed and burned."

"Oh, no…"

"Yeah. He told me that he'd had a beautiful time with me and he would never forget me, but he would only mess things up if we tried to have more."

"Mess things up? But why? I don't get it."

"He said it was different, that *he* was different, there with me, on the island. He said he wanted to remember me that way, remember *us* that way. That his marriage had ended not that long before, and it was his fault. And he wasn't ready to try again. He didn't think he'd ever be ready. He wanted to stick to the agreement we'd made."

"That's just so sad."

"Believe me, I wanted to argue. I wanted to ask him why he couldn't at least give it a try. But then, I was pretty much reeling that I'd put myself right out there for him—and gotten instant and total rejection. Plus, well, he was right that we did have an agreement. It wasn't as if he owed it to me to change everything up just because I'd decided I wanted more. So I went home and tried to forget him. Unfortunately, a few weeks later, I realized I was having his baby. I agonized for another few weeks."

"You should have called me. I would have come running." At the time, Rory was still living in her family's palace in Montedoro on the Cote d'Azur.

"I couldn't. I felt that I should tell him, tell Dalton, first of all, before anyone else."

"Well, fair enough. I can understand that."

"So I started trying to figure out how best to reach him..." Clara stared out the breakfast nook window. It was already dark. All she saw was her own reflection, a reflection that blurred as pointless tears rose. She swallowed, hard, and brushed them away.

Rory got up again and circled the table. This time, she just stood by Clara's chair, looping an arm around her shoulder, then smoothing her hair so that Clara gave in to the comfort she offered and rested her head against Rory's side. "I take it you found him."

"It wasn't hard, really. A little searching online and I learned he was a big shot from a Denver banking family."

"Wait. 'Ames' of Ames Bank and Trust?" There was a branch right there in town.

"That's right." Clara tipped her head up and caught

Rory's eye. "And the supposed ex-wife? Maybe not so 'ex'…"

Rory gasped. "You're kidding. He lied? He had a wife the whole time?"

"No. They *had* been divorced. But there were recent pictures of the 'ex' on his arm at some big charity event. She's gorgeous, by the way. Beauty-queen gorgeous. Blond. Willowy. Perfect. In the pictures she was smiling at him in this teasing, intimate way. The gossipy article that went with the pictures hinted that maybe a remarriage was in the offing."

Rory stroked her hair some more. "So that's why you put off contacting him?"

"Yeah. I kind of lost heart, you know? I didn't want to mess up his reunion with his ex—really, I didn't want to deal with him at all by then."

"Completely, one hundred percent understandable."

"I decided there was no real rush to tell him about the baby. At that time, I wasn't due for months and months."

"I get that."

"But then those months went by. I continued to put it off, kept avoiding the moment of truth when I would have to face him. And in the middle of that, there was all that frantic planning for the wedding to Ryan that ended up not happening. And, well, now it's April and my due date is six weeks away. I couldn't put it off anymore."

"So you've done it. You've told him."

"Yep."

"And…what next?"

"What do you mean, what next?" Clara stiffened. "I've told him, that's it."

"But what does he plan to do now?"

"How would I know what he plans?" Clara pulled sharply away.

Rory took the hint and stepped back. Gently, she suggested, "Well, I was thinking he might want to—"

"I *said* I don't know." Clara got up, grabbed their empty bowls and carried them to the sink. "We didn't get into any of that," she added without turning.

Rory, still standing by the table, asked, "So you have no clue whether or not he wants to be involved with the baby?"

Clara put the bowls in the sink and flipped on the water. "It's not like we had a real conversation. I told him that I was pregnant and that I didn't expect anything from him. I gave him a card with my numbers on it, so he can contact me if he wants to. That was it."

"But—"

"Look." Clara left the water running and whirled on Rory. "How would I know what he'll do next? Probably try to figure out a way to tell his wife that some woman he boinked last summer on Anguilla is having his baby."

Rory marched over and flipped the water off. "Sweetheart." She pulled Clara close. "It's all right. You've done what you had to do and you were brave to do it. I'm not getting on you."

Clara stiffened—and then let her defensiveness go and wrapped her arms good and tight around her cousin. "God. I hate this."

"I know." Rory gave her another good squeeze, then took her hand and led her past the breakfast nook to the sofa in the great room. They sat down together. Rory asked, "So he *is* remarried, then?"

"How would I know?"

"Well, you just mentioned him telling his wife about the baby."

"I don't *know*, all right? I'm just assuming he married her again, from what I read in that article."

"Today, when you told him about the baby, did he say anything about a wife?"

"No."

Rory offered gingerly, "So, then, maybe you're jumping to conclusions a little, don't you think?"

"It doesn't matter."

"Of course it matters."

"Not to me." She wrapped her arms around her belly and her precious unborn child. "I don't care what he does. He's nothing to me."

"Clara—"

"No. No, don't do that, Rory. Don't look at me like that, all tender and patient and sorry for me. I don't need anyone feeling sorry for me. I'm fine."

"I know you are. Darling, I love you and I can see how hard this has been—how hard this *is* for you, that's all."

Clara let out a moan. "Oh, Rory…"

"Come here. Come on."

So Clara sagged against her cousin again. And Rory held her close and stroked her hair and whispered that it was going to be all right. Clara cried a little. And Rory dried her tears.

And Clara said, "I'll probably never see the guy again, you know? And that's okay. I can live with that. I don't like it. It's a long way from my fantasy of how things would go. It's just…what it is. I'm having my baby and we're going to be a family, the two of us. I have a whole lot to be thankful for in this life, people I can count on, people who have my back, a successful business and a beautiful home. I may not have a man to stand beside me. But I have everything else, and that's plenty for me. I've done what I needed to do, told Dalton Ames about the baby. And now I'm going to buck the hell up and get on with my life."

Rory left an hour later.

Clara went to bed and slept the whole night without waking up once. She felt…better. Calmer. More able to cope. She'd done what she needed to do; then she'd shared the whole long, sad story with someone she trusted, and she'd had a good cry over it.

Now, at last, she could move on.

Two days later, Dalton Ames knocked on her door.

Chapter Two

It was a busy day at the café, with every table taken and customers lined up to get a seat.

The lunch rush went on and on. They turned the place over four times before things started easing off. Between eleven and three, Clara never sat down once. It was exhausting, especially in her pregnant state. Also, fabulous. More proof that the Library Café was a bona fide success.

After the rush, she had meetings with salespeople, scheduling and ordering to deal with, followed by a trip to the bank. It was almost six when she finally walked in her front door.

She headed straight for the shower, shedding clothes as she went. Twenty minutes later, barefoot in her softest, roomiest lounge pants and a giant pink shirt with Mama Needs Ice Cream printed across the front, she had a light dinner. Then she stretched out on the sofa to veg out with a little mindless television.

Her head had just hit the sofa pillow and she was point-ing the remote at the flat-screen over the fireplace when the doorbell rang.

What now? She wasn't expecting anyone, and her tired, pregnant body had zero desire to get up from the comfy sofa and walk all the way to front of the house.

However, she just happened to be one of those peo-ple who answered phones and doorbells automatically. It could be something important and you might as well deal with it now as later. So she put down the remote, dragged herself to her feet again, shuffled to the front door and pulled it wide.

And there he was. Dalton. As tall, dark and wonderful to look at as ever. In a suit even more beautiful and pricey-looking than the one he'd been wearing two days before.

Her hopeless heart gave a leap of ridiculous, giddy joy just at the sight of him. The rotten SOB.

He said, "Hello, Clara." And those eyes, which were a deep crystal blue surely not found in nature, swept from the top of her head down over her giant pink shirt all the way to her bare feet—and back up again.

And she said, "You've got to be kidding me."

"May I come in?" Stiff. Cool. So completely unlike the man she'd once been idiot enough to think she loved. "We need to talk."

Oh, did they? She braced a shoulder against the door-frame and folded her arms on top of her baby bump. "About what, exactly?"

He looked vaguely pained. "Not on your doorstep. Please." It came out more like a command than a request.

She stayed right where she was and just stared at him for a long, hostile moment. "I thought I gave you all my phone numbers."

"You did."

"Then why didn't you call? A little fair warning isn't that much to ask."

"I apologize."

"You don't sound sorry in the least."

The blue gaze swept over her again, rousing a thoroughly uncalled-for shiver of excitement. "Let me in, Clara."

Oh, she was so tempted to shut the door in his face. Because she was tired and her feet hurt and there was a really good tearjerker on Lifetime.

She didn't want to deal with this. Not now.

Not ever, really.

But she and the stranger on her front porch had made a baby together. And the baby trumped everything: including her burning desire never to have to see his face again.

With elaborate disinterest, she dropped her crossed arms and stepped away from the door. "By all means. Come on in."

Giving her no opportunity to change her mind, he stepped right over the threshold and into her private space. She blinked and looked up at him and couldn't believe this was happening.

"Nice house," he said, his fine lips curling upward a fraction at the corners.

"Thanks. This way." She took him through her formal dining room to the combination kitchen, breakfast nook and great room at the back. Stopping at the long kitchen island, she turned to him. "Do you want coffee or something?"

"No, thanks."

"Well, all right, then. Have a seat." She gestured at the sitting area across the room.

He went on past her, all the way to the wing chair next to the sofa, but he didn't sit down. For a moment, she hovered there at the end of the island, reluctant to get closer to him.

Dread curled through her. He wore the strangest look on his face, and a great stillness seemed to surround him. The moment felt huge, suddenly.

What in the world did he plan to say to her? Something awful, probably, judging by the seriousness and intensity of his expression.

Reluctantly, she approached him. He simply waited, watching her come.

She stopped a couple of feet from him. "Aren't you… going to sit down?"

He didn't answer. He didn't sit. Instead he reached for her hand.

The move surprised her enough that she didn't jerk away. His fingers closed over hers, warm. Firm. So well remembered. Tears scalded the back of her throat. She pressed her lips together and swallowed them down. "What?"

And just like that, he lifted his other hand and slid a beautiful diamond ring on her finger.

She gasped and gaped down at it, a giant marquise-cut central stone, surrounded by twin rows of glittering smaller stones, more diamonds along the double band.

"Marry me, Clara. Right away. You can move to Denver and we'll work this out. We'll make a family for our child."

She gaped down at that sparkling, perfect, beautiful ring. And then, slowly, her breath all tangled and hot in the base of her throat, she lifted her head and looked at him.

The really terrible, awful thing was, somewhere inside herself, she longed to throw her arms around him and shout *yes*!

And that made her furious—at herself, as much as at him.

Because who *was* he, anyway? When he touched her, she felt the thrill, yes. Her body seemed to know him. But her mind and her confused, aching heart?

Uh-uh. No. She didn't know this man at all.

She pulled her fingers free of his grip and took off the ring. "No, Dalton."

"Clara…"

"Take it. I mean it." He shook his head. But he did hold out his hand. She dropped that gorgeous thing into his palm. "No way am I marrying you, let alone moving to Denver. Justice Creek is my home. I have my family, my friends and my very successful business here, so this is where I plan to stay."

"Listen to me, I—"

"Stop."

Miraculously, he did.

"We need to get straight on something here right from the start," she said.

He eyed her sideways as he dropped the ring into his jacket pocket. And then he asked carefully in that voice of his that was so gallingly manly and deep, "By all means. Let's get it straight. Whatever the hell *it* is."

"Are you married or not?"

"Excuse me?" He gazed at her as though he had his doubts as to her sanity. "Married? Me?"

"That's right. Do you have a wife?"

The blue eyes, impossibly, got even bluer and that square jaw went to rock. "Of course not. I'm divorced, and have been since before the island. And I know that you know this. I told you myself."

She had to get away, get some distance from him. So she turned and marched over to the fireplace. Better. She straightened her shoulders and turned to face him again. "Look. I saw you, okay? I saw pictures of you online, with your supposedly ex-wife on your arm at some fancy party. The two of you were looking very chummy."

"Chummy? Astrid and I are not the least bit chummy."

"You looked pretty damn chummy to me."

"Astrid is a lovely woman. She's active in her community, doing what she can to help disadvantaged children and victims of natural catastrophes and such. Occasionally she asks me to support her various causes. I'm happy to help. Once or twice, I've acted as her escort."

"Well, isn't that civilized?"

"Yes, it is, as a matter of fact. Is there something wrong with being civilized?"

She decided not to answer that one. "There was talk about the two of you getting married again."

"Talk? Who said that?"

"I don't know who. It was just…somewhere online, is all."

"And you always believe everything you read *somewhere* online?" His eyes were practically shooting sparks.

Ha. As though he were the one who'd been shabbily treated. She wrapped her arms around herself again as she had at the door and held her ground. "Just answer the question. Are you married or not?"

"No."

"Are you *dating* your ex-wife?"

"No. I told you, we're on good terms, Astrid and I. But the marriage is over and it has been since before you and I were together on the island—as I made perfectly clear the first night that we met."

A small but definite *humph* escaped her, a sound she honestly hadn't meant to make.

"I heard that," he muttered darkly. "And what do you want from me? There is absolutely nothing going on between Astrid and me. We're cordial. And we're civil with each other and when she wants help with one of her causes, I do what I can."

She knew it was petty of her, but she couldn't resist remarking, "And if I believe that, maybe you've got a bridge you want to sell me?"

He regarded her, those laser-blue eyes boring twin holes right through her. "You think I'm lying to you? You think I would come here and ask you to marry me if I was already married?"

Okay, maybe he had a teeny-weeny point there. She tried to dial it back a notch. "You didn't exactly *ask* me, Dalton. You *told* me." It came out sounding plaintive and she couldn't decide which was worse: being a raving bitch or coming off as pitiful.

He demanded, "Do you think I'm lying to you?"

"I…" She gave up all pretense of angry defiance, dropping her arms away from her body, letting out a low, sad sigh. "I don't know. I don't know anything—not about you. Not really. On the island, you were…like someone else entirely, completely different from how you are now. It's very disorienting."

He looked almost stricken. For about half a second. But then his jaw hardened again and his eyes narrowed. "I think you should call Astrid and ask her if there's anything going on between her and me."

Her mouth dropped open. "Excuse me. Did you just say I should call your ex-wife?"

"That is exactly what I said."

"Not. Going. To. Happen."

"Why not? Afraid to find out I'm not a lying, cheating would-be bigamist, after all?"

"Of course not."

"Then you will call Astrid."

"Hello. Are you there, Dalton?"

"That's a ridiculous question."

"Just trying to be absolutely sure you can hear me."

"Of course I can hear you."

"Good. The last thing I'm up for is a little chat with your wife."

"*Ex*-wife," he curtly clarified. And then he lifted a hand and pinched the bridge of his nose. Was he getting a headache? She certainly was. "All right," he said. "This has not gone well. I need to regroup and come up with another plan to get through to you."

"Get through to me about what? Because, honestly, Dalton. Two strangers getting married is not any kind of viable solution to anything."

"We've lost months because you read something on the internet and jumped to conclusions."

"Don't forget that you put a detective on me."

"…And learned that you were getting married."

"But I *didn't* get married."

"Which I didn't find out until Tuesday when you finally came and talked to me. The heart of the matter is you should have come to me earlier."

She clucked her tongue. "Fascinating analysis of the situation. Also totally unfair. Why would I want to come to you? You made it way clear on the island that you were done with me."

"I wasn't *done* with you."

"It certainly sounded like it to me."

He pinched the bridge of his nose again. "It was different on the island. *I* was different."

"I'll say."

"I didn't want to ruin something beautiful and I was afraid that if we continued when we returned home, it would all go to hell."

"So you're saying that on the island you were pretending to be someone you're not."

"No, I'm…" He stopped himself, glanced away, and then said, way too quietly, "By God. You are the most infuriating woman."

She started to feel a little bit bad about then. In his own overbearing way, he really was trying. And she wasn't helping. Because he had hurt her and she just couldn't trust him. And his proposal of marriage had actually tempted her—at the same time as it had made her want to beat him about the head and shoulders with a large, blunt object. As she tried to think of something to say that might get them on a better footing with each other, he pulled a phone from his pocket and poked at it repeatedly. Her cell, on the coffee table, pinged.

He put his phone away. "I've texted you her number."

"Her, who?"

"Astrid. You have her number now. You can call her and she'll be happy to tell you that she and I have no plans to remarry, that we are amicably and permanently divorced, that we are not dating or in any way romantically or sexually involved with each other."

Now Clara was the one pinching the bridge of her nose. "I don't need your ex-wife's number."

"I mean it. Call her. And once you've talked to her, call *me*. Because you and I are not done yet. Not by a long shot. Good night, Clara."

And with that, he turned on his heel, crossed the great room, went through the kitchen and disappeared from sight. A moment later, she heard the front door open and close.

That motivated her.

Even hugely pregnant, Clara could move fast when she wanted to. She zipped through the kitchen and straight to the window in the dining room that looked out on her porch and front yard. She got there just in time to see him duck into the backseat of a limo.

A moment later, the limo slid away from the curb and drove off down the street.

"Astrid." She scowled. "No way am I calling Astrid."

And she didn't call Astrid.

But in the days that followed, she did think about Dalton a lot. She felt guilty, actually, for the way she'd behaved that night—so bitchy and angry, ready for a fight.

The hard truth was she still had that thing for him—for *both* of him, actually. The wonderful man she'd known on the island. *And* the sexy stuffed shirt who'd shown up at her door out of nowhere with a ring in his pocket and the arrogant assumption that she would pack up her life and move to Denver because he told her to.

She needed to buck up and deal, to reach out to him again, and do a better job of it this time. In the end, he was her baby's father and she had a duty to do what she could to encourage some kind of a coparenting relationship with him.

However, she didn't deal. She put it off, just as she'd put off telling him about the baby in the first place. Every day that passed, she had less respect for herself and her own behavior.

That Sunday night, Ryan dropped by with a pizza from Romano's, that great Italian place across the street from the bar he owned and ran. She got him a beer and they shared the pie and he told her about the new woman in his life, a gorgeous redhead with a great sense of humor. Clara said she couldn't wait to meet her.

Ryan, who was tall and broad-shouldered with beautiful

forest-green eyes and thick brown hair, gave her his killer smile. "Yeah, we'll have to set something up…"

She knew by the way his voice trailed off that the red-head wouldn't be around for long, which made her a little bit sad. Rye loved women. But he never stayed in a romantic relationship for very long.

After they ate the pizza, he hung around for a couple of hours. They made small talk and played Super Mario Kart 8 and she kept thinking that now was a good time to tell him she'd finally contacted the father of her baby, a good time to explain that she'd gotten pregnant during her Caribbean getaway last summer, that the baby's father was a banker who lived in Denver and had proposed to her out of nowhere just three nights before.

But she didn't tell Ryan any of that, even though he had been ready and willing to step in to marry her just months before. When Rye asked her if she had something on her mind, she just said she was feeling stressed, that was all, what with the baby coming soon and the restaurant keeping her so busy.

Rye's brow furrowed. "But I thought you were feeling good about Renée running things when the baby comes." Renée Beauchamp was her head waitress and manager.

She rushed to reassure him. "Renée is a godsend and already she's handling a lot of extra stuff for me. It's going to be fine, I know it. I just worry is all."

"You need anything, you know to call me."

She thanked him and told him he was amazing and promised that yes, she would totally take advantage of his friendship if she needed to.

But she failed to say a word about the father of her baby.

The next night, Dalton called. "Astrid tells me you haven't gotten in touch with her yet."

I need to get along with him, she thought. She said,

"How many times do I have to tell you that I have no intention of calling your wife?"

"*Ex*-wife," he corrected in a tone that said he was quickly losing patience with her. "You would know that by now, if you would only call Astrid."

I need to get along with him. "I'm, um, thinking about it."

"Think faster."

"Har-har."

"Last week, you said the baby was due in six weeks."

"Yes. On the sixteenth of May."

"Which is five weeks away now."

"I may not be a banker, Dalton, but I do know how to count."

"We don't have much time."

She pressed her lips together to keep from saying, *Time for what?*

And he went on, "I should be with you."

Okay, that sounded kind of sweet. She tried to think of something nice and helpful and conciliatory to say.

But before she could come up with anything, he said, "You could have the baby any time now. What if I'm not there?"

She had never expected him to be there, so she had no idea what to say to that.

And then he said, "Are you still on the line, Clara?"

"Yes."

"Call Astrid. I mean it."

And then he hung up.

And she did not call Astrid. But she *was* thinking about it. A lot.

The next weekend, Rory and Walker, Ryan's brother, had a little party out at the Bar-N, their ranch. Clara went.

So did Ryan and a bunch of their mutual friends and Clara's sisters and three of her brothers.

Rory took her aside and asked her how she was doing, how it was working out with Dalton. And Clara was vague and unhelpful in her answers, causing Rory to ask if she was all right.

Clara lied with a big, fat smile and said she was doing just fine and no, she hadn't told Ryan about Dalton yet. She hadn't told anybody, she confessed.

"I will," she promised her favorite cousin and dear friend. "Soon…"

Sunday night, Dalton called again.

It was just more of the same. He told her get in touch with Astrid and she said again that she was giving it some thought.

"Four weeks left until the baby comes," he said bleakly. "This is wrong, what you're doing, Clara. It's wrong and you know it."

And, well, after she hung up, she felt really depressed. Mostly because he was pretty much right.

So she did it. She called Astrid.

Dalton's wife—all right, all right, *ex*-wife—answered the phone on the first ring and sounded quite nice, actually. She said that yes, she would be happy to meet with Clara at Clara's convenience.

"Will you come to the house?" Astrid asked. "We can chat in private, just the two of us."

Clara took down Astrid's address and said she would be there at two the next afternoon. Then she called Renée, who said that she would have no problem handling the restaurant tomorrow without her.

But of course, Clara went in anyway. She might be about to have a baby, but the café was her *first* baby. She didn't like deserting her business or her staff with hardly any warning. And it turned out to be another busy day, so she was glad she'd gone in—and hated to just walk out on the lunch rush.

But Renée reassured her and sent her on her way, adding that she really ought to start cutting back on her hours. She was about to have a baby, and she needed to take better care of herself.

Clara promised she was fine. And then wondered the whole drive to Denver why she was even going to meet Astrid. She didn't really believe that Dalton was still married to—or even dating—his ex. He'd been right that she'd totally jumped to conclusions.

And now she was too proud to give it up and admit that she'd been wrong.

Astrid lived in an exclusive gated community. And she was every bit as beautiful as the pictures Clara had seen online. She congratulated Clara on her upcoming motherhood and Clara wondered if she knew that the baby was Dalton's.

Astrid led Clara into her beautiful home and served her a delicious late lunch of penne pasta with fennel sausage, broccoli, garlic cream and *grana padano* cheese.

As they enjoyed the wonderful food, Clara went ahead and admitted, "This is Dalton's baby."

Astrid nodded. "I had a feeling that might be the case. I…wish you both the very best."

What to say to that? "Thank you."

Astrid confirmed what Dalton had already told Clara, that Dalton had occasionally helped her with her causes and served as her escort at a couple of events. "But that was months ago. I'm actually seeing someone now. Someone very special." A slight, tender sort of smile curved her perfect lips. "Dalton and I are *not* getting back together. The marriage is over. It's been over for a long time."

"What went wrong?" Clara dared to ask.

Astrid only shook her head. "It's never a good idea to ask the ex what went wrong. You should take it up with Dalton."

Clara could hardly picture herself taking anything up with Dalton. But she only nodded and agreed that yes, he was the one she ought to ask about that.

She left Astrid's house at a little after four and fought rush-hour traffic until she finally got north of the metro area. All the way home, she stewed over how she needed to get straight with Dalton. She needed to start working with him instead of avoiding him; they needed to begin to adjust to their roles as parents of the same child.

At home, she dug her phone out of her purse, dropped the purse on the hall table and carried the phone through to the great room, where she sank to the sofa and kicked off her shoes. With a tired sigh, she let her head drop to the sofa back.

Dalton. She needed to make peace with him for the sake of the baby. But she hated that she was still attracted to him, even though he'd turned out to be nothing like the man she'd fallen for on the island.

Plus, hello. Extremely pregnant, big as a cow. And tired. Tired to the bone. She just couldn't talk to him right then.

And she wouldn't.

Tomorrow. Yeah. She'd get a good night's rest and call him in the morning.

The phone rang in her hand.

Dalton Ames, read the display. She put the damn thing to her ear. "What?"

"Astrid tells me you went to see her."

She stifled another groan. "Yes, Dalton. Astrid has set me straight."

"Good. Let me take you to dinner tonight."

She cradled her enormous belly with her free hand and sighed. "I'm eight months pregnant, Dalton. I just drove five hours round-trip to and from Castle Pines Village."

"You should have called me. I would have sent a car."

"The point is, I'm not going anywhere this evening but to bed."

Dead silence. Then, "My God, Clara. Are you all right?"

She wasn't, not really. She felt torn in two. But she was much too tired to do anything about that at the moment. "Dalton, we'll talk, I promise."

"When?"

"Soon. I really have to go."

"I'll be there by nine at the latest."

"What? Here? No. Why?"

"I want to see for myself that you're all right."

Clara gathered every last ounce of will and determination she had left and she told him, "Don't you dare, Dalton. You had better not knock on my door tonight."

More silence. Finally, "Are you sure you're okay?"

She wasn't, as a matter of fact. But no way was she telling him that. "Yes. I'm fine."

"Get some rest, Clara."

"That is exactly what I plan to do."

He said good-night then. She breathed a careful sigh of relief as she hung up the phone. Then she dragged her poor, tired body up off the sofa and into her bedroom, where she fell into bed.

In spite of her exhaustion, she didn't sleep well.

In the morning, she considered taking the day off. But that seemed wrong, after cutting out on her crew the day before.

So she pulled herself together, threw on a comfy blue dress with a handkerchief hem and a sturdy pair of flat-heeled sandals. She gathered her hair up into a scraggly ponytail and went in—and found Dalton there, sitting at a window table, sipping coffee and eating a Tuscan omelet. At the sight of him, in yet another of those beautiful tailor-made suits of his, looking fresh and rested and ready to get right to work bossing her around, her heart actually seemed to skip a beat.

Seriously?

What was the problem with her heart, anyway? It had no business skipping beats over him. She was as big as a barn and her ankles were swollen. The last thing she needed now was to get all excited over the guy who'd gotten her into this condition in the first place.

Some people's hearts just never learned.

Through a monumental effort of sheer will, she put on her calmest expression and toddled over to deal with him.

The first words out of his mouth were "You look terrible."

As if that was news to her. Of course she looked terrible. She was beat. Just completely exhausted from the constant, months-long strain of this whole situation.

And her restaurant was packed, as usual. Which was a good thing—except that all of her customers seemed to be staring at her and the big, handsome man in the great suit who gazed up at her critically, as though he, and only he, knew what was good for her.

Wonderful. Just what she needed. The whole town up in her business all over again, the way they were when she almost married Ryan.

And then he did something even more annoying than telling her she looked like crap: he actually put on a smile. And damned if that smile didn't tug at her silly heartstrings.

"I like your café." The blue gaze scanned the two-story

wall of bookshelves that gave the café its name. He took in the tan-and-coffee-colored walls hung with art by local artists. He glanced approvingly at the many windows, most with mountain views. He nodded at the cast-iron spiral staircase in the center of the room, which led up to a second dining room open to the floor below. "It's beautiful, Clara. And the food is excellent."

"Thank you," she said with careful control, keeping her voice just loud enough to be heard by him and him alone. "Tell you what, why don't you join me in my office when you're finished eating? We can speak privately. It's through that arch on the right as you're facing the counter."

He frowned up at her. "Are you sure you're okay?"

"Why are you always asking me that?" She spoke through clenched teeth.

"Because you look like you're about to fall over."

She lifted a hand and smoothed her scraped-back hair. "I'm just fine, thank you. My office, then?"

"I'll be right there."

"No hurry. Take your time." *Take forever. Please.*

He nodded and picked up his fork again. She seized the moment and made her escape. Head high, giant belly leading the way, she turned for the back rooms.

In her office, she shut the door, sagged against it and stared blindly at the tiny window high on the back wall that looked out on the alley. Really, she didn't feel well.

Her hands were chilly; her forehead was sweating. Her stomach churned and her overworked heart pounded away like a herd of wild mustangs trapped inside her chest.

What did he want from her?

To break her heart all over again?

For the past eight months, her previously well-ordered life had veered right off the rails into Crazyland. Her life had been one giant, tangled ball of anxiety and upheaval for way, way too long.

Logically, she knew that it wasn't Dalton's fault, that they'd had an agreement on the island and *she* was the one who'd wanted to make it more than it was. But in her heart, she blamed him. For not being there. For not wanting her more, for not being the perfect man she'd let herself imagine he was.

A tap on the door.

Time to face him again.

She pressed cold fingers to her hot, itchy eyelids and dragged herself up straight.

"Clara?" His voice, from the other side of the door. Gentle, for once. Maybe even a little concerned.

She didn't need or want his concern. "Yes. Yes, all right." She pulled the door wide.

And there he was, looking so good she wanted to break down and cry. He couldn't get away from her fast enough on the island. And now, since she'd told him about the baby, she couldn't get rid of him.

It was all so very confusing.

She opened her mouth to tell him…what?

She didn't even know what to say to him.

And then it turned out it didn't matter that she couldn't think of what to say. Because before she could get a word out, she fainted dead away.

Chapter Three

"Clara?" Dalton watched in horror as her eyes rolled back in her head and she swayed toward him.

Her face had gone dead white; her forehead and upper lip bloomed with sweat. He caught her automatically as her knees buckled, her body folding in over her big belly, gravity dragging her to the floor.

Stunned, he stared down at the top of her head. She was limp as a rag doll, out cold.

He knew terror then. Stark, raw terror. "Clara, my God…"

No response. She sagged in his arms.

Bracing one arm at her back, he bent to get her behind the knees with the other before she could slither from his grip. Then, hoisting her high against his chest, he carried her over to the gray velvet love seat under the window and carefully lowered her down onto it.

"Clara…" he whispered, and put his hand to her damp

forehead. No fever. If anything, her soft skin was too cool. The scent of her drifted to him. Sweet as ever. He wanted to touch her stomach, to somehow reassure her and the baby within her that everything was going to be okay, that he would make it so.

But before he could move his hand from her forehead to her belly, she stirred and moaned. Her eyelids fluttered open.

"What am I...? Dalton?" She put her palm to her stomach—just as he'd wanted to do—and looked down the length of her own body, frowning. "How did I...?"

"You fainted." He pulled his phone from his pocket and punched in 911.

She tried to sit up. "Listen, I—"

"Don't." He clasped her shoulder. "Stay down."

"But I..."

"Shh. Rest."

Wonder of wonders, she settled against the cushions with a long, weary sigh, lifting the back of her hand to cover her eyes.

The 911 dispatcher answered, "What is your emergency?"

"I need an ambulance at the Library Café."

The dispatcher started in with her series of questions.

Simultaneously, Clara gasped and dropped her hand away from her eyes. She glared at him accusingly. "An ambulance? I don't need—"

He put a finger to his lips and shook his head. It worked. She actually fell silent, though she did continue to glare at him as he rattled off answers to the questions coming at him from the other end of the line.

When the dispatcher let him go, he stuck his phone back in his pocket. "They'll be here within five minutes."

She had her hand over her eyes again and she grumbled, "I agree I should see my doctor, but an ambulance is overkill."

"Have you ever fainted before?"

"Never in my life."

"Think of the baby, then, and humor me. You're going to the hospital."

She made a low, unhappy sound. "If I'd known you were this controlling, I never would have had sex with you."

He almost laughed. "Too late now—give me your doctor's number. I'll call his office and get him to meet us there."

"Us?" she groused. "I'm guessing that means you're coming, too?"

"Yes, I am."

"Fabulous. And it's *her* office."

"The number, Clara."

Another tired sigh. "My cell. In my purse, second desk drawer."

"If I leave your side, will you promise to stay where you are?"

"Overbearing," she muttered. "Impossible…"

"Answer the question."

"Yes. All right. I'll stay right here."

So he went and got her shoulder bag from the drawer.

"Phone in the side pocket," she said. "Dr. Kapur."

He made the call. "All set. She'll meet you there," he said as he tucked the phone back where he'd found it.

The sound of a siren swelled in the distance, coming their way.

Clara was gently stroking her stomach. "You told them to pull around into the parking lot, didn't you?"

"That's right. Closest exit from here."

"I will try to be grateful that at least I don't have to be carried flat on my back through my own busy restaurant."

Clara knew she probably shouldn't have given in and let Dalton take over. She should be strong and sure and independent.

She *was* strong and sure and independent. Just not right at that particular moment.

The paramedics—both of whom she'd known since elementary school—arrived. By then, Renée and half the kitchen staff had realized something was wrong. They crowded in behind the med techs, making worried noises, wanting to know if she was all right.

Dalton herded them back out again, explaining as he went that she had fainted, that they were taking her to Justice Creek General, that there was nothing to worry about, her doctor would take good care of her and she would be fine.

He sounded so wonderfully confident and certain that Clara found herself feeling reassured. Of course she would be all right—and the baby, as well. There was nothing wrong with her that a good night's sleep wouldn't cure.

Roberta and Sal, the two med techs, finished taking her vital signs. They transferred her to a stretcher and carried her out to the parking lot in back.

Dalton came out with her. "I'll meet you at the hospital," he promised.

"Not necessary," she said. "I'll be fine." And then she waited for his answer, a thoroughly annoying little ball of dread in the pit of her stomach, that he would say, *All right, then. Good luck with that*, and be on his way.

But what he did say was "You won't get rid of me that easily," in a voice that seemed somehow both tender and gruff.

She barely kept herself from flashing him a trembling, grateful smile. "Oh, all right." She played it grumpy and ill-tempered for all she was worth. "Suit yourself."

"I will, don't worry."

"My purse…"

"I'll bring it," he promised.

The techs, Sal and Roberta, loaded her into the ambulance. Sal got in with her, while Roberta went around to get in behind the wheel. Dalton was still standing there, outside the doors, when Sal pulled them shut.

At Justice Creek General, they transferred her to a wheelchair, rolled her into one of the little triage cubicles, lifted her up onto the bed in there and hooked her to an IV. Fluids, they said, to make sure she was hydrated.

They'd just left her alone when Dalton walked in. "How are you doing?"

She was ridiculously glad to see his stern, handsome face. You'd think it had been years since she'd seen him— rather than twenty minutes, tops. "I'm getting hydrated."

"Excellent." He settled into one of the two molded plastic chairs.

"I think this is overkill," she grumbled, heavy on the attitude, which helped to remind her that she wasn't going to count on him.

"You've said that before."

"What about the bank? Aren't they expecting you eventually today?"

He flashed her a cool, oh-so-confident glance. "I've called my assistant and rearranged my schedule."

"Are you sure you should do that?"

He gave a one-shouldered shrug. "Perks of being the boss. No one's going to give me a hard time about taking a personal day."

"Ah." So, okay. He was staying. What else was there to say?

Nothing, apparently. He got out his smartphone and started poking at it. She stared up at the ceiling for a while, until her eyes drifted shut.

She realized she'd been snoozing when a giant, muscular guy with coffee-dark skin and dreadlocks came in to draw blood. Then a nurse came in and went over her medical history with her. After that, she dozed some more.

Eventually, she had to ask for the ladies' room. A blonde in purple scrubs pointed the way. She wheeled an IV pole with her when she went and reminded herself to count her blessings: at least Dalton hadn't insisted on going in there with her.

Back in the little room with him, she waited some more. She slept a little and felt generally mind-numbingly bored. Through all that, he remained, sitting there so calmly, now and then taking out his phone and checking things on it. She would have thought a high-powered control freak like what he'd turned out to be would be climbing the walls with all the endless waiting. But he took it in stride.

At half past eleven, Dr. Kapur showed up. Clara told her what had happened. Dr. Kapur left the room so that Clara could put on a paper gown. Dalton went out with her. The doctor came back in alone for the examination and Clara wondered if maybe Dalton had gone.

It was for the best, she decided. He didn't need to hang around for this. She was fine on her own.

But then he came right back in to hear the doctor's conclusions.

"Your baby seems to be doing well, no signs of fetal distress," Dr. Kapur said with a reassuring smile, gazing steadily at Clara—and then turning to share that smile with Dalton.

He's told my doctor that he's the father, Clara realized. And somehow, knowing he'd done that both pissed her off—and made her feel like crying. With a little bit of warm fuzziness thrown in for good measure.

Dr. Kapur continued. "But you've been pushing too hard, I think. You're dehydrated and you need rest. To start, I'm going to keep you overnight for observation and then tomorrow we'll decide where to go from here."

Clara longed to argue that she was fine and where she wanted to go was home. But if her doctor thought she needed to stay, so be it.

Then they put her in another wheelchair and rolled her to a regular room.

Once they'd had her change into a very ugly pink floral hospital gown—Dalton left the room for that, which she truly appreciated—and made her comfortable in the bed, they offered her lunch. They fed Dalton, too.

After the meal, she tried to get up and get her purse, which Dalton had stuck in the locker across the room.

"Stay in bed," he commanded, rising to loom over her. And then his dark eyebrows drew together. "Or do you need to use the bathroom?"

"I want my phone."

"Why?"

"I need to make a few calls."

"You should rest."

She only glared at him until he gave in and went and got it for her. She called Renée and said she was fine, but they were keeping her overnight, which meant she most likely wouldn't be in tomorrow—or if so, not until after the breakfast rush. Renée reassured her that things were under control and told her to take all the time she needed. They said goodbye and Clara started to autodial Rory.

"You're supposed to be resting," he said in a low and gentle tone that still, to her, managed to sound overbearing and superior.

"I *am* resting. And also making a few necessary calls."

"You just told your manager that you would be in tomorrow," he accused.

"No, I said I probably *wouldn't* be in. If you're going to eavesdrop on my conversations, you should listen more closely."

"There's no 'probably' involved here. You're *not* going in tomorrow."

"We'll find out about that tomorrow. The decision will be made between me and my doctor."

"You passed out, Clara. You've let yourself get dehydrated." He cast a baleful look at the bag of clear fluid hanging next to the bed and still connected to the back of her hand. "You need rest. And I'm going to see that you get what you need."

"Tell me, Dalton. Just when did you become the boss of me?"

He didn't even have the grace to take a little time to think about it, but shot right back with "This morning. You remember this morning, when you fainted in my arms? That was when I realized that *someone* has to take care of you or you're just going to keep on pushing yourself until you do real damage to yourself or the baby."

Was there even a smidge of truth in any of that? Well, okay. Maybe a little. A very, very little.

And what did he mean, *take care of her*? He made it sound as if she had become some ongoing project. Surely he wouldn't be hanging around for *that* long. He would have to go home to Denver and his banking empire at some point—like in the next hour or two.

Wouldn't he?

He was glaring at her. She glared right back at him and said with admirable composure, "Here's a hint. Your attitude needs some serious adjusting, because as of now, I'm not finding being around you the least bit restful."

He actually blinked. And then he allowed gruffly, "You're right. I'm upsetting you. I apologize. Will you please put the phone away and settle down?"

The thing was, he looked so sincere in his pompous sort of way. And even if she didn't want to let herself start to depend on him, she couldn't help appreciating that he was doing everything he could to look after her.

It was way too little too late. But that was almost as much her fault as his. She'd jumped to conclusions and thought he was married. He'd hired a detective and found out she was *getting* married. And neither of them had bothered to clear up the misunderstandings until months and months had passed.

Now he'd started to look worried. "I do apologize," he said again. "I mean that."

She gave in and muttered, "Apology accepted." And then put up her forefinger. "One more call. And then I'll lie back and relax. Promise."

He shook his head, looking all stuffy and put-upon— but then he shrugged.

She went with the shrug and autodialed Rory, told her about fainting at the café and being stuck in the hospital for observation overnight. After Rory finished saying all the right things about how she was there if Clara needed her and please to take it easy, Clara told her about the really hideously ugly hospital gown she was wearing.

Rory knew right away what she wanted. "I'll go by the house, get whatever you need and bring it right over there." Rory had a key to the house, just as Clara had a key to Rory and Walker's place at the ranch. "You're at General, right?"

"I'm at General, yes. And here we have yet another reason why you're my favorite cousin in the whole world. You know what I want without my even having to tell you."

"Back at you. Let me get a pencil…"

Clara told Rory what to get and Rory wrote it down.

And then Rory said, "I'll be there. An hour, max."

They said goodbye. Clara set the phone on the rolling hospital bed table thingy and felt better about everything.

Dalton was watching her, wearing a softer expression than usual, an expression that reminded her of the Dalton she'd known on the island. Which made her feel somehow a little less good about things. Where had that Dalton gone?

He asked, "Was that the cousin who's a princess, the one who'd planned to live in Colorado someday?"

Had she told him about Rory? "Yes, and now she does live here in Colorado—and how did you know that?"

"You told me on the island."

"I did? But we didn't talk about our real lives…" Sadness wrapped around her heart—a glowing kind of sadness. It had been a beautiful two weeks.

A smile twitched at one corner of his way-too-sexy mouth. "We had an agreement not to talk about our real lives, but you didn't keep it."

"No," she admitted. "I guess I didn't."

"You were careful about the basics. You never mentioned Justice Creek or that you own a café. But you talked about your family and your friends. All those random things you told me made it a lot easier for that private investigator I hired to find you."

"You were more careful than I was." At his nod, she went on. "I had your name, that you lived in Denver and that you were divorced. Luckily, you're a big shot, so it wasn't that hard to find you myself once I put my mind to it."

"To find me and then decide I was remarried and not bother to get in touch with me until three weeks ago."

"The important thing is, I *did* get in touch with you."

"Finally."

She looked at him dead-on. "Do you really want to go there right now, while I'm *resting*?"

Those blue eyes were on her, so focused, so determined. "No. You're right. I don't."

She shoved at her ponytail, which had sagged rather sadly and would be coming completely undone any minute now. "May I have my purse, please?" He got right up and brought it to her. "Thank you." He sat down again. She foraged around in the central compartment until she found her brush. And then she redid the ponytail, brushing it up and into her fist, then twisting the elastic back into place. "There. Much better."

He got up again and put the purse back in the locker. He was just shutting the metal door when the baby kicked her a good one.

"Ouch!"

He turned, fast, looking freaked. "Clara! What?"

She laughed and rubbed the spot. "It's just the baby. She's a kicker."

He came to her side. "She?"

She started to grab his hand and put it where he'd feel the next one—and then hesitated, suddenly self-conscious, a little embarrassed.

Which was silly. She'd let complete strangers touch her tummy. Yeah, okay, the guy had done a number on her heart. But he *was* the father. And he was trying. She nodded, pushed the covers out of the way, took his hand and put it on the side swell of her stomach. The baby promptly kicked her again. She winced. "There. Feel it?"

"I do." He had that look, a look of wonder, of awe. It made her almost start to love him a little again, in spite of everything—scratch that. *Like.* It made her like him a little. Those blue eyes were shining. "By God, I feel it. I do."

She laughed again and held his hand as he pressed his big, warm palm to the side of her belly. Another kick. She chuckled. And Dalton made a low, marveling sound. His hand felt so strong, long fingers spread, against the side of her belly.

And then her gaze went to his. They just stared at each other. With zero animosity. Only shared delight.

He asked, "A girl, you said?"

"Yes. I had an ultrasound."

"A girl," he repeated, as if he'd never heard anything more miraculous in his life. "I never thought…"

"What?"

He looked faintly abashed. She found that way too charming. "I don't know," he said almost shyly. "A girl, that's all. A little girl. What do you think of that?" It wasn't really a question. More an exclamation along the lines of *Isn't that awesome?* Or *How completely cool.*

Clara watched his face and remembered the sweet, passionate, caring man she'd fallen in love with. Why was he hiding from her? Where had he gone?

She was actually considering asking him, when her half sisters Jody and Nell appeared in the open door to the hallway.

He must have caught the shift in her gaze. Pulling his hand away, breaking that tenuous connection, he turned toward the door.

* * *

Rocked to the core by the feel of his daughter's tiny foot poking against his palm, Dalton turned to the two women standing in the doorway. One was conventionally pretty, with light brown hair and a big vase full of flowers in her hands. The other? An auburn-haired stunner, in a short, tight dress, she wore boots straight out of a *Sons of Anarchy* episode and had brightly colored tattoos from shoulder to elbow down her shapely left arm.

The family resemblance was clear—between the two women in the doorway and the woman in the bed behind him. Sisters, probably. On the island, Clara had told him she had two half sisters and one full sister. Plus, there was someone named Tracy, wasn't there? Tracy had come to live with Clara's mother's family, been raised as one of them, after her parents died tragically in a fire.

"Jody. Nell," Clara greeted the two with real warmth in her voice. "Come in, come in. Did Rory call you?"

The tattooed stunner came first. The one with the flowers, following close behind, said, "Roberta Carver came in the shop an hour ago. She said she and Sal Healey carried you out of the café on a stretcher this morning."

Clara groused, "Shouldn't patient confidentiality apply to paramedics and ambulance drivers?"

"Not in Justice Creek, it doesn't," said the stunner.

Clara jumped right to denial. "This is not a big deal. I'm only here overnight. Just for observation. It's nothing to worry about."

Dalton considered stepping in and arguing the point. But before he made up his mind whether to say anything, Clara started in with the introductions. Jody was the one with the flowers and Nell the one in the biker boots. Clara gave the two women Dalton's full name, but no explanation as to what he was doing there.

"I whipped this up so you'd know how much we love you," Jody said, looking proud, holding up the giant vase of flowers.

Clara gave her a beautiful misty-eyed smile. "It's fabulous. Thanks, honey." Jody went to put the flowers on the windowsill and Clara told Dalton, "Jody's a genius florist. She owns Bloom, on Central Street."

"They're beautiful," he said in the general direction of the flowers.

And then the stunner, Nell, popped in with "Hold it. Hold it right there!"

Jody blinked. "What?"

Nell turned on him and accused, "You're *him*, right? You're the father."

Her candor startled him. But he pulled it together and tried to reply. "Yes, I—"

"Nice suit." She cut him off with a sneer.

He decided to call that a compliment. "Thank you."

"Oh, don't thank me. Where the hell have you been?"

Jody groaned. "Nell, please…"

And Clara chuckled fondly. "Nellie. You never hold back."

"I asked the man a question." Nell braced her hands on her hips and scowled at him furiously.

He cleared his throat. "There was some confusion. It's a long story."

Nell whirled on Clara. "You just now *told* the guy?"

"Not *just* now." At least Clara had the grace to look sheepish. "I told him a few weeks ago."

"And he hasn't shown up until today?"

"We've been…in touch. And, as Dalton said, it's a long story."

Nell made a snorting sound. "He shoulda been here long before now."

"We're, um, working it out, Nellie. I promise we are."

Working it out? Not to *his* satisfaction, they weren't. But that was going to change. He would make sure of it.

Nell whirled on him again. She was not only gorgeous, but she had a certain scary energy about her. She made a man feel that it would not be wise to get on her bad side. "But you're here to do right now, aren't you, Dalton Ames?"

At last, a question he could answer without hesitation. "Absolutely. I'm going to look after Clara, and I'm going to take care of my child."

Clara started to speak—probably to insist as usual that she could look after herself.

But Nell beat her to it. "You'd *better* look after her," she warned. "Clara's tenderhearted. She's not as tough as some of us in the family. But we all have her back. Including her five brothers—three half, two full. Bravo men all. Big men. Strong. Protective of their sisters. Not men you want to mess with, men who will—"

"Nell," Clara cut in sweetly. "I think he knows where you're going with this."

Nell made a low noise in her throat. "We'll see about that."

Jody piped up with "Is there anything we can do, Clara, to help out?"

"Thanks. Just knowing I have so many people to count on helps a lot."

"Anything," said Nell as she pulled up the chair Dalton had been sitting in. There was one other chair, and Jody took that.

Dalton considered telling the two women that Clara needed her rest. But she *was* lying down and she seemed relaxed, so he didn't interfere.

A few minutes later, another sister arrived, the full sister, Elise. She came with Tracy Winham, the one who'd been adopted into the Bravo family when her parents were killed. Dalton ducked out to get more chairs as Nell informed the newcomers that he was the father and had promised to do right by Clara and the baby.

When he returned, two of Clara's brothers had arrived. They were big men, as Nell had warned him. But neither took a punch at him when they found out he was the father of Clara's baby.

The women left after about half an hour, and the men went soon after. The princess arrived. She had brown hair and eyes, like Clara's, and was almost as beautiful. She smiled and shook his hand and insisted that he must call her Rory.

Then she helped Clara wheel her IV drip into the bathroom. When they came out, Clara had changed into turquoise pajamas. She got back in the bed and Rory tossed the hated hospital gown into a laundry bin in the corner.

Two more men appeared, a full brother and a powerfully built half brother named Quinn, who had moved back to Justice Creek recently, having retired from a successful career as a mixed martial arts fighter. Quinn was a single father, Dalton learned, with a four-year-old daughter named Annabelle.

Quinn and the full brother, Jamie, didn't stay long. Rory left shortly after them. Dalton was just daring to hope that Clara might let him turn off the light and shut the blinds so she could sleep for a while.

No such luck. In sailed a slim, sweet-looking, impeccably groomed white-haired lady who wore giant round-lensed glasses with yellow plastic frames, dangly earrings, a mink coat held together at the throat by a brooch the size of a tarantula, and pointy-toed red high-heeled shoes.

Clara introduced her as her great-aunt, Agnes Oldfield.

Nothing got by Agnes. "Ames?" she demanded. "Dalton Ames? As in the Ames banking family?"

He said that yes, he was president and CEO of Ames Bank and Trust.

It took her about two more seconds to deduce that he must be the missing father of Clara's unborn child. "Where in the world have you been, young man? Your child will be arriving any minute now."

"Well, I—"

"Aunt Agnes." Clara came to his rescue. "Leave Dalton alone. He's here to help out and he doesn't need you picking on him." He felt rather mollified at that. It was the first time she'd openly admitted that he was trying to take care of her.

Agnes wasn't finished with him. "Of course I'm not picking on him. I'm just trying to find out where he's been all these months and what his plans are now that he's finally here."

Clara said sternly, "That's between Dalton and me."

"But does he realize you almost *married* someone else?" Agnes's rather protuberant eyes seemed to bulge even more behind those yellow-framed glasses.

"Yes," Clara replied wearily. "He knows about Ryan. He knows all about the wedding."

Agnes clucked her tongue. "I don't understand you young people today. It's important for a child to have both a mother *and* a father who are married to each other. *This* is the all-important nuclear family and it is the bedrock of our society, the bulwark of civilization, ordained by God Himself."

"I completely agree, Agnes," Dalton couldn't resist putting in. "I've proposed. She turned me down."

Clara piped up with "Dalton!"

"See?" And Agnes nodded approvingly in his direction. "This young man is not only from an excellent family. He knows what's right. I simply can't bear to *ask* why you've refused him."

"Then don't," advised Clara hopefully.

Agnes barreled right on. "Of course, after the way your father behaved, I can see why you might be a bit confused as to your responsibilities as a parent, Clara." The way her father behaved? Dalton made a mental note to find out more about that. Agnes kept on. "And I can't imagine how difficult these past months must have been for you."

"You're overdramatizing, Aunt Agnes," said Clara.

"No. No, I am not. I am sympathetic. I love you. I'm a traditionalist at heart, so I can't say I approve of your becoming pregnant without being married first, but I—"

"Aunt Agnes, stop!"

Agnes put her wrinkled, perfectly manicured hand to her chest. "There is no need to shout."

"Then listen to me. Are you listening?"

"Well, of course I am, dear."

"I love you, Aunt Agnes, but I want you to stay out of it, please."

"But I—"

"Please."

Agnes sputtered a little more, but she did finally back off—which was too bad, really, as Agnes had been arguing his case for him. The old lady stayed for half an hour. She talked the whole time, gossiping about people he didn't know and delivering several grim pronouncements concerning the frightening state of the world today.

Right after Agnes said goodbye, one of the nurses came in to check on Clara. Dalton left them alone.

When the nurse emerged from the room, she told him dinner would be served soon. Would he like a tray? He thanked her and said he would appreciate that and went back in with Clara.

He'd no sooner settled into the chair by the bed than yet another visitor appeared in the doorway. Tall and broad-shouldered with light brown hair, the guy was too damn good-looking. He carried a large stuffed teddy bear. In the teddy bear's fist were three red satin ribbons attached to three big red, shiny heart-shaped balloons.

Dalton knew instantly who he was. He'd seen the pictures of him in that private investigator's report back in December: Ryan McKellan, the one Clara had almost married.

"Ryan!" Clara cried his name with way too much delight. She held out her arms.

"Damn, Clara." The guy went straight to her, dropped to the side of the bed, propped the teddy bear on the bed table and gathered her into his arms. "I just heard."

"Thanks for coming," She hugged him way closer than Dalton thought was appropriate and the guy hugged her right back. The hug went on for far too long.

Finally, Ryan pulled back and Clara settled onto the pillow again. He touched the side of her face, a gentle touch that made Dalton want to break something—preferably that too-handsome face. "Are you all right?"

She had her hand on his shoulder and gave it a squeeze. Did she really need to keep touching him that way? "Honestly, Rye," she said. "It's not a big deal. I'm fine…"

Dalton wasn't letting that stand. "As a matter of fact, she fainted. She was dehydrated. And her doctor's keeping her here overnight for observation."

Ryan turned to look at him then. Frowning, he glanced at Clara.

Clara sighed, "Ryan, this is—"

"I'm Dalton Ames. The father of Clara's baby."

The other guy didn't look happy. Not happy in the least.

Clara didn't, either. Too damn bad. But then she said, "Dalton, will you leave us alone for a few minutes, please?"

It was the last thing he intended to do. "What for?"

The other guy tried to smooth things over. "Clara, it's all right. We can talk later." He started to rise.

But damned if she didn't grab him back. "No. We'll talk now." She shot Dalton a look of mingled exasperation and defiance—a look that asked, *Now, don't you feel guilty for being a complete ass?*

He didn't feel guilty. Not in the least.

She said, "Dalton, will you please step out of the room—and close the door when you go?"

He stayed where was, though he knew he'd pushed the issue to the limit.

She asked him again. "Dalton. Please."

He longed to simply tell her no, that he was going nowhere, not as long as this Ryan character was in her room.

But if he did that, it would cost him. He could see it in those big brown eyes of hers. If he didn't do as she'd asked, she was way too likely to *tell* him to get out—and not come back.

So he rose without a word and left them, pausing only to swing the door shut in his wake.

Chapter Four

Once the door had shut behind Dalton, Clara took Ryan's hand. "Thank you for the teddy bear…and the balloons. I love them."

Ryan lifted one shoulder in a half shrug. She knew the guarded look on his face. He was hurt. "So. That's him, huh? At last." He pulled his hand from her grip.

She suppressed an unhappy sigh. "It's him."

"You finally told him."

"That's right. Ryan, I'm sor—"

"He gonna do right?"

Exasperation curled in her belly. "I really, really wish that everyone would stop asking that. What does it mean, anyway, *do right*?"

"You don't know?"

"Of course I know."

"Then why'd you ask?"

"Because I'm tired of hearing it. Because marriage is not necessarily the right way to go in a situation like this."

Ryan made a face—one that meant he didn't agree with her, but he wasn't going to argue the point. "The kid needs a dad who's around, a dad who'll be there for her."

"Judging by the way Dalton has behaved since I told him about the baby three weeks ago, I don't think we need to worry about whether or not he'll be around."

Rye grunted. "Three weeks since you told him, huh?"

She waited until he met her eyes and then said softly, regretfully, "I should have talked to you, kept you up on what was going on, I know. I just…felt so tired. And I didn't know where to begin."

Another half shrug. "Where's he from?"

"Denver. He's a banker."

Ryan chuckled dryly and shook his head. "He looks like a banker."

She took his hand again. At least he let her keep it that time. And then she told him all the stuff she should have shared earlier, so he would have been prepared when he and Dalton finally came face-to-face. She went through the basics of what had happened on the island, and the misunderstandings that had kept Dalton from contacting her, and her from getting in touch with him.

At the end, Ryan said, "So he turned you down, on that island?"

"Yeah."

"What an idiot."

She squeezed his hand. "Spoken like the best friend any girl could ever have."

"He messes you over again, he answers to me."

"Rye, come on. He's trying."

"Trying isn't enough."

"Give the guy a break, huh?"

"He needs to know you've got people looking out for you."

She blew out her cheeks with a hard breath. "Are you serious? The family was here. All my sisters, all but one of my brothers. Aunt Agnes. And Rory. And now you. Believe me, at this point he's very well aware that there are people looking out for me."

"Good," he said. "As long as he knows." He gazed at her for a long moment. "Is he staying the night here? Or do you need me to come get you in the morning?"

"I don't know."

"Clara. You want me to stay?"

She thought of Dalton, out in the hallway. He really was trying and he *was* the baby's father. She pressed her lips together and shook her head. "No. You go."

"You sure?"

As if on cue, there was a tap on the door and Dalton stuck his head in. He scowled right past Ryan and locked eyes with Clara. "You need to rest."

She opened her mouth to tell him to butt out.

But Ryan spoke first. "I suppose he's right." And then he pulled her close for a second hug—and whispered in her ear, "I mean it. He gives you grief, send him to me." There was humor in that whisper and her heart felt lighter.

When he pulled back, they grinned at each other and she said, "Will do."

And then he got up. "You need anything, you call."

"Thanks, Rye. I will."

Dalton stood by the door wearing a smoldering expression that said only his excellent breeding was keeping him from punching Rye's lights out.

Rye paused a couple of feet from Dalton. "You'd better take good care of her."

"I intend to."

Rye did that ridiculous two-finger, *I'm watching you* gesture, playing the moment for all it was worth, and then glanced back at her one more time. "Later, Clara." He said it lightheartedly, with his famous sexy grin.

And then he was gone.

She waited for Dalton to start quizzing her about what had been said in his absence.

But he only asked, "Are you okay? Do you need anything?"

Which made her feel way too tenderly toward him.

She thanked him and assured him there was nothing she needed.

He took the chair by the bed. She settled back and dozed for a while. Dinner arrived. After the meal, he went out for half an hour or so and came back with a leather duffel.

When she asked what it was, he said, "A shaving kit, something to sleep in."

"So…you're staying the night?" She wasn't really sure how she felt about that.

He looked at her intently from under his dark eyebrows. "You have a problem with that?"

Did she? She still couldn't decide and ended up saying kind of limply, "I think it's unnecessary, that's all."

"Do you want me to sleep on a chair in the waiting room, then?"

"I—"

"Because I'm not going anywhere until we've seen your doctor in the morning."

She gave in. Because, really, she wanted him there more than she wanted him gone. "No. You can stay here in the room with me."

"Thank you," he said in a tone edged with irony.

At a little before nine, the nurses rolled in a bed for him. He took his duffel into the bathroom and came out wearing sweats and a blue Henley shirt that hugged his powerful shoulders and arms and made an absurd little ache in the center of her belly—to have those arms around her again, holding her close, the way they had done every night on the island.

Clara banished that ache. She took her turn in the bathroom and then he switched off the light and they settled in for the night.

She expected to lie there awake for hours, staring into the darkness, listening to the unfamiliar hospital sounds all around her, wondering what he was thinking, wishing she didn't care.

But she shut her eyes and pulled the blankets up more snugly around her—and that was it. Sleep just kind of mowed her down.

They drew her blood again very early in the morning. Dr. Kapur came in several hours later, at nine thirty. Dalton went out so the doctor could give Clara a quick exam.

He came back in to hear the prognosis.

"You're simply under too much stress," the doctor said. "Your cortisol levels are elevated and your blood pressure's higher than it should be. You need to take it easy."

Clara gulped. "What, exactly, does that mean?"

"I want you on modified bed rest until the baby's born. No working, no driving, limited activity. You may sit on the sofa and surf the Web, stand up long enough to take a shower or make a sandwich. Basically, you're going to be splitting your day between the couch and the bed. Catch up on your daytime television," the doctor advised with a grin.

"I don't watch daytime television." Was this really happening? "I don't have *time* for daytime television."

"Now you will," said Dalton a little too firmly. Clara opened her mouth to tell him to stay of it.

But then Dr. Kapur asked, "Are there stairs at your house?"

Clara's head was spinning. "Yes, I…"

"Avoid going up and down them."

"I… No stairs? And no *working*? At all?"

"None. That's of major importance. Whatever arrangements you've made for the birth and recovery go into effect as of now. You're going to be taking it very easy." Dr. Kapur turned to Dalton. "Reducing her stress is the key. We need to keep a close eye on her. Lots of liquids, too."

"Of course," Dalton answered gravely. "I'll see to it she gets proper care."

Clara wasn't sure she liked the sound of that. But there was no point in arguing with him in front of her doctor. "No driving, even?"

"That's right. No driving," Dr. Kapur confirmed. "I'll want to see you again in one week. Call my office and set up an appointment."

Clara sputtered out a reluctant agreement.

"All right, then," said the doctor. "I'll release you. Take it easy and I'll see you in a week."

Dalton was ready for her objections. And to be told he could go.

The minute the doctor left them alone, she turned a rather frantic-looking smile on him. "Thanks so much for everything, Dalton. But I know you have to go back to your own life and I'll just call—"

"I'm not going anywhere," he cut in before she could really get rolling, rising from his chair to move to her side. "My driver's waiting to take you home."

She gulped and stared up at him. "Home?" Her dark eyes sparked. "You mean to Denver?"

He asked, gently, "Would you like to come to Denver to stay until the baby comes?"

"Of course not. I told you. I live here."

"Well, then. That's where I'll take you. To your house."

She drew in a slow, shaky breath. "Really, it's okay. You don't have to—"

He sat down on the bed beside her. "Let me take you home, Clara. Come on. I'm here and I'm willing."

Her face was flushed. "God. Modified bed rest. I don't believe it."

"You're three weeks from your due date." He kept his voice even and calm. "Really, don't you think it's time you cut back?"

Her slim shoulders slumped. "I… Well, yeah. You're right. Dr. Kapur is right. I know that. It's just, I like to keep busy. And I'm used to being independent. And now I'm suddenly supposed to be home all day, lying around watching TV."

"There are other options. You could read. Knit. Do you knit?"

"I tried once." She pulled a pouty face, which he found way too adorable. "I was lousy at it."

He took her hand and felt a small surge of triumph when she didn't jerk away. "It's only for a few weeks."

She gave a little laugh that sounded way too much like a sob. "Right. And then the baby will be here. And then I'll never sleep again."

He chuckled. "It's not going to be *that* bad."

"How would you know? You've never had a kid, either." And then her big eyes got bigger. "Or have you?"

He reached out with his free hand and guided a few soft strands of hair out of her eyes, tucking them behind her ear. Her skin was cool and smooth as velvet. "No. Our daughter is my first."

She nibbled nervously on her lower lip. He wanted to bend close and steal a kiss. But he knew it was too soon. She whispered, "You're being so nice to me. Why?"

He told the truth. "I want to take care of you."

Her eyes were so wide, her mouth so damn soft. "Right now you remind me of how you were on the island. It's kind of disorienting. Whatever happened to that guy, anyway?"

He didn't really know how to answer that question. So he ignored it. Instead he rubbed his thumb lightly across the back of her hand and insisted very gently, "Let me take you home, Clara."

"I…" A small, soft sigh. And it happened. She gave in. "All right."

At her house, he herded her straight to the downstairs master suite, which was large and comfortable, with a walk-in closet on the other side of the roomy bathroom.

In one corner of her bedroom, she'd set up a bassinette, a changing table and shelves and a rocking chair. She explained, "For the first weeks after the baby comes home, she'll stay here in my room. Eventually, I'll move her to her own room upstairs."

Did she have the baby's room set up and ready? If not, he would take care of it.

But they would get to that later.

The bed was a king, a four-poster in dark wood with a cheery quilt for a bedspread. He went right over and folded the covers back.

She stood in the doorway, cell phone in hand, looking recalcitrant. "I need to call the restaurant. Then I want a shower."

"You can call the restaurant from bed."

"I want a shower before I get in bed. And I *don't* want you ordering me around."

He kept his tone mild. "Please."

She pointed at the easy chair by the window. It had a nice, soft-looking ottoman. "I'll sit in that while I make the call."

"That'll work." He waited.

"Oh, fine." With a huff and an eye roll, she went over and lowered herself carefully into the chair, cupping her big stomach in a spread hand as she did it. "There. Happy now?" She leaned back against the cushions. But she still had her sandals on and her feet on the floor.

He dared to approach. Slowly.

She watched him coming, narrow-eyed. "What?" He dropped to a knee beside her chair. She blinked down at him. "What in the…?" She looked pretty worried.

He figured it out. She feared he might be about to propose again.

No way. He might be overbearing. But he wasn't stupid. It hadn't worked the first time, to whip out that big ring out of the blue. Next time he asked her, it wouldn't be on the fly.

Gently, he picked up one of her feet—the one nearest the ottoman—and slid off the sandal. "Just helping you get comfortable." He eased that foot onto the ottoman and reached for the other one. She allowed him to remove that sandal, too, but she swung it over to the ottoman on her own.

She rotated her right foot, wiggled her pink-painted toes. "Ugh. Cankles."

"Cank…?"

"Cankles. I have cankles." She leaned forward to

smooth the hem of her blue dress over her knees. "You've never heard of cankles?"

"Never."

"That's when your calf hooks to your foot with no discernible thinning of the leg where the ankle should be. Calf-ankle. Cankle."

He had no idea what she was babbling about, and he supposed that fact must have shown on his face, because she finally explained in plain English, "My ankles are swollen."

Which provided him an opportunity to pleasantly remind her, "Another reason to stay off your feet."

She groaned and flopped back against the cushions again. "You've been great, Dalton, and I really appreciate all you've done—and shouldn't you be going?"

No, I shouldn't. "Later. After you get settled in."

"But I *am* settled in."

Pretending she hadn't spoken, he stood. "I'll leave you alone to make your call." And then he turned and got the hell out of there before she could tell him again to go. Behind him, she made an exasperated sound—but she didn't call him back to insist that he leave.

He slipped out the door and shut it silently behind him.

And then, shamelessly, he went about checking out the house.

It was charming, really. Well laid out, furnished in a simple, inviting style, and well maintained. She was young to have both a nice place like this and that successful café. She'd either worked her sweet ass off all her adult life, or she had an inheritance, or some combination of the two. Judging by all the loyal relatives who'd shown up at the hospital yesterday, she did have people to look after her.

So. Comfortably self-supporting, with a family who cared. Good for her.

Not so good for him, however. It would be much better if she needed—really needed—the father of her unborn child.

But a man had to play with the hand he was dealt.

He made a quick circuit of the downstairs, moving through the great room, past the breakfast nook, into the kitchen and through the archway to the dining room. Another wide arch took him into the foyer. He went up the stairs and came out on a balcony with a carved rail that was open to the great room below and a nice view of the handsome fireplace flanked by half-bow windows.

He kept going, making another circuit of the upper floor, which had three bedrooms and one large bath.

The baby's room, all done up in pink, green, yellow and white, with a mural of butterflies and cartoon animals on one wall, overlooked the backyard. Baby clothes and tiny blankets, all neatly folded and stacked, filled the white shelves. In the corner on the floor, he found a pile of books on pregnancy, childbirth and how to care for a newborn. He bent and scooped them up. They would make good nighttime reading. By the time she went into labor, he intended to be well informed on how to help get her through that, not to mention how to care for their little girl.

Another rocker, similar to the one downstairs, waited by the window. He found the room charming—and Clara all the more admirable to have pulled it together on her own while working long hours at her restaurant. No wonder she'd collapsed.

The woman didn't know when to take a break.

She would be taking a break now, whether she liked it or not. He would see to that.

Carrying the stack of baby books, he left the nursery and checked out the other two rooms up there: a spare bedroom and a sort of makeshift office/storage room, with a long folding table and an office chair, a laptop, stacks of file boxes. Deep shelves lined one wall and held rows of large plastic storage bins.

All good. The spare bedroom and the office/storage room would do for his purposes.

He left the baby books on the folding table, went back downstairs, grabbed a seat at the breakfast table, took out his phone and checked his messages and alerts. After dealing with the ones that couldn't wait, he brought up the memo app and began listing what he would need to get himself set up for the next several weeks.

Two hours later, he still hadn't heard so much as a peep from Clara's bedroom. During that time, the house phone had rung two separate times. He assumed she'd picked up from the bedroom as both times, the phone had rung only twice.

It was almost noon. He stared at Clara's refrigerator for several seconds, calculating the risk in making himself at home in her kitchen.

No. He had to be careful at this point, to presume nothing, to do nothing that could be construed as commandeering her space. He needed to respect all her boundaries—at least until he had her agreement as to how it was going to be.

He called his driver, Earl, who was waiting in the limo out at the curb, and asked him to go and dig up some lunch. Twenty minutes later, Earl stood at the door, arms full of to-go bags. Earl—who dressed like Johnny Cash, called Dalton "boss" and wore a black cowboy hat—was a prize.

Dalton accepted the bags and told Earl to take some time for himself. "Be back by three."

"Will do, boss."

Dalton shut the door, turned for the kitchen—and spotted Clara, wearing pink workout pants and a huge purple

T-shirt with Does This Baby Make Me Look Fat? printed across the front. She was standing in the arch opposite the dining room.

Her face looked soft and slightly flushed, her eyes heavy-lidded. Her hair was flat on one side. "I had a shower."

"Great."

"After I talked to Renée, I got a couple of calls. And then I guess I fell asleep."

"Even better. Things okay at the restaurant?"

"I can't believe it. They seem to be managing without me—and something smells amazing. What's in the bags?"

"Lunch. Hungry?"

"Starved. Please don't tell me I have to eat my lunch in bed."

"How about the sofa? You can put your feet up."

"Were you a nurse in your last life?"

"Are you saying you think I missed my calling?"

She propped a shoulder on the archway, rested her arms on her belly and tipped her head to the side, studying him. "You're being absolutely wonderful."

"Thank you. The sofa?"

"Sure. Why not?"

Clara did it the way he wanted it. It wasn't so hard.

She sat on the sofa, propped up on several pillows, with her legs stretched out across the cushions. He tore open the bags and set the food on the coffee table, then took one of the wing chairs.

They had pastrami on rye and chicken noodle soup from that great deli on Elk Street. She gobbled down several amazing bites before demanding, "How'd you know to go to David's?"

"I didn't. I have Earl."

"Earl. The Man in Black driver, right?"

"Earl always knows where to get the best lunch. Or dinner, for that matter. Denver. Boulder. Colorado Springs. Aspen. And Justice Creek. Wherever Earl drives me, he always knows where to eat."

She couldn't resist teasing him. "David's is terrific. But my café is the best."

"I told him not to go there. You eat there all the time. Variety never hurts."

He was right. "It's delicious," she said. "Thank you."

He nodded. They ate in silence for a minute or two as she tried to decide how to approach the subject he kept evading.

Finally, she just asked him, "Are you ever planning to go back to Denver?"

Deli paper crackled as he set down the remains of his sandwich. "I have something to confess."

"Great. But you haven't answered my question. And I've asked it more than once today."

"I went upstairs. I looked around. The baby's room is beautiful."

"I'm glad you approve. But when are you leav—?"

He put up a hand. "Hear me out?"

She picked up her soup and slurped down a big spoonful. "Talk."

"I want to move in here, with you."

She barely kept herself from choking on a noodle. "*What*? Whoa, Dalton. Not a good idea."

He chided, "You said you'd listen." And then he waited. So she made a big show of pressing her lips together and widening her eyes to let him know she *was* listening. "I can take the spare bedroom, and set up a rudimentary office in that room with the folding desk and the storage bins. I would go back and forth to the Denver office one or two times a week. And there's a branch here in town I might make use of if I want a bigger space or need my assistant with me. I'll look into that, see if that's workable. And I'll be cutting back my hours anyway, for now. Even the president is entitled to a little family leave at crucial times. So I'll work a shortened, flexible workweek. And then I'll be here to help out, to take care of you until the baby's born."

"Wow," Clara said weakly. She had no idea what to say. It made her feel a lot better about the future, about what kind of father he would be to their child, that he would offer to turn his life upside down to take care of her until their daughter came.

But then...no. Just, no.

She had to remember that she really hardly knew this man—and that he'd rejected her without even thinking twice last August. She couldn't *afford* to become too dependent on him, couldn't afford to let herself start trusting him in intimate ways.

He spoke again. "Your due date's three weeks away."

"I'm very well aware of when my due date is."

Patiently, he continued. "I haven't been here, to help you, up till now, and I regret that. If you think back on it honestly, I think you'll see that I had no *chance* to help you, until now."

"Because you turned me down, on the island." She tried to keep her voice even and reasonable. It was only a fact, not the end of the world. But still, she couldn't completely keep the hurt from showing.

"I was wrong."

"Too late now."

"That's not fair, Clara."

Carefully, she set her half-full container of soup back on the coffee table. "All I wanted then, with you, was a chance. To get together in our *real* lives, to see how it might go, to take it one day at a time. I made that very clear to you. But you wouldn't even consider it, you didn't even take a few minutes to think it over. And that really hurt me. It hurt me bad. I…I'd never felt about anyone the way I felt about you. I had this ridiculous idea that I'd finally found the guy for me. I really thought we had something special."

"We did," he put in gruffly. "And I didn't want to ruin it."

She scoffed. She couldn't help it. "You didn't want to ruin it—so you crapped all over it?"

He was silent. His face had that carved-from-stone look it got now and then. But then, finally, he started to talk, to actually explain himself a little. He said, "My marriage had failed. My divorce was barely final. I'd decided I was just not cut out for…I don't know, romance, whatever you want to call it. I'd told myself I wasn't ever going there again. And then, there you were, on the island, with your big smile and your beautiful, honest eyes, offering me something I thought maybe I could handle. Just a couple of weeks, magic time, an escape. Away from everything that makes me who I am. With you, for those two weeks, I gave myself permission to be…what I never am. It wasn't meant to last and when you wanted to take it further… Look. I blew it. That's all. And when I went looking for you, I thought you were taken."

Okay, he was kind of getting to her. She was weakening, softening toward him. How could she help it when he said she had beautiful, honest eyes, when he told her how it had been for him, and said it all so simply and directly?

She could kind of see his side of it now.

Damn it.

The baby kicked. She put her hand to the spot and

rubbed at it absently as she tried to get him to see how it was for her. "It's a scary time for me, okay? There's been so much stress and confusion. I don't know what I want or what to do, anymore. I'm just trying to get through this, you know?"

He gazed at her, unwavering, so sure of himself and his plans. "I want to *help* you get through this. You only need to let me do that."

"But…to have you living in my house with me. Dalton, I just don't think it's a very good idea."

"Why not?" Patient. Reasonable. But so very determined, too.

"Because you confuse me and I *feel* sometimes that I know you. But I don't, not really. We had a two-week affair. That's all it was. I can't let myself start to count on you. It wouldn't be right."

"Of course it would be right. You're having my baby."

"Yes, I am. And I'm willing, to work through this whole coparenting thing with you, over time."

"Over time? What does that mean?"

"It means we need to take it slowly, to figure out gradually how it's going to work for us as two single parents."

Something flared in his eyes. "There's nothing to figure out. I *will* be there for my daughter." His voice left no room for argument.

And the thing was, she *liked* it. A lot. Liked how sure he was, how he seemed to know what he wanted—and that was to take care of her and the baby they'd made.

What woman wouldn't want exactly what he was offering? To have the father of her child absolutely determined to do everything in his considerable power to make sure that she and her child were safe and well and taken care of?

It was programmed in the DNA, for a woman to want

a man who could stand up for her, stand beside her when she needed him—when their *children* needed him.

It was too tempting, what he offered.

This was dangerous ground.

She said so—gently, "And that's good. It's as it should be, that you know what you want—and what you want is to be here for the baby. But I keep trying to make you see. I'm *not* so sure. I just don't know if I could have you living in my house." She paused. "Dalton, I can see how hard you're trying. But I'm still not over what happened on the island. I'm just not. I…gave you up. Completely. I accepted that it was all just a fantasy, you and me. But now you're here and you're definitely real and, well, it has my head spinning. I can't just snap my fingers and say it's all worked out now, that of course you can help me and thank you so much."

"I don't expect it to be suddenly all worked out."

"And yet, two days after I finally got up the courage to face you and tell you about the baby, you showed up on my doorstep with a big diamond ring. Like all you had to do was put a ring on it and everything would be all better. What was that about?"

He leaned forward, elbows on his spread knees, and said in that take-no-prisoners, ruler-of-the-world deep voice of his, "Doing the right damn thing, that's what."

Doing the right thing. "Dear God, if people would only stop saying that."

"You're being unreasonable. People *will* say it. Because it's a true thing. A man ought to step the hell up when he's going to be a father."

"It's not the answer, Dalton, just to go and get married and hope that somehow it will all work out. Most of the time in this world today, it *doesn't* work out. And then it only brings more heartache when it all falls apart."

"Fine. Great. So you said no."

"Yes. And *that* was the right thing for me to do."

"I don't agree. I'll never agree."

"That's what I'm afraid of."

"What?" He pinned her with those laser-blues. "That I'll keep trying to do the right thing as I see it?"

"Yes. That you'll keep after me until I bend to your will."

"Not fair, Clara."

"Are you going to tell me that I'm wrong?"

"The facts are simple. You turned me down and I have accepted it. And now I'm *not* asking you to marry me. I'm asking you to let me move in here and do what I can for you and our baby."

"It's just…"

"What?"

"It's too late. That ship has sailed."

He fisted one hand and wrapped the fingers of the other around it. "But I realized my mistake in letting you go and I did hire someone to find you. You *were* going to marry your good buddy, Ryan. I was told that the baby was *his*. I had no reason not to believe that. So I stayed away. But now I'm here. And you've pushed yourself so hard for so long, you collapsed. You need someone with you. And as I'm the baby's father, why the hell shouldn't that someone be me?"

God. He was right. She really, really hated that he was right.

And he wasn't finished, either. "You do need me, Clara, whether you're willing to admit it or not. You need me and the baby needs me. And I need to be here, damn it. I need to do what I can to make certain that both of you are all right."

"But I—"

"Don't give me any 'buts,' Clara. Just put your damn pride aside for once and say you'll let me stay here and do what I can for you until our baby is born."

Chapter Five

Dalton knew he'd convinced her when she said wistfully, "You were so easygoing on the island. You took things as they came. The man you were on the island was not a relentless man."

He gave her the truth. It seemed a good time for it. "Right now the last thing you need is the man I was on the island."

She looked at him, huge eyes full of hurt. "Given that that man didn't really exist, it doesn't matter if I needed him."

"That's right." He said it gently, firmly. Even though, in a certain sense, the man he'd been on the island was as much his real self as the one who sat in the chair beside her now. The man on the island was the man he might have been given different parents, a different childhood. But he had no intention of going into any of that now. Now he needed to get her agreement so he could move forward with his plans. He pushed to close the deal. "Tell me I can move in here."

"How long do you plan to stay?"

"For as long as you and the baby need me."

"Who gets to decide that?"

I do. And I'm not leaving. "We'll know, I think, when it's time for me to go."

"What if it just doesn't work out for me?"

He almost chuckled. "I have zero doubt that you'll let me know immediately if it's not working out for you."

"You *will* have to go if I say so, Dalton. This *is* my house."

"Point taken."

"And you definitely can't stay past the birth. As soon as I'm back on my feet, you have to move out."

"How about this? After the baby comes, we'll discuss what to do next."

"Unless I simply want you out. Then you'll go."

"Absolutely." But she wouldn't want him out. She needed him. All he had to do was get her to see that. "Now finish your soup."

"I've had all I want, thank you."

He only looked at her patiently.

She stared back at him, defiant. But not for long. Finally, with a put-upon little scowl, she picked up the container and started spooning it in her mouth.

Dalton slept in the upstairs bedroom that night. Clara lay in her bed downstairs and thought about him up there, in that room that just happened to be directly above hers, sleeping in the old cherrywood sleigh bed that had once belonged to her mother's mother.

Life was so strange, really. You could give a man up, totally accept that it wasn't meant to be. And then six months later, have him sleeping in your spare room, determined to take care of you whether you wanted him to or not.

In the morning, he cooked oatmeal with raisins and honey for breakfast. She ate a nice, big bowlful.

Then she camped out on the couch with the TV remote, her phone and her laptop. Renée was under orders to call in and report between the breakfast and lunch rushes, and then a second time once they closed the doors for the day.

It was during the after-breakfast report that all the stuff Dalton had ordered brought up from Denver started arriving. She heard the front door opening and closing, men's heavy footsteps going up and down the stairs. They were pretty quiet about it, actually, and that made her smile. She could just picture Dalton scowling at them, ordering them to keep it down because there was a pregnant woman on the couch who was supposed to be resting.

The men's footsteps came and went for over an hour. Ryan came by to see how she was doing as Lord knew what all was still being hauled up the stairs.

He came and sat in the wing chair beside her and said, "I don't think your new boyfriend likes me very much."

She was instantly on full alert. "He's not my boyfriend. Did he say he was? Tell me the truth. What did he do? I'll talk to him."

Rye gave her his most charming grin. "Leave it alone. It was just a dirty look."

"I mean it. If he gives you any grief, you had better come and tell me."

For that she got one of those guy looks, a look of simultaneous patience and dismissal. "Come on, Clara. You know damn well I'm not going to do that. We'll work it out, him and me, in our own way."

"As long as there's no bloodshed involved."

"I'm making no promises—and are you even going to tell me why it looks like the guy is moving in?"

"Because he *is* moving in. I'm on modified bed rest and Dalton wants to help."

"Help." Another guy look. The kind that said she was a woman and women had no idea what was really going on.

"Yes, Ryan. Dalton is here to help."

"If he wants to help, he should man up and marry you."

There it was again. Marriage. Everybody seemed to think it was the only solution when the stick turned blue. "I love you, Ryan. But right now I just want to kill you."

"Why kill *me*? *He's* the one who—"

"I am so tired of having this conversation over and over. He asked me to marry him, okay? I turned him down."

Ryan opened his mouth—and then shut it without speaking. And then finally, he said, "You turned down his marriage proposal, but you're letting him move in?"

"What's so hard to understand about that? He wants to help, okay? He wants to be sure that I take care of myself."

Ryan frowned. "I don't get it."

"You don't *have* to get it."

A one-shouldered shrug. "Whatever you say."

Clara suggested, "Let's just change the subject, okay?"

So they talked for a little longer about nothing in particular. And when he got up to go, he asked her if she needed anything.

She said, "Just stop by and cheer me up now and then. It's looking like I'll be right here on this couch or in my bed until this baby's born."

He bent over and kissed her on the forehead and said he'd be back soon and she should call him if she needed him. "Anytime, day or night."

There was lunch. Earl brought it. Dalton sat in the wing chair and shared the meal with her. She kept waiting for him to make some disparaging remark about Ryan's coming by.

But apparently, he had more sense than that. He seemed cheerful and upbeat. And he never mentioned Ryan at all.

By then, she was getting pretty tired of the couch. She switched to the bedroom, took a long nap and woke up when the phone rang with Renée's afternoon report.

After Renée said goodbye, Rory called. She already knew that Dalton was moving in. Clara wasn't surprised. Rory lived with Ryan's brother, Walker, after all. And news traveled fast in Justice Creek.

That night, Earl brought Italian from Romano's. After they ate, Dalton went back upstairs to work some more. But then he came down around eight when she was starting to feel kind of forlorn and lonely and he asked her if she'd like to stream a movie.

"Do I get to choose the movie?" she asked.

And he said, "Anything you want."

She picked a romantic comedy. He watched the whole thing with her and didn't complain once.

Having Dalton living at her house? Maybe not as bad as she had expected it would be.

So far, anyway.

The next morning she woke up at six thirty and grabbed a quick shower. She dressed in yoga pants and a black maternity T-shirt that warned Keep the Oreos Coming and No One Gets Hurt. Then she headed for the kitchen to see what Dalton would be fixing for breakfast today.

He wasn't up yet. And the house seemed much too quiet, somehow. She put on water for strawberry leaf tea and sat at the counter to decide whether to wait for him or pour herself a bowl of granola.

The sound of the front door opening and closing surprised her. She got up and waddled down the hall in time to see Dalton on his way up the stairs in a tank shirt, mesh shorts and cross-trainers. His skin was all shiny with sweat, his shoulders wide and strong, every muscle in his powerful arms and legs sharply defined.

God. He looked good. So very good…

He paused in midstep at the sight of her. "Morning."

The nights on the island came sharply back to her: the scent of his skin, the feel of those big, strong arms around her, the way he would cradle her with his hard body as they slept…

She gulped and shoved those memories down into the deepest, darkest corner of her mind, where they would never rise again to torment her. "Hey."

He armed sweat from his forehead. "Thought I'd get in an early run."

"Um. Great. Keepin' healthy. Good idea."

"I met up with one of your half brothers. Quinn? He was out for a run, too." At her squeak of acknowledgement, he added, "I might check out that gym he's opened, Prime Sports and Fitness. He says that beyond the fitness classes and the mixed martial arts he specializes in, there's a fully equipped workout room."

But you won't be here long enough to join Quinn's gym. She almost said it out loud, but stopped herself at the last possible second. If he wanted to visit Prime Sports, more power to him. "Sounds good."

Twin lines formed between his black eyebrows. "You feeling all right?"

"Wonderful, why?"

"You seem a little…strained, maybe?"

"Uh-uh. No. Not strained at all." The kettle whistled. Just in time. "That's my tea…" She braced a hand under her belly and took off for the kitchen.

"I'll grab a quick shower and be down to make breakfast," he called after her.

"Sounds good." She kept going, not pausing, and definitely not glancing back.

In hindsight, as the days went by, Clara marked that moment in the front hall. She began to realize that her feelings for him had started to get really out of hand right then, early on that sunny Thursday morning, when he stood on the stairs in his exercise gear, looking so fit and strong and deliciously sweaty.

Before that morning, at least she'd felt she had a handle on her emotions when it came to him, that she knew how to control them, how to exercise a little constructive denial.

But after those few, seemingly innocuous moments in the front hall, control was a much bigger issue for her. Because they just kept happening, over and over again, more and more frequently—"they" meaning inexplicably powerful attacks of...what?

Longing? Desire?

Ridiculous for her to feel this way. She should have learned her lesson. She was fat as an old cow with the baby they'd made precisely because of these dangerous yearnings, the ones that she'd pushed way, deep down into darkness, the ones that were not supposed to keep rising to torment her.

But they did.

She would glance up when he entered a room and her breath would catch in her throat, her heart contract in her chest. In the evening, when they sat together in the living room watching TV or a movie, she would find herself glancing over at him, feeling that catch in her throat, that stutter in her chest.

Ridiculous.

And infuriating.

But undeniable.

Because, well, she might have turned her back on any possibility of a future with him. She might have told herself that she'd put him behind her. She had even told *him* that, repeatedly.

But as the first days of her modified bed rest went by, she couldn't help realizing that her heart was not through with him. And neither was her bloated, overburdened body.

Just the sight of him made her yearn. And beyond the thoroughly inappropriate desire that tormented her, she couldn't help feeling gratitude toward him, too.

He was here, after all. Here when she needed him, here for their baby, here when it mattered most.

How could she help starting to think that maybe she ought to consider giving him a chance again? At the very least, she should take this opportunity to get to know him as she hadn't gotten to know him on the island.

Even if it went nowhere and she learned all over again that he was not the man for her, it couldn't hurt to find out more about him. They might not end up together as a woman and a man, but they could never completely walk away from each other. He'd made it more than clear that he intended to play a major role in his daughter's life. So for a couple of decades at least, until their child was grown, they would have to deal with each other.

She started thinking that she really did need to reach out to him, to seek a common ground with him.

But then Monday morning came. And she got a serious dose of reality as to what a pushy, overbearing SOB Dalton Ames could be.

* * *

That morning, Earl had driven Dalton to Denver for a series of meetings that would last all day. Clara was alone in the house, in the bedroom. She'd been going over the accounts for the café, but she must have dozed off.

She didn't hear the woman come in.

Some random sound must have woken her. She opened her eyes and groggily blinked at her laptop, which remained perched on her thighs, exactly where it had been when she dropped off.

And then she heard something else, faintly. A cupboard closing in the kitchen?

Rory had a key and so did Ryan. Maybe one of them had come by…

But no. They would have knocked. They had keys for emergencies and such. Neither of them would just barge in unannounced, and then stay without letting her know they were there.

Clara put the laptop aside and rolled out of bed.

What now? Should she arm herself before leaving the bedroom? But arm herself with what?

The faint noises kept on. Someone was bustling around out there.

She scanned the room for a makeshift defensive weapon. She could unplug the bedside lamp and use it for a bludgeon. Or grab a pair of hiking boots to throw at the intruder…

No. Maybe not.

She decided she would skip the weapon and go with stealth. Just sneak out there, see if it was anyone threatening-looking and then, if necessary, retreat to her room and call the police.

It wasn't a great plan. But she didn't really believe a

burglar or home invader would show up at ten in the morning and then bustle around the kitchen.

So she tiptoed out into the hallway and around the corner into the great room—and found a tall, slim middle-aged woman taking the clean dishes out of the dishwasher and putting them away.

The woman spotted her and beamed. "Ah. There you are, Ms. Bravo." She frowned. "Did I wake you? I peeked in on you when I got here, and you were sleeping so peacefully…"

Clara smoothed a sleep-tangled hank of hair out of her eyes. "Uh, I don't know what woke me, really. But it's fine. And you are…?"

"Mrs. Scruggs, your new housekeeper." The woman lifted a stack of plates from the dishwasher and set them on the counter. "I'm also quite good with children, so I told Mr. Ames I would be happy to step in as your new baby's nanny when needed."

Clara grumbled, "Mr. Ames, huh?"

Another beaming smile. "I came in Thursday afternoon to interview. And he called me Friday to say I'd been hired. I clean and I cook. I'll be in five times a week. Full day on Monday. Afternoons on Tuesday through Friday. Those days, I'll just be cooking."

Dalton. Of course. The man had a pair on him for sure.

"Er…anything wrong, Ms. Bravo?"

"Not a thing. Call me Clara—and I have a question."

"Of course, Clara."

"Last Thursday, when Dalton interviewed you, did you come here to the house?"

"Yes. Yes, I did. Around two? I believe you might have been napping then, as well. Now that you're awake, how about if I put some fresh sheets on your bed, tidy your room and get the vacuuming out of the way?"

What could she say? The dust bunnies were piling up. No reason to jump all over Mrs. Scruggs, who was only doing what she'd been hired to do. It was Dalton she needed to have a little talk with. "Yes, of course. Carry on."

And Mrs. Scruggs did carry on. She vacuumed, made beds, dusted, did laundry and roasted a lovely leg of lamb with new potatoes and glazed carrots. She also whipped up a fresh and tasty-looking asparagus salad and a burnt-almond torte for dessert. Then she bustled on out the door at a little after four with a promise to return the next afternoon to make dinner again.

Dalton got home at a quarter of six. Clara met him in the front hall. He wore one of his perfectly tailored, impossibly expensive suits and he carried a Lederer alligator briefcase that cost as much as a Subaru. In fact, he looked so handsome and pulled-together she wanted to sidle up nice and close, breathe in the scent of his aftershave—and kiss him hello.

But of course, she did no such thing. Especially not right now, when she was seriously pissed off at him.

He smiled at her. "Clara." And then he sucked in a long breath through his nose. "It smells great in here."

"That would be the leg of lamb cooked by the housekeeper you hired on Friday."

"The impressive Mrs. Scruggs."

"The one and only."

"How's she working out?"

"She's fabulous. But Mrs. Scruggs is not the issue."

Twin lines formed between his dark eyebrows. "There's an issue?"

"Dalton, you do not get to hire someone to take care of my house and to cook my meals—and apparently to play nanny to my baby when the time comes—without even mentioning it to me."

"Clara…" He said it in a chiding way. It was very attractive, the way he said it. It was fond and also a little bit intimate.

And that pissed her off even more. "I had no idea she was coming. I woke up from a nap and found her putting the dishes away."

"She's a housekeeper. She's *supposed* to put the dishes away."

"You hired her without even consulting me. And then you didn't bother to tell me she was coming."

"Even excellent takeout gets old. I'm tired of it. And I'm more than happy to pay someone to do the housework I don't want to do—and *you're* not supposed to do."

"Maybe I would be happy about hiring someone, too, if you'd asked me. Which you did not."

"I wanted to surprise you."

"And you did. At first, I thought she was a home invader."

That kind of got to him. For a split second, he actually looked a tiny bit regretful. "I had no idea she would frighten you."

"She didn't do it on purpose. She was trying to be quiet. And I got over it. It's not the real issue. The real issue is that this is my house and *I* decide who comes to work in it. Also, you gave her a key. You don't just get to give people keys to my house."

"She's bonded and insured."

"Give me the keys to *your* house. I'll find some people to give them to and then not bother to mention what I've done."

"Clara." Tender. Patient. "I think you may have some issues with control."

That had her gaping. "*I* have issues with control?"

He took a step toward her. "Clara…"

"Stop that."

One black eyebrow arched. "Stop what?" He took another step.

"Getting closer."

He looked way too pleased with himself. "I like being closer."

She almost fell back, but it seemed a bad idea to show weakness. "Um. Mrs. Scruggs?"

"Yes?"

"I like her," she grumbled. "She can stay."

"See?" Too smug by half. "I knew she was the right choice."

"But don't do anything like that again. If you want to hire someone or change the way things work around here, you come to me and we discuss it. And I have to give my approval ahead of time if someone's getting a key."

"Fair enough. Agreed."

"And how much does the amazing Mrs. Scruggs charge, anyway?"

"I hired her." Mr. I-rule-the-world was back. "I'll pay her wages."

"Once again, Dalton. That wasn't the question."

A frown of mild irritation. "If I'm paying her, you don't need to worry about the cost."

"I most certainly do have to consider the cost. She's working for me. *I* should pay her wages."

"Clara, we don't need to argue about this."

"No, we don't. And we're not. We're *discussing* this. How much does she charge?"

"You're like a damn bulldog when you set your mind to something, you know that?"

"Whereas you are so easy-natured and laid-back." She piled on the irony.

"I'm just trying to be helpful, just doing what I can to make things easier on you."

"I had a question back there. You didn't answer it."

"What question?"

"How much does my new housekeeper charge?"

"Shouldn't you be lying down?"

That did it. She leveled her darkest scowl at him and threatened, "I'm not going to ask you again, Dalton."

His expression turned infinitely weary. And then he actually quoted a figure.

It was more than she wanted to pay, but having seen what Mrs. Scruggs could accomplish in a day, she knew that the housekeeper would be worth it. "All right. I can manage that."

A muscle ticked in his square jaw. "But you're *not* going to manage it, because *I'm* going to pay Mrs. Scruggs, and my paying her is only fair."

"Fair? Suddenly you're all about what's fair?"

"I'm living in your house, using your upstairs office and not paying rent. Paying the housekeeper—whom *I* hired—is the least I can do."

When he put it that way, it sounded way too reasonable. "All right. You can pay her for as long as you're staying here. But as soon as you move out, *I* pay her."

"Agreed."

She eyed him warily. "There's a gleam in your eyes. I don't trust that gleam."

"Gleam? Clara, I have no idea what you're talking about."

And then the baby kicked. She winced and rubbed her side.

"Let me feel." He said it softly. Hopefully.

And she just stood there, staring up at him as he took that last step that brought him up close and personal, and then put his warm, long-fingered hand over hers.

It felt good, his hand on hers. It felt really, really good. "Um…here." Her voice kind of broke on the word. And then she slid her hand out from under his and clasped it, moving it to where she felt the kick. "Yeah." She smiled in spite of herself. "That's it."

"I feel it," he agreed as the baby poked at his palm, then poked again. He was watching their hands, all his attention on the movement beneath them. And then he lifted his gaze and met her eyes. His were the clearest, most beautiful blue right then. "Clara…" His voice was rougher now, even lower than usual.

She just stared up at him, still annoyed with him for not even telling her about Mrs. Scruggs, and at the same time swept up in the moment, in the intimacy of it—their baby kicking, her hand over his. She should have glanced away.

But she didn't.

And he saw it, saw the yearning in her eyes. She knew he saw it by the way he said her name. Again. "Clara…"

Step back, her wiser self commanded. But she didn't listen to her wiser self. It felt too wonderful, to be so close, so…connected. It made her forget that she was pissed off at him, forget the hurt that still lingered between them, forget that if she *was* going to kiss him, first she wanted to talk to him.

Really talk to him. For a long time, in detail. She wanted to know all the things he'd never told her on the island. About his parents and his childhood, about his work—did he actually *like* being a banker?—about his marriage to Astrid and what had gone wrong with it. About why he sometimes seemed like two different people: the domineering, oh-so-well-bred banker on one hand. The sexy, adventurous charmer from the island on the other.

Who *was* he, really?

But his hand was on her belly, and his eyes were holding hers. His briefcase dropped from his other hand and hit the floor with a definite *thunk*.

And when he lowered his mouth to hers, well, there only seemed one thing to do in response to that.

Lift it up and take it.

Chapter Six

Damn. It's good to be home, Dalton thought as Clara swayed toward him.

Her lips—softer even than he remembered—met his. He breathed in the sweet, unforgettable scent of her skin. She let out a tiny moan.

And broke the kiss.

Too soon.

But he wasn't deterred. He let the hand on her stomach slide on around to clasp her lower back, bringing her belly, so full with their baby, to press against him. It felt good, that hard roundness pushing at him. Insistent, undeniable, this new life that they had made.

He lifted his other hand to cradle her face. "Ah, Clara…"

She scowled up at him. "I don't know why I just kissed you. I shouldn't have. It's wrong."

"Uh-uh. Not wrong. Very, very right."

"You piss me off. And we should talk first. There's so much to say."

"Shh."

"See?" She pouted up at him. "Now you shush me."

"Shh…"

He dipped his head and their mouths touched again, brushing. So sweet, the scent of her, Ivory soap and apples, all clean and fresh and crisp.

This time, she didn't jerk away.

Instead she opened on a sigh. He deepened the contact—not too much. Enough to run his tongue along the edges of her upper teeth. On the island, sometimes they would kiss for the longest time, sitting on the white sand beach under the shade of a big umbrella, or in bed, their bodies joined, holding out against the rising wave of pleasure, making it last.

Kissing and kissing until he knew he couldn't hang on one second longer. He was going to go over the edge and there was no way he could stop it…

She always tasted so good, like sunshine and sugar cookies. And freedom, somehow. All the freedom and ease and fun he'd never allowed himself.

Oh, there had been women. Lots of them. Before Astrid. Before he'd decided it was time to find the right wife, before he'd finally accepted that the thrill of being wanted by a stranger never seemed to last beyond the first encounter.

So he'd given up on one-night thrills. He'd pursued and married Astrid. And had it all gone to hell.

Only to meet Clara, on the island, while he was still reeling from how completely he'd messed up the commitment that should have been for a lifetime.

Clara.

It had never occurred to him that a woman could be so many desirable things at once. Thrilling and funny and cute. More than cute, beautiful. A pure temptation and a true companion.

Clara. He had found her when he wasn't ready. And then he'd blown it royally. He'd let her get away.

He wouldn't make that mistake a second time.

And it was so good, to be kissing her again. It made him ache. It made him hard. It made him want to *keep* kissing her.

He only cared that they didn't stop. He eased his fingers up into the warm, thick fall of her hair and cradled the back of her head, gathering her marginally closer.

Her hands slid upward, hesitating at his chest. For a second, he was afraid she would push him away.

But no. With a soft little moan, she grabbed his shoulders. And then she twined her arms around his neck.

And kept on kissing him.

He took advantage of that long kiss to touch her some more, to learn again the silky texture of her skin, to track the tempting indentations of her spine. He clasped her waist, thickened now with the baby. But still, that feminine curve was there, inviting the span of his hands.

He knew it couldn't go on forever, that kiss. Still, a groan of regret escaped him when she took her mouth away from him and settled back onto her heels.

She looked up at him, mouth plump and red from kissing him, eyes soft as melted chocolate, cheeks beautifully flushed. "Kissing," she said, reproaching him. "We shouldn't be kissing."

"Too late." He bent and scooped her up under the knees with one hand, keeping the other at her back.

"Dalton!" She laughed in spite of herself as he cradled her snugly against his chest. "Put me down."

"Bed or couch?"

"Put me down," she ordered again, shoving at his chest a little—but she was still laughing.

The bed was closer. He carried her through the arch to the side hallway, detouring into the master suite, taking her straight to the bed and putting her down on it, then dropping to sit beside her. "Scoot over."

"What?"

"Make room for me." He toed off one shoe and it fell to the rug.

"Wait a minute, Dalton. We have to—"

"Too late." He dropped the other shoe, turned and swung his stocking feet up on the bed, using his shoulder to nudge her a little more over to the center of the mattress, clearing the space he needed beside her. "Ah. There." He raised his arms and laced his fingers behind his head. "That's better."

"You're going to get your gorgeous designer suit all wrinkled."

"Sometimes a high price must be paid."

She'd rolled to her side so she and her giant belly were facing him, and she braced her elbow in the pillow, her head on her hand. "You remind me of the island Dalton right now...so free and fun and easy."

"I *am* the island Dalton."

She only looked at him, her expression growing serious. "Tell me about your parents."

He didn't particularly want to talk about them. They had done their job, fed him, clothed him, brought him up to be a functioning member of society. And now they were gone. What was there to say about them?

But it seemed she wanted him to talk about his parents. *Really* wanted it. And he understood that to get what he needed from her, somehow he was going to have to give her the things that *she* needed.

"Dalton?" she prompted.

So he told her, "They were older. My mother was in her early forties when I was born."

"*Were* older?"

"My father died a decade ago, of heart disease. My mother of cancer a couple of years later." He rolled his head toward her.

"I'm so sorry…"

"Why? It's not your fault."

She gave a sad little laugh. "Dalton, it's just what people say, that's all. An expression of sympathy for what you've lost."

"I know. It's the right thing to say. And you said it sincerely. I believe you. But still, it's not your fault."

She reached out and touched the side of his face. Cool and soft and welcome, her touch. "Did they…hurt you somehow?"

He studied her face. He really liked her face, the pretty oval shape of it, the fullness of her mouth. From the first, she'd seemed the most open, accessible person he'd ever known.

"Dalton?" She was waiting for him to answer her question.

"No, they didn't hurt me. They were distant, both of them. They wanted a quiet house, with everyone speaking in hushed tones. I don't think they really wanted children. But they did want an heir, an Ames to take over when my father stepped down. And then I finally came along. They were glad on one level. The bank would be run for another generation by an Ames. But they also found me messy and loud and inconvenient."

"I cannot imagine you as messy and loud."

"They eventually whipped me into shape—figuratively speaking, of course. There was no actual whipping. Just constant and steady pressure to conform to the life they had laid out for me."

"And you did conform?"

"I did. There were a lot of time-outs. Sometimes I lived in my room for days at a time. I was very resentful."

The big eyes brimmed with sympathy. "They didn't… love you?"

"I don't know about that."

Again, she brushed the side of his face with her tender hand. He felt that light touch all the way down to that place inside him that only she had ever reached. "You don't know if they loved you," she echoed in a sad little whisper. At his slight shrug, she said, "I'm so sorry…"

He tried a smile to lighten the mood. "There you go being sorry again."

"You try to make a joke of it, but I think they were hard on you. Too hard."

"Maybe. Their expectations were high, and I learned to rise to them. I am now the man they wanted me to be."

"Except…on the island?" she asked only slightly sheepishly.

He admitted it. "Yes."

She made a small, thoughtful sound. "So on the island you were your natural self, the person you might have been, if your parents hadn't been so strict and controlling."

He stroked her hair—and she let him. "I suppose you could look at it that way."

"Because it's the truth."

"Clara, who knows how I would have turned out with a different set of parents? I might have ended up a hopeless slacker, totally lacking in focus and drive."

"Oh, I seriously doubt that."

"But you never know."

She searched his face. "Do you plan to be strict and controlling with our daughter?"

"I plan to take care of her and make sure she gets whatever she needs."

Her expression had turned severe. "If you're too strict, you'll be dealing with me."

"I have no doubt on that score."

"Rules and boundaries are important. But there has to be love and leeway, too."

He turned on his side, rested his head on his arm. "I promise to be guided by you—or at least, to listen if you tell me I'm being too harsh."

She looked so hopeful. "You mean that?"

"I swear it." He watched her smile. Like the sun peeking out from behind a gray cloud, that smile. "Your turn."

"For?"

"I have questions."

She gave a low chuckle. "Anything. Just ask."

"At the hospital, your great-aunt Agnes said something disparaging about your father and his 'behavior.' What behavior was she talking about?"

"That detective you hired didn't tell you?"

"I didn't hire him to find out about your father."

"Right." She winced and reached behind her.

"What?"

"Pillow…" She felt around at her back. He reached over her and grabbed the pillow she was searching for. "Thanks." She took it and propped it between her thighs.

He touched the tip of her nose. "So. Your father…?"

"It's beyond tacky. You won't approve."

"Tell me anyway."

"Fair enough. My father had a mistress while he was married to my mother."

"Shocking," he teased.

She wrinkled that pretty nose at him. "It went on for two decades."

"It? You mean he messed around with different women?"

"No. Just one. Her name was Willow Mooney, and he was with her for more than twenty years. My father essentially had two families at the same time. There was my mom and my brothers and sister and me, living the good life in the big house my dad built when he and my mom got married. And then there was Willow, with her five kids, in a smaller place across town. That went on, him going between my mother and Willow, for over twenty years. And all along, he publicly claimed my half siblings. All nine of us have the Bravo name. I'm glad for that, on the one hand. I love my half sisters and brothers. But that he rubbed his other family in my mother's face, well, that hurt her. A lot. And the day after my mother's funeral, my father married Willow and moved her into the house he'd built for my mother. He's gone too now, my father, but Willow's still alive."

"Your father sounds like a man who never worried about what people might say."

"No, he did not. He never considered who he might hurt, either. He just did whatever he wanted to do. He was a big man, with a lot of charisma. And when he would look at you, *talk* to you, he made you feel like you were the only other person in the world." A faraway smile tilted the corners of her mouth. "I was always so certain that I was his favorite, of all his kids. But then my sister Elise told me she knew that *she* was the favorite. And my half sister, Nell? The really hot one, with the tats and the auburn hair?"

"Yes. I remember her."

"Nell told me a year ago that she always knew Dad felt

she was the special one. Even if you didn't like the things he did, somehow you couldn't help liking *him*, couldn't help feeling you were special in his eyes."

"Including your aunt Agnes?"

"*Except* for Aunt Agnes. She never liked him. And she can hold a grudge. She never forgave my father for keeping Willow on the side, for having children with her, children that he treated just the same as his children by my mother. My father sent all nine of us to college—or at least, those of us who wanted to go. And when he died, he left each of us a nest egg, a trust fund that matured when we reached the age of twenty-five. Agnes believed that my mother's children should have gotten more than Willow's kids. And to this day, she's furious that Willow ended up with my mother's house."

"You all appear to get along, though—your siblings and half siblings. At the hospital, everyone seemed on pretty good terms."

She reached down and readjusted the pillow between her thighs. "We've had our issues, but we've mostly worked through them. Our parents' choices are not our fault. But my mother, well, he hurt her so bad. She was proud, my mother. From a wealthy, respected family. Before she died, when she was so sick, she whispered to me that she wanted to hate my dad, that he had humiliated her for most of their married life."

"Then why didn't she leave him?"

"She loved him. Loved him enough to live with the humiliation of him having another woman. To her, having him half the time was still better than not at all."

"What about the other woman?"

"Willow?" Clara made a scoffing sound. "Are you kidding? Nobody knows what goes on with Willow, not even her own kids. I suppose she loved him, too. She started in with him when she was only eighteen. And I'm pretty certain she was true to him, through all the years he was married to my mother. And since he died, there's been no other man in her life—at least, not as far as I know. And in this town, if Willow Mooney Bravo started dating, it would be major news." She taunted, "Admit it. Your parents would never approve of my crazy family."

Probably not. "We'll never know. They're not around to judge."

"Judge? Is that what they would do?"

Absolutely. "I have no idea. And I don't care."

She tipped her head a little, studying him. "Liar."

"I'm not lying. I honestly don't care what they would think or do."

"But you can guess."

"Clara. It doesn't matter."

Her gaze turned assessing—and then softened. "Well, that's kind of sweet…"

"What?"

"You're trying to protect me, trying not to hurt my feelings."

"I'm trying to keep you focused on what matters. *You* matter." He put his hand on her belly. It felt good there. "Our baby matters. The life we're going to make for her, *that* matters."

"We'll have to work together—I mean, to make sure there's consistency for her, between your house and mine."

He considered letting that question stand and simply answering it as a what-if. But no. "You're assuming that you and I will be living apart."

She chewed on her lower lip a little. "That *was* our agreement, remember? You're only here to help out. You go when the baby comes, or when I say I want you to go."

He lifted his hand from her stomach and laid it, lightly,

on her soft cheek. "I think you're going to need a lot of help from me, Clara. For a very long time."

She drew a tiny, hitching breath. "What does *that* mean?"

"It means…" He canted closer. Until their lips were only an inch apart. Her warm breath touched him. He stroked her hair and whispered, "I'm going nowhere. You're mine and so is the baby. I keep what's mine. You should start getting used to that."

Her eyes went wide—and then narrowed. "Overbearing much?"

"I'm tired of dancing around the truth, that's all."

"What truth? I mean, wasn't Astrid yours? And look what happened there."

"That was different."

"How?"

"It just was. Take my word for it."

"Who's dancing around the truth now?"

Instead of answering that one, he said, "Oh, and with Astrid, there was no child involved."

She seemed to puzzle that through. Then finally, "Well, okay. I can see that. Kind of. But that hardly makes *me* yours."

He thought, *You are mine*. He said, "I just think you should start to accept the fact that I'm not going away."

"And yet you had no problem sending *me* away on the island."

Terrific. Back to that again. Patiently, he said, "My mistake."

"Yeah, and it was a doozy."

"I'm not denying that. I thought I could walk away from you—I even thought that walking away was the best thing to do. I had it all wrong and it took me a while to figure that out."

"What about the next time you're confused about something that means the world to me, the next time you walk all over my poor little heart?"

"There won't be a next time. Not about this."

"I'm not going to end up like my mother, Dalton. Lying on my death bed, feeling like I was cheated of what I wanted most in life."

"You won't end up like your mother."

"Suddenly, you can guarantee that? Mr. *I'll only mess it up if we try to take it off the island*?"

It would be so easy to become impatient with her. "Have you been listening to anything I've been telling you? I know what I want now, and that isn't going to change. I want our baby. And I want you. I'll take care of both of you. And there won't be some other woman in another house across town. I'll be true to you, to our family." He eliminated that inch between his mouth and hers. She gasped as his lips touched hers. He kissed her fast. And hard. "You need to get over what happened on the island so we can move on." He gentled his touch, stroked her hair some more.

She caught his wrist and pushed his hand away. "The really scary thing is I want to believe you."

It was more than he'd expected her to admit at that point. He felt a warm curl of satisfaction. "I will take care of you, Clara."

"I don't need taking care of."

He ran the back of his fingers down the side of her smooth, cool throat. "Yes, you do."

Her eyes went wide again and her mouth had gone so very soft. He moved in to steal another sweet kiss.

And the doorbell rang.

She immediately tried to rise.

He clasped her shoulder and eased her back down. "Stay there. I'll get it."

She wore a mutinous look. He was preparing to remind her that she was supposed to be staying off her feet. But then she only said, "All right," and settled against the pillows with a sigh.

He sat up, slipped his shoes back on and headed for the foyer, pausing to tuck in his shirt and straighten his jacket before he opened the door.

Wouldn't you know? It was the best friend she'd almost married. Just the guy Dalton *didn't* want to see.

Ryan had one arm braced on the doorframe and a smirk on his much-too-good-looking face. "I was beginning to wonder if anyone was home."

"Sorry," Dalton replied with zero sincerity. "Clara and I were relaxing…in the bedroom."

Ryan gave him nothing for that but a quirk of one eyebrow. "I came to see how she's doing." He straightened from the doorframe and waited for Dalton to step back and let him in.

Dalton held his ground. "She's doing fine. Resting."

The other guy grunted. "Come on, man. She's not going to be happy with you if she finds out you wouldn't let me in to see her."

Unfortunately, he was right. Dalton gave it up and moved aside.

Ryan circled around him and headed for the side hall and her bedroom.

Dalton really wanted to follow. But he knew what would happen when he got to Clara's room. She would ask him to leave so that she and her good friend Ryan could have a little quality time together. And then he *would* leave—after making himself look like a jealous fool.

No. Better not to issue a challenge he couldn't hope to win.

So he conceded the field. For now. He went upstairs and changed into jeans and a T-shirt. Then he settled in his temporary office and dealt with messages and email for a while, ears tuned for the sound of footsteps in the foyer downstairs.

He never did hear Ryan leave.

After an hour upstairs, he grew impatient. So he went down. A glance out the front window in the dining room showed him that the other man's quad-cab was no longer parked at the curb.

"Dalton?" Clara called to him from the great room. He went on back there and found her sitting on the sofa, propped up on the pillows, her laptop open on her stretched-out legs. She closed it and set it on the coffee table beside her. "Ready for dinner?"

He nodded. "I'll dish it up."

"May I please eat at the table like a normal person, without you on my case to sit on the couch?"

"Why not?" He didn't see that it could hurt. She seemed rested. And her color was good.

He set the table and put out the food. They sat down together and ate.

"Excellent," she said. "The admirable Mrs. Scruggs knows her way around a leg of lamb."

He probably ought to keep his mouth shut about Ryan. But to hell with that. "So, what did your good buddy Ryan have to say for himself?"

She sipped her ice water. "Not much. He just wanted to see how I was doing."

"I didn't hear him leave. How long did he stay?"

Another sip of water, followed by a wary look. "Half an hour or so." Her voice was a little too offhand.

Leave it at that, he told himself. And then didn't. "What is it with you two, anyway?"

She set down her glass. Slowly. "Rye's my friend. Has been since the second grade. We're the same age, so we went up through high school together. We just always got along. We both like camping and hiking, so over the years, we've gone on a lot of wilderness trips together."

"Always as…just friends?"

She thought that one over—and then answered obliquely, "Ryan's always been there for me whenever I needed him."

So he asked her directly, "Are you in love with him?"

"No."

"Were you in love with him in the past?"

She ate a glazed carrot. Slowly. "No. And where are you going with this, Dalton?"

"I'm just trying to understand, that's all."

"You've never had a really close woman friend?"

"No."

"What about Astrid?"

"We're on good terms now. But no. We're not what you would call close."

"Well, try and imagine that. A really close friend who just happens to be female. Rye's like that for me, a really close friend who's a guy. We trust each other and enjoy being around each other. We have a good time together. And we're there for each other."

"Has he ever been in love with you?"

She met his eyes—and then glanced away. Bingo. "I don't know how to answer that."

"Yes, you do. You just don't *want* to answer it."

Clara started to warn him to mind his own business. But then she couldn't quite do it.

Because of the kiss they'd shared in the hallway earlier. And the way they'd talked honestly together, lying on her bed, side by side, facing each other. Because of the way he'd touched her face and stroked her hair—so tenderly, as though he really did care.

Because he'd said she was his, and when she'd called him on that, he hadn't backed down. He'd insisted that he wasn't going away, and he'd seemed to mean it.

Every day he spent with her brought her closer to believing that he really did want more from her than a chance to do right by the baby they'd made. That he really did still want *her*, that there was more between them than their mutual obligation to their child.

No, she wasn't sure of anything. Not yet.

But tonight he had let her know him a little. And that gave her hope, all shiny, bright and new.

She said, "Rye's always claimed to be in love with me."

Dalton's jaw got that twitch in it and his blue eyes flared hot. "I knew it."

She took a bite of the excellent lamb. "You don't understand."

He made a low, growly sound. "You just told me straight out that the guy wants you. And an hour ago, he was in your bedroom with you."

"It's not like that, not at all. Not to mention, have you *looked* at me lately?" She patted the giant mound of her belly.

He seethed where he sat. "I look at you all the time. You're beautiful." What a fine thing to say. Too bad he was grinding his teeth as he said it. He went on, "Before Ryan was in your bedroom with you, I told you that *I* want you—which means I'm not okay with him being in your bedroom."

She didn't know whether to laugh—or groan. "He's

my *friend*, Dalton. How many times do I have to say it? There is absolutely nothing romantic or sexual going on between Ryan and me."

He wouldn't leave it alone. "But you almost married him and you just said that he's in love with you."

"I said he *claims* he's in love with me."

"You're splitting hairs."

"Not really. I think it works for him to believe he's in love with me. I'm safe to be 'in love' with, because I'm his friend and I don't want anything from him but to *be* his friend. And he knows that. He's not ready to get serious with a woman, but he can tell himself that if I'd only give him a chance, he would go for it." She cut another bite of lamb. "He's kind of a player, actually. The women come and go."

Dalton looked at her sideways. "Have you ever told him what you just told me?"

"Repeatedly."

"And he tells you you've got it all wrong, right?"

"That's only because once he admits I'm right, he'll have to start asking himself why he doesn't fall for someone who'll fall right back."

"Women," he muttered. "Always making the simplest damn things so complex."

"Speak up." She cupped her hand to her ear. "I can't hear you."

"Clara. He's a guy. Guys aren't all that deep."

"That's just not true."

"Yes, it is. He wants you or he doesn't. He's told you that he *does*. When you try to argue with him about it, he *still* says he wants you. He was going to marry you, for God's sake! You should take the man at his word—and stay the hell away from him."

"You haven't been listening to me, Dalton."

"Yes, I have. I heard every word you said."

"Well, just for the sake of clarity between us, allow me to repeat myself. One, Ryan is my friend. I will not be avoiding him and he's always welcome in my house. And two, he's *been* my friend for the last twenty-plus years. I think I understand him better than you do."

He glared at her for a full count of five. And then, at last, he asked with excruciating civility, "Could you do me one favor?"

"What?"

"When he comes over, could you bring him out here to the great room?"

She longed to tell him he was being ridiculous, that he should get over his jealousy of Ryan, as there was absolutely nothing to be jealous of.

But then again, it did seem important to him. And there was this tender new closeness she was starting to feel with him. She didn't know where it might lead them, but she wanted to encourage it.

Plus, she really had no special need to have Ryan in her bedroom. She could take it to the sofa, if that made Dalton feel better.

"All right," she agreed. "I'll bring him out to the great room—but you should know that Rye's friendship is important to me. He *will* be around. He's not going away."

"You've already said that."

"But were you *listening* when I said it?"

"Yes." Flatly, matter-of-factly. And maybe a little wearily, too. "Look. We'll work it out, him and me, in our own way."

Clara blinked and couldn't help gaping. *We'll work it out, him and me, in our own way.* It was word-for-word what Ryan had said when she'd told him to tell her if Dalton gave him trouble. What did they mean, exactly, when they said that? Was it some kind of guy code?

He must have noticed her surprise. "What's the matter now?"

"How, specifically, will you 'work it out' with Rye?"

He didn't answer. Suddenly, he was all about the leg of lamb again.

She refused to let it go. "Dalton. How?"

He chewed and swallowed. "You don't need to worry about it."

"If there's going to be trouble between you and Rye, of course I need to worry about it."

"I didn't say there would be trouble."

"You didn't say there wouldn't, either."

He dug into the asparagus salad. She kept her mouth shut and waited him out.

Finally, he sent her a grim glance. "Leave it alone, Clara. It's all going to be fine."

Did she believe him? Not exactly. He seemed much too determined. She had a very strong feeling that he would be taking the whole thing up with Ryan, just the two of them, one-on-one.

That felt like a bad idea.

But was it, really?

Or was it only what both men had told her? That they needed to work it out between them, without her trying to control the outcome?

She could easily get acid indigestion trying to decide how to proceed from here. Already she regretted being so frank with him about her relationship with Ryan. It was a sensitive subject between them, and Dalton didn't need to hear right out loud that Ryan thought he was in love with her.

Except. Well, if she and Dalton were going to try to

build something together, he deserved to know the truth about stuff like that, didn't he?

Ugh. Who knew? She certainly didn't.

"Finish your dinner." He said it gently.

She left her fork where it was. Chin high, she met his gaze across the table. "I need for you and Rye to get along."

"And I'm going to see that you get what you need."

"You'll be civil to him, maybe even try to get to know him a little?"

"Yes. I'll get along with him."

"Promise me?"

His gaze didn't waver. "You have my word."

Chapter Seven

Dalton regretted his promise the minute it came out of his mouth. When two men got into it over a woman, anything might go down. Sometimes a man needed to prove a point and do it strongly. Sometimes words just weren't enough. Things could get broken. Furniture. Heads.

He considered himself a civilized man. His well-bred, strictly controlled parents had seen to that. They were relentless in their calm, cold-blooded way. And they had drummed good manners and exemplary behavior into him, brought him up to be a pillar of his community. But in his heart, in his blood and his bones, he had a wild streak and he knew that.

The wild streak had its uses. It made him competitive, made him want to win. And that kept him at the top of his game at the bank, kept his instincts sharp and his mind focused.

The wild streak did, however, require effective managing.

Over the years, he'd learned a number of ways to keep it under control. The three top methods of wild-streak management? Sports, sex and not really giving a damn.

Sports were always useful. He worked out every day, played tennis and racquetball. He'd played football at Yale. Because there was nothing so satisfying as getting together with your peers and knocking each other around over a piece of pigskin.

As for sex, he and the wild streak had very few issues during the years he'd chased an absurdly long string of women. In fact, if he could have uninhibited sex with Clara right about now, the wild streak probably wouldn't be all that obsessed with neutralizing whatever threat Ryan posed to his future with her. But Clara was in no condition for enthusiastic lovemaking—and they hadn't reached that point again yet anyway.

And as for not giving a damn?

Not an option. Not when it came to Clara. He cared for her. A lot. From the very beginning, back on the island, she had somehow slipped right through all his carefully constructed and rigorously maintained defenses. Ending it when the vacation was over had failed to make him care less. In fact, as time went by, he only cared more.

And now there was the child, too.

Bottom line: he cared too much, she refused to marry him and they weren't having sex. Even working out like a madman couldn't neutralize the wild streak under these conditions. The wild streak needed an outlet. Spilling a little of Ryan's blood would certainly take the pressure off.

Except that he'd gone and promised Clara he would get along with the guy. To her, that meant no violence.

It was a problem.

So at first, he tried not to think about it. He put the matter out of his mind. He ran four miles the next morning and the morning after that. Both days, he visited Quinn Bravo's new gym, where he pushed his body to the limit, trying to open the valve a little and let out his pent-up frustration.

The next day, Thursday, he took Clara to see her doctor. The doctor looked her over and expressed approval that her blood pressure had gone down. Not only that, but the circles beneath her eyes had faded and her color had improved. The doctor's prescription: Clara should keep on doing exactly what she'd been doing.

Clara groused all the way home. She'd had about enough, she said, of living between her bed and the couch. And *next* week, when she would see Dr. Kapur again, she planned to insist that the doctor allow her to get out of the house for at least a couple of hours each day.

Dalton tried to be sympathetic. He wasn't really good at sympathy, but he understood that most people needed it. And for Clara, he was willing to make an effort to deliver it.

He said he knew she must be frustrated.

She muttered, "You try lying around the house all day when you should be getting things done. See how much *you* like it."

He reminded her that her job right now was to take care of herself and the baby, that she was doing really well and she ought to focus on the positive, rather than on temporary restrictions, which were for her own good and the good of the baby.

That really pissed her off. The minute they got home, she went into her bedroom and slammed the door behind her.

So much for sympathy.

He considered whether or not to knock on the door

and try to work it out with her. But he had a bad feeling that attempting to employ reason with her right then would only make things worse. So he went upstairs and got some work done.

At dinner, which she insisted on eating at the table, she was quiet. At first.

And then she shocked the hell out of him by putting down her fork, delicately wiping her mouth with her napkin and announcing, "Okay, I was a bitch this morning. It's not your fault that I'm on bed rest and you were only trying to make me feel better. I'm sorry I jumped down your throat."

He put down his own fork, wiped his mouth with his napkin and pushed back his chair.

Her eyes wide and worried, she watched him circle the table to get to her. When he reached her side, he held down his hand.

She gave him a look of pure suspicion before cautiously laying her fingers in his. He tugged her upright, grasping her chair with his free hand and sliding it back as she rose to her feet.

"What's the matter?" she asked nervously.

"Not a thing." He let go of her hand—so he could wrap his arms around her. "Apology accepted."

She pressed her palms to his chest and refused to lift her gaze to his. "I just hate lying around all the time." She stuck out her lower lip when she said it, which was way too damn cute.

He bent close. "Yes. I think you might have mentioned that once or twice already."

Finally, she looked up at him. "You're being wonderful to me."

"Would you prefer it if I were meaner?" He wanted to kiss her. A lot. But he kept himself in check until he could be more certain of her mood. A kiss might set her off again.

"I…"

"You…?" He rubbed his hand up and down her spine, enjoying the shape of her under his palm and the feel of her belly—and their baby—pressed against him.

She murmured, "There are things I want to talk about."

Talk. He probably should have known. "Such as?" He caught a lock of her hair and wrapped it slowly around a finger.

"Do you actually like being a banker?"

"Yes. I do."

A puzzled frown. "Why?"

"I like variety in my work. Banking uses a number of different skill sets. A banker has to deal quickly, make decisions and act on them. I like that. I like a fast-moving environment. I'm tenacious and detail-oriented—both good qualities for a banker. But I'm also flexible. I don't get stuck. If one way doesn't work, I'll come up with another. I like things rational. Banking is extremely rational. Also, in banking, there are clear rules. Bankers should be rule-followers. And I am. I know what's right and I do it."

A laugh burst out of her—and then she blushed and covered her mouth. "Sorry."

He wasn't offended. Why should he be? "No apology is necessary. You see more shades of gray in the world, and in life, than I do. I think we're both aware of that."

"Ah," she said, her face glowing up at him.

He couldn't resist. He dipped his head and took that sweet, soft mouth of hers. She stiffened.

But then she sighed and kissed him back.

It was a slow kiss, one he was careful not to sink too far into.

When he lifted his head, she said, "You realize the

qualities you just named off could work in any number of fields."

"But I'm an Ames. Born and bred to run the family bank. It's convenient that I actually *like* doing what I was born to do—and are you through eating?"

When she nodded up at him, he scooped her high into his arms. At her squeak of protest, he suggested, "Let me help you get back to lying around."

She made a delicate grunting sound. "As if I have a choice."

He carried her to the sofa and gently set her down on it, quickly bending to remove her open-backed shoes and then lifting her legs up across the cushions. "There. You're off your feet."

She pulled a face, but she stayed where she was. "I have another question."

He dropped into one of the wing chairs. "Of course, you do."

"When I went to talk to Astrid…?"

Astrid. Hadn't they said all they ever needed to say about her? Cautiously, he offered, "Yes?"

"Well, I asked her what went wrong between you two. She said that I should ask *you*. So, um, I am." She swallowed and licked her plump lips and he wanted to kiss her some more. He wanted to pick her up in his arms again and carry her to her bedroom. He wanted to spend the night in her bed with her, with his body wrapped around hers, his hand on her belly, so he could feel it every time the baby moved. "Dalton, why did you and Astrid get divorced?"

He hardly knew where to begin. "Well. I suppose the simplest way to put it is that I didn't understand her. I thought that she and I wanted the same things from our marriage. I had it all wrong."

"Wrong, how?"

"I married Astrid because I liked her."

"Liked?" She made the word sound as though it tasted bad.

He tried not to become annoyed with her attitude. "Yes. I liked Astrid. I respected her. She's intelligent and I found her pleasant and easy to be with. She's beautiful and well connected and she can really work a room. I was certain she would make me the perfect wife."

Clara had her lips pressed tightly together. He knew she was trying really hard not to ask the big question.

He let her off the hook. "Go ahead. Say it."

"I, um, notice that you've yet to use the word *love*…"

"It was time for me to get married." He sounded stuffy and pompous even to his own hears. "Astrid was an excellent choice for a wife."

"You're saying that no, you didn't love her?"

"As I said, I felt she would be a fine wife and that we would get along well together."

"Dalton, how many times do I have to ask you? Did you ever tell your wife that you loved her?"

"I did. Yes. It seemed the right thing for a man to say to his wife."

Clara groaned. "The *right* thing? Oh, Dalton. I don't even know where to start."

"Then don't?" he suggested hopefully.

She drew in a slow breath and let it out hard. "Let me guess. You said that you loved her. But she didn't believe you."

"Correct. She didn't believe me."

"Because you *didn't* love her. She was only a function to you. You married her for all the wrong reasons."

He couldn't let that go. "Excuse me. I admired her. I enjoyed being with her, found her intelligent and attractive. And I actually *liked* her. There was nothing wrong with my reasons."

"Except that none of them mattered, because you didn't *love* her, and for a marriage to work, it has to start with the love."

"I disagree. Love is…unquantifiable. It's not a basis for anything."

"Oh, Dalton." She shut her eyes, shook her head. "You just don't get it. Love is the basis for *everything*."

"I'll say it again. Compatibility, friendship and mutual respect. Those are the best foundations for a successful marriage. And I'll have you know that I *was*—and still am—very fond of Astrid."

"Fond?" She looked at him as though he'd just poked a puppy with a sharp stick. *"Fond?"*

"Yes. Fond. And you can stop groaning and rolling your eyes. You're right. For Astrid, love was the issue."

"Of course love was the issue. It always is."

He disagreed. But he knew that saying so wouldn't help his case. Instead he said, "I thought highly of Astrid. I enjoyed being with her. But whatever kind of love she was looking for from me, she never got it. And so she left me. At first, I was furious. And then I was…bewildered. I'd thought we were on the same page about what we wanted from life—and from each other. I misunderstood her completely and never managed to give her what she wanted."

Clara's outraged expression had softened. She said in a marveling tone, as if it was big news, "So that's what you meant on the island, when you said you didn't want to keep seeing me because you would only screw it up—you meant you had screwed it up with Astrid and you were afraid it would only happen again with me."

"Isn't that exactly what I told you at the time?"

"But don't you see? You *telling* me and my *understanding* it are not the same thing."

Would he ever truly comprehend the female mind? Doubtful. "By the time I met you on the island, I was past the bewildered stage and had moved on to being reasonably certain that there was something wrong with me, something I just don't get about women."

"Well, I don't think there's anything wrong with you, Dalton. I really don't. But I would definitely have to agree that there's something you're not getting about what a woman wants."

Annoyance prickled along his skin. *Patience*, he told himself. He said, "It had been so good with you and me, I was hoping to skip the part where it all goes to hell."

"Uh-uh," she said, her sweet mouth all pursed up.

"Uh-uh, what?"

"At the time, I just didn't get that. When you said you didn't want to see me anymore because you would screw it up, I took it as one of those 'It's not you, it's me' lines, just a bunch of crap you put out there so I wouldn't make a scene while you were dumping me."

Carefully, he reminded her, "How could I dump you? We'd agreed on the two weeks together with no strings and—"

She cut him off with a sharply raised hand. "I remember the agreement. It's way too clear in my mind. Please don't tell me about it all over again." Her cheeks were flushed.

"You're getting upset. That's not good for you."

"You're wrong. It's good for me to get this off my chest."

Was it? How? As if he knew. He was completely out of his depth here, and sinking fast.

She had more to say. "I was thirty years old on the island, Dalton. By thirty, if a woman isn't happily married to her high school sweetheart, chances are she's listened to a whole bunch of garbage lines and never wants to hear another one."

"Didn't I just tell you it wasn't a line? Didn't you just say that you finally *understand* that it wasn't?"

"I… Yes." She stared at him, narrow-eyed. And then she sagged back against the cushions and confessed, "All my life, I've been careful about romantic relationships, you know?"

An encouraging sound seemed appropriate there, so he made one. It worked. She continued. "I saw the way my mom suffered over my dad. Sometimes he would be gone for days at a time. It was like she never had a whole husband of her own. I didn't want anything like that to happen to me. So I've been careful. Maybe too careful. I dated, I even had a couple of steady boyfriends. But I never let myself get in too deep. I had my family, and some really good friends. I had Rye."

He felt his gut clench. He didn't want to hear about her precious Rye—and she knew it.

"Dalton." She said it softly, but her tone held rebuke. "It was never like that, with me and Rye."

"Like what?" he demanded, before he had a chance to think about whether or not he could actually deal with her answer.

And then she said, "Before you, I slept with two other guys. Neither of them was Ryan. We've never been lovers, Rye and me. That's just not who we are together. We're friends. Best friends. Not friends with benefits. Not ever."

The knot in his stomach untied itself, just like that. He felt very glad he'd asked. "Well, all right, then." He prompted, "So you dated, but you never got in too deep with any guy…"

"That's right." She picked up her story where she'd left

off. "And I've always been something of a workaholic. I knew I wanted my own restaurant and I drove myself to make that happen, then I drove myself harder to make the café a success. I didn't start feeling like maybe I'd missed out on finding something good with a guy until last year. Suddenly, I was thirty and it occurred to me that maybe I was never going to find someone special. And then I went to the island and there you were and it was like…" Her sentence faded off.

And just when it was getting really interesting, too. "Keep going."

She shook a finger at him. "Don't you dare laugh."

"I won't."

She lay back and spoke to the ceiling with a sigh. "It was like it was meant to be, you and me."

Meant to be. He considered himself a practical man, in no way romantic. But *meant to be* sounded damn good coming from Clara.

She went on, "On the island, by the end of those two weeks we spent together, I was way too invested in my fantasies of how it would turn out with us." She rolled her head toward him.

He captured her dark gaze. "I really blew it, huh?"

A smile ghosted across her mouth. "You could say that."

"By trying *not* to mess it up, I messed it up bad."

"Well, yeah." At least she said it softly. And her cheeks were sweetly flushed.

He asked, "Do you think that maybe you could let all that go now—or, if not now, possibly sometime in the near future?"

For several very long seconds, she only stared at him. He began to resign himself to being told that she could never forget that he'd turned her down on the island.

And then she held out her hand to him.

Now, there was a fine moment. He caught her fingers, got up from the chair and sat on the edge of the couch, beside her.

"I'm working on it," she whispered.

His heart tap-danced in his chest. At that moment, he was absolutely certain that it was all going to work out. She *would* marry him, as she needed to do right now or sooner, for the sake of their little girl.

Impatience spiked within him, to get things settled, get a yes from her so they could move it along, get the license, step up in front of the preacher or the justice of the peace, have it all properly sorted out before the baby came.

And what about Denver? He needed to get her to move to Denver. And he didn't delude himself. That would not be easy. The woman had deep roots in her hometown.

There was so much to work out. And the first step was getting her to say she would marry him.

But then she went on. "I'm glad we have this time together, to get to know each other in a deeper way, to find out if maybe we might have some sort of future together— I mean, beyond the whole coparenting thing."

Maybe?

She hadn't moved past *maybe*?

Maybe didn't cut it. Not by a long shot.

"Dalton, is something wrong?" Those big eyes begged him to tell her what he knew damn well she didn't want to hear.

He ordered himself not to get discouraged. They *were* making progress. And if he jumped down her throat now, he could lose the ground he'd gained. "Something wrong? No. Not a thing."

She chided, "I don't believe you."

He bent close and whispered, "Nothing is wrong."

And then he kissed her. Slowly. With feeling.

When he lifted his head, she gazed up at him dreamily.

Yes. Everything would work out. She just needed a little more time.

He felt confident, good about everything. It was all going his way.

And then, the next morning, her best buddy, Ryan, showed up at the door. Again.

Clara kept her promise and led the other man to the great room. She even invited Dalton to have a seat, too. So he took one wing chair and Ryan took the other.

It was awkward—for Dalton, anyway. They talked about Ryan's bar and Clara's restaurant, about Clara's friends and relatives. And about how he, Dalton, was managing to run Ames Bank and Trust from Clara's home office.

Yesterday, Dalton had been relieved to learn that Ryan had never been in Clara's bed. But the longer he sat there across from the other man, the more he found himself thinking that it might have been better if the guy had been her lover, after all. Clara had said that Ryan had a lot of girlfriends. And he was a charmer, good-looking, with an easy smile and an infectious laugh. For a man like Ryan, an unattainable woman would be rare, a prize.

About fifteen minutes into the visit, Dalton got a call from the main office, one he had to take. He went upstairs and dealt with it and the chain of memos that resulted from it. When he went back downstairs, he heard Clara laughing in the great room.

"Rye. Stop it. I mean it." And she laughed some more.

She sounded so happy. Dalton tried to remember how many times she'd laughed like that with him. Not enough times, that was for damn sure. He entered the great room through the kitchen just in time to see the other man bending over the sofa and kissing her on the cheek.

Yes, all right. It was a friends-only sort of kiss. But he didn't like the adoring look on Clara's good buddy's face when he did it.

"Call me if you need me." The guy was still bending over her, one hand braced on the sofa back.

"You know I will."

Ryan straightened and spotted Dalton standing there. "Later, man," he said flatly, with a quick dip of his chin.

Dalton gave him an answering nod. "Have a good one." He tried not to grind his teeth when he said it. The other man headed down the side hall toward the front door and Dalton told Clara, "I'll see him out." It might be a good moment to have a private word with Mr. Best Friend Forever.

But Clara nixed that. "Don't be silly. Rye knows the way."

A few seconds later, the front door opened and closed.

Right then, as he heard the door shut, Dalton made up his mind.

He and Ryan needed to talk. And it would be better to do that somewhere away from the house. Better if it was just the two of them, without Clara there to run interference.

Yes. Away from the house.

And soon.

It was easy to set up.

That afternoon, from upstairs in the office, Dalton called Ryan at McKellan's. "This is Dalton Ames. We need to talk."

The other man didn't seem the least surprised to hear from him. "I'm listening."

"Face-to-face."

"Fine. You want to come here?"

"That'll do. Ten minutes?"

"I'll be looking for you." And Ryan hung up.

Downstairs, Dalton discovered that Clara had moved to her room. She had the door shut, which worked for him. She could be sleeping. No reason to disturb her and then have to decide whether or not to lie to her about where he was going.

He found Mrs. Scruggs bustling around in the kitchen. He let her know he was going out and would return within an hour.

"Good enough," the housekeeper said. "If I'm finished here before you get back, I'll leave a note for Clara that you won't be long."

"Perfect. Thanks."

McKellan's Pub took up most of a block on Marmot Drive. It had lots of windows in front, with blue awnings that sheltered café tables right there on the sidewalk. Inside, it was all dark woodwork, accent walls of aged brick and cozy nooks where good friends could share a pitcher and order burgers.

Ryan was waiting at one end of the long wooden bar behind which ranged shelf upon shelf of gleaming liquor bottles. There were three rows of beer taps spaced along the bar. And even at two thirty in the afternoon, the place had enough customers to make a visitor feel confident he'd come to a popular, well-run establishment.

"You want a beer?" Ryan asked when Dalton reached the stool where he sat.

"No, thanks."

"Have a seat." The other man nodded at the stool next to him.

"A private word would be better."

Ryan didn't argue. "My office, then?"

"That works."

So Ryan led the way under an arch at the other end of the bar and through a short hallway to a pair of swinging doors. The doors led into the kitchen. The cooks called greetings and nodded as Ryan went by. He led Dalton through another door. In there, row upon row of metal shelves were stacked with restaurant and bar supplies. They went down one long row with full shelves to either side, finally reaching Ryan's office.

Ryan shut the door and went around to drop into the chair behind the desk. "Sit."

Dalton took a chair next to a sad-looking plant and considered where to start. As he did this, he and Ryan stared at each other—or maybe *glared* was more the word for it.

Finally, Dalton spoke. "I want to marry Clara."

Ryan swung his booted feet up on the desk. His chair squeaked as he leaned back. "Yeah. She told me." And then came the taunting grin. "Too bad you're having zero luck getting a yes out of her."

Dalton kept his breathing slow and even. "She's having my baby and I'm living in her house, taking care of her. We're working it out."

Ryan made a dismissive sound low in his throat. "In other words, she's told you no and she's letting you stay with her because she's got a big heart and you're the baby's dad."

That stung. Dalton decided a change of focus was in order. "Clara says that you think you're in love with her."

The pub owner didn't even flinch. "That sounds like Clara. I 'think' I'm in love with her. I more than *think* it. I *am* in love with her, always have been. She's turned me down over and over—but I almost got my ring on her finger at Christmas. Maybe one of these days I'll get her to actually go through with the wedding."

Over Dalton's dead body. "Don't you think if she wanted to marry you, she would have done it by now?"

"I could ask you the same question." Ryan studied his boots. "And I've got a business to run. So whatever it is you came here for, can we get down to it?"

"She's having my baby. She needs me and the baby needs her father."

"So?"

"Back off. Get out of the way."

The other man glanced up from his careful contemplation of his boots. The two locked eyes. Ryan said, "I'm not *in* your way, man. You're in your *own* way. She's not going to marry you just because there's a baby. She's a hopeless romantic. She wants it all—your life in her hands, your heart on a platter. She won't settle for less."

It wasn't anything Dalton didn't already know. "You're distracting her from making the right decision."

Ryan just kept on. "Plus, she's always been kind of trigger-shy in relationships. She told me she really fell for you on that Caribbean island. And then *you* called it off. Major fail. You might never get past that."

"I'll say it again. You're a distraction for her."

"No, I'm not. I'm her friend. At a time like this, she needs her friends."

"You're all over the map," Dalton accused. "You say that you're in love with her one minute, and that you're not in my way the next." He brought out the big guns, the ones Clara herself had provided. "My take is you love chasing her—you love it because you know it's safe. You know she's never letting you catch her and you're never going to have to step up and make it real."

That struck a nerve. Ryan's boots hit the floor and he

jumped to his feet. His eyes were ice as he rounded the desk. Adrenaline spurting, Dalton rose to meet him.

When they stood toe-to-toe, Ryan muttered, "You know jack about what goes on between Clara and me."

"I know enough. Do the right thing. Go find yourself a woman of your own."

Ryan got that look, eyes narrowed, every muscle ready.

Dalton gave him the necessary nudge. "Go ahead. Take your shot."

Ryan did just that. He feinted left, followed by a clean, swift uppercut.

The punch took Dalton hard on the jaw. He saw stars as his head snapped back. But he recovered quickly, regained his balance and faced the other man eye to eye. Slowly, he raised his hand to his face and shifted his jaw from side to side, causing a faint crackling sound.

Ryan held out both arms to the sides and groaned at the ceiling. "Are we doing this or not, man?"

Dalton tasted the copper tang of blood on his tongue. He wiggled his sore jaw some more and admitted, "I told Clara I would get along with you."

Ryan let out a bark of laughter. "Too late for that—and she's asking too damn much, anyway."

Dalton scowled. "You know…"

"What?"

"You're right." He jabbed twice with his left, just to throw the other man off.

Ryan laughed some more, easily leaning clear of each blow—and into the right cross that Dalton finally sent crashing into the other man's very handsome nose.

Chapter Eight

Ryan flew backward with a heavy grunt and staggered against the desk. He shook his head to clear it, and blood flew from his nose.

Then he jumped right up again and waded back in.

Dalton was ready for him with a left hook. Ryan blocked it and delivered another dizzying right.

They went at it for real then, knocking over both chairs, breaking the pot the sad plant was sitting in, ending up on the floor, where they grappled for dominance. Blood streamed from Ryan's nose, more so when Dalton gained the top position and punched him in the face again. They rolled. Ryan was on top. He punched Dalton in the eye. They rolled some more, neither of them managing to stay on top for long, both of them grunting and breathing heavily by then, grinding pottery shards and loose potting soil into their clothes.

It ended when the door opened. A guy in a chef's hat stuck his head in and shouted, "All right, enough!"

The whole thing was so damn stupid. Apparently, Ryan thought so, too. He started laughing again. He was a mess, blood all over his face, his nose and left eye swelling. Dalton didn't kid himself that he looked any better.

They rolled apart and sat up, arms on their bent, spread knees, sucking in air hard and fast.

The chef asked, "Anybody need a doctor?"

Ryan sent Dalton a questioning glance. When Dalton shook his head, Ryan said, "Thanks, Roberto. We're okay."

The chef watched them with mixed resignation and disdain. Finally, he announced, "Tim from Diageo is waiting out front."

"Have Benny deal with him." Ryan prodded the cut under his left eye.

"If I leave, are you two gonna behave yourselves?" Roberto glared from Ryan to Dalton and back to Ryan again.

"Yeah," Ryan said.

"We're finished," agreed Dalton.

The chef ducked out. Dalton got up and held down a hand. Ryan took it and Dalton helped him to his feet.

Dalton said, "Well, that didn't solve a damn thing."

Ryan shrugged. "Kind of satisfying, though."

Dalton stared around at the general devastation. "Sorry about your office."

"No big deal. That plant was half-dead anyway."

Dalton looked down at his bloody, dirt-smeared shirt and slacks. "I need to clean up a little before I go."

Ryan swiped drying blood from under his nose. "It's not going to help. She'll know exactly what you've been up to."

Dalton only looked at him.

Finally, Ryan grunted. "Men's room is back out past the kitchen, through the swinging doors. We walked right by it on our way in here."

The scent of Mrs. Scrugg's savory chicken and dumplings filled the air, and Clara was working on her laptop in the great room when she heard Dalton let himself in.

She expected him to come looking for her the way he always did when he entered the house. The baby kicked. She put her hand on the spot, knowing he would want to feel it, too. A smile of greeting rose to her lips—and faded when she heard his footsteps on the stairs.

He must have work he had deal with...

But then, a minute later, faintly, she heard the water running up there.

A shower? At four in the afternoon?

She shrugged. Maybe he'd been working out over at Quinn's gym and needed to freshen up. She focused again on the restaurant accounts, and then Renée called.

Clara was just wrapping it up with Renée when she heard Dalton coming back down the stairs. She sat up a little taller against the pillows, aiming a smile of welcome his way as she heard his footsteps approaching down the side hall.

Her smile died a quick death when she saw his face. He stopped near the kitchen island and stared at her, one-eyed. Because his right eye was swollen shut.

And the shiner wasn't all. He had a giant purpling bruise on the left side of his jaw, a mean-looking cut on his forehead that he'd doctored with those little bandage strips—and his lower lip was split.

She said into the phone, "Renée, I need to go."

"Sure. We're pretty much done anyway. Tomorrow, then?"

"Bye." Clara hung up and swung her feet to the rug.

"Don't get up." He came for her.

Ignoring his command, she gained her feet, braced her belly with one hand and rounded the couch to meet him. "Oh, my God. What happened? Were you mugged?" Instinctively, she reached to touch the giant swollen bruise on his chin.

He caught her outstretched fingers and kissed them with his poor, battered lips. "It's nothing."

"Nothing?" Her heart was beating much too fast and her stomach churned. "Wrong. My God, look at you. Is anything broken? We need to call an—"

"Clara, we don't need to call anyone. Don't get excited, okay?"

"I damn well *will* get excited." She rubbed her belly in an effort to soothe both herself and the baby, and said furiously, "This is outrageous. We need to get you to the hospital. You could have a concussion, broken bones…"

"Shh…" He looked down at her fondly, with a twinkle in his good eye.

A *twinkle*? Somebody had just beaten the poor man to a pulp and he could stand there and *twinkle* at her? She said smartly, "Don't you dare shush me. Not now. If someone's attacked you, we need to—"

"No one's attacked me." He put his hands on her shoulders, turned her around and pointed her toward the sofa cushions. "Go on. Lie back down. Please."

She shrugged off his hands and faced him again. "Tell me what is going on."

That twinkle? Gone now. He looked suddenly somber. She peered at him more closely, frowning.

Wait a minute. Did he look just a little bit guilty?

She demanded, "Tell me. Now."

He put his hand to his jaw and winced as he prodded at it.

She accused, "See? Your jaw is broken. I knew it."

"My jaw is not broken," he said wearily. "Please go back to the sofa."

"Fine." She reached around to rub that sore spot at the base of her spine. "I'll sit down and put my feet up. And then *you* will tell me what happened and how."

He didn't look happy. But he did give her a reluctant nod. "All right. The sofa."

So she marched back where she'd been, lowered her body with slow care and stretched out her legs across the cushions. "There. I'm on the sofa." She made a space for him next to her and patted it invitingly. "Sit here." He hesitated. And then, at last, looking a little like a condemned man on his way to the gallows, he trudged over and dropped down beside her. She patted his thigh. "Are you *sure* you don't need medical attention?"

"Positive."

"All right, then. Talk."

Another hesitation. And then finally, "I went to see Ryan."

In the space of an instant, her fear and worry vanished, to be replaced by a burst of sheer fury. "Wait. No. I don't believe it."

"Clara, I—"

She cut him off. "You got in a *fight* with Ryan, didn't you?"

He put up both hands. "Now, Clara. Take it easy. It's not good for you or the baby if you let yourself get worked up."

"Answer the question."

"Clara, I—"

"*Did* you get in a fight with Rye?"

He muttered a low curse. "Yes."

She gaped at him, the hot ball of anger in the center of her chest gradually increasing in size. And intensity. "I don't believe this. This isn't happening. You're a *banker*, for heaven's sake. Bankers don't get in brawls."

"Look. I apologize. It shouldn't have happened."

She sputtered, "You…you *apologize*? You can't see out of one eye, your lip's split, your jaw is the color of a ripe eggplant—and all you've got is you're sorry?"

"Clara, I—"

She didn't even let him finish. "One thing I asked of you. One thing. To get along with Ryan…"

"Clara, come on…" He reached out a placating hand.

She batted it away. "How messed up is *he*?"

Dalton scowled through his bruises. "He's fine. About the same as me."

"The same as you?"

"Isn't that what I just said?"

"The same as you is definitely not fine."

"Damn it, Clara, I—"

She cut him off again. "Where is he now?"

He rubbed his sore jaw some more and muttered, "I left him at that bar he owns."

As mad as she was at him, she still worried he needed to see a doctor. And should she trust him when he said that Rye was fine? She had to know for herself. So she grabbed her phone and autodialed his cell as Dalton protested, "Clara, come on. I said he's all right…"

She sent him a fulminating glance and gestured sharply for silence.

Rye answered on the second ring. "How's your boyfriend?" He actually dared to sound smug.

Oh, she was going to kill him—as soon as she finished murdering the man beside her. She glared at Dalton and muttered to Rye, "I take it you're okay."

Rye actually chuckled, causing Clara to feel as if the top of her head might pop off. "I'm not all that pretty at the moment. But neither is he, right?"

"I swear, Rye. If you were here, I'd beat you up myself. Did you *have* to get into it with him?"

"Good question. Let me think. Uh, yeah. Yeah, I did—and if you ask him, I'm betting his answer will be the same."

"Men," she grumbled to herself. And then she said to Rye, "I can't talk to you now."

"Hey. *You* called *me*."

"Goodbye, Ryan." Disconnecting before he could say another annoying word, she tossed the phone on the coffee table.

Dalton said, "See? He's fine. We're both fine."

She folded her arms and rested them on the high swell of her stomach. "You could have broken a bone, gotten you head bashed in, ended up in the hospital breathing through a tube."

"Now, Clara, come on. You know you're overdramatizing."

"Dear Lord, give me patience."

"We just needed to get a few things straight, Ryan and me."

"By beating the crap out of each other?"

He swore low—as if that was some kind of answer.

She sneered. "So, now do the two of you have it all worked out?"

"It's a guy thing. I don't expect you to understand."

She seethed at him for a good count of five. And then she realized she couldn't talk to him any more than she could to Ryan right now. "Get up, please."

He frowned—or at least, she assumed it was a frown. Hard to tell with all the swelling. "Why?"

"I want to go to my room and you're in my way."

"Clara…"

"Get up."

Looking all grim and put-upon—as though *she* were the problem and not two pigheaded, ridiculous men—he rose and moved away from the couch. "All right. Maybe it's a good idea if you give yourself some time to cool off a little."

She pressed her lips together, pushed herself to her feet, grabbed her laptop and phone and headed for the bedroom.

He called after her, "I'll bring you some dinner. That chicken smells wonderful."

She stopped just past the kitchen island and turned to him. "I'm not hungry, thank you. All I want is for you to leave me alone." And then she turned on her heel and lumbered to her room.

When she got there, she couldn't quite stop herself from slamming the door behind her.

Clara stayed in her room all that evening, only opening the door once at around seven when he knocked and insisted that she had to eat something. She took the tray from him and shut the door in his face.

The next day was Saturday. She ate breakfast sitting across the table from him, but she resisted his efforts to make peace. Once she'd eaten, she returned to her room.

She wasn't really angry anymore by then. Just deeply disappointed both in Dalton *and* in her lifelong friend.

And of course, word spread quickly among her family and friends that Dalton and Rye had come to blows in the back of McKellan's.

Elise and Tracy came by that afternoon. They made sympathetic noises at Dalton, whose face was a rainbow of colors, his jaw enormous, his right eye looking as if he would never be able to see out of it again. Clara took the two women to the back deck and gave them iced tea. They tittered and whispered that she ought to see Ryan.

"He's at least as bad off as Dalton," Tracy announced with something way too close to glee. "His nose looks like a giant tomato."

Tracy sighed in an absurdly dreamy way. "A lot of people think it's kind of romantic, the two of them fighting over you."

"A lot of people are idiots," Clara replied.

That snapped Tracy out of it. "Ahem, well, yes, Clara. They certainly are."

"Dogs fight. Tomcats fight. Men should be better than that."

"True," intoned Elise. "Too true." But Clara didn't miss the look she shared with Tracy, or the way the two of them were trying so hard not to grin.

Aunt Agnes came by after church on Sunday. She took one look at Dalton, pressed her perfectly manicured hand to the giant turquoise necklace that draped halfway down her bony chest and let out a cry of dramatic distress. "Oh, you poor man. I heard about what happened. I'm so sorry you were attacked."

Clara couldn't let that stand. "He wasn't attacked. It was a backroom brawl. And Dalton gave as good as he got."

Agnes did a little tongue-clucking. And then she told Dalton, "Ryan McKellan was not properly brought up. Hasn't Clara told you? His father deserted the family when he was only a baby. He and his brother, Walker, were raised by their mother and a bachelor uncle." She turned accusing eyes on Clara. "Without the steadying hand of a father, children grow up wild and undisciplined, lacking in self-control." Her gaze swung back to Dalton and she poured on the sugar. "I do hope Clara is taking good care of you."

Clara couldn't help remarking, "Actually, Aunt Agnes, I'm in no condition to take care of anybody. Dalton is supposedly here because *he* wanted to help take care of *me*."

"Of course I remember that, dear. I'm not as young as I once was, but I'm far from senile. And a man and a woman should care for each *other* in difficult moments of life. Even if you can't be up and around, you *can* be supportive in an emotional sense."

Clara reminded herself that you could never win an argument with Aunt Agnes. She kept her peace.

Agnes gave Dalton a beatific smile. "I just hope you're all right."

Dalton said he was doing fine and then Agnes mentioned what a beautiful day it was and she would just *love* a little private time with Clara out on the deck.

Private time with Agnes was the last thing Clara needed right then. But her great-aunt insisted. So out they went. Dalton brought them cold drinks and left them alone.

At which point Agnes started in with one of her lectures. "You need to marry that man, dearest. You need to do it right away. He's a good man from a fine family. With a man like that, you'll never want for anything."

"I'm not wanting for anything right now. I have plenty of my own money."

"Money isn't all of it. You know that very well. And you must face the fact that whatever happened to cause that altercation between him and Ryan McKellan had to have been greatly exacerbated by poor Dalton's frustration that you keep dragging your heels about marrying him. You've driven him to distraction and violence with your shilly-shallying and you need to stop stalling and let him do right by you and the child."

"I'm not stalling. And it is in no way my fault that he and Ryan behaved like a couple of yahoos and beat each other's faces in. Plus, I've never said I would marry him."

"Of course you will marry him."

"Aunt Agnes. Stop. Please. Dalton and I are...working on this." Or they had been, until he traded blows with Ryan and thoroughly pissed her off.

"Working on it? What does that mean?"

"Just what I said. We're working on our relationship, trying to figure out if maybe we could make a life together, after all."

"There is nothing to figure out."

"I disagree."

"The man is ready to marry you. And you're hanging back, hesitating to make the right choice because of the emotional damage inflicted upon you by a father who refused to honor his marriage vows and broke your poor mother's tender heart."

"That's your opinion."

"An informed opinion that happens to be correct."

"You need to let it go, Aunt Agnes. It's not your decision to make."

Agnes harrumphed. "Well, at least you're finally admitting that you're trying to work it out with him." She heaved a giant, weary sigh, followed by, "I only hope you come to your senses and say yes before your baby grows up into another fatherless hooligan, brawling in bars and unable to hold a productive place in society." There was more in the same vein. Finally, Agnes seemed to run out of steam.

She finished her lemonade and admired Clara's xeriscape garden and got up to go, bending as she left to give Clara a kiss on the cheek. "I only want what's best for you and the child."

"I know, Aunt Agnes. And I love you."

"I love you, too, dear—I'll see myself out."

Clara remained on the deck alone for a while, enjoying the May sunshine, and admitting to herself that some of what her overbearing great-aunt had said did make sense. Her mother's longtime suffering over her father's betrayal had gotten to her, made her warier than she might otherwise have been, made her more careful about giving her heart.

That night at dinner, when Dalton tried again to make it up with her, she said, "There are two things I won't put up with from you, Dalton, if we're ever going to make it work together."

He stared across the table at her through his one good eye and said, "Let me guess. Cheating and lying."

Her heart softened toward him—minimally, anyway. "That's right." It came out sounding almost tender.

And he replied gently, "I told you I would never cheat on you. And I won't. And I have not and will not tell you any lies."

So much for tenderness. Her fork clattered against her plate. She scoffed, "Oh, please. Did you or did you not tell me that you would get along with Ryan?"

"I did. And I *am* getting along with Ryan."

"Have you *looked* in a mirror lately?"

He set down his own fork, but quietly, and enjoyed a slow sip of the pricey red wine he'd served himself with dinner. "What a woman sees as 'getting along' and what a man has to do to reach a mutual understanding with another man can be two different things."

She was having that exploding-head feeling again. "Are you trying to tell me that when you said you would get along with Ryan, to you, 'getting along' meant it was perfectly okay for you to beat each other up?"

"No. When I said I would get along with him, I fully understood that to you, getting along does not include hitting, punching, kicking or physical aggression of any kind."

"So, then, you lied to me."

"No. I did what I had to do to get along with your good buddy. I went to see him to talk it out with him, and when talking didn't get us anywhere, we...did what men do. It wasn't any fight to the death, Clara. It was more on the order of a conversation. With fists."

"A conversation."

"Yes. Exactly."

"Right this minute, Dalton, I feel like we're not even from the same planet."

He drank more wine. "I am no liar. And I admit I do regret promising you that I would get along with your friend. But that's because 'getting along' in this case means something different to you than it does to me. And while we're on this subject, for the record, I just want to say that when you asked me to 'get along' with Ryan in the way that *you* mean 'getting along,' you were asking too much."

"Asking too much because I didn't want you two beating the crap out of each other? That's insane."

"No, it's not. Ask Ryan. He thinks you were asking too much, too."

"How can you possibly know that?"

"He told me. After he punched me the first time and before I hit him back."

"Wait a minute. Ryan threw the first punch?"

"Yes, he did. But only after I egged him on."

Clara decided she'd had more than enough of this bizarre conversation. "I can't talk about this anymore."

He picked up his fork again. "Maybe you ought to ask Ryan."

"Ask Ryan what?"

"If he thinks that the two of us are learning to get along."

After the meal, Clara went to her room and did just that.

Ryan answered on the first ring, his voice full of good cheer. "Hey, beautiful. What's up?"

"How are you feeling?"

"A whole lot better than I look. How's your boyfriend holding up?"

"About the same as you. I have a question…"

"Shoot."

"Would you say that you and Dalton are learning to get along?"

"Yeah," he answered breezily, without even giving it a second thought. "I would. I wasn't sure about him at first. I knew that he'd hurt you and I didn't like that. And initially, he kind of comes across like he's got a poker up his butt. But I'm getting used to him, beginning to think he's for real. After our conversation the other day, I'm starting to see he's an okay guy."

"Your *conversation*…?" Good grief. Dalton had called the fight a conversation, too.

"Yeah. You know the one. It started with talking and ended up on the floor."

"I just… Rye, I don't get it."

"Get what?"

Where to even begin? "You. Dalton. Beating each other up in the interest of communication."

Rye chuckled. "You're thinking too much. Guys aren't that complex." And again, he was sounding way too much like Dalton. Then he spoke more softly. "I think you ought to give the guy a chance."

Her throat clutched. "Oh, Rye…"

"You and me, Clara, we're good friends. I've tried for years to tell myself that someday it will be more. But I'm getting a clue finally. It's not going to happen, is it?"

Softly, she answered, "No, Rye. It's not."

"Yeah. Got it." His voice was tight, pained. He was quiet. And then he said, "You and your boyfriend need to work a few things out. And you know what? I'm kind of an idiot sometimes, but I get it. I'm not helping by getting in the way."

She insisted, "You're not in the way."

He grunted. "Yeah. I kind of was. But not anymore."

Tears burned at the back of her throat. She gulped them down. "What does that mean? Are you saying you won't be my friend anymore?"

"No way am I saying that. I'm your friend, Clara. And I'm here for you. Always."

She still didn't get it. Not really. But it did seem that he and Dalton had come to some sort of understanding, after all. So maybe she needed to just leave it alone for now.

And maybe Rye thought so to, because he changed the subject. "How about you? How're *you* feeling?"

She sat up a little and rubbed at that achy spot at the base of her spine. She'd been having some cramping. And then there was the heartburn and the swollen ankles. "Like I swallowed a whale. I cannot wait for this little girl to be born."

"Follow the doctor's orders. Stay off your feet."

"I am, I am."

"You need anything, call."

"I will." She thanked him and said good-night.

Faintly, from the great room, she could hear the TV,

which meant that Dalton hadn't gone upstairs yet. She considered getting up, going to him, making up with him, and telling him all about her surprising conversation with Rye.

But her back was achy and the cramping was getting to her. She didn't have the energy to crawl out of bed. She just wanted to rest a little. Maybe after a nap, if he was still up, they could talk.

Turning onto her side, she put a pillow between her knees and one under her belly. As she closed her eyes, the bedside clock showed nine thirty. Her whole body ached and she feared it would take her forever to drift off to sleep…

Clara woke with a startled cry.

She stared in disbelief at the clock. Somehow, hours had passed. It was one in the morning—and she was right in the middle of a full-on contraction.

She rode it out, holding her belly, watching the clock, trying to relax, to breathe slow and even, and switching to panting when the pain got too bad.

After about a minute that went on for a decade, the contraction faded off.

Then she realized that the bed was wet. With a whimper, she pushed back the covers and stared at the soggy sheet.

Her water had broken.

Chapter Nine

Clara crawled from the bed and staggered to the door that led to the hall. Flinging it open, she shouted up the darkened stairs.

"Dalton!" And then she sagged against the doorframe and waited for him to come.

He did, and quickly. Not twenty seconds after she called his name, he came racing down the stairs to her, wearing only a pair of boxers, his thick dark hair, slept on, standing on end, his battered face grim. "The baby…?"

She didn't know whether to laugh or cry. So she kind of did both as a chuckling sob escaped her. "I woke up." She looked down at the little puddle at her feet. "My water broke."

He took her by the shoulders, his big hands so careful, so gentle. "Do you need an ambulance?"

She bit her lip and looked up into those beautiful eyes of his—well, one beautiful eye, anyway. The other was still swollen shut. *Oh, dear Lord. Let our baby have his eyes.* "I just need you to get dressed and dig out my suit-case." It was all packed and waiting in the space under the stairs. "And take me to the hospital."

"You got it." And then he pulled her close for a quick hug, tipping up her chin afterward, bending close and brushing his nose against hers in the sweetest, most reas-suring little caress. "Don't move. I'll be right back."

She forced her lips to turn up into a smile for him, and gave him a nod.

And then he let her go. The instant he did, she wanted to grab him back. She swallowed the cry that rose in her throat. Slumping against the doorframe again, she watched him race up the stairs.

"Dressed," she reminded herself out loud. "I need to get…"

And then another contraction took her. She groaned and slid down the doorframe, ending up on the floor on her hands and knees, riding it out, hearing the strangest animal grunting sounds and then gradually realizing they were coming from her.

He was back at her side wearing jeans and a T-shirt just as the pain eased again. He dropped down to the floor with her and put his wonderful, warm hand on her back. "You sure you don't want me to call an ambulance?"

"No. No, I think I'm doing fine." Fine being a rela-tive term when you're pushing a baby out. "But maybe we ought to time a few contractions and call Dr. Kapur to make sure I'm far enough along that I need to go the hospital."

"Clara. You're on your hands and knees and your wa-ter's broken. We're going to the hospital. You can call the doctor on the way."

With a groan, she eased back and sat on the floor. Her

nightshirt, which had Not Everything Stays in Vegas printed down the front, was gooey-wet around the hem. "I need to get my clothes on."

"How about a pair of flip-flops and a robe?"

"And a clean shirt and panties—and a pad for all this dripping. Please?"

He wrapped his big hand around her neck and pulled her close enough to press a kiss to her forehead. His lips felt warm and soft and so reassuring against her skin. "Don't move," he whispered.

"Not a problem," she groaned.

And then he was up and heading for her bedroom closet.

He got her the dry clothing, which she changed into between contractions. He grabbed her purse for her, dug out her suitcase from under the stairs and herded her toward the back door. "Car keys?" he asked as they went out.

"I have them in my purse."

He helped her climb into the passenger seat and hooked the seat belt loosely, by holding it extra-extended as she worked the clasp. Then he took her purse from her, dug out the keys and went around to get behind the wheel.

Another contraction hit as he backed down the driveway. She groaned and panted as they sped off down the dark street. As soon as that one faded, she autodialed Dr. Kapur's office and got the night answering service. They promised to have her doctor call her back "very soon."

It was a short ride to the hospital complex, which stood in a wide curve of Arrowhead Drive southeast of town. Dalton pulled up under the porte cochere at Emergency and helped her inside. She leaned on the admission desk, groaning through another contraction and he went back out to park the car.

When he returned, she was sagging against a wall.

She'd preregistered a month before, so all she'd had to do was sign in.

Things were pretty quiet tonight, so she didn't have to wait long to be loaded into a wheelchair and rolled down a series of hallways to Labor and Delivery. There, they put her in a suite.

A nurse came. There were questions. And an exam.

It all got a little hazy after that. The pains came and went, growing longer and closer together. There were ice chips on her tongue and people speaking gently, encouragingly to her.

Dr. Kapur appeared and told her she was doing fine, spoke of dilation and effacement and all those words Clara had learned in order to try to understand what would happen when the baby came, all those words that seemed like nonsense syllables to her now that it was really happening. Now that her baby was actually being born.

And there was Dalton. Right with her through it all, letting her take his hand and bear down hard on his poor fingers every time the pain struck.

In the end, with her sleep shirt up to here and her knees spread wide and her hair dripping sweat into her eyes, they told her it was time to push and she pushed and pushed and screamed. And screamed some more.

Once, right after Dr. Kapur said the head was crowning, she turned to Dalton, who was still there beside her. She yelled at him that it was all his damn fault and she couldn't do this.

And he said, "You can, sweetheart. You know you can."

She blinked the sweat out of her eyes and wondered if he'd really called her sweetheart—or if she'd only imagined it in the endless, unreal agony of the moment.

It didn't seem the kind of thing that Dalton might say.

Not the rich banker Dalton, the Dalton of the Denver Ameses.

But maybe the island Dalton. Yes. The island Dalton *had* called her sweetheart. More than once, now that she thought about it.

"Did you just call me sweetheart?"

Before he could answer, Dr. Kapur said, "Push, Clara. Push."

And after that the pain was worse than ever as she bore down, moaning and crying, mangling Dalton's hand in her clutching, clawing grip.

"Here she is," said the doctor. "Just a little more…"

And Clara gave one more mighty, never-ending push— and her daughter slid out of her and into the world.

At first, there was no sound. The baby was quiet.

Clara clutched Dalton's hand even tighter than before. "Is she okay, is she—?"

"She's fine, fine," promised Dr. Kapur, clearing the airways with two swipes of her fingers, then lifting the gooey, white-streaked little body, still attached to the cord, and setting her on Clara's belly.

Clara touched the small head covered with slimy dark hair. "Are you…all right?" she asked the baby in a broken whisper.

And then the tiny mouth opened to let out a whine, followed by a squeal and then a full-out lusty cry.

Clara held the little body to her and turned her streaming eyes to Dalton. "Oh, Dalton. Look. I did it. It's okay. She's here."

And he bent close and kissed her sweat-slick forehead and whispered, "Great job, sweetheart," breathing the sweet words onto her clammy skin.

And she cried a little harder. Because their baby was with them, and safe. And he was right there beside her, calling her sweetheart, being absolutely wonderful when for months she'd been telling herself she had to learn to accept that she was doing this alone.

He straightened beside her. And she stared up at him. He was looking at the baby, a slight smile curving his beautiful black-and-blue mouth, his eyes alight from within—even the swollen one had a gleam in it. The swelling had gone down just enough that she could see a sliver of the eye beneath.

Oh, dear God, she thought. *I love him…*

And then, as though he'd heard her say those words aloud, he turned his eyes to her. He frowned. "Clara? What is it?"

She swallowed, forced a wobbly smile and lied, "Nothing. I'm just…happy, that's all."

"Are you sure? You seem—"

"I'm positive." She cut him off before he could get specific about exactly how she "seemed," while at the same time, her heart was chanting, *Dalton, I love you. I love you so much…*

Outside, dawn was breaking. Clara cried some more and watched the rim of light growing brighter above the mountains. She held her newborn baby and promised herself that she wouldn't think anymore about loving Dalton.

Not for a while yet.

Chapter Ten

Two hours later, after Clara and Dalton had eaten breakfast and Clara had nursed her newborn for the first time, it was just the three of them in the room.

Dalton sat in the comfortable chair by the bed with the baby cradled in his arms. He looked up from her tiny red face and caught Clara's eye.

She smiled at him and started to think how she loved him—but cut that thought off right in the middle. It was *I lo*—and nothing more. She pushed her love deep down inside her and asked, "What is it?"

He touched the tip of the baby's nose, brushed at the wisps of dark hair at her forehead. A tiny sigh escaped her little mouth. To Clara, it seemed a trusting sort of sound.

And he said, "I was thinking we need to decide on a name."

"I hadn't really thought about names," she confessed. "Is that odd?"

"Not particularly." His voice was low, a little bit rough, wonderfully tender. "You've had a lot to deal with in the past several months."

She teased, "I'll bet you want to name her after some stalwart banker ancestor. Or maybe your mother."

"Not a chance. I would like it better if she wasn't named 'after' anyone. I want her to have her own name—I mean, if that's okay with you?"

"Yeah. That's kind of nice, actually." And surprising. She would have thought he'd insist on some staid-sounding name suitable for an Ames.

The baby yawned hugely. He fiddled with the blanket, readjusting it around her scrunched-up face. "I was thinking maybe you could choose the first name. I'll take the middle one."

"All right." And just like that, the name came to her, as though it had been waiting inside her all along for her to simply let it out. "Kiera. I want to call her Kiera."

He tipped his head to the side, considering. And then, "I like it." He touched the baby's red cheek. "Kiera," he whispered. The baby made a cooing sound. "She likes it, too."

"Good, then. And her middle name?"

"Anne," he said, with certainty. And then he shot Clara a look both hopeful and hesitant, a look that did something lovely to her heart. "Is that too old-fashioned, do you think?"

"Uh-uh. I love it."

"Kiera Anne, then," he said softly.

And she agreed. "Kiera Anne it is."

They stayed the day and that night in the hospital.

Family and friends came and went. Each of Clara's brothers and sisters put in an appearance. And Rory and her fiancé, Walker. And of course, Great-Aunt Agnes.

Ryan came, too, sporting a shiner of his own and a very swollen purple nose. He brought a big basket full of baby gear, including a large pink stuffed rabbit. He and Dalton chatted easily, like a couple of old pals—old pals who'd just happened to beat each other bloody a few days before. When Ryan bent to kiss Clara on the cheek as he was leaving, Dalton didn't seem to mind at all.

Later, Earl came. He brought Dalton's assistant, Myra, down from Denver, along with a couple of colleagues from the bank.

Myra was a handsome middle-aged woman, tall and thin in a high-quality lightweight jacket and pencil skirt. She took one look at Dalton and demanded, "What in the world happened to you?"

"I fell down the stairs."

"And into someone's fist," muttered Earl on a low chuckle.

Myra wisely refrained from asking any more questions. She and Earl and the others stayed for half an hour and then headed back to Denver.

After they left, it was just the three of them—Clara, Dalton and Kiera Anne. It had been a long day and they went to sleep early. But of course, now there was Kiera, so they didn't sleep for long.

The baby woke up three times during the night. Clara practiced nursing her. Kiera latched right on and sucked like a champion. Clara glanced up and, through the shadows of the darkened room, Dalton's eyes were waiting.

They shared a smile that was intimate and companionable. She thought about how far they'd come since that day in the park in Denver.

And now she'd finally admitted to herself that she loved him.

She had no doubt that he still wanted to marry her. For Kiera's sake, if nothing else.

But were they ready for marriage yet? She just wasn't sure.

How *could* she be sure? She was thirty-one years old and in love for the first time in her life, with no real experience of what made a happy marriage work. All she knew was, if she ever did get married, she wanted to be absolutely sure it was the right choice. She wanted love and passion and honesty and a true, lasting commitment.

She whispered, "That day in Denver, when we met in the park and I told you about the baby...?" He made a questioning sound. And she said, "I never would have guessed that you would be here with me now."

He got up from the cot they'd brought him to sleep on and tiptoed to her side, dropping to a crouch so his face and Kiera's were on the same level. "You need to have more faith in me."

She almost came back with a snarky remark. After all, the way he'd treated her on the island hadn't exactly been faith-inspiring. But then, well, no. She was kind of getting past what had happened on the island. She drank in his beautiful, bruised, upturned face.

And she whispered, "You're right. Maybe I do need to have more faith in you."

He looked at the baby then, lifting his hand to touch her, running a finger across Kiera's cheek—a finger that kept going, until it brushed Clara's breast.

She caught her breath as his finger took a lazy, meandering journey over the pale, blue-veined slope of her breast and upward, leaving a sweet trail of sparks in its wake.

Kiera just kept nursing.

And Dalton's finger kept moving, across the top of

Clara's chest, over the twin points of her collarbone and then, in a smooth, knowing caress, up the side of her throat to the tip of her chin.

She asked, breathless, "Dalton?" And she lifted her head to track his movement as he straightened and rose to stand above her.

His mouth kicked up on one side. And then he bent down, bent close...

She sighed as his lips touched hers. "Dalton..." He kissed his name right off her lips.

Too soon, he was lifting away again. She grabbed his shoulder before he could escape and tugged him back down to her. "Again," she commanded.

He chuckled low.

And he gave her what she wanted, slow and light and very sweet.

Dalton drove them home the next day.

Clara half expected him to start pushing her to move to Denver. But he didn't.

And Clara didn't bring it up, either. He took excellent care of her and the baby. She didn't want him to go yet—and wait. Scratch that.

She didn't want him to go ever.

But they would get to that—to what the future would look like, to how she hoped he might be willing to relocate permanently to Justice Creek. Later. She saw no reason for them to rush into any big decisions, no reason to start asking each other the scariest questions, the ones about love and the future.

They had a newborn, which was more than enough to deal with right now. They were up half the night every night that first week. He took the baby monitor upstairs to bed with him and he came right down to help whenever she called him, no matter what time of night it was. Sometimes he came down when she didn't call, because Kiera had cried and he wanted to make sure that they didn't need him.

Also, he'd become wonderfully affectionate. He kissed her often, soft, sweet kisses. And he touched her a lot. When they sat together in the evening, sharing the sofa, he would put his arm around her and draw her close to his side. He didn't hesitate to brush a hand down her hair, to stroke her cheek or twine his fingers with hers.

At the end of that first week, Dalton took her and the baby to see Dr. Kapur. It was a satisfying visit. Kiera nursed like a champion and had gained seven ounces. And Clara's blood pressure now registered normal, her white blood cell count was back up and her iron levels were right where they should be.

And those cankles? Gone.

Dr. Kapur gave her permission to drive and return to her regular activities. "But take it easy," the doctor ordered. "I understand that you'll want to check in at that restaurant of yours. But only for a couple of hours a day at this point. If you push too hard and become exhausted, I'm ordering you back to bed again."

Clara promised she would take care of herself.

Dalton muttered, "I'll make sure she does."

Clara shot him a sharp glance for that—a glance he either didn't see, or pretended he didn't.

That evening, when they sat down to another of Mrs. Scruggs's excellent dinners, Clara tried to explain to him that she would really appreciate it if he didn't treat her like a child in front of her gynecologist.

And he growled, "Like a child? What the hell, Clara? When did I ever treat you like a child?"

"Maybe that was a poor choice of words. How about

this? I would appreciate it if you wouldn't announce to my doctor that if I don't take care of myself, you'll do it for me."

"Why not? It's the truth. If you don't, I will."

She stared across the table at him and almost wished she hadn't said anything—but then again, no. She schooled her voice to sweetness and asked teasingly, "Is this going to be our first argument since Kiera was born?"

He refused to be teased. "Answer the question. When did I ever treat you like a child?"

She set down her fork, though she knew it was a bad sign. When forks got set down at their table, arguments ensued. "All I'm trying to say is, when I promise my doctor I will take it easy, you don't have to chime in with threats."

"Threats? What threats? There were no threats. I said what I said because I care about you, because I *am* going to make sure that you don't overextend yourself."

"Sounds like a threat to me."

He set down *his* fork. "I don't make threats. I state facts."

She glared at him, at his dear, handsome face and his granite jaw where the bruising from his fight with Rye was only a shadow now. She couldn't decide whether she wanted to throw her plate of delicious stuffed pork chops at him—or march over there and kiss him until neither of them could see straight.

In the end, she didn't do either. She just started laughing.

He looked slightly bewildered. "What now?"

She laughed harder.

He asked, "Is this some kind of minibreakdown you're having?"

And by then, she was sagging in her chair, tears leaking from the corners of her eyes, waving her hand in front of her face. "I don't… It's just…"

He shoved back his chair and came around the table to her. "Clara? Sweetheart…"

She stared up at him. His dark eyebrows had scrunched together in worry and bafflement. Slowly the fit of laughter ended. She said, feeling suddenly shy, "You just called me sweetheart again."

He reached down, took her arm, pulled her up into his embrace.

She swayed against him, resting her hands on his chest. She could feel his heart beating, right there, under her palm. *Could you love me? Do you still want to marry me?*

The questions were there, on the tip of her tongue. But she didn't ask them.

She was too afraid of what his answers might be, too unsure of what she wanted in the end, anyway—oh, not about the love thing. She most definitely did want his love.

But the marriage thing…?

She was all turned around about that. They had come a long way together. But marriage seemed so huge. So final.

Better not to go there. Not yet…

"Clara." He cradled her so tenderly. And he watched her so closely, still with that worried, wary frown. "Are you all right?"

She held his gaze and nodded. "I am, yes. I…suddenly it just seemed so funny, that's all. You and me. Setting down our forks. Preparing to do battle."

With his thumbs, he wiped the tear tracks from her cheeks. "I can't promise I'll never be overbearing again. I'm an overbearing kind of guy."

"True." But she said it fondly, wearing a smile that trembled just a little.

He tipped her chin up with a finger. "Clara…" And his head swooped down. His lips met hers.

It felt so good, so right. His arms around her, his mouth brushing hers. She let out a small cry of eagerness and delight and slid her arms up to wrap around his neck.

And then they were *really* kissing, in the way that they hadn't done since the island. His tongue touched her lips and she opened for him and…

Oh, it was lovely. Her whole body tingled, coming alive. Her skin felt extra-sensitized as sweet, hot arrows of sensation zipped through her, shooting off sparks. Her breasts ached a little and she had a moment's fear that her milk might come.

But then she realized she didn't care. *He* wouldn't care. After all, he'd seen her on her hands and knees in a soggy-hemmed T-shirt in the foyer, weathering a contraction. He'd seen her push their baby out. And he was still here, still kissing her as though he couldn't get enough of her. What was a little leakage compared to all he'd already seen?

She could have stood there by the table and kissed him for hours. But then he lifted his head and framed her face in his two lean hands. For a long, glorious moment, they simply looked at each other. She stared up into those blue, blue eyes of his and never wanted to look away.

He said, "I want…" And then he didn't finish.

Tenderness filled her. He was a man who always knew how to finish whatever he started to say. But now he seemed strangely stymied.

Gently, she prompted, "You want what? Please tell me."

He touched her hair, stroking. She leaned her head into his touch. And he said gruffly, "I want to sleep with you. I want to move out of the room upstairs and into your room."

Okay, she *liked* that idea. She really, really liked it. "You should know that I can't have intercourse for—"

He stopped her with a smile—and a finger against her parted lips. "Four weeks, at least, maybe five or six. I know. I read the books."

"Um…what books?"

"The ones you left on the floor in the baby's room."

A few minutes ago, she'd been laughing hysterically. Now she wanted to cry. But in a good way. A very good way. "You read my baby books?"

A hint of alarm crossed his face. "Wait. I didn't ask you, right? You're mad because I didn't ask you…"

"Dalton, I think it's *beautiful* that you read those books."

He made a low sound in his throat, a totally charming, embarrassed sort of sound. "Well, I wouldn't go that far. It was purely practical. I needed information, and those books provided it."

"Information…"

"So I would know what to do, how to help, how to take care of you—and Kiera, too."

Tears filled her eyes again. "Dalton."

"Now you're definitely going to cry. Why are you going to cry?"

She sniffed and swallowed. "I'm not. Truly."

"Are you sure you're all right?"

"Positive—plus, if I *were* to start crying now, they would be happy tears."

"Happy."

"Yes. Happy."

His slow-growing smile made her pulse race. "So, about your bed…?" She tugged on his collar, though it didn't need adjusting. He said, "About me. In your bed…" He cleared his throat officiously and declared in a thoroughly bankerlike fashion, "I think it's a logical next step for us."

She almost laughed again. But she didn't want to scare him. "Logical, is it?"

"That's what I said, yes."

She pretended to have to consider. "It would certainly be easier for me, with you right there when Kiera cries."

"Exactly. I need to be there, not all the way upstairs when you need me."

"You'll get less sleep," she warned.

"As though I'm getting much now. No, I'll sleep better, if I can be there in the room with you."

It occurred to her that she might sleep better, too. Especially if he wrapped himself around her and held her close the way he used to do on the island.

"Say yes," he commanded, all gruff and low and overbearing.

She thought how sometimes his being overbearing wasn't such a bad thing. Sometimes it was a very sexy thing, a totally exciting, manly thing.

He bent his head and kissed her again. "Repeat after me. It's only one word. Yes." He said the word against her lips, pressing it there, feeding it to her.

"Dalton…"

"Yes."

She pulled away enough to tell him, "Sometimes there's just no backing you down, is there?"

He swooped in for another kiss. "Yes. Say it. Yes."

She wrapped her arms around him again, because she longed to hold him, because it felt so good. "All right, yes."

"Excellent." And he took her by the waist and lifted her high—and kissed her long and slow and deep as he let her slide down his big body until her feet touched the floor.

Unfortunately, that kiss got interrupted by Kiera, who

needed a diaper change and some dinner. Dalton changed her and carried her around, patting her little back, soothing her, while Clara finished her pork chop and string beans.

Then he passed her the baby, gave his hands a quick wash and finished his dinner as Kiera nursed.

Dalton moved into Clara's room with her that night. She had plenty of space for his things in her walk-in closet.

As he put his clothes away, he felt pretty good. Even a little smug. Those kisses at the table earlier had been deep ones. She'd seemed to enjoy them as much as he did.

Getting into her bed with her had been a stroke of genius, if he did say so himself. From now on, he would be right there beside her nightly. All kinds of good things might happen while sharing her bed with her. True, weeks of sleeping next to her without actually having sex with her could end up driving him close to insane. But a man always had the option of a cold shower or his own hand. Not ideal solutions, but he would work with what he had.

"What are you grinning about?" Clara stood in the doorway to the master bath, barefoot in shorts and a striped T-shirt, watching him.

He pushed in the drawer he'd just filled with his boxers and turned to her. "I was just thinking over my plans to seduce you now you've let me in your bed."

She was grinning, too. And her cheeks were pink. "You're a dangerous man, Dalton Ames."

"No. Just determined."

Those brown eyes narrowed. "Determined to do what?"

"Come here."

"You didn't answer my question."

"And I'm not going to. Come here."

She took two steps—and then hung back, tipping her

pretty head sideways so that her shining sable hair tumbled down along her arm. "What are you up to?"

"Come here. I'll show you."

She laughed. It was a happy sound. He drank it in. And then he reached out and grabbed her wrist and pulled her to him. She tipped her beautiful face up to him and teased, "So show me, then."

He did. He lowered his head and kissed her, right there in her closet. He took his time about it. And she lifted her slim arms and twined them around his neck and kissed him right back.

The days went by.

They were good days, Dalton thought. Long, full days. His daughter enchanted him. He'd never planned to have children, had considered himself a little too distant, too well trained by his aging, cool-natured parents to be a good dad.

But now there was Kiera, and he could hardly remember the time when having kids had seemed like a bad idea. When his daughter looked up at him, her little fingers clutching his thumb, making those goofy, chortling baby sounds...damn. He was done for. Kiera owned him, body and soul.

And being with Clara—*really* being with Clara? The best part of any day or night. He slept with her in his arms, the way he had during those unforgettable two weeks on the island. And when Kiera needed him, he was right there, just a few steps from her bassinette, ready to change her if she needed it, to hold her and comfort her until she went back to sleep.

Twice a week, Earl took him to Denver for meetings and to deal with anything that couldn't be handled from Justice Creek.

It was working out well, he thought. He could do much of his work remotely, but could always get to the main office in an hour and a half by car if he just had to be there for some reason. He was beginning to see that living in the town Clara didn't want to leave would be fine for him.

He would sell the ten-thousand-square-foot house in Cherry Hills Village and build another house, here in Justice Creek. And he could expand the Justice Creek branch of the bank and install himself in an office there. Myra, his longtime and extremely able assistant, probably wouldn't be willing to make the move with him.

But he would find someone else for Justice Creek and leave her in Denver. The woman could almost run the damn bank anyway. Might as well give her a promotion— chief operations officer, maybe. Dan Foreman, the current COO, was ready to retire. Myra could be groomed to take over for him. It would give her a chance to spread her wings.

It was all going to work out at last. He couldn't wait for Clara to have that checkup, the one where her doctor gave her the go-ahead to do more than sleep in the same bed with him.

Then he would finally make love to her again, after which he was sure he could convince her to say yes to that diamond ring he'd bought back in April.

She *had* to say yes. He refused even to consider that she might still hold out against him.

Because they needed to be married. They had Kiera, after all. And their daughter deserved everything— including a mother and father who were married to each other.

Chapter Eleven

"I'll reschedule the meetings, move them to tomorrow, and go with you," Dalton said at breakfast on the thirtieth of May.

Clara shook her head. "Some things a woman needs to do on her own." Like find out from her doctor if she was healthy enough to resume sexual relations.

Okay, it was kind of silly. They'd seen each other naked—oh, did he look good naked! As good as he'd looked on the island. No, better. She slept with him every night now. And they *had* been fooling around a little. And it had been lovely and intimate and she really, really wanted to be freed up to let that intimacy go wherever the feeling might take them.

But she did not want him sitting there beside her when Dr. Kapur gave her the go-ahead. She just didn't. End of story.

He said, "If it helps, I won't go into the exam room with you. I'll stay in the waiting room, look after Kiera."

"Dalton."

"What?"

"No."

He studied her for several seconds. She was certain he was regrouping to keep pushing until she gave in—which she would not.

But then, wonder of wonders, he let it go. "You need me, you call me."

She thought how dear he was. A little overprotective, maybe—or even a lot. But so wonderfully manly and hot. And so very, very good to her. "I will. I promise."

Half an hour later, with Kiera in her arms, she kissed him goodbye at the front door.

"Back by six at the latest," he said. "If you need me—"

"Dalton."

"What?"

"Have a good day."

He started to say something else. She braced herself to hold her ground. But then he only eased the blanket away from Kiera's face and kissed her on the cheek.

Rocking Kiera from side to side, Clara lingered in the open doorway and watched him go down the steps and along the walk. He gave her a wave before he ducked into the waiting car.

At five forty-five that evening, she was standing in the same spot with the baby in her arms when Earl dropped him off. Dalton ran up the steps to her, eyes locked with hers.

She stepped back so he could come in.

He knocked the door shut with his Italian shoe and dropped his high-dollar briefcase on the floor. "Well?"

And for some ridiculous reason, she was blushing. And then she was smiling. And then she nodded.

He said, "Tell me that's a yes."

And she said, "Yes, Dalton. It's a yes. We have the, um, all-clear."

And he reached out, wrapped his hand around the nape of her neck and pulled her close, bending his dark head for a scorching-hot hello kiss. *Oh, my!* If the baby hadn't been between them, she would have dragged him to the bedroom on the spot.

"Go on," she said with a nervous giggle. "Change into something you don't mind Kiera drooling all over."

Dalton traded his suit for jeans and a knit shirt. Then he set the table. By then, Kiera was snoozing. Clara took her to the bedroom and tucked her into her bassinette.

She rejoined Dalton in the kitchen. They sat down to eat.

It was a quiet meal. They didn't say much, but they kept trading glances. Every time he looked at her, she felt shivery flashes of heat sizzle across her skin. Her pulse beat a little too fast in anticipation of the night to come.

"Eat," he said finally, in that overbearing way of his. "You've hardly touched your food."

"It's the butterflies," she answered softly.

"Not following."

"In my stomach. Taking up all the room…"

He gave her a glance filled with equal parts desire and tenderness. And then he slid his napkin in beside his plate and pushed back his chair.

She rose to meet him as he came for her, letting out a cry of nervous joy as she wrapped her arms around his neck and he gathered her in good and tight. "Kiss me. Please…"

He answered by lowering his mouth to hers. She gasped in excited delight as his tongue swept past her parted lips.

Kiera chose that moment to start fussing. Whiny, questioning little wails erupted from the baby monitor propped on the edge of the counter.

Dalton kept kissing her. She kissed him back. Sometimes Kiera only fussed for a few minutes and then went back to sleep.

But not this time. The wails got louder. And longer.

Finally, he lifted his head. "Does she have radar for exactly the wrong moment?" He listened, cocking his head. "I know that cry. I think she needs her father…"

She laughed, took him by the shoulders and gave him a playful shake. "Go."

He turned and headed for the side hall. She cleared the table and put the food in the fridge.

When she entered the bedroom, he was sitting in the rocker. He sent Clara a wry smile—and kept on rocking the baby. Clara continued on through the bathroom and into the walk-in closet.

Dalton glanced up from the bassinette and his sleeping daughter to find Clara standing in the doorway to the bathroom, barefoot, wearing the same short, low-cut, man-destroying red and yellow summer dress she'd worn on the island that first night. Just weeks after Kiera's birth, it practically fit like a glove. Her dark eyes were full of secrets. A soft, tempting smile curved her lips.

His throat seized up and his heart felt suddenly too big for his chest. He tried to speak through the tightness, to tell her she was the most beautiful woman he'd ever known.

But she put her finger to her lips and came toward him. He watched her approach, his mouth gone dry, his weirdly expanded heart pounding way too hard. A few feet away from him, she stopped. He started to reach for her, to gather her close.

But she shook her head and held out her hand.

He took it.

She turned and pulled him toward the hallway door, leading him on through it and out to the great room, where she scooped up the baby monitor from the kitchen counter. Then she was moving again, taking him back toward the front of the house, but this time through the dining room.

"Where are we going?" he croaked, feeling ridiculous, sporting serious wood when all she'd done was take his hand and drag him around the lower floor of the house.

"You'll see." They entered the foyer. She headed straight for the stairs and started up them, pulling him along behind.

On the upper landing, he saw light spilling out of the bedroom he'd been using until three weeks before. She led him in there, where the bed was turned back and the lights were on low.

At the side of the bed, she set down the monitor next to the strip of condoms waiting on the nightstand. Then she let go of his hand and turned her back to him, smoothing her hair out of the way, indicating the zipper at the back of the dress.

She looked amazing in it. It seemed a shame to take it off so soon.

But then again, the sooner she had it off, the sooner she would be naked.

He took the zipper down and she eased the tiny red straps off her shoulders and let the dress drop.

She had nothing on underneath it. She turned to him. So beautiful, all womanly curves in all the right places. "Your turn."

He couldn't get out of his clothes fast enough. A little smile ghosted across that soft mouth of hers as he ripped his shirt over his head, whipped off his belt, and dropped trou—boxers included.

She pushed him back to sit on the bed. He went, his pants in a wad around his ankles. He really liked where this was going and saw no reason to take issue with any of it. She dropped to a crouch. In no time, she had his shoes and socks off. He kicked off his pants and boxers. She picked them up and tossed them across a nearby chair.

Now both of them were naked, which suited him just fine.

He said, "Come here."

She actually obeyed him without question for once, rising and bending toward him, the dark cloud of her hair swaying forward. He backed away, swinging his legs up onto the mattress, making room for her.

And then she was with him, there on the bed. He reached to embrace her and she melted against him, all that sweet-smelling softness right there, wrapped in his arms.

He needed to kiss her. And he did. He kissed all the best parts of her—which meant he kissed her everywhere. Her lush mouth, her cute nose, the tender, velvety lobe of her left ear. He laid a row of kisses down the silky side of her throat and lower. To her pretty breasts. He kissed them, but lightly. With care.

And then he moved on. He kissed that little mole on the crest of her hipbone. He rolled her over and pressed his lips to the bumps of her spine, to the full, tempting curves of her bottom. He kissed the backs of her thighs and the delicate, nerve-rich flesh behind her knees.

She moaned a soft "Please" as he turned her back over to nuzzle the dark hair where her thighs met.

She moaned some more—and opened for him. For the first time in too many months, he tasted her. So sweet, so musky and already very wet. He was cautious, at first, trying to judge her receptiveness for this, her first time after Kiera. But she pushed her hips toward him, her body moving eagerly in response to his caresses.

So he made her wetter, lifting her legs, settling her smooth pale thighs over his shoulders. That put him where he could watch her face as he stroked her with his tongue, with his fingers, as he teased her a little with his teeth...

"Come up here," she pleaded, urging him to claim her.

But he stayed where he was and kept on kissing her long and deep and slow. He wanted her to give in, let him take her there with kisses first.

And she did give in. She surrendered. He tasted greater wetness, and kept on kissing her. And she went over the edge, clutching his shoulders, whimpering his name. Still, he kissed her, feeling the pulse of her climax on his tongue, loving the taste of her, reluctant to let go.

When she finally sighed and settled, he realized he didn't want to wait any longer, either. He couldn't wait. Wouldn't wait...

He stuck out an arm toward the nightstand. Reaching, fumbling, he almost knocked the strip of condoms to the floor. But he caught them before they fell. And by some minor miracle, he even managed to get one torn off the strip and out of the packaging.

She chuckled softly. "Here." And she took it from him. "Come closer..."

He rose to his knees. She gazed up at him, her lips slightly parted, heat and trust in those impossibly fine dark eyes. Her fingers closed around him. A low, hungry sound escaped him as she rolled the condom down over his aching length.

When she looked up at him again, he bent close and took her mouth, kissing her as she tugged at his shoulders, pulling him down to her, along the soft, welcoming length of her body. With a groan of pure need, he nudged her thighs wide and settled between them.

He sank into her slowly, sure he would die of pleasure as her body surrounded him.

She wrapped her slim arms and strong legs around him. And he was gone, lost in the scent of her, in her softness and strength and complete willingness to have him. She held him close to her, stroking his back, his shoulders, the side of his face, fingers sliding up to thread into his hair. He kissed her and she returned his kisses, her tongue mating with his as she moved in rhythm with him.

It went on forever. He didn't want it to end. And he wasn't sure he could last long enough.

But somehow he held on. He managed to wait for her to go over again. And when she did, when he felt her inner walls contracting so tight and hot around him, he let his own climax have him, let it roll up from the core of him, spreading outward along his arms and legs, rippling down every nerve ending, opening him up, making his head spin and turning him inside out, leaving him completely satisfied—and Clara still with him, wrapped in his arms.

Clara couldn't remember when she'd ever been so completely happy as she was that night.

And they got lucky. They had two more hours before Kiera woke up again. They showered together in the guest bath, taking their time about it, making use of another condom before they got out and dried off.

"I realize I'm suddenly starving," she said when they were back in the bedroom.

She found a couple of old robes in the closet up there. They put them on and went down and raided the refrigerator. And then, with his head in her lap where she could bend down and kiss him whenever the mood struck, they watched television for a while.

Finally, Kiera needed attention. They took care of her and went back to bed—in the master bedroom that time. Clara fell asleep with Dalton spooned around her. It was the perfect ending to the perfect night of lovemaking.

Kiera only woke once more that night. Clara fed her and then Dalton changed her and held her until she slept again.

The next time Clara woke, she was alone in the bed and dawn was breaking. She sat up, shoved her tangled hair out of her eyes—and saw Dalton, bare-chested in a pair of workout pants, sitting in the rocker with Kiera in his arms.

She bent over the side of the bed and grabbed one of the robes they'd tossed on the rug last night. As she stuck her arms in the sleeves, Dalton rose carefully from the rocker. He only got one step before Kiera started crying. So Clara pulled the robe around her, tied the sash and went and got the baby from him.

He gave her his warmest, sexiest smile as he passed the warm bundle into her arms.

She settled back into the rocker. As always, Kiera latched right on, resting her little pink fist on Clara's breast as she gobbled her breakfast. Dalton disappeared through the door to the bath and dressing room, emerging a few minutes later dressed in khakis and a T-shirt. He bent over the rocker and pressed a kiss to Clara's forehead.

"I'll make breakfast," he whispered, and left them alone.

Half an hour later, when she had Kiera back down, she followed her nose to the kitchen. He had bacon and eggs and toast waiting.

"I think you might just be the perfect man," she said as they sat down to eat.

"Hold that thought."

She dug in. The food was so good and she was so hungry she hardly glanced up from her plate until it was empty.

When she did, she found Dalton watching her, his eyes the magical blue of the Caribbean.

Love you, she thought. *So very much*. She opened her mouth to say it at last.

But her courage faltered and she ended up whispering, "Thank you. For breakfast. For last night. For the island and the past two months when you've been here with me every step of the way, taking care of me when I couldn't even admit that I needed it, needed *you*. Thank you for—"

With zero warning, he shoved back his chair and stood.

She gasped at the suddenness of the move. His eyes were electric now. What was going on? "Dalton. What…?"

"Marry me."

Her heart stuttered to a stop—and then recommenced beating like a trip-hammer. She put her hands against her suddenly burning cheeks. "Oh, Dalton, I—"

He came to her, held down his hand. All nerves now, she took it. He pulled her up out of the chair.

"We're good together." He captured her face between his palms. "It's working, you know it is. And I'm willing to sell the Denver house, to move here, to your town, to make it work for me so that it will work for you."

She gazed up into his beautiful eyes. Oh, she did want to say yes.

But wasn't it too soon? It seemed too soon. Didn't it?

"Say yes," he demanded. And he kissed her, a quick, hard press of his warm lips to hers. "Say yes."

"I… It seems too soon, don't you think? I just want us to be absolutely sure."

"I *am* sure." No doubt in his voice. None at all. "Marry me."

The thing was, she wanted to. She really did. To say

yes, to move ahead with him, to commit to being with him forever. Together. To build the life their baby needed, the life she'd always dreamed of.

But forever was a long, long time. She needed to know she could trust him with that, with all the days to come. She needed to know he would never decide that she wasn't quite enough for him, that he needed something more.

Oh, dear God. What if it all went wrong somehow? How could she be sure that it wouldn't?

More time. Definitely. They needed more time.

He was watching her. He was waiting. For her answer.

And she knew he wasn't going to like what she said.

So she stalled—by blurting out what was in her heart for him. "Oh, Dalton. I love you. I love you so much. You're everything to me."

"Good. I love you, too." He said it really fast and not all that sincerely. "Marry me, Clara."

She just stared up at him, speechless now.

And then he dropped his warm hands away from her face. He fell back a step. And he insisted, way too stiffly, "Clara. Say yes. Marriage is important. You know it is. Marriage is the foundation of the family. And Kiera needs us to build a strong foundation for her. This living together, this being not quite married, it's not enough, Clara. Our daughter deserves a family bonded in the sight of God and the law."

She stared into his handsome, beloved face and she couldn't help picturing the lonely little boy he must have been once, with parents who didn't like noise or giving hugs.

She should say yes, she knew it. He needed her to say yes. And she loved him so much. She wanted him to have what he needed.

But then again…

No.

Hell, no.

She wanted more. She wanted… "Oh, Dalton. I want it all, you know?"

His eyes changed as she watched. From electric blue— to ice. "No, Clara. I *don't* know."

She tried to make him see. "I want your heart, given openly as I'm giving you mine. I don't want you to marry me just because of Kiera."

"But I'm not. I—"

"Yes. Yes, you are. And you have to see. I watched my mother suffer for years, because she didn't have all of my father."

"I've told you, I'm not going to cheat—"

"I know. You'll be true. I believe that you will. I do. But I…well, I almost made a huge mistake and married Ryan for all the wrong reasons. I won't do that again. And I refuse to end up like Astrid, having to accept that the man I love is never going to love me back."

"Didn't I just say that I love you?"

"Yes. You said it really fast and not the least convincingly."

"But I did say it. And I mean it. And, damn it, Clara. You are not Astrid. She's a wonderful woman, but she's not you. It's…different with you. It was different from the first. Why can't you see that? Why can't you trust me?"

"I do trust you. I just don't think we're ready for marriage yet."

His lip curled in a snarl. "Ready? What do you mean, ready? We have a *child*, for God's sake. How much more ready can two people get?"

"Kiera does not automatically make us ready for marriage. Come on, Dalton. You *have* to know that."

He didn't answer. The look on his face said it all,

though. He most definitely did *not* know that. In his careful, guarded heart, he still believed that Kiera should be more than reason enough for her to say yes.

And she simply didn't agree with him. "Dalton, please. It's just…not right. Not yet. It's not the right time."

"Wait a minute." He backed off another step. "What exactly are you saying? Is this your way of telling me you want me to move out?"

"What? Where did that come from? Move out? Dalton—"

"Answer the damn question."

"I… No. I don't want you to move out. Did I say that I wanted you to move out?"

"Who knows what you said, what you meant? I can't tell what you're working up to. So I asked you, all right? I just asked you directly. Are you trying to get me to go?"

Oh, dear Lord. How had this all gone so wrong, so fast?

She took a step toward him. He eyed her with fury and suspicion. "Stay," she said softly, coaxingly. "I do *not* want you to go. I love what we have, love living with you." She took another step. And another. And finally, she was close enough to reach for him. "I love—"

"Don't." He shifted back, jerking away from her touch.

She dropped her reaching hand, but she couldn't stop herself from trying—again—to make him see. "Please, Dalton. I love you and I love having you here."

There was a moment. Endless and awful. It was painfully clear to her that her refusal had wounded him. She hadn't meant to do that. The last thing she ever wanted was to hurt him. She only wanted to love him. She only needed more time.

Finally, he spoke in a low voice with careful, tightly held control. "I'm going out."

She cast about madly for a way to hold him there, a

way to get him to stick with this, stick with her, until they somehow came out on the same page. But she had nothing. She ended up mumbling miserably, "Well, okay."

"If you need me…" He seemed not to know how to finish.

Perfect. He didn't know how to finish. She didn't know where to start. "Look. It's okay. Don't worry, we'll be fine. I'll just…" The words ran out as he took her by the shoulders.

Hope flared and her heart started galloping. Oh, if he would only pull her close, kiss her, say something wry and patient—something to reassure her that he understood her need to wait, to be absolutely certain the time was right before they went ahead with such a life-altering step as marriage.

But of course, he didn't understand. And he didn't pull her close. He only guided her gently to the side, clearing his path so that he could leave.

Clara turned to watch him go, pressing her lips together to keep herself from begging him to stay. A sad little moan of frustration escaped her. But if he heard it, he pretended not to. He walked away and he kept going.

She stood there, staring at the spot where he'd been, until she heard the front door open and then close behind him.

Chapter Twelve

Dalton left the house with fury in his heart and a vague plan to head for Prime Fitness. He would punch a bag until his hands bled and the muscles in his shoulders gave out.

But somehow he found himself stopping in front of McKellan's, of all places.

The windows were dark. The bar wasn't even open yet. And he certainly had no interest in meeting Ryan.

Still, Dalton stood there on the sidewalk, first staring at the Closed sign inside the front door, then slowly tipping his head back until he was looking at the top floor of the building and the big windows up there.

What do you know? Ryan stood in of those windows, wearing a CU T-shirt and sweatpants, holding a mug of coffee, looking down while Dalton looked up. Several seconds ticked by. And then Ryan raised an index finger.

Dalton nodded. The other man disappeared from sight.

Two minutes later, the door of the bar swung open. "Want some coffee?"

"Coffee would be good," Dalton heard himself say.

"Come on up."

Dalton went in. Ryan locked the door again and then led the way through the empty bar and up some stairs in back.

The apartment was a large one, with good views of the mountains all around. At the counter in the roomy, chef-worthy kitchen, Dalton took the seat Ryan offered. A cup of really good coffee from a pod machine was ready in no time.

Ryan leaned on the counter across from him. "You've got that look."

"What look?"

"Pissed off. Dumped."

"Pissed off, yes. Dumped, no—well, not exactly." He glanced around vacantly, noted the high-end stove and fridge, and the splendid view of the mountains framed by the wide window over the nearby butcher block table. "I can't believe I came here."

Ryan gave a short laugh. "Why wouldn't you come here? Who knows what goes on with her better than me?"

Dalton sipped more coffee. "I've got this delusion that you might be on my side now."

Ryan shrugged. "I might be."

"Will you give it to me straight? You are, or you aren't."

Ryan refilled his own mug and came around the counter to take the stool next to Dalton's. "She's had a baby with you. She wants to be with you. I want her to have what she wants."

"So, then, what you're telling me is you're on my side."

The other man finally gave it up. "Yeah. I'm on your side. I think she's in love with you."

"Right. She told me that this morning."

One of Ryan's eyebrows inched toward his hairline. "She said she's in love with you and that pissed you off? You are seriously weird, dude."

"Before she told me she loved me, I asked her to marry me—for the second time."

"The light dawns. She said no again."

"Not no. Just not right now."

"And *that* pissed you off."

"Oh, yes, it did. I asked her to marry me for the second time. I said I was willing to live here, where she wants to be. I essentially said I'd do anything. Which is true. I would. Anything. If she would just marry me." He drained the mug. "Apparently, for Clara, anything and everything isn't enough."

Ryan got up and made more coffee. This time, he pulled a bottle of Crown Black from the cupboard and added a double shot to both of their mugs.

It was too early for liquor, but Dalton didn't refuse. He took his mug back and sipped. It went down hot and smooth.

Ryan said, "She's afraid to get married."

"I know."

"Afraid she'll get it wrong."

"I know."

"So you have to wait, man. You just have to hold steady. And wait."

Dalton knocked back more whiskey-laced coffee. "I need things settled."

"Well, right now you're not going to get what you need."

Dalton shook his head. "I don't like it."

"Got that."

"I'm a banker. I'm an Ames. An Ames is a pillar of the community. An Ames does not have a living-together arrangement with the mother of his child. When an Ames has children, he has the good sense and integrity to take that all-important walk down the aisle."

"I hear you. But you have to hold steady."

"There's something very…slipshod about what's happening here. I don't like it one damn bit."

"Hold steady."

Dalton set his mug down harder than necessary. "Hold steady. Is that all you've got?"

"Sorry to break it to you, man. But right now, for you, that's all there is."

When he left Ryan's place, Dalton went to Prime Fitness. He changed into workout clothes and went at it for two solid hours. Then he grabbed a shower and returned to Clara's house.

She came hurrying through the dining room to meet him in the front hall. "Dalton." She hesitated, a worried frown drawn between her smooth eyebrows. "Are you okay?"

Hold steady. "I'll live."

She let out a little cry and ran to him. He opened his arms and took her in. "Dalton…" And she kissed him.

He kissed her back. Hard and deep. "Kiera?"

"Asleep."

"Good." He bent enough to get her under the knees and hoisted her high against his chest.

"Dalton, what in the—?"

"When's Mrs. Scruggs coming?"

"After lunch sometime."

"Good."

"Dalton, what are you do—?"

He shut her up with a kiss and he carried her, still kissing her, into the great room. "Baby monitor?"

She pointed at the kitchen counter.

He carried her over there. "Grab it."

She did. He kissed her some more as he carried her back through the dining room and up the stairs to the spare bedroom, where he took off all her clothes and then all his clothes and made love to her until Kiera needed her again.

The sex helped, more than the talk with Ryan and the two hours at the gym. He figured as long as he could have her in his arms every night and make love to her often, he could do it.

He could hold steady. He could wait her out. He could be there for her the way she needed him to, the way Kiera needed him—until Clara finally saw the light, got over whatever was holding her back and said yes, she would marry him. That yes, she would finally be his wife.

In the days that followed, he gave himself a lot of pep talks. He reminded himself that he was part of her life now. A big part. He was in her house and in her bed and she wanted him to stay there. He reminded himself of how much he liked it there. In her bed, of course. But also her house. Clara's house was more like a real home than the giant Georgian mausoleum where he'd grown up, more like a home than any of the big, expensive houses he'd owned—because Clara and Kiera were in it.

Two weeks after he proposed at the breakfast table and she turned him down, he tried again to explain to her that to him, being married to her was a necessity, that it was how he'd been raised and what he believed. That he and she and Kiera were a family and they deserved all the rights and benefits of being a family. And the only way to get those rights and benefits was to stand up before a judge or a preacher, to say, "I do" and to sign a marriage license that would be filed at the courthouse, a legally binding document. They needed that kind of commitment.

They needed to be bound together in every way, for all the world to see.

Clara didn't disagree with him. She listened patiently to his excellent, thoroughly reasoned arguments.

And then she said that she loved him and she needed more time.

He went straight to the gym and worked out until he couldn't lift his arms and the muscles in his legs twitched and quivered. Then he returned to the house and went upstairs to his makeshift office and didn't come down until eight that night.

They made up in bed. A very sweet reunion. He buried himself in her softness and she cried out that she loved him as she came.

Hold steady, he reminded himself for the umpteenth time.

More days passed. Clara established a regular routine for working at the café. She managed to put in six or seven hours daily, starting around ten. Every few hours she would duck out of the restaurant, come home and feed Kiera, then head back to work. Dalton watched Kiera while she was gone. He was even able to do his work while she slept. On the days he went to the local branch of the bank or to Denver, Mrs. Scruggs filled in.

It was all working out fine.

Or that was what he tried to tell himself.

But inside, he was going more than a little crazy. Because he wanted to make things right and they wouldn't be right until Clara had his ring on her finger, until she finally said yes.

Clara knew Dalton was suffering.

She saw how hard he tried, how it got to him, not being able to do the right thing as he saw it.

And she loved him. Loved him so much.

She really did wonder at herself, at her own stubbornness, her deep-rooted fear that she would somehow mess it all up if she said yes. Strangely, that fear helped her to better understand why he'd called it off with her when they left the island. He'd been afraid, too, then, afraid and trying to protect himself.

At the time, the pain of his rejection had kept her from considering what might be driving him. If only she'd known then what she knew now, she could have forgiven him so much more quickly. She could have sought him out earlier, gotten past her silly assumptions about him and Astrid sooner.

If she'd gone to him sooner, she never would have put poor Rye through their almost-wedding. That whole sad little disaster wouldn't even have happened. Because Dalton would have stepped right up and stuck by her.

And that would have given them more time together. Time for her to learn to trust her own instincts, to put her faith in her love.

Instead now *she* was the one with the fear. And *he* was the one ready to move forward.

For a while, she self-righteously told herself that it was *his* fault, that he didn't really love her the way she wanted and needed to be loved. That if he really loved her, he would be able to say so, with feeling.

But as the weeks went by, she began to see that reasoning as the total garbage it was. With everything he did, Dalton proved that he loved her. Just to see him with Kiera in his arms was enough to convince any woman with a heart that the man would make an excellent husband.

She knew that she needed to get over this weird impasse within her, to shove her fear aside, to stand tall and say yes.

But she didn't. Her fear held her captive, suspended, unable to act.

And a full month after that morning he proposed at the breakfast table, she had yet to agree to be his wife.

Dalton stayed with her, in her house and her bed. He took care of their baby. He didn't make threats or stage any scenes. He made love to her often with a passion and intensity that left her limp and satisfied.

But he did withdraw from her in subtle ways. His dry sense of humor was less evident. He worked a little later in the evenings. He spent more time at the branch of his bank there in town. And he went to Denver more often.

She knew he was only doing his best, only trying to cope with his frustration at her continued refusal to take the next step. She did understand, even sympathize. And she didn't blame him.

But his careful, polite withdrawal did nothing to help her decide to say yes.

She needed to get it all out with someone she trusted. She needed reassuring hugs and good advice. She needed a pep talk, something to break the impasse in her mind and heart. Unfortunately, Rory and her fiancé, Walker, were off in Montedoro for the birthday gala of Rory's mother, the sovereign princess.

Ordinarily, with Rory unavailable, Clara would have gone to Ryan. But that seemed wrong somehow. Wrong, to go seeking romantic advice about one man from the man she'd dumped at the altar six months before. Plus, there had been the animosity between the two men. True, the bad blood seemed to be pretty much over.

But going to Ryan for advice about Dalton still didn't feel right.

So she told herself she would wait until Rory came home in the first week of July. And then the two of them could have a nice long talk over a jumbo tub of Ben & Jerry's.

She told herself that it would be fine in the end. That she shouldn't worry. It would all work out.

But still, it seemed to her that Dalton was more cut off from her every day.

The last day of June they had a ridiculous argument over paper products.

Apparently because of a clerical error, several boxes of paper napkins, biodegradable flatware and carryout containers were delivered to the house instead of the café. Clara, holding a fussing Kiera in her arms, let the delivery guy pile the bulky boxes on the front porch, signed for them and let him go.

Two minutes later, Dalton came in from his morning workout. He called her from the front hall. She emerged from the master bedroom, carrying the still-fussing Kiera in her arms.

He wanted to know what was going on with all the boxes on the front porch.

She explained about the mistake.

He armed moisture from his sweaty forehead and asked, way too calmly, "So you simply let him leave them here?"

Kiera was still crying. Clara rocked her, patting her little back. "I'll put them in the SUV and drive them to work." The restaurant was just around the corner. As a rule, on clear days like this one, she walked. But she had her own parking space at the café, right by the back door. Unloading would be easy and quick.

He gave her a burning look that really had nothing to do with the boxes and everything to do with his ongoing frustration that she wouldn't give him a yes. "*You'll* put them in the SUV?"

Kiera wailed. Clara kissed her temple and rubbed her back some more. "It's no biggie, honestly. They're pretty light. If you'll take Kiera now, I'll just—"

"I'm covered in sweat."

"Dalton, she's not going to care."

His scowl deepened. "The real issue here is that you can't do everything for yourself and you'll never admit that and let me help you. I'm not letting you carry all those boxes to the garage."

The baby cried harder. *Leave it*, she told herself. *Just let it be.* But he had no right to go all caveman on her ass. "Don't start in with what you'll *let* me do. You know I hate that." Kiera let out a long, angry wail.

Dalton glared at Clara, deep blue eyes full of anger and accusation. For a second, she thought he might grab her and shake her. But in the end, he only turned without another word and went back out the front door. She peeked out the sidelight to the right of the door and saw him stack three boxes, hoist them high and start down the steps.

That had *her* wanting to shake someone. She seriously considered marching out after him with their wailing baby in her arms, following him down the steps and yelling at him that he should stop right now, damn it, she would do it herself.

Somehow she held herself back from going through that door. Instead she took Kiera to the bedroom, checked her diaper and nursed her.

Sitting in the rocker, with her blessedly silent baby at her breast, she thought the whole exchange in the front hall seemed beyond ludicrous. Dalton had behaved badly.

And she hadn't been able to make herself let it go. What he'd said about how she wouldn't let him help her had made her want to scream.

She *had* let him help her. He'd been helping her for

months now. Why couldn't he see that? Why couldn't he...?

Well, okay. She knew why. It always circled back to the main point of contention: what he needed to do and what she wasn't ready for.

She heard Dalton come back in through the door to the garage. He went upstairs and didn't come down.

Kiera seemed a little more settled after nursing. Clara put her in the bassinette, grabbed a quick shower and got dressed for work. She hustled to the kitchen to get something to eat.

And Kiera started fussing again.

Dalton did not come down to help.

Clara ended up eating at the counter, a crying Kiera in her arms. Then she carried her around, trying to soothe her.

Time dragged by. No sign of Dalton. He knew very well that she liked to leave for the café by ten. And it wasn't like him to ignore Kiera's crying. He was always so considerate, always there when she needed him to take the baby.

Not so considerate today, however.

Then again, she could have gone upstairs after him. She could have reminded him that she needed to get going.

But she didn't go upstairs. She was still smarting from the harsh words they'd shared in the front hall—and damned if she'd ask him for anything.

When he finally appeared, at a little before eleven, he said gruffly, "Sorry. I had a few calls that couldn't wait."

If he had calls to make, he surely could have told her so. She longed to accuse him of...what? Failure to communicate? Making her late in order to get under her skin?

Uh-uh. Not going there. She drew in a slow, calming breath and took the high road. "No problem." She passed him the fussing baby. "Gotta go."

And she got out of there before she weakened and said something they would both regret.

The street around the café and the parking lot in back were already packed with cars when she pulled into her reserved space by the rear door. It was going to be a busy day. She went around the back of the vehicle and grabbed a giant box of take-out containers.

Awkwardly, bracing the unwieldy box on the rear bumper, she reached up to shut the hatch—and caught sight of four guys lurking near Renée's lovingly restored cobalt-blue '65 Mustang convertible. They were all cute, clean-cut and of high school age. One of them leaned against Renée's car, arms crossed over his chest, gaze scanning the cars around them. Another was bent over the interior on the driver's side. The third guy snickered.

And she distinctly heard the fourth one say, "Do it, Derek. Before someone sees us."

Clara shut the hatch. Hard. Four heads whipped around and four sets of startled eyes focused on her. She called to them, "Was there something you boys needed help with?"

The one who'd been leaning on the Mustang just had to play tough guy. He gave her a narrow-eyed glare and instructed, "Mind your own business, bitch."

Clara dropped the box and reached in her bag for her phone. She rooted around in there and didn't find it—at which point she recalled that she'd left it on the kitchen counter.

Terrific.

But then her fingers closed on a rectangular shape—her blusher compact. It would have to do.

She whipped it out, pretended to punch in 911, put it to her ear and said loud and clear, "Yes. I would like to report a car theft…"

The boys were already backing away. The mouthy one called her another crude name—and then, in unison, they whirled and took off. A moment later, they vanished around the corner of the building.

Clara dropped the compact back into her bag, left the box where it fell and followed them, but at a safe distance, and only far enough that she could see the path they'd taken between the café and the building next to it.

They were still running. They'd crossed Oldfield Avenue and were racing toward the library, which just happened to be next door to the town hall and the Justice Creek Police Department.

Clara almost grinned. Those boys must be from out of town. If they were locals, they wouldn't have fled in the general direction of law enforcement.

From out of town or not, though, they were flirting with big trouble. She hoped that maybe she'd scared a little sense into them. She stood there, watching them, until they disappeared from sight beyond the library. Then, with a shrug, she returned to her SUV by way of Renée's Mustang, which seemed undamaged. Grabbing up the fallen box, she entered the café through the back door.

The place was a madhouse, another one of those days like the one almost three months ago now, the day of the evening when Dalton first appeared at her door with a big ring in his pocket and a marriage proposal on his lips.

Dear Lord. Only three months? It seemed like forever since then. Like a lifetime.

She stood in the café's kitchen, her thoughts spinning back to that night, as her cooks and prep staff hurried to keep up with the orders and her waitstaff flew by the service window, grabbing up full plates and rushing off to serve them.

Barefoot in a tent of a T-shirt, she'd answered the door

and found him standing there. Her heart had soared at the sight of him. Even then, when her mind was dead set against him, her heart had known...

Her anger with him over their silly argument that morning vanished. Who did she think she was kidding? She'd never gotten over him. He was the one for her—as her father had been for her poor, long-suffering mother.

Dalton was the one for her. But he wasn't like her two-timing father, not in any way. She knew that he wasn't. He loved her as much as she loved him. He wasn't going to cheat on her.

So why did she keep holding out against him, against his need to be her husband, to claim her and their daughter as his family in the most complete and binding way?

The pot washer, Ivan, swung by her with a rack of steaming glasses in his hands. "'Scuse me, Clara..."

She shook herself. She could beat herself up later for not being brave enough to say yes to the man she loved. Right now it was time to go to work. She tossed the box into the storage room, stashed her purse in her office and waded right in.

Wherever the staff needed an extra hand, Clara stepped in to smooth the way. She expedited orders, greeted customers, helped to bus and set up tables. And she did grab Renée briefly, to warn her about the four boys in the parking lot. Renée ran out to check on the Mustang. When she came back, she reported that the car was untouched. No fledgling car thieves in sight.

After that, it was all about the work. The rush seemed to go on forever, turnover after turnover. By two, Clara's breasts were hurting. It was past time to go home and feed her baby.

She went to her office and called Dalton.

He said, "You left your cell. Do you want me to run it over to you?"

She ached with the longing to have him there, beside her, right then, so she could grab him and hug him. He was always taking care of her in a thousand little ways. She needed to be more appreciative of that, not be so prickly and insistent that she could do everything herself. They were a team, after all. They helped each other.

"It's okay," she said. "I don't need it right now. I know I'm late for Kiera's feeding. And I probably won't get back to the house until four or so. It's crazy busy here. Can you give her the frozen?" She regularly pumped and froze her milk.

"I'll do that."

Clara could hear the baby crying. "She's still fussing?"

"She's been fine. She just woke up." He said it flatly, distantly. Because she'd hurt him. Because she wouldn't let him give her what he needed to give her: everything. His heart, his hand and his name.

Clara swallowed down the tears that tightened her throat. "So…see you around four?"

"All right." And he was gone.

She stood there in the short hall that led to the restrooms, thinking, *I need to say yes. We need me to say yes…*

The sound of shattering crockery snapped Clara back to reality. Someone out in the kitchen must have dropped a plate. And she had a restaurant to run.

So she rushed to the ladies' room and washed her hands, then returned to her office and got out the breast pump she kept there for days when she didn't have time to go home. Ten minutes later, she was back out on the floor.

It was a little after three when things finally settled down. Clara cleared out the cash drawer, grabbed the day's credit receipts and returned to her office, where she locked the door, opened the safe and pulled the bank deposit together.

The bank was just down the block. And a walk would clear her head after the frantic workday. Maybe she could steal a few minutes on her favorite bench in Library Park, give herself a little pep talk about Dalton, about that all-important next step she really needed to quit waffling over and take.

She still hadn't gotten the SUV unloaded, but that could wait. She put the bank drop in a shoulder bag so that no casual observer would guess she was carrying a large amount of cash and she left the café by the front door.

Dalton, upstairs at his desk in the office room, heard sirens in the distance and wondered at the sound.

A house on fire? A high-speed chase? A medical emergency? You didn't hear a lot of sirens in Justice Creek.

The sirens faded off toward the southeast.

A few minutes later, the house line rang.

He grabbed it on the first ring, expecting it to be Clara, still hung up at work. "Hello?"

"Hi." A woman's voice, but not Clara's. "This is Renée. Renée Beauchamp, from Clara's café?" Dalton remembered the pretty, petite brunette. He eyed the baby monitor, which was blessedly quiet, as Renée, her voice oddly strained sounding, asked, "It's Dalton, right?"

"Yes, that's right."

"Dalton, is Clara there? I can't seem to reach her on her cell."

He felt it then: that first distinct stab of anxiety. "She left her phone here this morning. And no, she's not home yet." He stared at the time display in the corner of his laptop screen. Four-twenty. "She should be home any minute, though." There was a small, shaky exhalation from the woman on the other end of the line. Anxiety crept up the scale toward full-blown alarm. "Renée, what is it?"

"She left the café to make the bank drop at least forty-five minutes ago and she hasn't come back."

"Maybe she ran another errand."

"Oh, I don't know. I don't think so."

"Did you call the bank?"

"Just now, yes. She's not there. I…" And finally, she came out with it. "Five minutes ago, I got a call from Archie Sims, one of the policemen who eats here regularly? He recognized her SUV. He said it's on fire."

Chapter Thirteen

Impossible. Not happening. No freaking way.

Stupidly, he parroted, "On fire?"

"Yeah. Archie said her car is straddling the railroad tracks southeast of town, you know, where they cross Arrowhead Drive?"

"My God. Is she…?" He couldn't quite ask it. And he was thinking of all those damn paper goods. Had she unloaded them? If they were still in there, they would burn hot and high.

"Archie didn't know if there was anyone inside. When he called, they were just trying to put out the fire…"

He remembered the sirens. For Clara? The sirens were for Clara…?

No. Not possible. He wasn't even going to think it.

"I'm calling the police," he said. "I'll see what I can find out."

"Yes. All right. I'm—"

"I have to go." He disconnected the call and started to dial 911, but then realized he wouldn't be able to explain his emergency. He didn't have one, not really. Clara had one. But how to explain that?

No. Not going to work.

So he looked up the police department's main number and tried that.

Two minutes into that call, he knew it was hopeless. They weren't set up to randomly pass out information about burning cars and what—or who—might be inside them. He thanked the woman on the other end of the line and hung up, chillingly aware that soon enough the police would be calling *him*.

In the meantime, what the hell to do? He paced the floor, swearing.

Clara. My God.

If she was in that car…

No. No jumping to conclusions.

Think, damn it.

Arrowhead Drive, Renée had said. The railroad tracks at Arrowhead Drive…

He knew the spot. It was a short drive away.

He headed for the stairs. Halfway down them, he remembered Kiera. What to do with Kiera? Not a good idea to take her with him to the scene of the…whatever the hell it was. Uh-uh. He couldn't take her, and he couldn't leave her there. Mrs. Scruggs had gone home half an hour before. He whipped out his cell and autodialed her number.

Thank God, she answered. He babbled out something semi-incoherent, about an emergency, about Clara's car on fire.

"I'll be right over," the housekeeper said.

"God bless you, Mrs. Scruggs."

"Five minutes."

"Yes. Hurry."

As he hung up, Kiera started crying. He stuck the phone in his pocket and went to her, scooping her out of her bassinette and putting her on his shoulder, his eyes blurring with sudden moisture at the warmth of her tiny body, at the sweet baby smell of her.

He walked her, rocking her gently from side to side, whispering, "It's okay. She's going to be okay."

Kiera seemed to hear him. She gave a little sigh and stopped crying, stopped squirming. She snuggled against his shoulder.

He kept walking, kept up the gentle rocking, back and forth across the bedroom floor, as the recent weeks rose up before him, reproving him.

He'd been…cool. Cool to Clara. Cool in the interest of pressuring her to give in, to give him what he wanted, to say yes and marry him. Cool and getting cooler.

That morning, he'd picked a fight with her over nothing. He'd acted like an ass, making her late for work. He hadn't even kissed her when she left.

And later, when she called to say she wouldn't be home till four, he'd had no tender words for her, no warm and loving *See you soon*. Just a flat *All right*, after which he'd disconnected the call.

All right. That was what he'd have to remember, if worse came to worst. *All right*, the last dull and distant words he'd said to her.

Bad. It was bad, the way he'd been behaving.

He closed his eyes, rocked his daughter, whispered a broken, sorry prayer, "Just bring her back to us. Bring her back safe. Please let her be safe…"

The house phone rang. Kiera startled, but then only made a little cooing sound and settled against him again.

He strode to the bedside extension and grabbed it up. "Yes, hello?"

"Dalton, it's Renée. Clara asked me to call you."

Hope exploded through him. His heart felt as if it were going to sledgehammer its way free of his chest. "Clara? Where is she? Is she—?"

"She just left here. She's okay. She only went to the bank, then took a little walk through Library Park. She didn't even know the SUV had been stolen."

His throat had locked up tight. He coughed to clear it. "So, the car. She wasn't in it?"

"No. She's fine. She came in a few minutes ago. She's running home right now."

"Running home? I don't…"

"She should be there any minute. She said she needed to get to you. And she just wanted you to know that it's all right, that she's safe."

He heard the front door open, then Clara, calling him. "Dalton?"

"In here!" He spoke into the phone again. "She's here. I have to go." He hung up and turned to the hall doorway as swift footsteps approached.

And there she was. Safe. A little breathless. But whole and well. Standing in the doorway, her big eyes full of love and worry. "There you are. Renée said she'd called you about the car. You must have been scared to death…" Those eyes brimmed. "I went to the park, to think. I had no idea that someone stole my car. I had no idea of what was happening…"

"Clara." He couldn't cross the distance fast enough. Three long strides and he had her in his arms.

She trembled, "Oh, Dalton…" She tipped that beautiful face up to him.

"Shh." He kissed her forehead, her eyebrow, the tip of her nose. "It's okay. You're here. You're okay. *We're* okay."

"I love you, Dalton."

There was nothing to do but to give it back to her. And he did, with all the feeling he'd tried to deny, with all the yearning that welled in his racing heart. "And I love you, Clara. I love you more than I can say."

Her sweet face seemed to light up from within. She whispered, "Listen to you. Listen to what you said."

He used his thumb to brush the tear tracks from her soft cheeks. And he said it again, just to be perfectly clear. "I love you." And then he pulled her closer and stroked her hair. She wrapped her arms around him—around both of them—as on his shoulder, their daughter sighed and made another of those soft little cooing sounds. He had it all, the world, everything, right there in his arms.

Clara. Kiera. With him.

Safe.

A few minutes later, Mrs. Scruggs arrived.

Dalton and Clara explained what had happened as best they could with the limited information they had so far, thanked her and sent her home again.

The police came next. They'd already caught the car thieves—four teenage boys from Boulder, the same boys, it turned out, that Clara had confronted in the café parking lot that morning. They'd come back, hot-wired her SUV because she'd "pissed them off," one of them said, and gone for a joyride. When they were done, they'd torched the car on the railroad tracks.

Two witnesses had seen them setting the fire and both had called 911. The boys were caught within five minutes of lighting the match. Parents had been called. The boys would not be getting off easy.

Clara knew the two officers who came to talk to them. She made the men coffee and thanked them for everything.

As soon as they left, family and friends started calling. Word got around in a small town and everyone wanted to know what, exactly, had happened, and to be reassured that Clara was all right. Dalton and Clara took turns answering the phone and telling the story.

Dalton wasn't the least surprised when Ryan showed up to see for himself that everything was all right. Clara's great-aunt Agnes came, too.

It was dinnertime by then. Clara set two extra places and served them all Mrs. Scruggs's stellar pot roast.

Aunt Agnes made a lot of veiled references to wedding bells and the necessity that a child should have married parents. Clara gave her patient looks.

Dalton said gently, "Clara needs time, Agnes. I want her to have what she needs."

Clara gazed at him across the table, her mouth so soft, her eyes shining bright. "I'm getting there," she said. "I'm getting there fast."

"Well, I should hope so," declared Aunt Agnes, and then went on to mutter the usual timeworn platitudes, which included phrases like *the cornerstone of the family.* And *the imperative for a true and binding commitment in the sight of God and man.*

"Give it a rest," Ryan said to Agnes. "Look at them. They're doing fine."

It was after eight when Rye and Agnes left.

The door closed behind them—and Kiera, with her customary perfect timing, started crying.

Dalton volunteered, "I'll get her. I'll change her if she needs it, and then bring her to you."

"I'll clear off the dishes." She looked much too tempting, in snug jeans and a fitted red top.

And he couldn't leave the room without at least touching her. "Come here."

Smiling, she came to him. He reached for her, wrapped his hand around the nape of her neck, under the silky, warm fall of her hair. Her skin was cool and velvet-smooth. She tipped her head up for a kiss. He made it a slow one, nipping her lower lip a little before settling his mouth on hers. She sighed and her lips parted. He drank in the taste of her. She lifted her arms and wrapped them around his neck.

Kiera kept crying.

Reluctantly, he let go of Clara and went to get the baby.

An hour later, Kiera was fed, diapered and thoroughly cuddled. Dalton put her to bed. He straightened from the bassinette—and there was Clara.

In a white satin sleep shirt that buttoned down the front and came to midthigh, her hair curling loose and thick on her shoulders.

"You are so beautiful." The simple words seared his throat as he said them. She grabbed the baby monitor off the edge of the dresser and held out her other hand. He took her outstretched fingers, felt that hot, sweet bolt of longing shooting up his arm from the point of contact, headed straight for his heart.

"Upstairs," she whispered. He didn't argue, just followed along after her, satisfied to be wherever she might take him.

In the upstairs bedroom, she set down the monitor on the nightstand. He sat on the edge of the bed and took off his shoes and socks. "Sit beside me," he said. "There's something I need to tell you."

She gazed down at him, trust and light in her eyes. "Dalton…"

"Come on." He caught her hand.

She sat beside him and cleared her throat, a nervous sound. He tugged on her arm. She followed his lead, swinging her legs up onto the mattress, turning to face him.

For a moment, they just sat there, staring at each other.

The right words were there within him. He only had to let them out. "I love you, Clara Bravo. You're everything to me. I love you and I want to be with you. I want…our family. You, me and Kiera. I want it all with you. I want forever with you."

She made a soft sound, a tender sound, a little hum in her throat.

He reached for her, because he had to touch her. He traced the shape of her eyebrows, followed the line of her hair where it fell along her cheek. "And today, I learned something. Something important."

"Yes?" So sweetly, on a sharp, indrawn breath.

"Today I finally figured out that I'm more scared of losing you than I am of not being married to you. I will always want you to marry me. But if you don't want to do that, okay. As long as you'll stay with me and we can be a family, anyway, I'll learn to be happy with things the way you need them to be."

Her eyes shone diamond-bright then. "You mean that? You would do that, live with me, be not quite married to me? You would do that and not have to be distant, not have to hold yourself away, not have to pick fights over paper goods?"

"That was wrong, the way I behaved this morning. It was wrong that I pulled away from you. I won't do that anymore. Life's too short. You never know what might happen. I don't want to waste a moment I could have with you. I want to be with you. *Really* with you, Clara, for every day, every hour, every second that we have together."

She put her hand to her chest. "Oh, Dalton. I do love you. I love you so."

"And I love you. And I will say it. With feeling. Every chance I get."

"You really mean that." It wasn't a question.

He answered anyway. "Absolutely. I do."

She canted toward him. "A kiss to seal it…"

"I love you." He leaned in to meet her.

"I love you," she said. Their lips met in a kiss that started out tender—and quickly burned hot.

"Clara…" He had to hold her, to touch her, to feel her body pressed to his, so he pulled her closer, turning her and settling her across his lap.

Those dark eyes gazed up at him, full of trust in him, in what they shared together. "It means a lot that you would do that, that you would put aside what you want so much, what you believe to the core of you is the right thing, in order to make it good between you and me. But you know what?"

He stroked the back of his finger down the side of her throat. By then, he was kind of through talking. He unbuttoned the top button of her silky, sexy white shirt.

She caught his hand. "Are you listening?"

He bent close, pressed a hard kiss on those lips he would never tire of kissing. "Of course."

"Good. I sat on a bench in Library Park today, when I really should have been here, with you."

He unbuttoned the second button, peeled the fabric back a little, ran a finger across her nipple, causing her to let out the most adorable little purr of sound. He reminded her, "You didn't know what had happened. How could you have known?"

"That's not the point."

"Excellent. There's a point."

She laughed then, and shoved playfully at his shoulder. "Oh, you…"

"Tell me the point."

"The point is that I made a decision, sitting there, in the park. Or maybe not a decision, exactly. Maybe it was more that I had a realization. And what I realized is that I do believe in you. I believe in *us*. I believe in what we have together, that it can last. That you'll always be true, that you'll be there for me, as I will be for you. Because you *are* true, Dalton. You're the truest man I know. And that's how I know that we're finally ready."

"Ready?" His breath caught. He even forgot about getting her naked.

She gazed up at him so solemnly. "I love you. I'll stay with you. Just as you said a minute ago, we'll be a family. We *are* a family in all the ways that matter. Except one."

He could have a heart attack, his pulse raced so fast. "Clara. Tell me. I need to know. Is it possible that you've changed your mind? Is it possible that you…?" He couldn't quite bear to ask. What if she said no?

But she didn't say no. She nodded up at him, her eyes so bright they blinded him. "Yes, Dalton. I love you. I'll stay with you.

"And I will marry you, too."

* * * * *

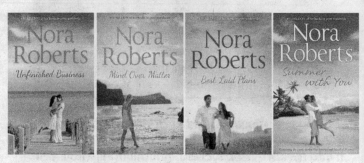

MILLS & BOON®

The Thirty List

* cover in development

At thirty, Rachel has slid down every ladder she has ever climbed. Jobless, broke and ditched by her husband, she has to move in with grumpy Patrick and his four-year-old son.

Patrick is also getting divorced, so to cheer themselves up the two decide to draw up bucket lists. Soon they are learning to tango, abseiling, trying stand-up comedy and more. But, as she gets closer to Patrick, Rachel wonders if their relationship is too good to be true...

Order yours today at
www.millsandboon.co.uk/Thethirtylist

MILLS & BOON®

Cherish™

EXPERIENCE THE ULTIMATE RUSH OF FALLING IN LOVE

The World of
MILLS & BOON®

With eight paperback series to choose from, there's a Mills & Boon series perfect for you. So whether you're looking for glamorous seduction, Regency rakes or homespun heroes, we'll give you plenty of inspiration for your next read.

WORLD_ M&B2a

The World of
MILLS & BOON®

HISTORICAL

*Awaken the romance
of the past*
6 new stories every month

MEDICAL ROMANCE™

*The ultimate in romantic
medical drama*
6 new stories every month

MODERN™

*Power, passion and
irresistible temptation*
8 new stories every month

By Request

*Relive the romance with the
best of the best*
12 stories every month